HOSTAGE

HOSTAGE

R.D. ZIMMERMAN

Delacorte  Press

Published by
Delacorte Press
Bantam Doubleday Dell Publishing Group, Inc.
1540 Broadway
New York, New York 10036

Library of Congress Cataloging in Publication Data

Zimmerman, R.D. (Robert Dingwall)
Hostage / by R.D. Zimmerman.
p.   cm.
ISBN 0-385-31983-5
I. Title.
PS3576.I5118H67   1997
813'.54—dc21   97-3233
                                                      CIP

Manufactured in the United States of America
Published simultaneously in Canada

November 1997

10 9 8 7 6 5 4 3 2 1

BVG

For David Grundy
1955–1996

Many thanks to many people:
Ellen Hart, Don Houge, Jonathon Lazear, Mary Logue,
Lisa Motz, Lars Peterssen, Gail Plewacki, and Katie
Solomonson. Special thanks to Leslie Schnur and Tom
Spain for their trust and insights.

HOSTAGE

You really don't think about dying when you're dancing, at least not if the music's fast and pulsing and the volume's so loud that you can feel the beat pummel your innards. There's nothing better than flashing lights, grinding hips, and bodies, bodies, bodies all packed together as the tunes pound on and on. It just makes you feel so full of energy, so incredibly alive. Maybe that's why Curt and I both loved going down to the bars. Maybe somewhere inside we understood we were doomed. Maybe we were merely trying to forestall the inevitable.

So that's how I'm going to remember Curt, out there on the dance floor in his white T-shirt and blue jeans, a big smile on that handsome face, a thread of sweat rolling off his brow as the Village People throbbed away. Nobody could dance better than him. We'd both come out in the last year—even the moms knew—and you could see his joy and relief as he bounced around, feet moving, fingers snapping, the music pouring into his body and out his soul.

Yes, that's how I'll remember Curt—so very happy, so very gay—even though I'll always, always feel guilty for what I did to him.

1

He'd spent a long time thinking how he was going to kill Curt. After all, they were best friends.

Turning a corner, the man parked on the edge of Powderhorn Park, a large, rolling space with a frozen pond in the middle, and then proceeded the rest of the way up the snowy sidewalk. No one was out, not in this neighborhood, not at this time of night, but he still pulled up the collar of his dark wool coat, he still kept his cap snug on his head. You never knew. Some insomniac could be up watching TV, some truck driver could be coming home late, and the last thing he wanted was any sort of complication. He just had to do it and be done with it.

As he approached the small brick building two blocks later he took note that all four apartments were dark. Very good. He'd thought about slipping down the side of the building and using the rear door, but, no, that wasn't such a hot idea. He knew this place well. All four apartments were identical, all four bedrooms were in the back of the building. The chances of waking anyone up were much slimmer if he just went in the front, entered Curt's ground-floor place, and proceeded to the back where Curt lay sleeping. If anyone heard him they'd think it was just someone getting up in the middle of the night to take a pee.

Off to the right he heard something, glanced over. Raccoons, three of them gathered in a concentrated huddle. Having obviously gotten into someone's garbage, they sat right in the middle of the street ripping apart a McDonald's bag. The biggest one, a gloppy packet of ketchup in his paws, glanced at the man, but confident that the frigid night belonged to them, didn't budge and continued with the feast at hand.

MAC, the Minnesota AIDS Coalition, had set up a rotation of friends to care for Curt, which meant there were maybe twenty-some keys circulating around town. Perhaps more, for Curt had been popular, a jovial sort with a big heart and a handsome face, and in return a lot of people now cared for him. Which meant it wasn't at all unusual, thought the man as he approached the front door, that he would have a key too. If all went well no one would suspect anyone had slipped in here tonight. If any suspicions were raised, though, the trail would be impossible to follow. Hadn't Curt mentioned that even a delivery service had a key?

He knew the place so well that when he unlocked the front door of the building and stepped inside, he didn't even have to turn on the light. A little lobby that they kept locked after nine at night. Four mailboxes on the right. Four steps up to the first landing. Curt's apartment was up there, the first door on the right, and the man paused only briefly. He listened, tried to suck in any and all of the sounds. But there was nothing, and so using both hands he slid the key into Curt's door, twisted the lock open, and entered.

It was hot.

The first thing he did was take off his cap and stuff it in his pocket; then he unbuttoned his coat. He didn't remove his gloves, however, even though this place was as overly warm as a nursing home. It smelled like one too. Stuffy. Stale. Moist. Medicinal. The gloves had to remain on though, lest he leave a careless print.

Sensing something move to his right, he looked into the living room and saw eyes staring back at him. Curt's cat, Girlfriend, sat perched on a window ledge, a tall, lean creature with short, jet-black hair. She stared at him for a long, soulful moment, knowing of course that something was wrong, terribly so. Aware in some wise animal part of her that she was powerless, however, Girlfriend turned back to the window, gazing out at the antics of the raccoons and their McDonald's bag.

He proceeded to the rear of the apartment, passing through the dining room and directly into the kitchen, where he paused in front of the old wooden cabinets, tall ones made of shellacked fir. Down the short hall lay the bathroom, where a faint night-light was burning, and beyond that was a dark doorway, the bedroom. Standing quite still he heard distinct noises, the hissing of a vaporizer, and finally Curt's slow, pained wheezing.

Knowing he had no other choice, the intruder didn't hesitate. He continued on, walking right into the bedroom, a small room with a dresser on the left, some big posters on one wall, a chair, a bedside table littered with vials, pills, a glass of water, and the bed in which Curt now slept. It was dark, of course, except for the light from the alley, which made everything glow as if a full moon were out. The man grabbed the back of the chair with one hand, dragged it across the floor, and sat down right next to the bed, surprised that Curt didn't even stir. Then again, who knew what drugs he was on today.

Poor Curt.

He was buried under a down comforter and three or four blankets, a near skeleton of a figure who didn't look as if he'd ever be able to stand again. Curt's best friend just sat in the chair, silently weeping, searching for an answer, wondering how could this once robust and vital guy now be so scrawny, so puny? How could this butch man have lost so very much weight and still be alive? He'd fought so ungodly hard, hung on as long as he could to this apartment. He should have been moved to one of the AIDS foster homes weeks ago instead of to a hospice tomorrow as was now planned, but of course that was what Curt had wanted least: to leave this place, the life and memories he'd had here.

Finally, he reached down and touched Curt on the shoulder—oh, Jesus, nothing but bones!—and nudged him gently, saying, "Curt, wake up."

As if in delirium, Curt stirred. "Wh-what?"

"It's me, buddy. Wake up."

Curt rolled to one side, struggled to open his sunken and hollow eyes, then managed a smile. "Oh, hi. So you're next on the roster. I . . . I didn't know you were coming tonight."

"Yep."

All the friends and then some were taking turns staying here, watching out for Curt, making sure he took his meds, trying to get him to eat something, anything, even a mere spoonful of mashed potatoes. And there *would* have been someone here to-night had Curt's visitor not fudged the schedule, twisted it around so that Mike thought that another guy would have been here, another guy who would have shown up if Carol hadn't called to tell him that Tony was on this evening, when in fact Tony was out of town. It was all an oversight that Curt's best friend had cleverly manipulated so that he could do the necessary deed.

"How're you doing?" he asked.

"Not so good," Curt said in a faint voice. "I think this is it. I think I'm in the departure lounge."

"Yeah, well, none of us is getting out of here alive." He reached out, pushed aside the thick layer of covers, found the skeletal hand, and shuddered, for it was like holding hands with death. "Who knows, maybe I won't be far behind you."

Curt looked down at the gloved hand wrapped around his. "You're all right, aren't you?"

"Just a cold," he lied, "that I don't want to pass on to you."

"What's the diff, I already have PCP." Reminded of the *Pneumocystic carinii* pneumonia that had plagued him from the start of his battle against AIDS, Curt suddenly began hacking, the cough coming from deep within and racking his body. "I . . . I—"

"Shh, buddy," he said, reaching out and smoothing Curt's forehead, the skin so translucent, so fragile that it seemed it might rip. "Don't say anything. Just relax. I'm right here."

The coughing deepened, desperately so, and at one point Curt's entire face twisted and he struggled to push himself up. He was gagging, and for a moment it seemed he might vomit, but then things subsided and the fit passed as quickly as it had come.

"That's it, Curt. Just get comfortable."

Curt gazed up, those soulful eyes so sincere. "Our soup of the day is a lovely lobster bisque."

At first he didn't know what to say or do. At first he thought it was a joke. But of course it wasn't. A deathly dementia was overtaking Curt's mind, and in the course of the last two weeks Curt, without realizing it, was saying far too much about everything and anything.

"And today our salad dressings are creamy pepper, honey mustard, and, of course, our house vinaigrette."

He smiled, ran his hand down Curt's sunken cheek. "Hey, man, I think you should have gotten out of that restaurant a little bit sooner. You're going to carry that shit with you to the grave."

Curt squeezed his eyes shut, seemed to fade away, but then came back, his lids bouncing open in panic. "What's going to happen to Girlfriend?"

"We'll find a nice home for her, don't worry."

"Promise me you won't send her to . . ." He closed his eyes. "Promise me not the pound. I don't . . . don't want my kitty to be gassed."

Tears started swelling his eyes. "I won't let that happen, sweetheart. I promise."

"Thanks. God, I've always been able to count on you, haven't I?" He started to cough again, then stopped, only to drift away again. "I'm sorry, man. I'm really sorry."

"Don't worry," he replied.

"But you're going to do it, aren't you?"

"Shh, don't talk."

"Do it for me, will you? Don't back out now."

"Just rest."

His face tensing with fear, Curt looked up. "I haven't told anyone. I promise, I—"

"Hey, it's okay."

"No one will ever find them down there," he muttered as his eyes fell shut.

And right there was the problem. Who knew what Curt had been blathering and to whom? For the past week his temperature had been dangerously high as his body had struggled to fight off the pneumonia and brain lymphoma, not to mention the various fungal infections and thrush and a half dozen other things. For days now he'd been babbling everything from daily specials to talk of the weather to messages for "Mr. Wonderful," his ex-lover, the shit who'd abandoned him when Curt had first tested positive. Curt's best friend had listened to a variety of nonsensical things, and now he only prayed that Curt hadn't let their plans slip.

"It's . . . it's not a . . . a *gay* disease," begged Curt, struggling to open his eyes. "Make sure everyone . . . understands."

"That's right, it's just a disease." He reached into his pocket and pulled out the small vial. "Look, buddy, I brought you something."

"A magic potion?" Curt smiled, caught his breath, and stifled a cough.

"Right, the one you've been waiting for. Don't worry, it's going to make everything all better."

What other choice was there? He'd been over and over this, trying to figure out any other way. But there wasn't, thought the man, reaching to the bedside table for the glass of water. He had to do it tonight too, not only before Curt was moved to the hospice, but before he let the proverbial cat out of the bag. Besides, it wasn't going to hurt. Curt'd be gone in an instant. And he was going to last only another few weeks anyway. Better he should be spared all the misery.

And so he poured the cyanide into the glass of water, swirled it around, and then leaned over to Curt, whose head he lifted up.

"Drink up, sweet prince," he said, his eyes beading with tears as he held the glass to Curt's lips. "Don't worry."

"Just get that fat-ass con . . . congressman for me."

"Whatever you say."

"Oh, and tell Mr. Wonderful I hate him."

Curt smiled, took a swig, and then a moment later, in one quick jerk, was released.

2

"God, I can't believe I'm going to interview Mr. Gay Public Enemy Number One," called Todd Mills from the kitchen of his fifteenth-floor condo. "Of course, it's only the biggest interview of my career."

"Nervous?" replied Steve Rawlins, seated somewhere out in the living room.

"Ah . . . yeah."

"Good. You should be."

The small kitchen was all white, from the cabinets to the countertops and even to the coffee maker, from which Todd now poured two mugs of very black coffee. Lost in thought, he headed out, one mug in each hand, and crossed onto the oatmeal-colored carpeting that ran throughout the entire two-bedroom apartment.

He said, "I just hope I don't screw it up."

"You won't." Rawlins, who was suffering from sinus problems, was settled in a black leather recliner by the balcony doors. "This sun feels so good."

Todd couldn't help but be apprehensive, however, because even though he was back on the air and had already done a couple of stories, this was his first actual interview as an openly gay reporter. Until last year he'd been about as deep in the closet as you could get, trapped in an image of his own making—that of a dashing reporter, brown-haired, square-jawed, broad-shouldered, ever-charming, and model-handsome. And straight . . . well, divorced . . . well, actually . . . well, not straight. Not really. Well, not at all. Nevertheless, for almost twenty years, ever since he was a punk out of Northwestern University, he'd worked like a secret agent to hide his sexuality, lying, conniving, twisting until he'd nearly lost his mind. Instead, his lover Michael had been murdered, which in turn had outed Todd and changed his entire world.

Todd handed Rawlins one of the mugs of coffee, then sat down in a nearby red chair, wondering how this had happened, how he'd found someone as wonderful as this man, Steve Rawlins. Though Todd had known in his teens that he was attracted to guys, though he'd once been married, though over the years he'd had anonymous sex and closeted relationships, this romance was different than any and all of them. Simply, never before had Todd been able to give himself both emotionally and sexually to one and the same person, male or female, and never before had he been so absolutely sure of one thing in particular.

He reached out and put his hand on Rawlins's knee. "I love you."

Rawlins opened his mouth, presumably to respond in kind, but his head kept tilting back until a huge sneeze burst out of him.

Todd laughed, then said, "Maybe I should go get you some tea instead of coffee."

"You know, I always wondered what it was like to be waited on hand and foot." He put his hand over Todd's. "But just sit and relax. I'm fine."

"Yeah, but maybe a little—"

"Don't worry, for you I'll live."

Todd took a sip of coffee and glanced outside. There wasn't anything particularly special about his apartment—except, of course, the view. And what a view it was, the likes of which were hard to find in this midwestern pancake of a city. The floor plan was bent slightly so that one large window faced northeast and overlooked the trees of the parkway below, the red tile roof of an old beach club, a bit of Lake of the Isles, and in the distance the Oz-like towers of downtown. On the other side of the room, south-facing glass doors opened onto a balcony and Lake Calhoun, a large oval shape that filled almost the entire view. And if the warm weather kept up, thought Todd, eyeing the soggy but still frozen body of water, the ice might be gone within a matter of days, and there was no place where spring was more intense, more appreciated, yet more short-lived than in these northern plains. Gazing into the near future, Todd pictured the two of them walking and jogging and swimming, packing as much activity as possible into a single worshiped season.

Noticing Rawlins squint with pain as he rubbed his forehead, Todd said, "Maybe you shouldn't go to work this afternoon."

"Neah." Rawlins eyed Todd up and down, taking in his dark-blue suit, pale-blue shirt, and black leather shoes. "You look great. But you can't do full execudrag without a tie."

"I'll put it on down at the station."

"Silk, I assume."

"Only the finest, thank you." He couldn't stop himself from asking, "Are you really all out of pills?"

With the sun spilling over him, Rawlins bent forward and, as he blew his nose, nodded. A detective on the Minneapolis police force, he usually looked pretty tough—not particularly tall, but broad-shouldered and muscular with cropped brown hair and a face that could look either sweet or much too serious. Today, however, with a red nose and wearing old jeans and a scruffy flannel shirt, he looked like a pathetic boy.

"Well, you'll see the doctor in a bit and I'm sure he'll give you some great drugs."

"Oh, my God," moaned Rawlins, reaching for another Kleenex. "I know the doctor said last week that I'm in good health, but I mean to tell you I'm in snot hell."

"Sinus infections are the worst."

"Maybe it's an allergy."

"It could be, which would explain why you haven't been able to shake it. I do have down pillows, you know. Are you allergic to feathers?"

"Who knows?" said Rawlins with a shrug.

"Or it could be—what do you call 'em—dust . . . dust . . ."

"Dust mites. That's what my sister's allergic to."

"Then you could be too," suggested Todd. "Be sure and ask the doctor."

"I will. Maybe I should see an allergist."

Nodding toward his new pet, Todd said, "God, I wonder if it's her."

Something small and black and lanky emerged from the hall that led to the two bedrooms. A cat. Todd had never seen a creature more languid or more aloof than this one; he'd had her for almost a month now and she still refused to let Todd pet her. She barely ate either. He'd never been overly fond of cats—Todd found them much too independent and finicky—and he would never have taken this one except for the special circumstances.

"Come here, kitty," called Todd, holding his right hand down low and softly snapping his fingers. "Come here, Girlfriend."

She paused, glanced at Todd with one eye, then turned and trotted behind the couch.

Rawlins watched the course of events and commented, "When are you going to give up?"

"She'll come around, you'll see."

"It's been almost a month."

"She's in mourning, that's all. Trust me, she knows Curt died and she just hasn't gotten over the shock."

"Yeah, well, that makes two of us."

Todd noticed the little face poke out from behind the couch. "She's making progress. At least she stays in the same room with us now." When Todd clicked his fingers together and Girlfriend disappeared a second time, he took a sip of coffee and said, "I wonder what she saw that night. If only she could talk."

"If only I'd been there like I was supposed to," Rawlins lamented, for it was he who had been scheduled to stay with Curt the night he died.

"You've got to stop beating yourself up about this. Either it was a genuine mix-up or . . . or somehow Curt finagled it."

"Or someone else did. I'm not sure Curt had it together enough that week to be so clever."

"Well, then he'd worked it out in advance with someone."

"Maybe, but with whom?"

Just exactly what had happened that night was still a mystery. It was clear that Curt Anderson hadn't died of complications from AIDS, but from cyanide poisoning; the autopsy as well as the glass of water found by his bed made that perfectly clear.

Whether it was a suicide, an assisted suicide, or a murder, however, had yet to be determined, and probably never would be. Given the huge number of friends and volunteers MAC had organized to take care of Curt and the fingerprints each and every one of them had left behind, there was no conclusive evidence to be found in the apartment.

"There's just nothing to go on," continued Rawlins.

Todd gazed out the window. "Yeah, but you know, there must have been someone else there. You just don't take a sip of cyanide by yourself and then calmly put the glass down on the bedside table. From what I understand it works a lot more quickly and violently than that. If he'd drunk it on his own he probably would have dropped the glass or spilled it or something like that. Someone must have helped him."

"I don't think we'll ever know the truth. No one else at the station is paying much attention, because Curt would have died soon anyway." Rawlins shook his head. "I should have been there."

"Hey," Todd said softly. "You gotta stop thinking like that. You can't blame yourself."

Ever since Curt's death Rawlins had been in a major funk, sleeping a lot, going about the days under a cloud of lethargy, and even losing his appetite. With that in mind Todd wasn't surprised that Rawlins had gotten so sick, that the sinus infection had taken such a strong hold.

"Anyway . . ." mumbled Todd.

Rawlins wiped his nose and asked, "What's your day look like?"

"I just have a couple more articles I want to check this morning. The interview will be right after one. Then I think I'll hang around for the edit this afternoon, see how the thing looks, and do a live intro of the interview on the five P.M. news."

Rawlins grinned. "Just a regular old working stiff again, aren't you?"

"Can you believe it?"

After a lengthy hiatus, Todd was back at it, back on television, which surprised him almost as much as the next guy. After much discussion and indecision, Stella, his agent—the tiniest shark, as she was known—had negotiated a hell of a contract for him with WLAK, Channel 10. His debut story had recently aired, a two-part series about the Megamall—the suburban shopping mecca that Todd personally hated—and the economic boon it was proving not to be for the cities of Minneapolis and St. Paul. And while Todd could have let things rest for a while, he was hoping today's interview would be even bigger. Already the station manager had told him that one of the networks had expressed interest in running a clip this evening.

Todd took another sip of coffee, set down his cup, and settled back in the chair. "You know, I don't know what's harder to believe—that he actually wrote this book or that people are really buying it!"

"What I can't believe is that they found twenty-five suckers willing to pay five thousand bucks each to have lunch with him. He's such a turkey."

"Which actually makes him an easy target," said Todd. "But I don't want to be sloppy." Todd checked his watch. "Listen, I gotta get going. It's not every day that I get to talk to someone like Johnny Clariton."

"Thank God for that."

"You know, I'm going to have a hard time being objective."

"Why bother?" Rawlins shook his head. "The way he goes on and on about the 'homosexual agenda' and the 'gay disease,' why should you have to behave responsibly?"

"Those are radical words for a cop," said Todd.

Still, queers everywhere were rallying against Johnny Clariton's calling AIDS the gay disease, and Todd was going to do what he could to amplify the comment, to make that the marker of his true values. But Todd had to be clever about it, intelligent, direct, sincere. He had to lead the interview down a particular path and make sure that Clariton said it all over again and said it even more horribly than before. And Todd could do it. In his own mind he'd conducted the interview more than a dozen times; in his imagination he'd nudged Clariton this way and that, antagonized, flattered, coerced, charmed, and finally caught the congressman in a trap of his own words.

Right. Todd stood up, looked out over the frozen lake. Curt

had been one of Rawlins's closest friends, and while Todd hadn't known him very well, watching that man's life waste and shrivel away had affected Todd like nothing else. He'd never felt sadder, more horrified, nor more proud, all the while wondering why and how he'd escaped, why he hadn't made that one innocent and disastrous step.

Which was why Todd was going to make sure that Johnny Clariton would be held hostage to his words about AIDS and gays for the rest of his political career.

"Here I go," said Todd, caught up by the task ahead and rising to his feet.

"Hey, I hate to bring up the nitty-gritty of our lives at this particular moment," said Rawlins, wiping his nose with a tissue, "but I'm going to do a couple of loads of laundry. Is all your stuff—"

"Yes, Mr. Policeman, I promise all my dirty clothes are in the hamper," replied Todd, who'd finally, after much nagging, quit dumping everything in a pile in the walk-in closet. "Now, you get yourself to the doctor, okay? You can't fly to New York next week with sinuses as messed up as yours." Todd went around, kissed Rawlins on the forehead. "You're the best."

For a brief instant they grabbed hands and squeezed. The upcoming trip had been Todd's idea, not only as an attempt to perk up Rawlins but a way to further cement their relationship. Hoping to make it as romantic a getaway as possible, Todd had already made reservations at a swank Midtown hotel and his favorite restaurant down in SoHo, as well as ordered tickets for a Broadway show. Now it all depended on whether a third course of antibiotics could clear Rawlins's forehead.

Todd kissed Rawlins again, then turned, going quickly for the front hall, where his briefcase sat by the door.

From his chair Rawlins called, "Let me know what His Honorable Congressman, the jerk, has to say. And don't forget your tie!"

"It's right here in my briefcase."

Suddenly something black shot in front of Todd. Watching as Girlfriend darted into the kitchen, he paused.

No. He didn't believe in bad luck, did he?

3

If only beauty could kill.

She fantasized about gunning him down with a double-barrel stare of her icy blue eyes. She thought about tripping him with one of her long, long legs and then stabbing him with her pointed heels. She visualized herself pouncing on him and clawing him to death.

Neah, clawing wouldn't do. Once elegant and much admired, her nails were now in shit shape, and for sure she'd break one. Besides, it was all set up for later anyway.

As she walked up Lake Street in south Minneapolis, the breeze filtering through her coiffed blond hair, Tina pulled up the collar of her black wool coat. The sun was out, most of the snow was gone, and the ice on the lakes was melting, but there was still a bit of a chill hovering over the city. She wasn't like these kids, these die-hard Minnesotans, like that one over there on the other side of the street bombing toward Lake Calhoun on Rollerblades, wearing nothing but a T-shirt and some long shorts! Or those people over there at the coffee shop, sitting outside in open jackets and drinking coffee, soaking up the sun as if it were July. Oh, no. She still hadn't shaken the chill of this past winter, and she didn't feel as if she ever would, particularly given how lousy she'd been feeling. Her entire soul was trembling, it seemed, which was why her coat was buttoned up snugly and why she was still wearing her leather gloves, not to mention the pale yellow turtleneck. Perhaps instead of the tasteful cream-colored skirt and white stockings, however, she should have worn slacks, something a little more casual as well as warmer. Then again, thanks to her years as a top model in New York, Tina knew how to dress for any occasion. And today, after all, she was going to see one of the most important men in the United States.

Exactly, she thought as she neared the place. One of the most important men and arguably the biggest asshole of them all. She'd never thought about killing anyone before, never, not a woman like her, once beloved in the fashion industry even more for her congenial Minnesota temperament than her wholesome beauty. But this guy was pushing it too far, his ideas too radical. No doubt about it, if she could kill one person it would be him. After all, someone had to stop him. Something had to be done.

Tina came to the corner of Lake and Hennepin, pausing right in front of the large Gap store. Outside of downtown, this was the busiest intersection in the city, with two- and three-story brick buildings filling each of the corners. And while the neighborhood had once been rather borderline, it was now booming, the hippest of the hip flocking to the trendy restaurants and shops. Even bored suburbanites, ever in search of new shopping, frequented the neighborhood. Especially today. Mr. Jerk himself was in there signing his book, and there were sure to be hundreds in line waiting for his smarmy autograph.

Crossing the street in a crowd of twenty or so, Tina could tell that the flow was definitely toward him. In this block-long set of old brick buildings, a small shopping mall had been carved, and as she ducked out of the sunny, almost-spring day and entered the complex, she could tell that everyone was going in and no one was going out. Great, she thought. So much for Hubert Humphrey and Walter Mondale. So much for the bleeding-heart liberal Minnesotan. No wonder this guy had to be gotten rid of.

Up ahead the central atrium of the mall was packed. So, she thought, the crowd was so big they'd moved the entire shebang out of the bookstore. Tina drifted to the side, peered around, saw a huge line snaking this way and that. Must be, what, four, five hundred people standing there waiting to meet him, Mister Big Shot Congressman. Did all these people really agree with him? Sure, the medical system in the United States was all messed up and as expensive as hell, but did they really want Medicare slashed and medical assistance all but eliminated? What kind of country was this anyway? Where were our values?

Tina hummed that old ABBA song, quietly singing, "Money, money, money, makes a rich man cry."

Shaking her head in disgust, she glanced to the side and caught her own reflection in a store window. She dabbed at her cheeks, tried to smooth her foundation, which she'd put on far too heavily in an attempt to cover the sores. Dear Lord, how was it possible to have aged as much as she had in the past year? With her dry blond hair and fading skin—what horrible color!— she looked as if she were over fifty instead of not even forty. Her pal Elliot was right. If her skin cracked and shriveled any more she was going to have to switch her name to Patina.

Forget how exhausted you are, she told herself. Just stroll along. Admire the lovely shoes in the window. What nice pumps! And the sandals! What fun colors! She casually moved to the next display window, glanced over, saw the crowd, checked out their clothes. Lots of khakis and loafers. Lots of women with perky hair. All of them white. And all of them Republicans. Blech.

But . . . not much security.

That was what she really needed to find out. Brushing a strand of hair out of her face, she moved into the open courtyard, glanced up at the balcony, then scanned the stairs. There were a couple of cops over there, another one or two by the newsstand. She surveyed the long line of eager fans. No, there didn't appear to be any FBI folk. And, most important, there weren't any Secret Service men. Of that she was fairly sure, because when the President was last in town there were guys with mirrored sunglasses and earpieces everywhere. No, it was just as they thought. This guy, His Honorable Johnny Clariton, wouldn't get Secret Service protection until he announced his presidential bid, which everyone expected he would do in a month or so.

So let's just see how close I can get, mused Tina.

She sauntered forward, her heels clicking on the tile floor, and came around a column. The line of fans twisted all the way through the atrium and down to the far end, where a mass of people were glommed around a low table. Tina bent over a bit, peered between a couple of people. And there he was. Her heart jumped. She'd seen him on TV countless times, doing his blather on CBS/NBC/ABC and CNN/CNN/CNN about how the country was in deep trouble with this and that and how we needed to return to the family values that had made this country great. She'd seen him on the cover of *Newsweek,* his handsome face lit up, the index finger of his right hand raised high as he lectured on the problems of the national deficit, medical care, and, of course, AIDS funding, stating bluntly that now that so much progress had been made on the "gay disease," research should really be left to the drug companies since they were already reaping such enormous profits. But this . . . this was different. Seated there at a banquet table, smiling endlessly as he signed book after book, he definitely seemed not larger than life but . . . small. Maybe that's why Johnny Clariton was so popular. With light-brown hair rimming his bald head, a square jaw, and a charming, white smile, he looked like the boy next door. And for that reason quite possibly the next President of the United States of America.

My, how she hated him, thought Tina with a fake smile as she moved into the atrium. A leader that would inspire the best in people he was not.

So just how close could she get?

"Excuse me, can I get past you?" said Tina to a young woman with a stroller. "This is so exciting I can't stand it."

"Isn't he wonderful?" replied the woman.

"Well, I just can't believe it." Tina's heart clutched when she glanced down at the stroller and saw a little girl, small and blond and adorable, for she reminded Tina so much of her own daughter. "I can't believe John Clariton is right here in Uptown."

"I know, that's why I came."

Her voice sweet yet raspy, Tina begged her way closer, maneuvering in and around clumps of people, around the line of book buyers, around a fountain, and almost right there, right up to the table where the Honorable Jerk was signing his tome. She paused once to catch her breath—she'd been running a fever forever and she really should be home in bed—then moved on, her heart beating faster and faster. Dear God, she was so near to him. Her hand, beaded with droplets of sweat, slipped into the pocket of her coat and clutched a Kleenex. If only it were the syringe. If only she could do it right now.

Suddenly a mountain of a man slid right in front of her.

"That's close enough, ma'am."

Forcing the classiest of smiles, Tina looked up into gorgeous dark eyes and said, "What?"

"This is a book-signing, ma'am, and all these people are waiting to speak to Mr. Clariton and have their books autographed. I'm afraid you'll have to step back a bit."

"Oh." She looked him up and down, noting his chestnut brown hair, his broad shoulders. "Oh, I see."

"If you'd like to buy the book they're selling it right over there," he said, pointing to a table by the fountain.

"And the congressman wrote it? What's it about?" she asked, even though she knew all too well and was perfectly disgusted by it.

"It's a science fiction novel."

"Really? How very interesting. Do you work at the bookstore here? Have you read the book?" She lowered her voice and her lips pursed into a sly grin. "Just because he's a member of congress doesn't mean he can write. Is it any good?"

"No, I don't work at the bookstore, but a lot of people like the book."

"Oh." Trying to appear innocent but titillated, like many of the suburban matrons here, she asked, "So are you his bodyguard?"

"Something like that."

"How fascinating."

"Lyle?" called a woman from behind Clariton's table.

He turned, listened to some apparent orders, then turned back to Tina. "Excuse me, but the congressman's aide would like everyone to move back a bit."

"Of course."

Okay, okay, thought Tina as she retreated. So now wasn't the time—not that it was supposed to be anyway. No. Just stop by, scope things out. See what you can find out. That was her job, that was what they'd instructed. And that was exactly what she'd done. Mission accomplished.

Stuffing her hands in her pockets, she turned around. No need to worry, for she was going to get her fifteen minutes of fame. They all would. Fifteen minutes and then some. Right. Mr. Johnny Clariton's interview was going to be just ever so explosive.

She moved on, treading her way through the crowd, and just as she came around an escalator bright lights burst against her face. Several people started zooming in on her. Oh, shit! Tina tensed, ready to bolt. Was it the police? How could they know what she was really doing here?

A woman pressed forward, some instrument held in her hand, and in an altogether perky voice said, "Hi, I'm Cindy Wilson from WTCN TV, and we're interviewing a few of Johnny Clariton's fans at this amazingly successful book-signing."

Tina held up her hand to shield her eyes from the bright lights, saw that the blond woman was in fact holding a microphone and that the lights were from a camera, and said, "What?"

"We'd like to know what you think of Johnny Clariton. Don't worry, this is just being taped. We'll run it at the midday news. Any comments for WTCN TV?"

It couldn't hurt. Not really. So what if the connection was made later on? Sure, she had a lot to say about this guy. Why not now?

So Tina nodded. "Okay."

"Great." The reporter nodded at her photographer to start taping, cleared her throat, and in her best TV voice began. "This is an amazingly successful book-signing, don't you think? There must be six or seven hundred fans here, maybe more, and—"

As the microphone was tilted toward her she bent forward and said, "Tina. My name's Tina, but I think there are only about four hundred people here."

"So have you bought your book yet?"

Tina hesitated, then forced herself not to be nice, but blunt and truthful, and said, "Hell, no."

"Oh, I see," replied Cindy Wilson, not really sure where to take the comment. "Does that mean you're not a Johnny Clariton fan?"

"No, not at all."

"Oh . . . oh, okay."

Tina saw Cindy Wilson's eyes as she turned to her cameraman and signaled him that this wasn't a good one. Tina couldn't stop herself. She used to be so timid, so polite. Everyone liked Tina. Pretty Tina from the Midwest. She never put up a fuss. She'd stay under the lights for hours until they got the perfect shot. But then in her mind's eye Tina saw Chris—those beautiful eyes!— and she reached out and grabbed for the microphone. If nothing else, goddammit all, she was going to do it. For the sake of Chris alone, Tina was going to make sure the world knew just what they'd been through. That was why she was here, why she was involved in all this, after all. Not for herself, but for Chris. And there was no turning back. And there was no time like the present to start speaking out.

"You know what, I want to change my mind," barked Tina. "I want Johnny Clariton to be elected the next President of these United States of America. I also want him to contract HIV, and I want him to develop full-blown AIDS. He's been going around saying the epidemic is over, but let me tell you, if he got sick then he'd find out it really isn't."

Shaking, Tina turned and started off. Exactly, she thought as she stormed away. If they were even the least bit successful Clariton would get sick. Very sick.

Behind her she heard Cindy Wilson mutter, "God, Bob, I don't think we can use that one, do you?"

Lyle had an uneasy sense about the lady and kept his eyes on her as she wove through the crowd and disappeared behind an escalator.

Behind him, Carol, the congressman's aide, scowled as she said, "What did she want?"

Lyle rolled onto his toes and tried to see far into the crowd. "I'm not really sure."

"She was kind of weird-looking, don't you think?" pressed Carol, a very average-looking woman with brown hair, a wide face, and wearing a predictable blue suit. "Did you notice all that makeup? I mean, it was caked on so thick it was falling off. At first I thought it was another one of them, another one of those drag queens. It wasn't, was it?''

A large man in the peak of condition, Lyle continued to scan the throng of people. To be sure, there was something odd about the woman, but it wasn't her sex, of that he was confident.

"No, it was a woman."

"God, then she looked like death warmed over."

Lyle, not a man of many words, nodded. That was what had caught his attention in the first place, her frail demeanor as well as the strange tone of her skin. And after the trouble that Clariton had had on the West coast—some AIDS activists had doused the congressman with a bucket of blood, which fortunately turned out to have been sterilized—Lyle was being especially alert. That, after all, was why Clariton's publisher had decided to bring in someone like Lyle, just in case something like that happened again. As far as Lyle knew, though, there hadn't been any threats here in Minneapolis.

"Well, be alert." Carol laughed, then kept her voice low as she said, "But you know, a lot of our people—the congressman's strategists and so on—are hoping something else will happen. After those guys threw that crap on Congressman Clariton in San Francisco, his popularity soared. Do you realize he gained fifteen points in the polls overnight? Fifteen points! Christ, the publicity we got out of it was utterly phenomenal! You can't buy coverage like that, believe me."

"No," said Lyle, his eyes once again searching the crowd and hoping that nothing happened while he was in charge, "I suppose you can't."

"It just goes to show," continued Carol, glancing over at her hero as he signed book after book, "that Congressman Clariton is right: Good Americans are fed up with gays and their agenda, and the more shenanigans they pull, the more they prove him right. Wouldn't you agree?"

Spying two well-dressed men with short hair move oddly through the crowd—men he assumed were queer—Lyle said, "Excuse me."

As he stepped into the swarm of people he put his hand inside his sport coat, resting his fingers gently on the pistol that sat snugly in his shoulder holster. Did he agree with Clariton's position on gays?

If the congressman and his aide only knew.

4

With all that had happened in the last year, Todd had wondered every now and then if he had lost it, his thirst for broadcast journalism. It used to be that he'd be up and going anytime of day to scoop a story, particularly as the lead investigative reporter on WTCN's CrimeEye report. Hoping to catch a crime of any kind on videotape, he and a photographer had chased around the city, following lead after lead, more often than not finding nothing, but sometimes hitting a bull's-eye. He recalled the rush of capturing that guy as he broke into the jewelry store—his jaded girlfriend had called to tip off Todd—and the charge of filming the suspects in a cop killing as they got together to brag about their murderous caper. Oh, yes, and there'd been almost a dozen cats in trees, a few of which had proved to be interesting adventures.

Then after Michael's death there'd been the long, empty spell where nothing seemed to make a difference.

No, what he'd lost professionally, Todd realized as he steered his dark-green Jeep Grand Cherokee to the studios of WLAK TV, wasn't his thirst for broadcast journalism, but something else: his arrogance. Or at least more than he could afford. To be in this business you had to be controlled, you had to be supremely confident even if you sensed you were doomed for failure. You had to boast that you were going to get a shot of a judge buying cocaine when everyone thought it was sheer stupidity, then sit there in a van for three, four, five days, until you got that very judge on tape, doing just that, buying drugs. Ever since Michael's death, however, Todd was more emotional than he could afford to be. He gave away too much. He got angry too easily. Exactly, he thought. If you're going to keep your job at Channel 10, if you're ever going to win another Emmy, you're going to have to revert to your old egotistical, arrogant self. But was that possible?

Okay, so he was nervous today. That was understandable, but he couldn't show it, not by any means. He was nervous, but as he drove along Highway 394 he realized, too, that he did feel confident, even strong. He wouldn't have been able to do this story a year ago, at least not in the way it should be done. To do a great interview you needed to be honest and blunt—and, yes, arrogant—and any earlier than this Todd would have been too afraid to ask Johnny Clariton certain questions for fear of what they might elicit. But now . . . now Todd was no longer afraid of having the spotlight turned on himself. Which meant that it no longer mattered to Todd whether viewers liked him or not depending on his sexuality or even the ties he wore. Deep inside he was no longer terrified of what people would think if they knew the real Todd Mills. No, first things first, and what mattered most to Todd now was the quality of his work. Odd, he thought as he pulled off the Louisiana Avenue exit and neared the station, but he'd lost sight of that over the years. Instead, he'd sought success. Accolades. Awards. Any and all external praise to bolster his own sense of self-worth.

Well, screw all that. He was back, and back for all the right reasons. Thank God for WLAK, the upstart station that had lured Todd back into the business with a generous offer. At first Todd had balked, but then they'd given him everything he'd wanted and then some. Pleading for him to accept their offer, Channel 10 management had said, we just want Todd Mills because who else around here has won a couple of Emmys?

"That's polite bullshit, doll," countered his agent, Stella, from her California office when he'd first told her about the offer. "They want you because your name was smeared everywhere up there and all over the country. You've probably got more name recognition out there in Minne-whatchamacallit than anyone else, between you getting the Emmys and poor Michael getting himself killed. Just be aware of that, and if you decide you want the job let me know. I'll make them pay through the nose. But don't forget, I'm sure I can—''

"Thanks, Stella, but I don't want to relocate right now.''

"Yeah, yeah, yeah, doll, but you did make a lot of the national papers, so for another six months or so I can get big bucks for a guy like you. After that—and no offense meant—the free ride is over, expired, kaput. You know, I still got some feelers out at CBS, like maybe they could use you to cover some of the gay issues. It could be great, ya know. Oh, and Todd, there's something I been meaning to ask you—what do people eat out there?''

Okay, okay, he thought, pulling into the lot in front of the low white building. Don't deceive yourself. WLAK hired you because of the sensationalism around your career. And they gave you the Clariton interview because you're gay and, given the good congressman's remarks, they're betting sparks will fly. It was like sending a black reporter to interview someone from the KKK. Sizzle. In these conniving times he also assumed Clariton's handlers were equally savvy, that they knew Todd was queer and perhaps had even sought him out for that very reason. Clariton's complicity in agreeing to an interview with a gay reporter, therefore, could only mean one thing: He hoped to turn it into political gain of some sort. Todd's challenge, on the other hand, was to trounce on Clariton and expose his true motivations and thoughts. Christ, realized Todd, this wouldn't be an interview so much as a duel. And he had to come into it as confident as an enraged bull.

He parked behind an entire row of dark-blue Ford Explorers emblazoned with the Channel 10 logo, then walked past a half dozen satellite dishes, twenty- and thirty-foot things aimed toward the sky. As he approached the employee entrance he pulled a passcard from the outer pocket of his briefcase, then swiped it in the door and buzzed himself in. The corridor he walked down was broad and softly lit, with awards and celebrity photos lining the walls.

A guy darted from a side hall and dashed toward the door.

"If it isn't Bradley, WLAK's top photographer,'' said Todd of the man who would be shooting his interview with Clariton.

"Please," joked the black man, who had short hair and one gold earring. "I'm a photojournalist."

"You're not going anywhere, are you?"

"Nope, don't worry. I'm just going to get something out of my car."

"Great." Todd glanced at his watch. "Listen, I think we ought to leave about noon and give ourselves plenty of time."

"Sure. I'll meet you in your office."

Todd turned into the newsroom, a huge space with exterior windows on one side, twenty cubicles grouped in the middle, the raised assignment desk looming over all, and various private offices and technical rooms on the other sides. Always fluttering with the hyperactivity of reporters, editors, and producers, the thirty-five people who toiled away in this one room were responsible for broadcasting almost six hours of news a day, beginning at five-thirty in the morning. To back up the anchors with news footage it took roughly twenty minutes of tape for each minute on air, and it amazed Todd how the creative anarchy back here emerged so cleanly and professionally on screen. They pulled it off in part because Channel 10 had been completely and thoroughly computerized, from the keyboards and monitors on each and every desk to the robotic cameras in Studio A that danced like angels with the touch of a computer screen.

Grabbing himself a cup of coffee from an industrial-size metal coffeepot that sat back in this corner, Todd ignored the newspapers from around the country that were stacked to one side. If there was any Clariton news this morning, which was the main reason Todd had come in, it would be found on the wire service.

Unlike the staff at Channel 7, the bunch here was a friendly group, and various hands waved and faces smiled as Todd walked through the center of the newsroom toward his office on the far side.

"Hi, Mary," he called to one of the reporters, who sat in her cubicle to the right.

"Knock 'em dead today, will you?"

"Just for you."

"It's still a go," called the assignment editor, Frank, a burly guy with thin brown hair, who was coordinating today's activities like a mad ballet. "One o'clock and he's yours."

"Great."

There'd been some worry, after all, that Clariton might cancel again on Channel 10; six months ago on another brief trip— before he had a book to sell—the congressman had backed out literally seven minutes before a scheduled interview. Using that as leverage, Todd had managed to get Clariton's PR person to grant him an exclusive today.

Todd entered his office, a small glass-walled space on the far side of the newsroom, and before he even put down his briefcase or took off his overcoat, he hit a couple of keys on his computer keyboard. As he hung up his coat his messages came up on the color screen, and he sat down and quickly scrolled through them. Nope, nothing that couldn't wait until later this afternoon. Next picking up his phone and checking his voice mail, he found five messages, including one from Janice, his girlfriend the lesbian, as he called her, with whom his life was so intricately entwined. She was visiting family in Santa Fe, and she had called to wish Todd good luck with the interview.

"But I wish you were here, Todd," she said on the message. "All of us do. It would have been really terrific."

There was a knock on the glass, and Cherise, one of the pro-ducers, a woman with rich black skin, poked her head in. "Todd, I just wanted to let you know that we're entering your pieces on the Megamall in all the awards."

"That's great."

"Yeah, they're both among our most widely watched segments of the year."

"Does that mean I get to keep my job?"

"It's been a rough decision, but I guess so," she said with a smile.

While Todd despised the Megamall because it threatened to turn Minneapolis into a doughnut city—another sprawling De-troit with its shopping and life drained from the city core—Todd knew that viewers first and foremost loved a someone-done-somebody-wrong story. With that in mind he had first focused on the crime at the Megamall that wasn't being reported because it was happening within the confines of a private establishment; with a tip from a former gang kid they had videotaped one mugging, two car thefts, and a handful of hookers scoring in one of the bars. Next a guide from some part of the dismembered Yugoslavia had taken him on a tour, starting at the Grand Balcony—a perch attached to the food court that overlooked the enormous indoor amusement park—and then continuing all the way down into the space where they were planning to build the humongo exhibit and ride called Journey to the Center of the Earth. But where they were about to start construction on buried dinosaurs and rivers of lava, Todd had failed to find any safety flaws. There was a rumor that payoffs had been made to building inspectors, and when Todd could find no evidence of that either he focused the second segment on how little taxes the mall actually generated since there was no sales tax on clothing in Minnesota.

"You know," added Cherise, "the Clariton interview will probably be even more widely watched. We've had promos running for the last two days."

"Well, don't worry, I'm going to give you guys fireworks."

"I'm sure you will. Good luck!"

Todd turned back to his computer, calling up Lexus-Nexis, a professional research database. Yesterday he'd printed out no less than a dozen articles from sources such as *The Washington Post* and *The New York Times,* and he'd taken them home and read them all last night, highlighting key points and any and all crackpot comments the congressman had made. In an interview such as this Todd liked to find the subject's main buttons and then, of course, hit the biggest one first. Naturally Todd was going to go right to health care and Clariton's comments on AIDS. Then he'd move to the book, which was drawing fire because of the millions of dollars he was earning from it. Hey, and wasn't the thing ghostwritten? And lastly, the national budget, more specifically Clariton's tax plan, which sounded good but didn't seem to add up.

Todd had stayed up late, scratching notes and questions on a yellow legal pad, and now he scrolled through the research program, hunting the wire services for last-minute news. There was news about a storm brewing in the Rockies, something about an overturned school bus in New Hampshire, more on the political problems of Russia, but only a couple of small mentions of Clariton's book tour. Searching for anything else, new or old, Todd scrolled on and on, through listing after listing. Although he couldn't convince himself, he really didn't need anything more, but he pushed on, at the same time trying to visualize how the interview might go, what might happen. Without ever thinking about it, Todd did a great share of his work in the shower, on the road, while he jogged, and now while he busied himself with an essentially unnecessary task.

An odd title popped up on Todd's screen, one he hadn't noted yesterday, and he hit the RETRIEVE button. Seconds later a short, humorous article appeared from the *L.A. Times* in which a reporter wrote how Clariton was the master of saying something totally weird right at the beginning of an interview. Todd pondered this a moment, then realized something quite important. So Clariton was that kind of ass, was he?

Completely consumed, Todd was startled when his office phone rang. Checking his watch as he picked up the receiver, he realized that nearly forty-five minutes had passed.

"Channel Ten, this is Todd Mills speaking."

"Hey, it's me."

Todd immediately smiled. Rawlins. Clutching the handset in his right hand, the interview and everything else vanished.

Todd said, "So what did the doctor say? We're on for New York, right?"

"What?"

"The doctor—what did he say about your sinuses? Will you be able to fly next week?"

"I don't know yet. I mean, my appointment's not until after lunch. I'm still at your place."

"Oh, just lying around, are you?" joked Todd. "So what's up?"

"You won't believe it: We got a witness."

"A witness? A witness for what?"

"I called down to the station to check on messages," continued Rawlins, referring to the police station. "And some old guy across the street from Curt's apartment saw something."

Todd had been so focused on the interview that at first he couldn't quite switch gears. Someone saw what?

"You're talking about the night Curt died?" asked Todd.

"Exactly. Granted, it's not much, but it's a start," replied Rawlins. "You see, there's this old guy who lives across the street from Curt's apartment building, and he hasn't said anything before this because he really hasn't gone out this winter. Something about a bad hip. I don't know how or why he wasn't questioned, but . . . but, anyway, the night Curt died he hears something right outside his back door. He puts on his glasses, goes into the kitchen, and turns on a light. And what do you think he sees?"

"Some kids?"

"No, a bunch of raccoons in his garbage. So he bangs on the door and scares them away, and they dart out front, dragging some junk with them. The old guy then goes to the front of his house without turning on any lights, and when he looks out the window he sees the raccoons in the middle of the street ripping apart a McDonald's bag. Apparently his grandson had stopped by and brought him some dinner. Gutsy little things, he thinks. Gutsy because they broke into the garbage and stole the last of his dinner. And gutsy because they're not even frightened by some guy walking down the street. Get this, a guy who turns and heads into Curt's building."

"You're kidding."

"Nope."

"So what does this guy look like?" pressed Todd. "Did the old man see much? Better yet, does he even remember?"

"He was wearing a dark coat and hat. And he was white."

"Great, I wonder how many white guys in Minneapolis own dark coats."

"True, it's not much to go on," replied Rawlins over the phone, "but it does prove someone went into the building. And whoever that was obviously went into Curt's apartment, because none of the other tenants had any visitors that night. None. That much we already know."

"Any idea what time of night this was?"

"Shortly after two. The old man is sure about that because he looked at his bedside clock when he got out of bed."

"Which is about when Curt died," said Todd, recalling the coroner's report. "So it obviously wasn't a simple suicide."

"Nope. Either it was an assisted suicide—which I suppose isn't all that bad, is it?—or . . . or just a plain old murder."

It probably wasn't the latter, pointed out Todd. After all, nothing had been taken, not Curt's stereo or his VCR or even his gold watch, which was sitting right on his dresser.

"So given Curt's health," commented Todd, "I suppose an assisted suicide is the logical explanation. I mean, if I were that sick I'd probably want something like that."

With a deep sigh Rawlins added, "Yeah, me too."

"But listen, I have to get going. We're leaving in about twenty minutes."

"Well, good luck. And Todd?"

"What?"

"Don't forget your tie."

"Thanks, I'll put it on right now."

"I'll be thinking of you."

"And I'll be thinking of you." Todd hesitated. "Listen, if your doctor says you can't fly, we can cancel everything in New York and just take a drive up to Lake Superior or something."

"Don't worry, I'll be fine."

Even though I had to do it before he said too much about our plans, I thought I would have been more upset about killing Curt. On the other hand, did I really kill him or did I merely help him catch an earlier train out of his own personal hell? I mean, let's face it, anyone would have done as much for a dog in half the pain.

I've never seen anything more cruel than AIDS, the way it attacks your entire body and creates all those sores and weird infections. They used to say the lucky ones got something like pneumonia and croaked overnight. Now they say the lucky ones get the pills, all those protease inhibitors or whatever. Frankly, I don't know which is better. No one does, actually. Over these long years of the epidemic I've just seen too many guys linger and linger, bouncing from crisis to crisis, hope to despair, Kaposi's sarcoma to blindness to fungal infections. Nowadays some guys are able to get their T-cells back up there, but who knows for how long. Sure, the new drugs are inching toward promise, but if you ask me, AIDS is like watching the end of your own life come racing toward you. You know it's going to smash right into you, eventually take you six feet under, and there's nothing you can do.

Watching Curt fade away over this past year has affected me like nothing else. So would I do it again? You bet.

5

These past couple of months Elliot had never been happier. He wasn't really sure why, everything just seemed so clear, all the complex questions so black and white. As he now walked down Nicollet Mall, the main street in downtown Minneapolis, with his small nylon backpack slung over one shoulder, he couldn't help it. He just wanted to stop there at the corner of Nicollet and Seventh, rip off his little black tam, and hurl it into the air just like Mary Tyler Moore. Sure, he thought, you can turn the world on with your smile. Everyone has that power, that magic. He used to spend so much time worrying—what was he doing with his life, why wasn't he more successful, when would he ever get out of the stupid restaurant business and become a real, serious artist?—and for what? Where had it gotten him? Everything was so much simpler. You live and you die. And he'd probably be dead by fall, if not a whole hell of a lot sooner.

A true Midwesterner from Omaha—Homoha, in his lexicon—Elliot had always been tall and gangly with long Ichabod Crane legs and arms, but of course he was now thinner than he'd ever been in his entire skinny life. He had a long face with a little mouth, dark eyes, and for the past few months he'd been sporting a little goatee, a sprout of light-brown hair on his chin and above his lip. He'd never been handsome, though some people found him cute, even now at forty-three, probably because of his lankiness, his smile, and, well, his artistic bent—namely his hip clothes, the gold hoop earrings that he wore in each ear, and so on. For a long time he'd been worried that he'd never had a longtime companion—he had a girlfriend once way back in his freshman year at college, and over the years a couple of guys he used to date—but being unattached was just making this so much easier. If he had a lover now, Elliot would worry about leaving him behind.

As he'd done for the last ten years he'd worked here, he ducked into the brick building on the corner, entering the marble lobby and walking directly to the escalator. The restaurant, Jerome's, was on the second floor, connected to the skyway, that system of second-floor passages and bridges that turned the entire downtown into one big ant farm, and as he rode the escalator upward he realized he could walk this route blind, no prob. Like his best chum, Curt, who'd worked here since the restaurant had first opened until over a year ago when his health really went to pot, Elliot had spent so much time here. He'd worked four evening shifts and two lunches a week, making a pretty good buck too, for he was a pro at humoring the customers and anticipating their every need. He got to paint as much as he wanted during the week and work an invigorating job—all in all not bad. Fun people too. Oh, the parties they'd had after work, drinking wine and smoking pot, laughing and dancing. God, he used to dance a lot, didn't he? He should, he knew, be doing more of that while he could still walk, but frankly he just didn't have the energy anymore.

As he neared the top, he switched his black nylon pack to his left shoulder and prepared to disembark. Stepping off the mechanical steps, however, he failed to see the figure to his right and, blam, he ran directly into an older woman, nearly knocking her off her feet.

"Oh, I'm sorry!" Elliot exclaimed, squinting at her. "I'm so, so sorry, ma'am. Did I hurt you?"

"No, no."

"You sure?"

The lady, short with gray hair, wasn't the least bit fazed, and without even bothering to reply she scurried on to some store. Elliot, however, just stood there. Oh, brother. His peripheral vision was the pits and getting worse not by the week but by the day. You just gotta remember to turn your head side to side, he told himself. Scan. You gotta scan, man. Scan from left to right, right to left.

Jerome's was one of the fanciest restaurants downtown, a smart place known for its elegant atmosphere, its Paris-trained chef, and the wine. A great list. Fabulous reds, the best in town. No sandwich joint, this was where top execs came to linger over pheasant consommé, medallions of lamb, and corporate strategies. In the evening the place filled with first the pretheater crowd and later the wealthy romantics and still later the sopranos, baritones, actors, and rock stars who sought out anything but flyover food. Elliot himself had waited on Joni Mitchell, Julie Andrews, and, with trembling hands, the hot, hot Keanu Reeves, his fave.

"Hey, Leo," said Elliot as he cruised in the entrance.

"Elliot, how great to see you!" replied the owner, a paunchy red-haired guy, from behind a podium. "You're looking good."

"Feeling good."

"Well, that's wonderful."

"But you know what," said Elliot, stopping and leaning an elbow on a corner of the podium and studying the other. "You look tired. Man, are you still putting in eighty- and ninety-hour weeks?"

Leo smoothed the lapels of his crisp tuxedo, tightened his bow tie. "Something like that anyway."

"Shame on you, Leo. You gotta get out of here. You gotta get out and take a bite of life before life eats you."

"Ah, so says the wise man who's here for the free lunch. Go on, get outta here," said Leo. "We've got a really busy lunch hour, but why don't you go into the kitchen and nab something to eat. Everyone will be thrilled to see you."

"Will do."

A waitress whooshed by. "El, you look great!"

"Hey, Kate, feeling great."

"Hi, Elliot, long time no see!" shouted one of the busboys.

"Hey, Rob." And then, "Hey, Tim. Hey, Pete. Hey, Liz."

And on and on. Elliot knew all of them, even these folks on the lunch shift. All of them except one new waitress who'd been hired after Elliot had left five months ago. He cruised into the kitchen, a cramped space packed with stainless-steel counters, huge refrigerators, and gas stoves with blazing flames. The lunch dance was just cranking up to disco speed, and lest he smash into something Elliot made a concerted effort to turn his head from side to side. You are, he told himself, the Scanman.

"Hey, Paul!" Elliot called to the chef, who was darting around.

The head chef, a stout fellow whose energy level was permanently stuck on full tilt, waved his chopping knife and managed what was almost a smile. "Have you come back to work, you lazy bum?"

"No way! I like my Ragú from a jar."

He snarled.

Looking around, Elliot saw that the chef de cuisine and chef garde-manger were busy slicing and dicing a cornucopia of definitely non-Midwestern veggies, from huge mushrooms to furry green stalks. Everything here was made from scratch, and back in the corner the pastry chef, a young woman with a flushed red face, was furiously blowtorching ramekins of crème brûlée, one by one, to a sinful crunchy brown.

"Wow, busy," said Elliot. "And what is it, not even eleven-thirty. What do you got, a banquet or something today? This joint's hoppin'."

"No shit," said Kate, a trim woman with short brown hair, coming in from behind. "Haven't you heard?"

"No," replied Elliot, feigning ignorance.

"Big, big V.I.P. day," called someone else.

"Yeah," shouted one of the waiters. "Featuring one Very Ignorant Prick in particular."

"Cool," said Elliot. "Who is it? Movie star?"

"If only." Kate shook her head. "Johnny Clariton—you know, the congressman—is having a roundtable lunch here."

"Ew, icky, the devil himself," replied Elliot, wrinkling his nose. "Glad I don't work here anymore."

"And don't I wish I had the day off. Instead, we're going to be waiting on him and about twenty-five bigwig execs whom Clariton is coddling for donations. Five thousand bucks a plate, can you believe it?"

"Paul," called Elliot from across the room, "be sure and cook up something yummy! Oh, and stir in a little bit of that salmonella that you, ah, hit a few patrons with every now and then."

Paul flung a paper-thin tomato slice at him.

Kate charged off, grabbing some salt and peppers and then scurrying back into the main dining room. Elliot stood there. Not a good time to help himself to a free lunch, which the owner, Leo, always made available to Elliot—Elliot, who was getting more sympathy from more frightened people than he would ever have imagined, particularly since Curt had croaked. If they hadn't understood before, they did now: Elliot was going to die too.

Oh, big deal, he thought with a roll of his eyes.

There was no time for such thoughts, not today. And there was no time to grab a meal. Much too chaotic. Everyone looked so uptight, so busy. He drifted over to the stainless-steel bread drawers, slid one of them open, and pulled out a hot roll. This would do, he thought, munching down on it and glancing around. He really couldn't stay anyway. Just get in, do your business, and get out, those were his instructions.

Elliot backed away, turned his head from side to side, and took it all in: the madhouse kitchen with the sterotypical uptight chef, the stereotypical gay waiters, the stereotypical pretty and fun waitresses. He loved them all, didn't want to hurt them. That was the one thing he'd insisted on when they were planning all this— nothing that would injure any of his friends. They were way cool.

But it should be okay. It really should.

So, carrying his backpack, he slipped down the side hall as if he were going to the employees' john. Instead, he stopped in front of the third door, glanced once toward the kitchen, and ducked in. It was the supply room, with paper towels and sponges and dish soap and chemicals lining one wall, stacks of clean laundry on another, and bags of soiled linens on the floor. Oh, yes, he'd been right, this would do nicely.

Working quickly, Elliot did exactly as he'd been told, unzipping his backpack, reaching in, and pressing the START button on the device. Immediately the red digital numbers came to life and started ticking down the seconds. Very good. He then zipped up the backpack and buried it beneath several bags of linen. Simple. No one was going to find it back here. Nope, not in the next ninety minutes anyway. He checked the scene one last time, smiled to himself—if only everything else went so easily—and opened the door.

Stepping into the hall, he slammed right into Hal, one of the waiters and an old pal.

"I'm sorry, Hal!" exclaimed Elliot. "I'm really sorry. Did you know I'm going blind? I mean, I really am. It's this stupid cytomegalovirus retinitis—it's a herpes virus, and it's eating at my eyes. You know, blurriness, floaters. Actually, I'm losing my peripheral vision and I didn't even see you."

"Don't worry, man," replied Hal, a tiny guy, who was unable to hide his surprise at Elliot's candor.

Elliot started squinting and looking around. "I thought this was the guys' room. But obviously—"

"No, it's the next door."

"Oh, cool. I see. Yeah, I see. Right there." Elliot put on a big grin. "Thanks, man."

As Hal scurried away, Elliot went into the men's room. It always freaked people out whenever he talked about AIDS or any of his symptoms, but he didn't care. He believed in being real up-front about the whole thing, about not hiding what was wrong or how it was affecting him. His appetite, or lack thereof. His loss of weight. His pathetic eyes. And how he'd been on AZT four or five years ago, but hadn't been real careful about taking the pills—okay, okay, so he skipped a day every now and then— and hence the virus within his body had developed a resistance to the drug. He was as frank as he could be because, after all, he'd contracted a virus and people needed to know about it, understand it. HIV and AIDS were everywhere, lurking unseen more often than not. So if he could make it a little more visible, that would make it a whole lot more real. He was the first to admit that it was a brutal disease, and if he could shove people's faces in it, well, then, maybe they'd be a little more careful when it came to sex. Besides, there'd been enough shame in his life—he was one of those queers who'd played with dolls when he was a little kid, ever since he was five or so, and he'd hid that part of him for years. But not now. No more hiding anything. Particularly not with AIDS. No way was he going to keep quiet, no way was he going to make a silent exit. No, he thought with a sly grin, he couldn't wait to tell his story, blurt it out to the entire country. Sure, he was pissed about having AIDS and everything, but he had his own agenda, and he was going out in fucking style. Big fucking style.

Exiting the restroom, Elliot passed down the short hall and back into the kitchen, where Paul was barking orders, pissed about the quality of the salmon, stressed to the max by the five-thousand-dollar plates he had to get out in a half hour. The sauté chef was going full tilt, madly adding some twenty-five-year-old balsamic vinegar to a sauté pan of delicate mushrooms. And the pastry chef, looking more like a spot welder at this point, was torching the last of the crème brûlées.

Taking it all in, Elliot departed, amazed at how quickly life could spoil.

6

You didn't have to be a rocket scientist to figure out that Cindy Wilson's career at Channel 7 was in a distinct nosedive, and no one knew it better than Cindy herself. In fact, she'd been slipping ever since the Todd Mills fiasco last year. There'd been all that botched business with him and that murder, and instead of taking over for Todd Mills as the lead reporter on WTCN's CrimeEye segment, the whole concept had been canned. Cindy still couldn't believe it. She'd been so sure she'd take Todd's spot and that would prove to be her stepping stone to an Emmy or two, just as it had been Todd's, but instead management had bagged the whole bit. Too much Todd's, they'd said. People associated it entirely with him. Better to start something else than try and relaunch it with a new lead reporter.

Bullshit, thought Cindy Wilson, an attractive blond woman, as she sat in her tiny office at the station. When it looked as if Todd Mills was guilty as sin, Roger Locker, the station director, had made the decision to go after Todd hook, line, sinker, rod, and fishing boat. It was news, hot news, and it was far better to cast the first stone than sit there with mud on their faces at having a murderous reporter on their staff. True, Cindy had been in on the decision and had been the reporter covering it—which might be part of why her popularity had plummeted, for at least one editorial in the gay papers had branded her a homophobe—but in any case the whole thing had backfired. Todd came out a big winner in the sympathy department, and rather than try to relaunch the CrimeEye segment without Todd and have to explain just why he was no longer working there, WTCN management decided to jettison the entire thing.

Oh, brother. Didn't anyone out there understand that it was about ratings and viewership, that by going after Todd she'd just been doing her job? And didn't anyone out there understand that she was just as good as that squirrelly Todd Mills? Better, even. She didn't push things like Todd did. She didn't try to expose the ugly underside of things. No, she gave people a story that made them hopeful, that made them feel good. And recently, as a matter of fact, it seemed that viewers were appreciating her more and more. At least until Todd Mills reappeared last month on WLAK.

The return of Todd Mills, she thought with a slow shake of her head.

That jerk cast such a big shadow. He was cute, he was smart, nice voice, broad shoulders, and so on and so on, but so what? She'd never bring in her personal life as he had, she'd never let her problems air like a soap opera for everyone to see. Yet he had, and look at where it had gotten him. Channel 10 had thrown all sorts of money at him, and his first story for them, the one on the Megamall, hadn't gotten so much advance publicity or so many viewers because Todd had done such a great job and it was such a hot piece. No, it got all that attention because everyone wanted to witness the reappearance of Todd Mills, the infamous homosexual. So maybe that was what it was all about after all, mused Cindy. Sex. What was she supposed to do, then, go out and sleep with the governor?

It just wasn't fair. How was an ambitious woman like her supposed to make it? And on top of it all, she thought as her anger rose to a pitch, Todd was getting an exclusive interview with Johnny Clariton!

Cindy Wilson shuffled through some papers atop her desk. Channel 10 had somehow finagled the interview, then assigned the one reporter who was most certain to clash with the congressman. And it was going to be hot, she was sure of it. Lots of people would watch. It'd be a tough interview, but Todd would do it and do it beautifully. She was certain he would, for Cindy had worked in his shadow—literally so because Todd was such a hog he barely shared the spotlight with anyone—and she'd watched him burrow in, bite hold, and not let go until his point was made. Which meant lots more people would admire Todd Mills.

Okay, so give Todd a great big gold star. What could she do about it anyway?

The intercom on her phone cracked, and a deep, gravelly voice commanded, "Cindy, get in here."

She wasn't ready for this, but she pressed down on the button anyway, and called back, "Sure, Roger."

Her boss, Mr. Type A, the original prime candidate for a heart attack. That Todd had rejected Channel 7's late and lame offer—presented to Todd only after the grapevine brought news of Channel 10's offer—still infuriated Roger Locker. They'd had Todd, lost him once, then lost him a second time, for Mills's agent had quite ceremoniously told Locker to go take a flying leap. And Cindy of course knew what was driving up Roger's blood pressure this morning: the Clariton interview that Channel 7 was not conducting.

Cindy rolled her chair back, headed out of her office and down the narrow hall. She brushed aside a wisp of her blond hair, then smoothed her ivory-colored blouse, fussed with her gold bracelets. Of course she knew what this was going to be about. And of course she knew it wouldn't be pretty.

Stepping into the doorway of his office, she put on a big smile, and said, "Hi, Roger."

A heavyset, balding man, he looked up, a scowl on his face. "What the hell were you doing in Uptown all morning, sipping on a nice café latte or something?"

Roger specialized in intimidation, and Cindy fell for it every time. Even though she should have expected something like this, her face began to flush with embarrassed warmth.

She replied, "Ah . . . interviewing some of . . . of Mr. Clariton's fans."

"Well, that's what I just saw on the tape. Imagine my surprise. And what did I tell you to do?"

"Roger, that was impossible."

"Which is exactly what I expect you and everyone else here at WTCN to do—the goddamn impossible! I wanted our lead tonight to be the first interview with Johnny Clariton."

"You don't understand, there was no way he'd talk with me."

"Why?"

"Roger, I couldn't even get close to him."

"Why?"

"Because he's got this bossy aide as well as this incredible hulk for a bodyguard who wouldn't let anyone near him. It was a book-signing, and a book-signing only." Cindy shrugged. "Sorry, Roger, they wanted and encouraged me to film his fans, which is to say voters. That's what they wanted to get across, not his book, not his politics, but his popularity—I mean, everyone knows he's going to run for president." She shrugged. "I did my best, but there was no way I could speak to him directly. Trust me, Roger, I got as much as I could, and besides, none of the other stations had a crew there, not even WLAK."

"Well, all you got is drivel—just a bunch of gushy folks and one nut case—and drivel isn't news. Our viewers are no dummies, and if we put that on the air everyone will know it's because Clariton wouldn't speak directly to us." He shook his head. "Don't you see what I was trying to do? Don't you see that I just wanted to steal some of Channel Ten's sizzle? That's my job, to make you look good, to make Channel Seven look good."

"I know, Roger, but—"

"But what, you don't want to be the best?"

"Of course I do, you know that," she fired back, at the same time thinking, If I were the best would I put up with this kind of crap?

"So this is what I want you to do. . . ." He spun his chair around and stared out the window. "Yeah, this'll work."

"Uh-oh."

Roger's main job, it seemed, was to sit around the station and, first, get mad and, second, concoct wild schemes. No one knew that better than Cindy, who had bought in to far too many of his plans, none of which actually had led to the big break Cindy was in search of.

"Cindy, I want you to get all dolled up." He swiveled back, looked her up and down, really seeing her for the first time that morning. "Well, you look good already, but take a couple of minutes and just sort of fuss yourself up, put on some nice perfume.''

"Oh, come on, Roger," she moaned, fully knowing where this was going.

"Just do it up, make yourself glamorous. Then I want you to grab a photographer—take anyone—and head down the street to Jerome's."

"Gee, let me guess—you want me to take another stab at him, so to speak?"

"Exactly." Locker checked his watch. "Clariton's roundtable is scheduled to start in only twenty minutes. Get your rear down there and see what you can turn up."

"You mean, before our turncoat friend, Todd, shows up."

"You got it. I want you to sweet-talk your way into that lunch. Maybe you could sneak into the back of the room, listen in." He reached into his coat pocket, pulled out his wallet. "Here. Here's a hundred bucks."

"A hundred? At five grand a plate that isn't even going to buy me a carrot stick."

"No, my dear, I want you to bribe the maître d' to let you in. Clariton's going to make a speech or a toast or something, and I want you to be right there. Maybe you can take along a pocket recorder and tape it. And then when the lunch is over, just rush over and start talking. Get him to say something, anything, even if it's just a few words, so that you can be the first Twin Cities reporter to talk with Clariton. And don't forget to get some footage of you and Clariton together. If you snuggle up right next to him I'm sure he'll wrap his arms around you. Make it look like he's in love with you. Then we can edit in what you got this morning and you can do a voice-over."

"Oh, I get it." Well, pondered Cindy with a smile, it might work. "We piece it all together to make it look like we've got the most extensive coverage of Clariton's entire day."

"Right. Trust me, all you need to do is catch his eye and he'll give you a few minutes. There's no doubt in my mind that Mr. Clariton would rather talk to a gorgeous girl like you than . . . well, a gay guy like Todd."

"But—"

"Don't worry," said Roger, reaching for the phone. "I'm going to make sure things go our way because, after all, this—"

"—ain't no dress rehearsal." Cindy shook her head and moaned, "Oh, brother, how did I ever end up working here?"

And with that, Cindy Wilson headed back down the hall. All she had to do was dab on some makeup, grab her black leather coat, get a photographer, and she'd be on her way—destined, she sensed, to stir up as much news as possible.

7

Matthew had not one but both feet in the grave. And the realization of that made him deliciously happy.

He'd been a model, one with a super future. The crowning piece of his career—which had ended not quite two years ago when he was thirty-four—had been when his face and physique had graced Times Square in a Calvin Klein ad. A mere two years ago the sharp-cheeked face that was more striking than it was handsome, the dazzling teeth, the chiseled chest, and the straight, light-brown hair were poised to take him to the very top. But then in the space of a mere twenty-four hours everything had fallen apart. The day before he was to do a shoot for the cover of *GQ* a red bump erupted on his forehead. Even though they could have put makeup over the sore—which the modeling agency desperately encouraged Matthew to do because, after all, everyone got a pimple now and then—Matthew canceled, for he recognized the bump, knew immediately that it was no zit. He'd seen that type of cancer on at least four of his friends and now he was seeing it on himself, a fact that Matthew's physician confirmed within a few days. Yes, that was Kaposi's sarcoma and, yes, Matthew had been expecting some such crisis, for he'd tested HIV positive three years earlier.

Who would have thought, mused Matthew as he drove his light-blue van on 35W toward downtown Minneapolis, that this farm boy from central Minnesota would escape the family farm, rise literally to the heights of the fashion world, then tumble to his present situation? He'd always wanted to be famous and had always known that somehow, someway he would be. Thirteen years ago he'd come to Minneapolis, determined to be a playwright and hoping that one of his plays would bring him the national recognition he was expecting. When that failed to happen and he was completely destitute, a friend of his gave him two phone numbers: one for a temporary employment agency that had a filing gig for three months minimum, and the other for a small Twin Cities modeling agency. He dreaded the first so he called the second, and that in turn had lit the fuse that had nearly blasted him all the way to the stars. And although he didn't quite make it out of the solar system that time, he knew this wondrous deed they were about to enact would make him a household name. It was odd, though, for he was only just realizing that his life hadn't been headed all this time for glorious fame, but instead for infamy of a most calculated kind. Yes, by tonight his deed, if not his face, would be broadcast on every national evening news show.

Too bad he'd never looked worse. Too bad his illness had progressed with a speed that alarmed even his doctors. Too bad his immune system was too severely compromised for the new drugs to have anything but a temporary effect. In fact, he looked like shit, which was why he could no longer bear even a glance in the mirror.

For starters all that straight, silky, luxuriant hair was completely gone. All of it. What the chemotherapy hadn't zapped Matthew had shaved, a nick here, a nick there. His skin looked like hell too, a brownish blob of a lesion here, another lesion there, particularly on his back, where he was nearly as spotted as a leopard. Of course, the fact that he'd lost almost thirty pounds from his already lean frame didn't help, especially since his cheekbones stuck way out and his cheeks themselves had fallen in, giving him *the look,* that kind of death-camp visage.

What the fuck, at least he was going to live long enough to do one important thing with his life. And this was important. You bet, he thought as he steered the van up the ramp into downtown. This wasn't about getting mad or getting even. Hell no. It was about taking action. Doing something. Taking a stand. And fighting back. Too bad Curt couldn't be here to witness this, but at least he'd gone toes up before he'd ruined the whole goddamn thing, which was what Matthew had been so worried about. Worried that in his delirium Curt would blab. But now that Curt was dead—shit, would Matthew ever stop feeling guilty?—their secret was safe, or so it seemed. And while it was obviously too late not only for Curt but for Matthew as well—the average life span for a person with KS was eighteen months after the appearance of the first lesion, so he was already pushing it—at least their little plan might speed things up and save a few others. It would have an effect, he was sure, unlike those guys in Italy, the big ninnies, the three men with AIDS who had robbed those banks. What exactly were they trying to prove? That queers could be tough guys? Or that in Italy criminals with AIDS should have a right to be imprisoned instead of being forced to go free? Jesus Christ, the world was nuts, fucking nuts.

Ignoring a sharp pain in his forehead—he prayed this wasn't the start of another bout of cryptococcal meningitis, like the god-awful one he'd had last year—Matthew turned left and proceeded into the heart of the city, eventually crossing Marquette Avenue and Nicollet Mall. How this place had changed, turned into a big city of sorts. He remembered his family—his parents and two younger sisters—driving all the way from the farm each Christmas, getting rooms at the Leamington, gawking at Dayton's Christmas windows, scarfing mountains of chow mein at the Nankin, then seeing two, three, four, and five movies. Life had seemed so simple. Of course then puberty had struck, and the day his father found him in the barn half-naked with another boy had changed the rest of his life. For starters, everyone stopped expecting that one day he'd take over the farm, and Matthew started plotting his escape to the big city. It took years, but he made it.

Shrugging off the memories, Matthew turned right, glanced at his watch, and saw he was perfectly on time. Bravo. Practice makes perfect, and the three of them had gone over and over this, getting the times and approaches just right. And as planned he pulled into the rear of the building, drove to the service door, leaned out the window, and punched in the security code. In the blink of a second the huge garage door started lifting up, and Matthew drove into a large loading area. He pulled to one side, then reversed the van to the loading dock. Not wasting a moment, he grabbed a broom from the back of the van, jumped out, then ran across the platform, reached up, and with a single swipe of the broom aimed the security camera away from the dock and at the garage door. The guards checked the monitors only once every thirty minutes, so there shouldn't be a problem, he thought as he hit the CLOSE button and watched the garage door rumble shut. Next he rushed back to the van, climbed in the back, and stared at the large laundry basket on wheels. Of course everything was in there, the guns and the gas masks buried beneath the pile of white sheets. Matthew had been over it and over it, checked and rechecked. Not to worry. Everything was going to go great.

Suddenly there was a *rap-tap-tap* on the rear door and a voice calling, "Are you a friend of Dorothy's?"

Excellent, thought Matthew with a grin. He flipped open the back door and there they were: Elliot in his tam and plaid wool coat, Tina with her blond hair and black wool jacket and now wearing a jeans skirt and heavy wool sweater vest.

"Hey, Matthew," called Elliot. "Everything's groovy on this end."

"It's all right on schedule," Tina said with a nervous smile.

"The luncheon started on time?" asked Matthew.

Elliot nodded. "Exactly. Johnny and all his bigwig buddies are upstairs chowing down."

"Excellent," said Matthew. "Are we all ready?"

"One sec," said Tina.

She quickly kicked off her high-heeled shoes, flinging them into the back of the van, then reached into her large purse for a pair of white running shoes. She put those on, then chucked her bag into the vehicle as well.

Matthew saw how pale Tina was and asked, "You gonna be okay?"

"Absolutely," she said, although her voice was noticeably weak. "I won't turn back."

"Okay, let's go."

"Right, right, right," mumbled Elliot.

They got things under way, with Matthew pushing the laundry

cart to the rear of the van, then lifting it onto the loading dock. Elliot grabbed it, but swung it wide and right into Tina.

"Oh, sorry, gorgeous! I forgot to scan! It's the eyes!" he pleaded.

Matthew jumped out of the van and helped Elliot while Tina hurried ahead and opened the service door. Passing through that, they entered a long corridor, a bleak concrete-block hall that proceeded into the heart of the building. Tina again rushed ahead, disappearing around the first corner. A few seconds later she reappeared.

"Still nothing," she reported.

"Very great," said Matthew.

No security, at least not down here. No one noting any comings and goings. Yes, very great indeed, thought Matthew. It was just as they had thought, just as Tina had observed this morning. No Secret Service in sight. And so they continued rolling the laundry cart full of weapons and masks down the hall, around the corner, and right to the large service elevator.

The luncheon was scheduled to end at one. Of course it could go longer, which would pose problems. The execs who'd paid through the nose for lunch with Johnny Clariton could demand a few more words, pose a few more questions, beg for a buddy-buddy photograph. But Clariton was famous for his punctuality. A tight ship, that was what he ran, he always claimed, and that was how the United States should be run. Efficient. Effective. No more two-hundred-dollar toilet plungers. As for himself, he had a hired timekeeper on staff, someone who kept him going from place to place, from speech to book-signing to congressional hearing. Just in case, though, Matthew had decided to give themselves a little extra time. Things wouldn't, well, explode until 1:10.

Elliot tapped the call button, and when the elevator doors eased back he said brightly, "Going up?"

"In flames," said Tina, trying to manage a joke.

"Of course, that'll be second floor. Step to the rear."

They rolled the cart into the large elevator, but when the car started rising upward all three of them fell silent. They were really going to do it, thought Matthew. Incredible. Fucking incredible. And, given that he didn't expect to survive the next few days, he was surprised he wasn't more nervous.

Dismayed that his headache was growing worse—he'd gone off his suppressant therapy last month—he rubbed his forehead. Then he glanced over, saw the beads of perspiration forming on Tina's brow, saw her makeup blistering.

"What's the matter?" he asked.

"Just tired." She dabbed at her brow with the back of her right hand. "I've been running a temperature for three weeks now and I'm just a little warm. But don't worry, I'll make it."

"Of course you will." Thinking back to sweeter times, he said, "Remember when we met out on that shoot in the Badlands?"

She nodded, tried to smile. "Yeah. Wasn't that for a Banana Republic ad?"

"I think so. And, you know, you were so beautiful, standing out there in chinos on the edge of the world. I thought you were the prettiest thing I'd ever seen."

"You should talk. God, we had some fun, didn't we?" Tina tried to laugh, but instead her eyes started to mist up.

"Nervous?"

She nodded. "A little. But then I think of Chris and I know I'm doing the right thing."

"Absolutely."

"Man," volunteered Elliot, his sad eyes fixed on the floor, "when Chris kicked the bucket I just sat down and cried and cried. That's when I realized for the first time that, man, this really is a big, bad, ugly world. Let me tell you, I sobbed for days."

"Yeah, and I cried for days when Curt finally died," said Matthew, glancing at the others, wondering if they even knew how hard it had been for him. "If there was a God, Curt would have made it at least until today. If only he could be here—he'd be one proud son of a bitch."

Elliot shrugged. "Yeah, but you gotta go when you gotta go. I mean, loose lips sink ships, and he could've sunk us, you know."

"Well, he didn't," snapped Tina.

The elevator chimed and the doors opened, bringing them

back to their mission. Matthew poked his head out, saw that the service lobby was empty. He signaled Elliot, who pulled out the stop button on the elevator, thereby freezing the lift on this floor. He then helped Elliot roll the laundry cart into the small lobby.

Now all they had to do was wait for the roll of applause that would signal the conclusion of the roundtable luncheon. Then, of course, Mr. Johnny Clariton would step into the adjoining room for his interview with Channel 10's own Todd Mills. And things would really explode.

8

One of the first things Todd learned in the biz was that if you didn't know how to dress you didn't belong on television. Aside from Stella, his agent, who'd advised him to always dress conservatively—"Okay, doll, so shoot me, a little dash of Ralph Lauren won't kill anyone"—no one in television had ever told him what to wear. He knew, though, that if the clothes were wrong he'd lose viewers and eventually his job, and while he was sure that the dark-blue suit looked good, he was hit with a rare twinge of insecurity.

"So just tell me, do I look okay?" he asked Bradley, the photographer, as they cut immediately left at the restaurant's entrance and entered the room where the interview would take place.

"Hey, man, you look great. Don't sweat it." The tall black man looked him up and down. "My wife says I have impeccable taste, and you look impeccable."

"Thanks."

Todd put down his briefcase and surveyed the room, a small space off the main dining area at Jerome's. Used primarily as a private dining room for corporate lunch meetings or, from time to time, as a refuge for fan-beset rock stars, it had a high ceiling with an elaborate wrought-iron chandelier, terra cotta–colored walls, and a beige carpet. There were three or four tables pushed to one side, a dozen chairs, no windows, and heavy, draping tan curtains lining one wall. Checking it all over, Todd thought that the curtains might prove a good backdrop.

"What do you think, we set up a couple of chairs over here by the curtains?'' asked Todd. ''There were a couple of plants out by the entrance; maybe we could put those in the background.''

''Sure.''

''And the camera right about here,'' he continued, stepping more into the middle of the room.

Usually Todd liked to get to a place only about ten minutes early, for it really didn't take more than a good seven minutes to set up, but today he'd given them extra time. Not only did he not want to be rushed and he did want to make sure things were set up perfectly, Todd wondered if there wouldn't be a way to listen in on the luncheon, at least the end of it. Or perhaps Bradley could dash into the hall and tape the guests as they filtered out. Thinking of that, Todd wondered if he should try to corner a couple of them and get a few words. That could serve as the background to the start of the interview. Or was it better to leave all that alone and just set up and stay in here, focused on what was really important?

Bradley unzipped the large equipment bag and started pulling out endless cords, a tripod, a handful of proBeta tapes, and finally a professional Beta camera, the very latest, loaded with computerized gadgetry. Then he started digging for something, opening and closing various pockets of the bag.

''Don't tell me you forgot one of the batteries,'' said Todd.

Everything had a battery, from the camera to the lights to the cords, and more than once Todd had had a story ruined by equipment failure. All you had to do was forget one little battery that went in the mike cords and that was it, interview shot.

''Found it,'' Bradley smiled, lifting out a pack of gum. ''Just be cool, Todd. I checked all the batteries, brought backups for them all.''

Oh, brother, thought Todd. He had to get a grip and be calm; no, he had to be confident and arrogant. Oh, shit. You're going to mess this one up royally, he told himself, if you don't relax. But what was it? Why was he so worried? Suddenly he knew. Although he was sure Johnny Clariton wanted to talk about anything but gays and AIDS, Todd was going to do his damnedest to make sure those issues were addressed. Yet, Todd realized, he himself had never talked about these things on air.

Always another bridge to cross, wasn't there?

"Bradley," said Todd, "I want to make sure this interview doesn't look impromptu, so let's make sure Clariton is lit really well."

"Backlit?"

"Yeah. Why don't you set up the light umbrella? And let's double-mike this one, okay?"

"Wireless or Lav?"

"Lav."

Right, he thought. He'd bring Clariton in, seat him, and then clip a Lav mike to each of their lapels. Todd wanted the interview double-miked like that to make sure Todd's questions were well heard. A lot of times the questions were more important than the answers; too often you could simply ignore a person's answer, because that could just be bullshit. A politican's answer in particular. What you wanted to get was the look, the reaction to a question, which more often than not provided a glimpse at what the person really thought.

Bradley opened up the light kit, and then the two of them made careful business of getting everything set up. When the lights were adjusted, the camera positioned, Todd took a deep breath. Yes, he could do it.

Several minutes later Todd heard a prolonged roll of applause from behind the curtained wall. Time for the main event.

"Bradley," said Todd, clipping on his mike and sitting down, "let's do a quick test."

"What?"

"I want to see some footage just to make sure."

"Todd," said Bradley, clearly exasperated, "everything's perfect."

"Come on, just do it."

Rolling his eyes, Bradley turned on the camera, checked the focus, and let it roll.

9

This was too perfect, thought Cindy Wilson, barely able to contain her excitement as she tape-recorded Congressman Clariton's words.

"Let's face it," Clariton calmly said, leaning against the podium at the far side of the restaurant as if he were leaning against the fireplace in his own home, "the biggest threat to the American economy is the national deficit. It's just too damn big. Simply, the government has its hands in too many pies. We're spending far more than we're taking in. And it's got to stop. It's just not good financial practice, as all of you business people here today fully know. When you spend more money than you have you eventually go bankrupt. It's that simple: The American economy is on the road to bankruptcy."

Hidden in a wait station stocked with cutlery, napkins, and bus trays, Cindy held the small tape recorder up to the speaker in the ceiling. This wasn't as good, of course, as plugging directly into a soundboard. And it certainly wasn't as good as getting this on tape, for nothing mattered more on television than image, image, image. But this was pretty good, just getting his voice. Actually, this very well might be the lead story tonight, and Cindy peered out at the man who now spoke so evenly, so casually, that it seemed he could explain nuclear fusion in a mere sentence or two. He was making that much sense. He was taking the complexities of big government and putting it in terms that people like Cindy could understand. No wonder he's so popular, she thought. WTCN was going to love this.

"We could raise taxes, I suppose." Clariton shrugged. "Raise 'em enough to cover what we're spending. But do you want your money going to pay for a two-hundred-dollar toilet bowl plunger or a hundred-dollar hammer? I sure as hell don't. No, we need to take hold of big government and, in fact, get rid of it before it gets rid of us. I mean, let's face it, the United States government is well on its way to becoming just as big, just as unwieldy, just as bureaucratic as the government of the former Soviet Union. And we know what happened to them, don't we? Good Lord, isn't that place a mess.''

Cindy swept the small tape recorder around to get the audience reaction, a mixture of groans and laughter. When she and the photographer had tried to enter Jerome's like proper folk, the guy in the tux had promptly given them the boot, particularly when she'd flashed the hundred bucks. On her own, Cindy had then slipped past the host's desk and into a side dining room. She just assumed that the room, with its tall ceiling and wrought-iron chandelier and long wall of curtains, had to somehow connect to the main dining room. And she was right. After a quick search she located a door at the far end of the curtains, inched it open, and found herself right in this wait station, which at least afforded her the opportunity no other reporter had, the chance to observe the entire luncheon and record everything Johnny Clariton said.

''And one of the biggest challenges facing us right now, of course, is medical care. Yes, we've got wonderful doctors. Yes, our technology is fabulous. But as a nation we have to decide just what the government's role is and how far the individual is supposed to go.'' Clariton stepped around the edge of the podium and with a shrug said, ''Frankly, I believe—and I've stated this numerous times—that we've got to rein in the federal government's responsibility. Let me ask you this: If some fool is stupid enough not to wear a helmet while riding a motorcycle and he breaks his neck, is it my responsibility if he's underinsured to make up for his stupidity and support him via medical assistance? Now, I don't have anything against smokers and I certainly don't want to go tangling with any of the tobacco companies, so please don't repeat this outside of this room . . . but if somebody—and, I mean, we're all aware of the health risks—smokes a few packs a day and then gets cancer, just what is the government responsible for? Should my tax dollars go to care for him, should he be eligible for Social Security for the rest of his life? Likewise with AIDS. I mean, gays know how you get it. And they should know how to prevent it. But if some guy goes into the bushes and comes out HIV positive, is the United States government supposed to pay for his medical care? Are American families responsible for homosexual practices? I think not. No, in all these cases I believe it's up to the individual to take care of himself, to seek and secure private health insurance. We are, after all, a capitalistic society. Insurance companies make money. Drug companies make money. Doctors make money. And so do you good business people. All I'm saying is it's your money, your country, and you have to decide how it is you want to spend your tax dollars.''

A round of applause broke out, and Clariton smiled and did his best to look as modest as possible. As the clapping continued, his aide took the opportunity to step up to the podium and whisper in his ear.

Clariton then said, ''I'm sorry, but my trusty aide Carol has informed me that we're running out of time. I can take a couple of quick questions, and then I've got to move on.''

Without saying anything new, Clariton answered exactly two rather benign questions. And then telling the audience how wonderful they were and how great Minnesota was—''But heed my words, your state taxes are too high, and you can tell the Democrats I said that!''—he was off, moving swiftly out of the room.

Cindy switched off the tape recorder and stood there beaming. This was too great. A true scoop. Granted, this wasn't video, only voice, but back at the station Roger was nevertheless going to love it, and on the news tonight her audience would eat it up. Dear God, this could be the break she'd been wanting. They'd run some footage of Clariton's book-signing this morning, then perhaps a still photograph of Clariton himself with a voice-over from the luncheon. There were some great excerpts, a few things he'd never publicly said—oh, the tobacco companies wouldn't like it, not one bit—and, yes, this was the stuff of great news.

As the applause began to subside, Cindy peered around the corner. The five-grand-a-plate lunch was winding up, but a num-

ber of these well-heeled executives were lingering over coffee
and political gab. Okay, so she'd stick around for a few minutes,
see if she could speak to a couple of them, then duck out the way
she had come in.

Oh, this was too incredibly perfect.

10

All Rawlins wanted was to get on that plane and go to New York. Maybe he was reading too much into it, maybe a long weekend in Manhattan wasn't that big of a deal for Todd, perhaps a mere lark, but Rawlins couldn't help looking at the trip as a signal, a sign that this was it, the big relationship of his life. He'd had his disco days, he'd had his fuckathon, dating one guy after another, but all he wanted now was one simple but seemingly impossible thing: someone to love who loved him too. And he prayed to God that Todd Mills was that guy at last.

So he just had to get well, and he had to do it fast.

But, dear God, his sinuses were killing him. If anything, the pain was getting worse, and now, driving to his doctor's and gingerly touching his forehead, he had the sensation of walnuts being stuffed up his nasal cavity. Ugh. This time he was going to get down on his knees and beg his doctor for the strongest possible medication. The drugs he'd been taking—a decongestant and an antibiotic—weren't even touching the pain.

True, you couldn't be gay these days and not be a hypochondriac, but Rawlins kept telling himself he had a good doctor and that they'd get to the bottom of it. Last week he'd had a thorough physical, and if nothing showed up in all those tests then he'd go see an allergist. After all, it could be something like dust mites. Or it very well could be Girlfriend. Rawlins had never had an allergic reaction to cats before, but then he'd never lived with one, and he'd been all but living full-time at Todd's for the last month.

And thank God for that.

Curt's death wasn't something he was going to get over, not

ever. Of that he was sure. Rather, Rawlins already understood that Curt's death was destined to become a marker in his own life, a before-and-after kind of thing, for watching the course of Curt's illness had altered something quite fundamental in Rawlins. Quite simply, he'd never seen anything as awful as what Curt had endured. First Curt's asshole of a lover of five years had dumped him—just walked out the door and never came back— the very day Curt had discovered both that he was HIV positive and that his condition had already progressed into AIDS. Next there was the endless assault of infections, the parade of doctors. And then Rawlins had witnessed how Curt had so quickly fallen apart, as if he were running for the grave. Rawlins had seen AIDS before, of course, but until Curt much of it had been at arm's length. This was Minneapolis and Saint Paul, after all. This was flyover land, about as safe from AIDS as any gay man could be. Thank God the epidemic hadn't hit as it had in New York and San Francisco, where Rawlins had heard of guys going to their hundredth AIDS funeral, of apartment buildings emptied of all the men, and of telephone lists rendered useless because all the numbers belonged to dead men.

For Rawlins, Curt's death had simply proved to be the proverbial straw. While he knew of death after death of Twin Cities men, Curt's was amazingly the first AIDS death he'd been involved with on a near daily basis. Was it because so many others had retreated to die at family homes and farms up north or in the Dakotas or Iowa? Or was it because Rawlins was a shit, a self-centered faggot who'd been too afraid to give his time to any of the charity groups? Both, undoubtedly. Regardless, until Curt he'd never seen anything so awful so up close, how AIDS didn't just attack one part of the body, but every part, the lungs, the skin, the mind, the inside of the mouth, even the fingernails. For Curt, however, Rawlins had been there, changing his diaper and spoon-feeding him broth and laughing and crying. Jesus Christ, he kept screaming inside, why couldn't Curt have hung on just a bit longer, why couldn't he have gotten any of the new drugs soon enough to make a difference? Rawlins nearly went insane watching Curt slip away, and he wouldn't have made it if Todd hadn't been there.

God, thought Rawlins as he drove through the sunny day toward Park and 26th, Todd Mills was the best thing that had ever happened to him. And there was no way Rawlins wasn't going to New York. The last thing he wanted was to give Todd some reason to back off, for it was only in the last month or two that they had crossed some sort of line—or rather Todd had crossed it, for Rawlins had been there, waiting, hoping. Shit, he was so in love with Todd Mills. And what he loved most about him was something he couldn't identify, something he'd never felt with anyone before. Simply, when they were together nothing else seemed to matter. And that was when Rawlins knew this was right, that there was a God or a Higher Power or whatever. You just didn't get the chance to feel that way about someone else, male or female, without an Almighty blessing you.

So as Rawlins parked his car and turned off the engine, he was determined to buck the pain and infection tormenting his sinuses. There was no other choice. I'm going to be okay, I'm going to be okay, I'm going to be okay, and I'm going to New York, he chanted as he got out, zipped up his leather coat, and started toward the short brick building housing his doctor's office. He pulled open the glass doors and entered a waiting elevator car. Boy, wouldn't he like to have his blood pressure taken right now. Must be way up there. And then the lift started, carrying him to the top. When he reached the third floor and stepped out, however, he was immediately dizzy. That was what was really driving him crazy, his sense of balance, for his blocked sinuses had caused fluid to build up in his inner ear. He took a deep breath, steadied himself. Just give me a drug that works, he prayed. The pressurized cabin of an airplane really would be torture.

Entering the first door, he went right up to the receptionist's desk and said, "Hi, I'm Steve Rawlins and I have an appointment with Dr. Samuelson."

"Certainly, Mr. Rawlins," said the woman, checking the calendar. "It'll just be a few minutes. Just have a seat and the nurse will call you."

It was stupid, but he searched her face. Late fifties, finely wrinkled skin. Plain features. Light-blue glasses. Light-blue sweater. Serious. He thought of all the tests he'd had last week, but there wasn't a trace that she knew any of the results. Then again, why should she?

He sat down, glanced around. An elderly woman sat across the room in a wheelchair. To his right a small boy was curled in his mother's lap. And on the other side a young woman was reading *Better Homes & Gardens* and sniffling. Rawlins picked up *Sports Illustrated,* made a weak attempt at thumbing through it, but didn't really see a single word or picture.

"Steven Rawlins?"

His heart jolted and he looked over. A nurse in a white uniform stood in a doorway looking at his chart. Feeling suddenly nervous, he slowly stood up, then didn't move for a second, surprised at his feebleness. He looked at the nurse; she smiled back.

With his heart ticking faster and faster and his armpits blossoming with anxious perspiration, he followed the nurse from the waiting room, down one narrow hall, down another, and to a small room for patients. Dear God, prayed Rawlins, please let there be a simple explanation why I can't rid the infection from my head, please let everything be all right. I've got to go to New York next week, because I've just found the most wonderful person. Please don't let me lose him.

"Just have a seat," she said with a smile as she ushered Rawlins into the room. "The doctor will be right with you."

Rawlins was too nervous to make a peep, and he went in and sat down on a molded-plastic chair. As the nurse shut the door and disappeared, Rawlins wanted to jump up, beg her not to leave. Aren't you supposed to take my blood pressure? How long will I have to wait to see the doctor? Oh, and why are my sinuses killing me?

Rawlins closed his eyes and touched his forehead, surprised at the panic suddenly surging through him. There was a gentle knock on the door and the doctor entered, a short man with a graying beard, balding head, glasses.

"Hello, Steve," he said, extending his hand.

Oh, shit, thought Rawlins as they shook hands, why does he look so serious? "Hi."

Dr. Samuelson sat down opposite Rawlins, opened Rawlins's chart. There was a moment of silence that seemed to last forever.

All of the tests they'd done flashed through Rawlins's mind, but of course there was only one that mattered—the very test that he'd blocked out all week, the very one that was now making him so incredibly nervous—and he blurted out, "Are my test results in? The one for HIV?"

"Yes," said the doctor, who took a deep breath, then looked right at Rawlins, his face as grave as an executioner's. "Yes, the results are back, and, Steve, I'm afraid I have some very unfortunate news."

It's me again, the guy who offed Curt, and today I want to get up on a soapbox and scream. I want to scream because I hate straight people. I mean, look at this letter that the Florida AIDS Ride received from a Florida state official:

"In my capacity outside the office, I again have no interest in your AIDS bicycle ride. It is my personal belief that AIDS as a disease was created as punishment to the gay and lesbian communities across the world. Unfortunately, due to their lifestyles, many innocent people have also had to suffer. For those people I am truly sorry and hope that one day we can cure this disease. As far as the gay and lesbians of this world . . . let them suffer their consequences!"

Now, that's exactly what I can't stand about AIDS in America—the rationalization that you're a homo and you're doomed to get these cooties. How can people be so warped? First of all, duh, no one deserves anything like this. Second of all, wow, there are 30 million people on this planet who've been infected with HIV—something like 6.4 million of whom have already croaked of AIDS—and do you think most of them are homos? Hell, no! For the info of straight white Americans who can't see beyond their own priggish noses, worldwide only five percent to ten percent of HIV infections have been transmitted via homosexual contact. Shocking, huh? Just think of it, every minute of every day six people are infected—that's 8,500 new cases a day, a 1,000 of which are kids. And almost all of them straight.

I curse the conservatives in America. I curse the religious right, for there is a God, but He or She or It certainly isn't theirs.

Trust me, this, the most politicized disease in the history of the *world, ain't never going to end until those guys in the boxer shorts—the straight white guys on Wall Street and in Washington who run the world—start getting AIDS from banging their secretaries and mistresses. Yup, that's when we'll see some real action—just as soon as they turn HIV positive.*

End of lecture.

11

It all happened much more quickly than Todd would have expected. The applause from the main dining room didn't simply signify that Clariton had finished speaking and it was time for questions, but that Clariton, with his politically flaunted punctuality, had concluded his roundtable luncheon and was moving on to the next item on the agenda. Todd and Bradley were still taping a preview when Johnny Clariton himself walked in.

"Oh, shit," muttered Bradley, standing up behind the camera.

Todd was so surprised that he jumped up and started walking around the lights, the Lav mike still attached to his lapel. He was almost all the way to the congressman when he reached the end of the mike cord and the clipped mike nearly pulled off his suit coat.

"Yikes," he muttered, unclipping the mike with shaking hands and tossing it over the back of a chair.

Straightening his coat and tie, he looked up just as the congressman, trailed by an assistant and an obvious bodyguard, approached him. Clariton was, thought Todd, taking a quick, nervous appraisal of him, definitely as wholesome-looking as reported, with a clean, smooth face, receding hairline, and wearing a crisp white shirt and gray suit. He was, however, definitely shorter than Todd had imagined, almost small, really. On first glance he seemed very much the average guy next door; on further study Todd could sense the energy burning within. The eyes were moving, the hands fidgeting. He was obviously very much a damn-the-torpedoes-full-speed-ahead kind of guy.

"Good afternoon, Mr. Clariton," said Todd, struggling to

regain his composure and holding out his hand. "I'm Todd Mills from WLAK TV."

"Hi. You the one doing the interview?" He looked Todd up and down, then turned to Bradley. "Or is it you? Which one of you's the gay one?"

As much as he would have liked to brush aside the comment as silly and inane, Todd was sure someone had just slammed a board into his gut. He tried to say something, but his voice was all but gone.

"I'll be doing the interview," Todd finally said, although his voice was weaker than he would have ever imagined. "And, yes, I'm gay." He paused, struggled to regain his mental equilibrium, and forced himself to add, "However, that's certainly none of your business."

"Well, of course it is," shot back Clariton, his voice big and authoritative. "I just want you to know how sick I am of all this AIDS crap. I just want you to know that I won't be talking about it. Understood?"

In disbelief, Todd stared at Clariton. He then glanced at Clariton's assistant, a woman with a smile permanently plastered on her face, and his bodyguard, a meaty-looking guy with brown hair. Getting no reaction from either of them, Todd turned to Bradley, who stood by his camera, so dumbfounded he wasn't even moving. Perhaps they should cancel, call the whole thing off before they even began. Todd wasn't going to take shit like this. No, not at all. Thinking it through in a flash, he realized that if worse came to worst he could always do a report simply on this conversation, explaining on air why the interview hadn't taken place.

Trying to maintain a steady presence, Todd drew a line in the sand, saying, "WLAK was not informed of any restrictions regarding this interview."

Clariton's assistant, a young woman wearing a navy blue dress suit complete with one of those white frilly things at the throat that was supposed to emulate a tie, jumped forward, blurting, "I believe I spoke to you, Mr. Mills. And you have to understand it's just been—"

"No, Carol, what he's got to understand," interrupted Clariton, "is that there are certain things—"

"By the way this is off the record," inserted Carol.

"Who cares," said Clariton with a wave of his hand. "I just was going to tell him that, frankly, I'm sick of gays screaming this and that and begging for special treatment."

Barely able to hold in his anger, Todd, his voice dripping with sarcasm, said, "Thank you for sharing that with me."

"I mean, like I was just saying in the other room, why should tax dollars of good American families go for medical aid and research to pay for a bunch of deviants who fucked too much? But like I said, I don't want to get into this today. I'm here to talk about my book. That's what I want to talk about—my book."

"Yes," said Carol. "We set up an interview with you, Mr. Mills, to talk about Mr. Clariton's novel. Do you know it's already on *The New York Times* best-seller list? Isn't that just super?"

He stared at this shrimp of a man. Did he dare tell him what he thought? Todd turned again toward Bradley. What should he do? Forget the whole goddamn thing?

It was then that Todd saw what Clariton obviously hadn't: the tiniest of LED lights on Bradley's camera. Not only was the light burning a very distinct and unmistakable red, but the camera was aimed right at Clariton.

"Excuse me," muttered Todd.

This might be too good to be true, thought Todd as he hurried over to Bradley. It might be too unbelievably incredible.

"Oh my God, Bradley," said Todd, his voice hushed. "Don't do anything real obvious, just tell me it's true—is your camera on?"

"What? Oh, I . . ." Bradley's eyes darted to the side, took it all in. "Holy shit, it is. I didn't turn it off."

"What about the Lav mike?" Todd nodded to the mike, which was dangling from a chair right in front of Clariton. "Would it have gotten what he just said? Tell me it did."

Bradley bit his lip, started chuckling. "Oh, yes. It's real sensitive. It would have gotten everything."

Barely able to contain himself, Todd clasped Bradley on the shoulder, and said, "There is a God."

He took a deep breath. And smiled. This was it, handed to him on a gold platter, Johnny Clariton's true thoughts as expressed bluntly and crudely in his own words. Nothing else mattered. Who cared now how the interview went? Todd had it all and then some. People such as his mother loved Johnny Clariton because of his freshness and vivacity, because he projected himself as a dynamic leader, a great American one. Kind, just, caring, wise. People such as his mother, however, would be disgusted to hear Johnny Clariton's personal views expressed so hideously. This was no wise man, no mythical leader who could lead America the Beautiful back to great times.

This guy was a pig, and Todd now had the tape to prove it.

Suppressing divine pleasure, Todd turned around, and said, "I know you're on a tight schedule, Mr. Clariton, so why don't we get started?"

"Yes, of course." Clariton called his bodyguard. "Lyle, stand by the door and make sure no one else comes in, all right?"

"Yes, sir," replied the large man.

"Let's be quick about this," continued Clariton. "I'm signing at another bookstore in . . . in . . ."

"Saint Paul," interjected Carol.

"Right, Saint Paul. And we have to be there at—"

"Two o'clock."

"Yes, at two, and then it's back to—"

"Washington." Looking at Todd, Carol said, "The congressman is very busy. He has a budget meeting this evening."

"Okay, then let's get going." Todd went over and took his dangling mike, then motioned to the chairs. "We'll sit over there."

"Yes, yes. Very good," said Clariton.

As if he had done this a million times in a million cities, Clariton let himself be directed into place and let Bradley attach the Lav mike to his lapel. Almost passive as people fussed around him, he seemed to drift away. Perhaps he was merely relaxing, zoning out for few seconds, but as soon as the lights came on the politician turned back on too, and Clariton's face brightened, his eyes opened wide, and a charming grin appeared.

Todd took his notes from his briefcase, glanced at them one last time, and tossed them aside. Actually, he didn't really need any of this interview, for he already had material and then some to skewer Clariton. That in turn afforded Todd some room. Sure, what the hell. He could take this almost any which way he wanted.

"By the way," said Todd as he attached his own mike and tried to hide the wire beneath the folds of his suit, "I read just this morning that you have a reputation for spouting off right before an interview. That wouldn't be your way of sabotaging things, now, would it? You say something cocky, it throws the reporter off balance, and you get the upper hand—is that how you work? And is that what you were trying to do by demanding to know who's gay?"

Todd looked up at Clariton, who was looking back, a smarmy smile on his face.

"Well, you have to admit, I did catch you off guard," said Clariton with a chuckle. "But, no, I was just letting you know what was out of bounds to talk about. If I wanted to throw you off I'd . . . I'd tell you who told us you were gay."

Todd tried not to swallow the bait, tried not to show the tension that went zipping through him. "I think you're doing it again, being unpleasantly devious."

"But wouldn't you like to know?" taunted Clariton. "I'm sure you'd find it interesting."

"Actually, I don't care," lied Todd as coolly as he possibly could. "First of all, I would hope your staff is astute enough to know what is common knowledge. Second, all anyone has to do is ask me."

"Well, I didn't even have to ask, did I?"

Todd glanced at Clariton, saw the triumphant grin on that boy-next-door face. No, thought Todd. I won't be beaten like this. I won't. Todd took a deep breath. Once he had known all too well how to control himself. From being closeted for so many years, he had learned to keep his true emotions from showing on the surface, which in turn had helped him get as far as he had in broadcast journalism. However, as he now struggled not to be paranoid, not to obsess over who was talking behind his back, he knew that he couldn't just sit there and take this. Hell, no. He had to go on the offensive, and so he drew his own weaponry, his favorite question for straight men.

In a hushed voice he asked, "Let me ask you this, Congressman Clariton, have you ever had a same-sex experience?"

The stupid grin on Clariton's face vanished, and he pulled back, his eyes tight and hateful, and then after a moment he said, "I won't even bother responding to that."

"You don't have to. When a straight guy hesitates like that it always means yes."

"Shut the hell up. That's ridiculous!"

"Maybe, maybe not." Todd then sat back and said in an almost cheerful voice, "But if you want to sabotage someone's self-confidence, that's how you do it." Almost out of nowhere Todd suddenly realized something else. "You know, I just now figured out why you agreed to an exclusive interview with me. You're using me to legitimize yourself. You want to be seen talking nicely to a very public gay man, so voters with gay sons and daughters and friends won't think you're too homophobic. Well, I'm not sure it's going to work." With a smile Todd turned to the camera. "Okay, Bradley, let's get things going."

Bradley bent down to the camera, focused one last time, then said, "Okay, here goes."

With the tape rolling, Todd, feeling stronger and more confident than he had in months, smiled and said, "Congressman Clariton, I want to thank you for joining me this afternoon."

Looking anything but thrilled, Clariton took a deep breath and forced himself to say, "It's a pleasure to be here in this wonderful city of hardworking citizens." He paused and added, "This is truly one of the great places in our country."

"Yes, actually it is. Now, just a few minutes ago you told me you would not be discussing AIDS or quote-unquote deviant sex. What is it, sir, that you are prepared to discuss?"

Clariton squirmed in his seat, and with a stern voice said, "My book."

"Of course. You're not here on a political campaign, you're

here as part of a book tour. Can you tell me a little bit about what you've written?''

"It's a science fiction novel set in the future, in the year—"

"Of course it's set in the future; that's what makes it science fiction.''

"Ah, right. And—"

Todd interrupted, saying, "I understand there are quite a lot of allegations surrounding the book, among them that you didn't write a single word of it. Is that true? Did you work on it at all?''

"People do gossip, don't they?''

"There's also criticism that you'll be making upward of four million dollars in royalties. What can you say about that?''

Clariton started to say something, stopped, then retrenched himself and put on a politician's smile, big and plastic. "Now, come on, Todd, must you really be so antagonistic? You know I didn't come to Minnesota to be attacked.''

"Sir, with all due respect, as an elected official it's your duty to respond to the people who elected you. I, for one, can only—"

A muffled explosion rocked the room, and not more than two seconds later a shrill alarm started blasting. Todd sat forward, looked around, saw Clariton's bodyguard, Lyle, become terribly alert. What the hell was going on? That was from somewhere inside the building, wasn't it?

"That's a fire alarm," said Bradley, standing up from behind the camera.

"Now what?" snapped Clariton.

Todd suggested, "Maybe something caught fire in the kitchen.''

"Oh, my God!" gasped Carol, pointing to one of the vents. "Smoke!''

A thick, dark waft of smoke came pouring out of the vent, and Lyle said, "Mr. Clariton, if you'll come with me, sir!''

The very next instant a single sprinkler kicked in, spraying water down on the equipment.

"Oh, Christ, my camera!" snapped Bradley.

Before he could be shocked Todd yanked off his mike, then lunged at Congressman Clariton and did the same. Working as speedily as possible, Bradley shut down the lights, next turned to the camera and started detaching it from the tripod.

"Bradley, give me the tape!" demanded Todd, for whatever happened he couldn't lose that very special tape of Clariton's comments.

Bradley popped open the camera and threw the videotape at Todd, who caught it and stuffed it in his briefcase. Quickly getting soaked, Todd returned to Bradley's side, the two of them dismantling the equipment and throwing it in the nylon bags.

"You all go ahead!" shouted Todd to Clariton. "We'll be right behind you! Go out the door and take two rights. The escalator's right there and then it's a clean shot to the front door!"

Lyle took the congressman by the arm and said, "This way, sir!"

"Come on, Carol!" called Clariton.

Just as they were heading to the main doors, though, three people burst in: two men, one of them skinny, one of them with a shaved bald head, and a woman with big blond hair. Wearing smoke masks, they were pushing a large cart, and the skinny guy turned around, took a chain, and padlocked the door shut behind them. The woman and the bald guy dug into the cart and pulled out two guns, which they trained on Todd and the others. Lyle immediately stepped in front of Clariton.

"Get down on the floor!" screamed the bald man, his voice only slightly muffled by the mask.

"Facedown, now!" seconded the woman.

Clariton half-emerged from behind Lyle and blurted, "You can't do this!"

"Just watch, dumbo!"

"I'm a U.S. congressman."

"Really?" said the skinny guy as smoke poured in through all the vents and water rained down on the far side of the room. "I thought you were Julia Child."

"That includes you, big guy! On the floor," shouted the bald man, training his gun on Lyle, "before I start blasting the shit out of you!"

Todd glanced at Lyle, saw his right hand ever so slightly begin to rise up the side of his sport coat. Would he resist or—

A small door at the end of the curtains was suddenly thrown open, and a woman came charging right into the room. Of all people, thought Todd, staring at her in total disbelief.

"Holy shit!" yelled the woman as she rushed into the room, completely panic-stricken, "there's a fire in the kitchen! You—" She suddenly froze, surveyed the situation, spotted Todd. "What's going on?"

Todd stared at his Channel 7 nemesis. "Cindy, where the hell did you come from?"

As the leader, the guy with the shaved head, rushed toward her brandishing his gun, Lyle reached beneath his sport coat and pulled out a pistol. With three bold steps he charged across the room, lunging at the woman with the gun. He batted the pistol from her hand, then grabbed her, spinning her around and pinning her from behind as if she were as weak as a paper doll.

Pressing his pistol against her temple, Lyle shouted at the other guy, "Put down your gun!"

"Fuck you, Rambo!"

And with that the bald guy in the smoke mask grabbed Cindy Wilson, jabbing his gun at her head. For a weird moment everything was oddly still as the alarm shrieked on and water poured from the lone sprinkler. Staring at the men and the women they each held, Todd and the others were completely still.

Knowing he held trump, the guy holding Cindy Wilson calmly declared, "Go ahead and shoot my friend. It doesn't make any difference, right?"

Not even struggling in Lyle's grasp, the skinny blonde calmly said, "Yeah, do it. I'm next to dead anyway."

"But this one . . ." He yanked on Cindy Wilson's arm, poked the barrel of his gun into her cheek. "This one doesn't want to die, do you, darling?"

"No!" Cindy struggled, then froze. "No, please . . . please!"

"Shoot her!" ordered the skinny blonde.

"No!" screeched Cindy, starting to buck.

"I'm going to do it!" yelled the leader. "On the count of three she's a goner unless you throw down your gun!"

"Please, no!" begged Cindy.

"One . . ."

Cindy's terrified eyes turned to Todd. "Oh, my God!"

"Two . . ."

Todd shouted at Lyle, "For Christ's sake, he's going to do it!"

The leader steadied the gun, smiled, opened his mouth as if to speak. And Lyle lowered his pistol, then tossed it aside.

"Very good," said the leader. "Now, let go of my friend."

As she was released and started picking up the weapons, the skinny blonde said to Lyle, "I wasn't bluffing. An early ticket out of here would've been just fine with me."

"Now all of you get down on the floor!" shouted the leader, still pressing his gun to Cindy Wilson's head. "Get to work!"

"Right-o," the scrawny guy said. "Better do just like he says, campers!"

Todd led the way, dropping to his knees and lying down on the now-soaking carpet. Carol and Bradley quickly followed his example, but Clariton hesitated and glanced at Lyle, who wasn't budging either.

Yanking on Cindy's hair, the head guy shouted, "I'd still be real happy to shoot this one!"

"That won't be necessary," replied Clariton, sounding very authoritative. "Now, Lyle, please do as they say. We don't want to aggravate the situation any further." Clariton looked at the masked leader. "But I would like to discuss this and perhaps come to some sort of—"

"Shut the fuck up! If you're not down on the floor in two seconds, she's dead meat!"

"Okay . . . okay. Let's not be hasty."

The two men lay down, and Todd wondered if this was it, the beginning of an execution-style assassination. Of course this was about Clariton. Of course he, the controversial politician, was their target. But his assistant? His bodyguard? And what about Bradley and Todd, not to mention Cindy Wilson, whom the bald guy still held at gunpoint? Would any of them be left as witnesses, or would they all be eliminated?

His heart surging, Todd's eyes darted about. Think. Fall back on your training, fall back on what you know. You've interviewed hundreds of people who've been through something like this. What did they do? How did they react? How did the police say they should have reacted?

Okay.

Yes, just three. Yes, one woman. Two men. Take it in. When he'd worked on the CrimeEye team he'd seen enough to know that you only had a few precious moments to get the most important facts, details that would be gone in an instant. Look at it all carefully. Record it in your mind. Masks. They're all wearing big black smoke masks. The woman has thick blond hair. She's wearing a black wool coat. Running shoes. Long legs. Skinny. One of the guys is kind of gangly. Torn jeans, ripped sweatshirt. Short, short hair. The other guy, the leader, is also thin and has a shaved head.

"Facedown now!" the leader shouted at Todd, aiming a pistol at him.

One last glance to the side told Todd that Bradley was on the floor by the tripod, while Carol was lying by a table.

Clutching Cindy Wilson and pressing a gun to her head, the bald leader shouted, "Hands behind your backs! Any troubles and this lady here gets a nice surprise!"

Smoke now gushed out of all the vents, and two of the intruders started dashing around, strapping everyone's hands with plastic strips.

"Do the big guy first!" ordered the leader. "Strap his feet too!"

Lyle shouted, "You—"

"Shut up, asshole!"

They were flex-cuffs, quick handcuffs made of plastic, realized Todd, the kind the police could strap on in seconds. Working like a pro, the woman bound up Lyle, hands and feet, then Carol and Bradley. The skinny guy put the cuffs on Todd, and then less than a minute later he and the blonde were grabbing Clariton and forcing him to his feet.

"I don't think you want to do this," began Clariton, trying to control his voice. "I am a United States congressman, you see, and the FBI's not going to like this. Perhaps we could talk. You're getting into a lot more trouble here than you may realize.

We could talk and I could help you. I'm sure there's something I can do for—''

"Do you know how full of shit you are?'' snapped the woman.

And with that she pulled out a roll of duct tape and ripped off a piece. She dragged her sleeve over his mouth to dry his face, slapped the tape over his lips, then turned to the cart and pulled out a few sheets.

"Get in the laundry basket!''

His clothes soaked from the wet carpet, Clariton blurted a muffled plea.

"Get in!'' shouted the woman.

She and the gangly guy grabbed Clariton and dumped him into the basket. They then piled the sheets back on top of him. Next the two of them ran around the room, first to Carol, then Todd, the bodyguard, and finally Bradley, strapping tape over each one's mouth.

Above the screaming alarm the leader shouted, "We're going to go in the other room. We're going to be right in there, and if we hear so much as a peep from any of you, I'm going to shoot both this lady and Clariton in the head! Got it? Don't any of you move and don't any of you try anything stupid!''

"Oh, my God . . .'' begged Cindy. "Just leave me! Don't take me! Please, I won't cause any trouble!''

"Shut the fuck up!'' he shouted, pressing his gun so hard against Cindy Wilson's skull that her head tilted to the side. "Now, listen carefully so you can spread the word. We are Americans, we are acting independently, and we are all three dying of AIDS. We are appalled by Congressman Clariton's position on the AIDS epidemic. After we give the congressman a small dose of our lives, so to speak, we intend to release him. So tell the cops to leave us alone unless they really want him dead. You'll be hearing from us very soon.''

"Ta-ta, kids,'' said the gangly one. "It's been a real . . . blast!''

His mouth covered with tape, Todd twisted on the floor. The leader was shoving Cindy Wilson along, and the other two were wheeling the cart loaded with Congressman Johnny Clariton through the back door, the one Cindy had used.

"Get down, asshole!" shouted the leader at Todd. "And don't do anything stupid or this chick's dead!"

Todd dropped his head, his right cheek sinking into the wet carpet. The fire alarm kept on shrieking, water from the single sprinkler rained down, smoke continued to pump into the room, and somewhere in the distance he could hear the cry of the fire trucks. But all of this seemed almost inconsequential, for the one thing that had seized Todd's mind was the image of the guy with the shaved head.

What the hell was so incredibly familiar about him?

12

They turned a sharp corner and Matthew slammed Cindy Wilson into the waiting freight elevator. Once the cart and the others were in, he released the STOP button, hit another, and as soon as they started to descend they ripped off their smoke masks. Matthew then slumped against the wall of the lift. His heart was pounding, to be sure, but his head felt as if it would explode. He closed his eyes, opened them, saw only dancing ribbons of light. He shook his head, tried to focus on something, anything, and saw the pile of linens shifting.

Jabbing his gun into the cart, he shouted, "I'd love to kill you right now, Mr. Johnny Clariton!"

The lump muttered an indistinguishable string of words and froze.

The elevator slowly stopped on the ground floor, the doors eased back. Matthew stepped out first, again saw no one, then seized Cindy Wilson by the wrist and started dragging her along. Not wasting a second, Elliot and Tina shoved the cart out, charging after Matthew down the long hall until they reached the service area, where a red light was flashing and an obnoxious alarm was honking. Their blue vehicle sat undisturbed, though, backed up against the loading dock.

Matthew, still clutching Cindy Wilson, looked at Elliot and snapped, "Open the goddamn van!"

"Yes, boss man."

Elliot hurled open the rear doors of the van, jumped in, and grabbed a piece of plywood. Using the wood to bridge the gap between the dock and the vehicle, Elliot then jumped out. As planned and practiced, he and Tina rolled the cart into the rear of the van, then climbed in the back, crouching on either side of the laundry cart.

Nodding at Cindy Wilson, Elliot asked, "So, what are we going to do about the weathergirl?"

"I . . ." Matthew began.

He clenched his eyes shut as a searing blade of pain stabbed his head. For a second Matthew was sure he was going to pass out. Then he opened his eyes, tried to say something, but no words passed his lips. Shit, he didn't need this, not now, and they didn't need her, not anymore.

With great effort he forced himself to speak, saying, "Let's . . . let's just get rid of her."

Hell, why not? And he lifted the gun up to Cindy Wilson's head. She yanked back, cried out. One clean shot, he thought, and—

"No, Matthew!" screamed Tina, leaping out of the van.

"Shit, we don't need her!"

"No!"

Matthew shrugged, pulled back the gun. Then punched Cindy in the head with the butt of the gun. Cindy staggered a half step and collapsed on the loading dock.

Tina stood there, dumbfounded. "I hope you didn't kill her."

He looked down at her still body. "Do I care?"

From the back of the van Elliot pleaded, "Guys, we gotta go!"

Matthew shrugged again, turned, and trotted over to the wall, where he punched in the code for the garage door. As the large door rumbled upward, he darted back to the van, jumped into the driver's seat, and revved up the engine.

From the cargo space of the van Tina tried to keep things under control, saying, "Just stay calm, Matthew. Everything's going fine."

"Yeah, yeah, yeah."

He roared out, shooting over the curb and pulling onto LaSalle Avenue with a screech just as two fire trucks came bombing around the corner, their sirens and horns blasting. He was on a dead-on collision course with the first, and he twisted the wheel to the right.

"Matthew!" screamed Elliot from the back.

He swerved around the back of the first truck, kept going, and raced right in front of the second. Veering around a stopped car, he drove straight through the intersection without taking a look.

And then everything was remarkably calm, even quiet.

With each second the noise of the sirens grew fainter and more distant. With each second the traffic returned to normal. With each second it became more apparent exactly what had happened.

"Oh, my God," exclaimed Matthew, "we did it!"

Elliot peered out the rear window, saw no one—not a single cop car—tailing them, and screamed, "Yahoo!"

Tina took a deep breath, slumped against the side. "Thank God . . ."

"Hey," called Matthew from up front, "you better unbury our hostage before he suffocates."

"Right, right, right," muttered Elliot.

Digging through the linens with both hands, Elliot grabbed Clariton by one arm and yanked him up. Beet red and perspiring, his hands bound behind his back, Clariton emerged only to slump against the side of the cart.

"He needs some air!" shouted Tina. "Take off the tape!"

Elliot grabbed the congressman, holding his chin with his right hand, and said, "This may hurt, Johnny boy!"

With a quick yank he pulled the tape covering Clariton's mouth. It came off with a quick ripping noise, and Clariton flinched and began gulping air.

"What . . . what . . ." he gasped, his lips bleeding. "What do you assholes want?"

"Be nice," chided Elliot, "or I'm going to have to put the tape back on."

"But . . . what . . ."

"I have AIDS," called Matthew, steering around a corner and heading for the freeway.

"Me too," said Tina.

"Me three," added Elliot. "And it's a real drag, man. I mean, I'm going blind by the day, which for your info is why I'm not driving, and trust me, we can all be thankful for that."

"And your position on AIDS, frankly, sucks," barked Matthew from the driver's seat.

"Not to mention all the nasty things you've said about homo*thethual th,"* lisped Elliot.

"I don't . . . don't understand," muttered Clariton. "What do you want with me? What are you going to do?"

"Oh, you'll find out soon enough, Mr. Clariton," said Tina. "But I should tell you that we've kidnapped you because of your distinct lack of compassion."

Matthew laughed. "Shit, if you become the President we're all dead meat—every person with AIDS."

Tina nodded. "If someone like you gets elected and pushes through all your stupid ideas on medical reform and assistance, what's going to happen to people like us?"

Bobbing around in his bed of linens, Clariton's eyes opened wide. "You people are crazy!"

"No, no, no!" shouted Matthew, the anger bursting out of him. "That's just the point, asshole—we're sick! We're goddamn sick as hell!"

"And we want to teach you a lesson," added Tina, looking him directly in the eyes.

"That's right!" chimed Elliot. "A big lesson for Mr. Gay Public Enemy Numero Uno!"

"Don't worry," continued Tina. "In a few days we're going to turn you loose, but first we're going to tell you about our lives and make a few videos."

"You see, we're each going to record a little story," said Matthew, actually eager to make his confession public.

"Right," continued Tina, "and then we'll send you back to Washington, where you're going to take it upon yourself to make sure AIDS is treated with compassion and to push through new legislation to fight for the only thing that's going to stop AIDS once and for all: a vaccine."

"You think I'm going to cooperate with you?"

"Oh, but I'm quite certain you will. Once we're done with you I'm quite positive you'll talk to all the people in congress, corner the President, and work as hard as you can. And if you get everybody going, if you get everyone's attention, then I'm sure someone will discover a way to end the AIDS epidemic once and for all.''

"You can forget about us—we're as good as dead,'' tossed in Elliot with a big moan. "But you, believe it or not, are going to be our great hope!''

"That's right, we're going to make a convert out of you yet!'' shouted Matthew, knowing all it would take was one stick of a needle. "God, this is so unbelievably fucking great!''

13

Lest he jeopardize the lives of Cindy Wilson and Johnny Clariton, half of Todd said he should just stay there, lying on the wet carpet with his hands bound behind his back, his mouth covered with tape. The other half said he and the others should just get the hell out of there before the whole building went up in flames. Todd twisted on his side, saw that the main doors were chained and padlocked, which meant that the only way out was through the same door they'd taken Clariton. And what if they really were right in the next room? Of course they wouldn't hesitate to shoot either Cindy or Clariton. Or both.

Above the alarm and smoke and chaos, Todd heard something, worked himself around, and saw Lyle, his feet and hands bound, flapping madly about as he struggled to break free. Bradley was lying completely still, his head turned away from Todd, while Carol, Clariton's assistant, was perhaps the only one dealing honestly with the situation. She was crying, tears streaming from her red eyes, rolling down her cheeks, and plopping onto the carpet.

When Todd moved his head again, he realized that one corner of the tape was peeling away from his mouth. He started rubbing his cheek on the wet carpet, and little by little the tape started coming more and more loose. Dragging his face as hard as he could, he kept at it until finally a third of the tape came free. He stretched his mouth, pulled his lips apart, then rubbed his cheek again on the carpet. With one more swipe the tape fell free.

Great, now what?

As the sprinkler continued to rain water down on one side of the room, he glanced up at a vent, half-expecting to see flames leaping out. Instead, the smoke had virtually stopped. Seconds later the water stopped too, and just after that the alarm ceased its screaming. After the chaos it was oddly quiet.

Like Bradley and now the others, Todd lay completely still as he tried to tell what was going on. Within seconds he heard voices and commotion from the main hall, but who was it: their assailants or a herd of firemen? When he was sure the sound was from many more than just three people, Todd didn't restrain himself.

"In here!" he hollered. "Hey!"

Within moments someone was banging at the chained door. Todd shouted out again, and then there was this incredible banging. Not realizing there was another door into here from the dining room—one that was not locked—a handful of fire fighters in rubber coats and boots burst through the door, their axes drawn.

"What the hell?" said one of them upon seeing Todd and the others tied up on the floor.

"Get the police!" shouted Todd. "The congressman has been kidnapped!"

While one of them radioed for the cops, the other three guys put down their equipment and quickly started freeing Todd and the others. One of them helped Carol, removing the tape and cutting the plastic handcuffs, then aided Bradley, while one worked on Lyle and the other on Todd. As soon as he was loose Lyle burst up like a bull.

"They went through here!" he shouted as he charged out the small door and into the main dining room.

"Oh, my God," said Carol, her blue suit and white frilly tie thing soaked, as she slumped in a chair. "There were three of them—two men, one of them bald, and a woman. You've got to stop them! They've got Congressman Clariton and . . . and another woman too!"

His wet suit hanging heavily from him, Todd clambered to his feet and looked around. Both the room and the situation were a complete mess. What a disaster. What an opportunity. His instincts seized the moment and went into overdrive.

"Bradley!" he said, turning around. "Get the camera going! Maybe we can catch up with Clariton!"

Bradley took a deep breath, exhaled, and with not quite as much enthusiasm as Todd, replied, "Yeah, right—the unblinking eye."

Though a quick search of the building didn't turn up Congressman Johnny Clariton and his kidnappers, it was only minutes before Cindy Wilson was found unconscious on the loading dock. An ambulance and paramedics were quick to arrive, and they administered emergency first aid, covering a bleeding wound on Cindy's head, making sure her pulse was stable, and loading her onto a gurney. Less than five minutes later the ambulance whisked her away to Hennepin County Medical Center, the best trauma center in the Upper Midwest.

Meanwhile, Todd and Bradley reverted to their own training, taping the unconscious Cindy Wilson as she was first cared for, then carried away in the screaming ambulance. And once she was gone they returned to the chaos of the room where the aborted interview had taken place, getting shots of the water- and smoke-damaged room as well as the skyway filled with the cadre of fire fighters. While it was still perfectly fresh in his mind, Todd walked alongside Bradley, microphone in hand, and narrated each scene, explaining what they'd seen, what had happened. Later, back at the station, he'd go back and figure out how they'd present it all, but for now he just wanted to record the details.

Within minutes a great switch of tides took place as the fire fighters receded and a swarm of cops and detectives swelled in. By that time it was clear there had been no real fire, but that some sort of smoke bomb had exploded in the rear of Jerome's restaurant and that Congressman Johnny Clariton had, indeed, been abducted. And, yes, everyone was quick to assume that the smoke had been part of one and the same thing, specifically a well-organized plan to seize the congressman. A more thorough search of the building, however, failed to turn up any clue as to his fate.

As the side dining room where it had all taken place was

cordoned off and the crime lab people began to descend, Todd paused in the second-floor hall. Uniformed men and women swarmed all around him, shouting out orders, barking into walkie-talkies, and continuing to search for any relevant clues. Dear God, thought Todd as the magnitude of the incident began to sink in, did this really happen? Did this twister of a story—an unprecedented act of domestic terrorism—really descend right upon him?

Lugging his camera, Bradley came up behind Todd and said, "They want to question us all. Individually. They're setting up in the main dining room."

Todd wasn't surprised, and said, "Of course. I'm sure this is just the beginning. I mean, the FBI is sure as hell going to be all over this one too."

"Yeah, like flies on shit." Bradley shook his head. "Man, I wonder what they're really going to do to Clariton."

"I don't know, but I don't think they'll keep us waiting very long." Todd looked up and down the busy hall, half-expecting to see one cop in particular, one who was sure to be worried about Todd's well-being. "I'm surprised Rawlins isn't here already. You haven't seen him, have you?"

Bradley looked around and shrugged. "Nope, but then again maybe he hasn't heard about it yet."

That, Todd knew, couldn't be. For something this major they'd page Rawlins and every detective on the force. After all, Minneapolis had never seen anything this big before, Todd thought, sensing that this might rate right up there with the Oklahoma City bombing.

Forcing away a shudder of worry, Todd added, "If he's not already here, then Rawlins has got to be on his way. Trust me, only an act of God would keep him away from this."

14

Lyle Cunningham, the bodyguard hired to protect Johnny Clariton, made sure he was the first one questioned at the restaurant and then again at the police station in the Minneapolis City Hall, where they were all taken. And his credentials ensured that he was the first one released. Now leaving the huge granite building, a fortresslike edifice, he stepped outside and hailed the first taxi.

Big and brawny from years of training, Lyle had been brought in by Clariton's publisher to provide security here in Minneapolis. It was an assignment Lyle had been most reluctant to accept, for he was anything but a supporter of Clariton and his politics. In fact, if anyone on Clariton's staff had inquired what Lyle thought of the congressman, Lyle would have openly and honestly replied that he was at the other end of the spectrum. No one, however, had made an attempt to screen him for his personal views, and so the job was Lyle's. Oh, well, he'd thought at the time. It was supposed to have been easy enough. This was Minneapolis, after all, and while they had proceeded with caution, no one had expected a repeat of something like the San Francisco debacle or certainly not what had actually happened.

Now riding a taxi out of downtown, he smashed a fist against the soft seat. This should never have happened. He should have posted himself by the door when they had first entered the room. He should have immediately suspected that the smoke could be a ruse and acted more defensively. Instead, the relative tranquillity of Minneapolis had lulled him into a false sense of security and a group of kooks had abducted his ward. And from experience he knew the next few hours would be the most difficult and tense.

"So, you ain't in any trouble, are you?" asked the driver, a tall guy with a stubbly beard and thick black glasses, as he drove south on Highway 35W.

"What?" asked Lyle, glancing toward the front seat.

"I mean, I pick up some people at City Hall, you know, and they just got let out of jail."

Disgusted, Lyle shook his head and glanced out the window. The last thing he wanted to do right now was make small talk.

There was no telling which way this would go, but if the kidnappers meant to harm Clariton they could have simply and easily assassinated him right on the spot. They'd had their chance then and there at the restaurant, so they most certainly had other plans. But what? A ransom demand? A political statement? Probably the latter, but there was scant time. With each passing moment the tension would twist tighter and tighter, making the situation worse and worse and Clariton's chance for a safe release slimmer and slimmer. Already the Minneapolis police force was all over this, and one of the detectives had mentioned that the FBI's special Hostage Rescue Team was swooping down from Quantico. A United States congressman kidnapped? One of the most talked-about men in Washington, someone who was sure to be a presidential hopeful, abducted by a few drippy thugs? It was an act of terrorism that wouldn't be tolerated.

Less than ten minutes later the cab driver was turning off the highway and heading east toward Powderhorn Park, Lyle's neighborhood. He didn't live that far from the park itself, just a few blocks southeast, and when the taxi pulled up to his small stucco house, Lyle pulled out a ten and a five, threw it at the driver, and hopped out.

"Hey, thanks!" said the cabby, scratching his beard.

Lyle's vehicle, a Ford pickup, was parked right on the street, just where it had been this morning when the limo had picked him up before getting Clariton. He darted around the vehicle, up the front walk, and entered his screened porch. Unlocking the

front door, he charged inside and up the narrow dark-oak staircase, ripping off his tie as he climbed. He ducked into the larger
of the two bedrooms, threw his nearly dry jacket onto the brass
bed, took off his shoulder holster, and examined his gun.

A sinewy, terribly black creature came slithering into the
room. A cat, yellow eyes, short jet-black fur. A little love machine, she trotted over to Lyle, rubbed up against his ankle,
purred.

"Hey, Koshka," said Lyle, bending over and patting her.
"Yes, you're my little girlfriend, aren't you?"

Two years ago he'd found her and her sister abandoned beneath an elm in Powderhorn Park, a pair of sickly kitties not
more than a few weeks old. Lyle had scooped them both up, able
to fit them in the crook of one of his large arms, taken them right
to a vet, and then in the ensuing weeks learned a great deal about
motherhood as he nursed them to health. A doting father, Lyle
had raised them both, eventually giving one of the feline crea-
tures to his cousin and keeping Koshka, the seductress of the
two, for himself.

Now sweeping down with his hand, Lyle whisked up Koshka,
gave her a quick kiss, and gently tossed her on the bed. He then
returned to the more mundane matters at hand, and he quickly
changed, tossing aside his coat and tie and reaching for jeans and
a loose plaid shirt. He next strapped the shoulder holster back on
and slipped his gun in place. A sweater, which would be far too
constricting, was out of the question.

He'd been very direct and precise in what he'd told the police,
recounting just what had happened, exactly what he'd seen. With
an eye trained for this type of situation, he'd recounted details he
was sure the others—Carol and those two guys from the television station—had missed. Not simply the clothes, the hair, or
even the shoes, but the scar on the skinny guy's jaw, the
woman's mangled fingernails, where the bald guy had nicked his
head with a razor. Lyle had told the cops everything—everything
with one exception. And that he couldn't reveal. If he did, a
million cops would be barreling down the same trail; it'd be like
leading an entire platoon down a tiny footpath.

Right, he thought as he charged downstairs, where he called the office and checked in with his boss. He had one strong sense of where the trail to Johnny Clariton might begin, and he, by God, was going to follow it.

15

It was the perfect spot to hide someone like Johnny Clariton, a room behind a room within a space beneath the surface and below endless piles of crap. Entering these windowless chambers—two small rooms with tall ceilings and an adjoining bathroom with a big sink and toilet—Matthew locked the door behind them. Who in their right mind would ever think of looking here? It was both the least and the most obvious place for them to hide, and over the past week they'd gone undetected as they stocked it with food, sleeping bags, almost an entire apothecary worth of drugs, a small television, and of course all the video equipment they would need.

"Shit," mumbled Matthew, staring at the key in his hand.

He couldn't remember if he'd just locked the door, so he did so again, twisting it tight. When he turned back around, his head spun. Grab on, he told himself. Grab on to the door frame. Take a deep breath. You can't fucking lose it, not now, you moron. Wishing to God he was still on the suppressant therapy for cryptococcal meningitis, he closed his eyes and stood still.

"Oh, isn't it lovely," exclaimed Elliot, looking around as if he'd never been there before. "I've always wanted to live in a sterile, anonymous environment. Don't ya just love white on white on white on white?"

Tina immediately started digging in the laundry cart in which they had reburied the congressman for his trip from the van into the building. Pulling him up, he again emerged red-faced and sweaty. Using the tip of one of her fingernails, she picked at the corner of a second piece of tape that Elliot had plastered over

Clariton's mouth, then pulled. This time Johnny Clariton cried out.

"Come on, let's get him out of this thing," said Tina, referring to the laundry cart as she blotted her own forehead.

Noting the beads of sweat on her brow, Matthew demanded, "You all right?"

"No, not really. I'm exhausted and my stomach feels like it's about to fall out."

"Just hang in there, babe."

But she did look like shit, he thought. So thin, so pale. What the hell, they were all horribly run down, and this had been the most major day any of them had experienced in some time, if not ever. Usually their days were an endless parade from bed to doctor's office to lab then back to bed, and Matthew could now see that Tina's adrenaline was going to last only so long, that the excitement was only going to take her so far. Without a doubt they had to secure Clariton before he realized how weak all of them actually were.

"Come on," ordered Matthew, "let's get him locked up."

Elliot nodded. "Right, right, right."

With his hands still bound behind his back, Clariton pleaded, "What are you going to do? Where are you—"

"In there," snapped Matthew, waving his gun through the doorway.

They led him into the adjoining room, an empty storage space not larger than ten by eight feet, the walls blank, a couple of large pipes in the corner. Elliot dashed to the side, where he opened a canvas bag and pulled out a set of shiny handcuffs. The metal things dangling from his left hand, he spun around and bashed right into Tina, nearly knocking her off her feet.

"Oh, sorry, doll. Didn't see ya." He looked at the cuffs, glanced at Clariton, then looked around the room. "Golly, I think I'm losing my mind. How were we going to do this?"

"The pipe," said Tina.

"Right, the pipe!" Elliot dashed to the corner, attached half of the device to the pipe, then just stood there. "Now what?"

"His wrist."

"Right, his wrist!"

Matthew and Tina pushed Clariton toward the corner, and then Elliot pushed up Clariton's left sleeve and locked the cuffs.

"Guess you aren't going anywhere for a while, huh, Johnny boy?"

"But . . ." Clariton shuddered and looked away. "You know, I really could help you if you let me go."

"Don't worry, we are going to let you go. That's part of our plan," said Matthew. "But until we do, let me make a couple of things clear. First of all, we're in a place where no one can hear you, so don't even bother trying anything. If you make any noise, shout out or anything, we're going to put the tape right back over your mouth. Got it?"

"Yes, but—"

"Second, we're going to cut the flex-cuffs off your wrists. That will leave just the metal handcuffs on your left wrist, but again, any trouble and we'll strap the flex-cuffs back on both hands and around your ankles too. Got it?"

"Yes, but don't you see that I—"

Matthew snapped, "Do you understand or don't you, asshole?"

Clariton hesitated, then nodded.

"Here's a sleeping bag," said Tina, pulling one out of the duffel. "You can sit on this or whatever."

"And here's a coffee can," offered Elliot, pulling out a large red can. "You gotta go potty, use this. Sorry, it's the best we can do."

"Elliot, where are the clippers?"

"Oh, right."

Elliot dashed out of the room, returning seconds later with a pair of garden snippers. Matthew gave him the signal, and Elliot pushed Clariton around and cut the plastic binding his hands.

"Remember, asshole, don't make any trouble." Matthew turned to Tina, "What do you think, time to do the—"

Clasping one hand over her abdomen, Tina spun around and darted out of the room. She raced through the next and into the large rest room, slamming the door behind her.

"Oh, dear," muttered Elliot.

Of course Matthew knew what was up. Like Tina he'd been

plagued with wasting syndrome and had had trouble with almost every kind of food; all three of them were living on almost nothing but graham crackers, bananas, mashed potatoes, and Coke. He just prayed that was all, that there was nothing more serious.

Turning back to Clariton, Matthew waved the gun and yelled, "Just sit down and keep quiet! If you do anything to make me mad I'm going to . . . going to . . ."

"Yeah, so just watch it!" seconded Elliot.

Matthew stormed out, followed by Elliot, who slammed the door shut.

Great, thought Matthew, going up to the bathroom and pressing his ear against the door. This was all they needed. He tossed his gun on a pile of clothes, then ran his right hand over his stubbly scalp. Christ. Standing there, he heard her moan, and then the next instant came the distinct passing of gas and liquid as Tina's bowels exploded. A moment of silence came next, followed by her very slight but pained crying. Staring at Elliot, Matthew waved him toward the door.

Elliot edged right up to the doorjamb. "Tina? Tina, hon, you okay?"

"There's blood."

Matthew had been there, and he snapped, "How much?"

"A lot," she moaned, stifling a whimper.

"Great," muttered Matthew, starting to pace. "Absolutely fucking great. This is all we fucking need."

What if she passed out? What if the bleeding didn't stop?

"Tina, hon," began Elliot, his voice gentle, "I think you'd better drink something. Will you do that for me?"

She coughed. "Sure."

When Elliot didn't move, Matthew barked, "Well, don't just stand there, you fool! Get her . . . get her some Gatorade or a Coke or something!"

Elliot jumped, rushing across the room to a large red and white cooler.

"And I hurt," came her small voice.

Matthew yelled, "And get her a Percodan! Make that two!" He moved right up to the closed door and said, "It's okay, babe."

Hearing her moan in pain, Matthew placed a hand flat on the door, wanting, wishing to send her comfort, release, but forbidding himself to do anything more unless asked. He was sick of people asking him what they could do for him, tiptoeing around, themselves horrified by what they were witnessing, this terrible disease that was attacking his skin, his lungs, his stomach. Fuck it, he was mortally ill, they all were, no doubt about that, but he hated being treated as if he were a fucking two-year-old. He was just so sick of people—these grown, healthy adults—whimpering around him, wanting to know if he wanted a glass of water or a cold washcloth for his burning head or a cookie. Matthew, want a cookie? Shit. Yet now that he heard poor Tina literally flushing her life down the toilet, all he wanted to do was hold her, rock her. Oh, God, he begged, banging his head against the wall, let this be over soon, this torture of life.

"Yo," said Elliot, pushing a couple of pills, a baked treat, and a bottle of Gatorade at Matthew.

Matthew turned, saw the offering, and started shaking his head. "Where in the hell did you get a Twinkie?"

"I brought a whole case of 'em. A psychic friend of mine says it kills HIV."

"But that'll be impossible for her to digest. Are you crazy?"

Elliot shrugged. "Queer, everyone knows *that.*" He pushed the stuff closer. "Come on, give it to her, it'll be good for her blood sugar."

Matthew took it all, then said, "Tina? Tina, open up. Here's some stuff for you."

The door cracked open and a deathly thin wrist, as skimpy as a twig, poked out. Matthew handed it all to her, wondering how in the hell she was even strong enough to hold it.

"Thanks," she said, her hand withdrawing and the door shutting.

Again she moaned as another burst of fluid shot out of her.

After a few moments of quiet Matthew said, "Tina, what do you think if I make the first video?"

"No," came her immediate response.

"But—"

"We've been over and over this, Matthew. It has to be me. I'm the straight one."

They had discussed this at length, the order in which they were going to make the videos of each of them with Johnny Clariton. And the order was important, very much so. The country, even the world, would be watching, and Tina, Elliot, and Matthew wanted to make it perfectly clear why they had done this, abducted a U.S. congressman. They had all agreed with Tina that the first image of them would be the most important, the one that would hit the hardest. And what could be a better, more shocking first glimpse at this band of AIDS terrorists than a straight woman, who some viewers might still recognize as a one-time top model, dying from this dreadful disease?

"I'm kind of dizzy. Just give me a few more minutes," said Tina, her voice weak. "But I've got to do it. I've got to do it for Chris."

"Sure. Sure, babe, whatever you say," replied Matthew. "You just rest a bit and we'll start getting everything ready." His head pounding, Matthew turned to Elliot and ordered, "Get me the syringe!"

16

Channel 10 was thrilled. Todd Mills, well, he was a god.

He'd already told his story on the 5:00 P.M. local news. And now he was on the national news, live with Dan Rather. Perched atop a WLAK TV van, which stood only feet away, was a mini-satellite connecting Todd via the stars to the preeminent television anchor.

". . . and, to repeat, Dan, in the almost six hours since three self-described AIDS activists abducted Congressman Johnny Clariton, there has been virtually no news as to his fate. His kidnappers have yet to make any demands whatsoever, and as far as I know, the FBI and the police have virtually no leads," reported Todd, holding a stick mike and looking straight into the camera as he stood in front of the large brick building where it had all taken place. "Otherwise, the only other person known to be injured thus far, WTCN TV reporter Cindy Wilson, remains unconscious but in stable condition at Hennepin County Medical Center."

It was the lead story not just in the Twin Cities, not just in the United States, but perhaps in the western world. And Todd was right in the eye of it, being sucked up and picked apart by not only the police and the FBI, but the horde of journalists who were descending upon Minneapolis. As not only one of the top journalists in the region, but as both a victim and a witness to the abduction, Todd was being all but consumed. What was it like? How many of them were there? Did you get any sense of what they wanted? Did you fear for your life? Was there really a fire? What do you think they'll do to Congressman Clariton? All afternoon he'd gone over and over and over it, first with the authorities, then with his colleagues, the piranhalike media.

"Todd," said Rather, his voice coming in clearly through the earpiece lodged discreetly in Todd's right ear, "as I understand it, you had just started an exclusive interview with Congressman Clariton moments before the assailants set off the smoke bomb and burst into the room."

"That's absolutely correct, Dan," replied Todd, looking squarely into Bradley's camera. "The congressman concluded his roundtable luncheon, left the main dining room of Jerome's, and came into the side dining room where we had set up our camera and lights."

Todd's voice was perfect. He looked fabulous, just right for the situation. Dressed in jeans, a crisp shirt, a Ralph Lauren cotton jacket—all clothes that someone at Channel 10 had darted out and purchased that afternoon at Dayton's, the behemoth department store, because Todd hadn't been able to return home to change—the image was not of a prepped and preened reporter but of a correspondent caught right in the middle of a maelstrom. Standing there, the lights of Bradley's cameras glaring in his eyes, a sidewalk crowd—not to mention the entire country—watching, Todd only hoped no one sensed how utterly exhausted he was. He'd been cranked on high all afternoon, telling, recounting, trying to recall every detail, and he now struggled to appear calm, insightful, sincere.

Rather continued, saying, "Can you tell us what Mr. Clariton was like in those moments before he was kidnapped? Did he have any intimation whatsoever of any danger?"

"I'm quite sure that the congressman didn't suspect a thing. He'd had a very successful book-signing this morning, a stellar luncheon—which was, at five thousand dollars a plate, attended by the region's top executives and completely sold out—and he appeared quite animated and pleased. However, after the incident in San Francisco when some AIDS activists hurled a bucket of blood on him, he did have a bodyguard assigned to him. Mind you, had Mr. Clariton already announced his bid for the presidency of the United States—which so many expect him to do within the next month—he would have had Secret Service protection. That, however, wasn't the case.''

"Of course not. He was ostensibly on a private tour promoting his book.''

"That's correct.''

"In your opinion, just how dangerous is this situation?''

"I would say extremely,'' ventured Todd. "Keep in mind that the kidnappers stated that they are in the last stages of a terminal illness and that they know they are dying. Consequently, that means they have almost nothing to lose.''

"A frightening thought.'' Rather shook his head. "So far all the top national AIDS organizations have issued statements deploring today's event. What has been the reaction there in Minneapolis?''

"Complete and total outrage. In fact, the Minnesota AIDS Coalition, the largest local AIDS group, has condemned the abduction and will be holding a meeting tonight to help its staff and volunteers deal with the trauma of the situation.''

Todd's mind started whizzing: Do I leave it at this? In a matter of a mere second or two his mind ran like a supercomputer and quickly came to one quick, firm conclusion: No. This is too important for me and others like me. Go on, just jump.

"Dan,'' began Todd, "I'd also like to add that in the moments before the chaos broke loose I personally found Mr. Clariton quite aggressive and, to be perfectly frank, rather hostile to the cause that his abductors claim to represent.''

"Really?'' came the surprised reply. "In what way?''

"Before we got started, he lambasted in a most derogatory manner all homosexuals and everyone with AIDS.'' Go on, just say it, he thought, staring into the lens. Out yourself to the universe. "He came striding into the room where I was to interview him and demanded to know who was gay. When I identified myself as a gay person but assured him that that had nothing to do with our interview and that, in fact, my sexuality was none of his business, he launched into a tirade of bigotry and vitriol.''

"I see,'' said Rather, unable to hide his own amazement. "Can you be specific, Todd?''

Okay, thought Todd. Now it's time for a little poker, and if you play it right this is going to draw a mountain of attention. So hint it, but hold it. Just tell 'em there's some great dirt coming. Soon. But keep 'em waiting. Channel 10 will wet its pants with glee.

"I don't think, Dan, it would be particularly appropriate for me to go into it at this time."

"Absolutely. And I'm sure we'll be hearing more from you in the near future. Thank you," concluded Rather. "That was Todd Mills, reporting from our Minneapolis/Saint Paul affiliate WLAK TV on the fate of Congressman Johnny Clariton, who was kidnapped early this afternoon by a radical group of AIDS activists."

Todd stood quite still, staring into the camera until there was a fuzzy snapping sound. An instant later the connection was severed and there was nothing, and Todd lowered his stick mike, then pulled the clear earpiece from his ear. He took a deep breath, glanced over at the crowd gathered behind the barrier. He suddenly felt as if he'd walked face first into this wall, an invisible but completely solid one.

Exhausted, he made his way over to Bradley and asked, "Was that okay? Did I make sense?"

"Great. Perfect," Bradley replied, adjusting a few things on his camera.

"How about you? Aren't you a little worn out?"

"If I weren't so wired I'd collapse right here on the sidewalk." He wiped one of his eyes. "But I don't think I'll make it until the ten o'clock news."

"Yeah, I'm kind of wondering if I will."

Todd walked over to the Channel 10 van, which was parked halfway up on the sidewalk, and climbed into the passenger seat. He sat there for a moment, rubbing his face with both hands, then reached for a Thermos on the dashboard and poured himself a cup of coffee. Taking a swig, he frowned, for it tasted like lukewarm, acidic brown . . . brown . . . something. But he was tired, in need of a jolt, and so he took a large gulp. Next he reached for the mobile phone, called the station, and dialed up his voice mail. There were two messages. Please, he prayed, let one of them be from him.

"Hi, doll!" came the voice of his West Coast agent, Stella, on the first message. "You're amazing, totally amazing! How do you get yourself into these things anyway? I'm so glad you're all right, and I'm so glad you were there. I mean, doll, do you have any idea what this is going to do for your career? Do you? If they don't already, then everyone in the country is going to know who you are by bedtime tonight. You were absolutely fabulous on the CNN spot this afternoon—and it's been repeating every half hour on *Headline News*. Oh, my God, it's just too great. This is going to make you rich. And don't worry, I'm going to milk this for all it's worth. We won't screw up like Wolf Blitzer did after all that Middle East stuff. He could be a real biggie on the networks by now, but instead, doll, it's going to be you. Congrats! Call me when you get a few."

Todd shook his head, rolled his eyes. Had Stella-doll just seen him on Dan Rather? Would his outing himself on one of the major networks cause his worth to go up or in fact drop a few hundred grand? He hit a button on the phone and deleted the message. Who cared?

What he really wanted was news from Rawlins. Where the hell had he been all afternoon? Todd had left numerous messages at Rawlins's home number, on his voice mail at work, and even on Todd's own answering machine just in case he returned to the condo. But so far Todd hadn't heard word one from him, nor had he found anyone who'd seen him or spoken to him all day. Could something have happened at the doctor's? Could he have been in an accident?

So when would it be time to panic?

Todd listened to the next message, left only moments ago.

"Holy shit, Todd!" came Janice's voice from Santa Fe. "I'm still down here in Santa Fe, and we just saw you on CNN. Thank God you're all right. I mean, you looked fine, but I'm sure you're a wreck."

He grinned slightly. Perhaps no one knew him better than his old college girlfriend, Janice Gray, the self-described lipstick-lesbian lawyer.

"Take care, sweetheart," continued her recorded voice. "We're all thinking of you. And please, please be careful. Just don't go pulling any of your usual stunts, all right? Call when you get a chance. Love to you and Rawlins.''

Todd smiled, hung up. Then frowned. Where the hell was Rawlins anyway?

Grabbing his briefcase from the back, he jumped out of the van, went over to Bradley, and said, "Listen, I have to take off for a while.''

"What?" replied Bradley as he finished packing up his camera.

"There's something I gotta check on.''

"But you don't have a car. How are—''

"Taxi," said Todd, half-turning and starting quickly down the sidewalk. "If anyone asks, tell them I'll be out at the station in an hour, hour and a half, okay?''

"Ah, sure.''

If he was going to hunt down Rawlins, the first place Todd would have to start was the last place he'd seen him: the condo.

With all good intents, I thought I'd feel nothing but relief once Curt died. I thought I'd feel nothing but a kind of happiness for helping him out of here.

Instead, he's beginning to haunt me.

I'm in a store and I hear someone coughing away, and then Curt's hacking starts echoing in my ears. I close my eyes to try and block it out, and I see the blood dribbling from his ears. I start crying, and then I hear him moaning with pain. Worst of all, and this is really the pits, I don't think I'll ever enjoy sex again because Curt has crept in there, right into my secret fantasies. To be perfectly frank, I'm having trouble getting a hard-on, because, instead of visualizing gorgeous men, all I can see is Curt's emaciated body. It was so gross, looking at him. So awful to put on a happy face, be all smiley and up when all I wanted was to run the hell away. What did he lose in the end—fifty, sixty pounds? How many times did the shit and the blood come oozing out his ass and all over the bed? About a gazillion, actually.

Crap, I wish I'd get plowed over by a Mack truck.

This could be something like post-traumatic stress syndrome. It could be plain old guilt. Instead, I'm afraid it's reality. My reality. Before all this I never imagined killing anyone. Certainly not two people. But as time ticks by—tick, pause, tick, pause, which is to say, things are really draggin' 'round here—it's becoming all too clear. That's right. Time for another cyanide cocktail. I'm going to have to play bartender to the devil once again just so I can fulfill my darkest fantasy.

Care for a drop-dead nightcap, dahlink? After all, by command of His Highest Honcho, the Almighty God, ain't no one gettin' out of here alive.

17

Shaken by the day's events, Todd sat in a near state of shock in the rear seat of the taxi. It was the first time all day he'd been both quiet and still, and he stared blankly out the left window as the cab whisked around the northern edge of Lake Calhoun.

Given the gravity of the situation that had overtaken not only his life but the entire nation, he hoped he'd done well in his coverage, conveying accurately what he had witnessed. He'd tried to be impartial, tried to be objective, but of course that had been impossible. On the one hand, after speaking face to face with him, Todd thought worse of Clariton than ever before. On the other hand, what had happened was horrific. Recalling it all with a shudder, Todd was only just now realizing how frightened he'd been.

He closed his eyes, took a deep breath. Just relax. You're okay. But he couldn't stop his mind from ricocheting from the abduction to national television—surely many members of congress and perhaps even the President himself had just seen him on TV—and then to matters more personal. Specifically, what had happened to Rawlins?

He opened his eyes and stared at the large grayish plain of the still-frozen lake, then pressed himself against the right window, saw his towering condominium building coming into sight. Lights dotted the structure here and there, and Todd quickly tried to find his apartment up there on the fifteenth floor. Lights on at his place would mean Rawlins was there and everything might be okay, right? Right? Starting from the ground, he tried counting floors, but then the car hit a pothole and Todd bounced in the backseat and lost focus.

Arriving at his tall building on Dean Parkway, Todd tipped the taxi driver generously, grabbed his briefcase, and bounded out of the vehicle. He waved briefly at the security guard, an older man who buzzed him in, and proceeded directly to the bank of mailboxes just off the main lobby.

"Hey," called the guard, hanging out the door of his small room, "I just saw you on the evening news with that Dan Rather fellow!"

Todd struggled for a reply, finally saying with a shrug, "Big afternoon."

"I'll say!"

Todd took out his keys, found the smallest one, and opened his mailbox. He pulled out a magazine and a handful of envelopes, then opened his briefcase and dropped in his mail. Glancing over to make sure the guard wasn't watching, Todd next pulled out the videotape of Clariton's comments and slipped it into his mailbox, which he locked tight.

Crossing to the other side of the lobby, he hit a button and the elevator doors opened. Stepping in, he began to ascend, he hoped, to some kind of truth. It flashed through his mind that something had happened and Rawlins had never even left the apartment this morning. What if he'd slipped in the shower and knocked himself out? Or had a seizure of some sort? Perhaps. Or perhaps something else had come up and Rawlins had simply left a note to that effect, like maybe his mother in rural Minnesota had had a heart attack and he'd been called out of town.

Good grief.

By the time Todd stepped onto the fifteenth floor, he'd visited and weighed every possibility, still unable to settle on any kind of reasonable explanation for Rawlins's absence and increasingly fearful of what it all meant. Hoping for some kind of immediate answer, he jabbed the key into the lock of his apartment, swung open the door.

Crap.

It was dark, not a light burning in the place. Todd stood in the doorway, wondering if he should just duck out and head straight over to Rawlins's apartment. Wait, he reminded himself, Rawlins could be lying unconscious in the bathroom, his head split open, or there could be a note, or . . .

Why was it so cold in here?

Peering into his darkened home, Todd didn't move. It wasn't simply that it felt unusually cool or chilly, but there was a distinct draft, a real gust of air blowing through the apartment, out the door, and into the hall. Was one of the windows open? Without turning on a light Todd took several steps, letting his front door swing shut behind him. He moved past the dark kitchen and right up to the edge of the living room.

Todd froze.

The sliding glass door to his balcony was pulled open, and Rawlins stood on the balcony. Rather, Rawlins had one foot on a chair, the other on the balcony railing. In one instant Todd's heart jolted with anger and a barrage of testy questions: Where the hell have you been? Why haven't you called? What's the matter with you? The next moment he understood something incomprehensible: Rawlins was about to jump.

An adrenaline-fueled rush of panic surged through Todd, but he didn't budge. Oh, dear God.

He cleared his throat and, his voice weak and shaking, called, "Rawlins?"

When there was no reply Todd took a couple of steps closer. The cool air gushed in, and from the street below he could hear the stream of traffic, rubber tires humming against pavement, frustration turning to a mad honk, the screech of a quick brake, somewhere far off the safe sound of a siren—safe because it was exactly that, so very far away.

"Rawlins?"

Nothing. The solid figure, black against the dark blue hues of the early-evening sky, didn't budge.

Todd inched still closer, wanting at once to dart forward, fearful at the same time of what that might precipitate. Trembling, he realized that of course he was right, of course Rawlins intended to jump. No fool would stand perched like that, poised as if to take a flying leap off a diving board. Even one wrong flinch and he'd lose his balance and go tumbling over.

"I'm . . . I'm here, Rawlins. It's me . . . Todd. I'm

home," began Todd, stuffing the panic charging through him. "Hey, buddy, I'm here. Let's . . . let's talk."

It was as if he'd lost his hearing, as if he were deaf as a rock. Rawlins just kept looking out, staring upward into the sky as if from here, from this fifteenth-floor balcony, he could leap right up there, into the heavens without touching earthly reality—and earthly pain—ever again.

God, no.

Todd wanted to scream, to go charging across the room, tackle Rawlins, pin him down, hold him here, and not let him go, not ever. Instead, a kind of surreal common sense shackled him, restraining him, holding him in control, and he crept across the soft carpet of his living room, one silent step at a time. More like an observer than a participant, he didn't take his eyes off the dark figure, afraid that if he even blinked Rawlins would be gone, vanished into the void. And thus he moved past the black leather couch, past the glass coffee table. Past a side chair, the TV. The sliding glass door was pulled back, the screen door as well. Only another ten feet. Just past the table. Todd didn't make a noise. Didn't say a word. No, obviously nothing he could say would bring Rawlins back. Only force might.

Finally he reached the doorway to the balcony, and the cold night air blew over Todd, rippling his hair, chilling his bones. His eyes fixed laserlike on the back of Rawlins—a shirt, no jacket, jeans, leather shoes—and Todd took a quick appraisal of just how it could be done. He stood as still as if he were about to slap a fly, for one wrong move and things could tip the other way.

Then he leapt into action.

Todd grabbed onto the doorjamb with his left hand and with his right lunged out and grabbed Rawlins by the back of his jeans. Plucking his lover from the edge, Todd heaved as hard as he could, eliciting an angry scream from Rawlins. Todd tripped and fell inside, and Rawlins came flying from his precipitous perch onto Todd, the two of them landing with an ugly crash on the carpet of the living room floor. In an instant Todd's lungs exploded as the weight of Rawlins crushed down on him. And as he lay wheezing on the floor, struggling for air, things truly blew up.

"You asshole!" screamed Rawlins. "You fucking asshole! What are you doing, goddammit all?"

For a brief instant Todd feared that Rawlins would do it, just get right back up and dart onto the balcony, hurl himself over with a flying leap. Instead, he was all over Todd, fists swinging, feet kicking. Unable to breathe, much less get up, Todd curled himself into a ball as Rawlins's fury burst over him.

"You did this to me, didn't you?" shrieked Rawlins.

"Wh-wha—" gasped Todd.

"You fucker!"

A fist plunged into his side, and Todd jerked back as the pain zipped through him. What the hell? He scrambled across the floor, scurrying on his hands and knees, trying to get away. Rawlins took another swing; Todd ducked. Gulping for air, Todd glanced over his shoulder and saw the rage—so absolute, so total—in Rawlins's red, hysterical face.

"I'm going to kill you!" shouted Rawlins.

As Rawlins lunged at him Todd didn't doubt he meant it, and Todd crawled across the room, grabbing for a chair, a pillow, something, anything, to shield the blows. Rawlins came at him shrieking, and Todd jabbed out a foot, catching Rawlins by the ankle and tripping him. Rawlins fell, crashing into the glass coffee table and smashing right through the top. The glass shattered beneath his weight, and then he lay there in the shards, his body heaving with sobs.

Todd, only just regaining his breath, half-reached out. "Rawlins?"

Amid the glassy mess the body moved, the head lifted.

Todd begged, "Wh-what is it? Rawlins, what the hell are you—"

He pushed himself up, his face a tight, wrinkled, crying mass, and sobbed, "I'm dead."

"What?"

"I'm dead!"

"Rawlins, stop it! You're being—"

"I have AIDS!" he screamed. "I'm going to die—just like John and Rick, just like Max, Al, David, Ed, Thomas, and Curt! You hear me? I have AIDS just like Curt did!"

Everything exploded, and Todd couldn't move. "No . . .
no . . ."

Rawlins sat back, staring at the palm of his left hand. There
was a large chunk of glass sticking into him, and he looked at it,
then pulled it free. As if he'd just uncorked a bottle, a deep, rich
flow of blood started pouring out of his hand, curling, dripping
down his wrist, trailing down his arm.

Oh, dear God, thought Todd. This couldn't be. Looking at
Rawlins's bloody hand, he didn't see the stuff of life dripping out
of his lover. He saw poison gushing, oozing out. Their future
flashed before him, his and Rawlins's future—the doctors, the
medications, the sores, the . . . No, he couldn't lose Rawlins,
and Todd grappled across the floor, his eyes welling with tears.
He had to hold him. Take him back. Not let him go.

"Stop!" shrieked Rawlins, holding up his bloody hand.

As if Rawlins had just pulled a gun on him, Todd jerked away,
staring at the ribbon of blood as if it were some sort of hideous
secret weapon, the plague to end all plagues.

"That's right," said Rawlins in a deep, ugly voice as he
pressed his hand closer to Todd, "you don't want to ever come
close to me again."

No. No, but . . .

This was insane. This was impossible. Todd did, indeed, pull
back. But then he scrambled to his feet. And then he started
running out of the lightless room. Down the dark hall. The door
to the linen closet was cracked wide and he threw it open. Plunging in his hands, he started groping for a towel. Suddenly some
unseen creature screeched and clawed him. Todd in turn
screamed and jerked back as Curt's cat, Girlfriend, who had been
curled up on the towels, came shooting out like a missile, whizzing past Todd and disappearing into the bedroom. Todd caught
his breath, reached a second time into the closet, grabbed a
towel, thought better of it, took another. Rawlins had AIDS? He
started shaking, trembling. Let there be some kind of mistake.
Don't let this be true.

He heard an odd noise from the living room, and it flashed
through his mind: Rawlins did it; he jumped.

Carrying the towels, he tore back down the hall into the living room, where he was greeted by the darkness and a cool gush of air. Rawlins was no longer on the floor. The balcony door was open, the balcony itself as empty as if something had just flown away.

Todd couldn't move and, his voice barely audible, gasped, "Rawlins?"

In response came a frightened sob. Todd ran across the room, found him there, curled in a ball and lying on his side behind a chair. He was sobbing. Todd stared down at this hysterical mass, saw Rawlins lost in his fears: Homo. Fag. Queer. You fuck with another man and you're dead. Bad boy. You deserve it. You deserve to rot on this earth. Shame, shame, shame. Die, faggot!

"Did . . . did . . . did you do this . . . this to me?" begged Rawlins, looking up through his tears.

Perplexed, Todd stared at him, this strongest of men who'd regressed to some kind of panicked child, and said, "What?"

"Do you have it . . . Do you have it too?"

Todd suddenly understood. It made sense. Of course that was why Rawlins had attacked him with such fury. Oh, shit.

"No, I'm okay, Rawlins. You know I tested negative." Todd knelt down next to him. "Give me your hand."

"But—"

"I'll be careful."

Rawlins gingerly held out his bleeding left hand, and Todd wrapped a towel around it. First one, then the second for added protection.

Todd tightened the towels and said, "Tell me what happened."

"I . . ." he began, and then stopped.

"You went to the doctor's?"

Rawlins nodded.

"And what, you got the results from some tests?"

Again Rawlins nodded.

Which meant, realized Todd, that of course Rawlins had had blood drawn last week. "Why the hell didn't you say anything before?"

Shit, never mind. That was a conversation for much later. Just stay focused. For now just get all the facts.

A hope flashed through Todd's mind, and he asked, "Are you HIV positive or is it . . . is it AIDS?"

The first meant there was more time. Time meant a greater chance. A chance for the new drugs to do their work. A chance for yet more drugs to be created.

"I'm probably just positive." Rawlins shrugged, wiped his nose with the back of his right hand. "But my doctor won't say for sure, not until he knows my T-cell count."

"Rawlins, we'll get through this. We'll make it." They had to, thought Todd. "They're doing all this great stuff now, all this wonderful stuff, you know, with the protease inhibitors and all that. They're talking about AIDS becoming a manageable disease, and—"

"Fuck you!" shouted Rawlins, kicking at Todd and pushing him away. "That's exactly what I used to say to Curt. 'Oh, don't worry, you'll make it, there's AZT, and they're doing all this great stuff now.' And that's exactly what he used to say to his friends. 'There are all these great meds out there. Don't worry, the scientists are working around the clock.' And did any of them make it? No, they're dead as dirt. Did they not suffer? You bet they did. Oh, Christ, don't you remember the pain Curt was in? And you know what? I'm spent. I've had so many friends die and I gave them all my courage, all my strength—little good it did— but now I don't have any energy left for myself."

Todd was on his feet. He was at the balcony, sliding shut the large door. And then he just stood there, staring out at the lake, at the distant planes circling the airport like blinking fireflies. He saw all that, just as clearly as he saw what lay ahead—all the tests, all the pills, all the stress and fear, all the desperate hope. Could he do it? Did he have the strength, the stamina, to be a martyrlike caregiver? He didn't know, not really. Couldn't be sure. Michael, the first guy with whom Todd had had a serious relationship, had been murdered, and Todd didn't think he could go through it again, invest and lose it all, have someone else die. And right then, right at the same time, he realized that Michael's murder was somehow easier than this was going to be. Michael had been whole when he'd left this world. Michael was gone in a blink.

Yes, he realized, HIV and AIDS were some kind of horrible test, just what of he had yet to learn.

His eyes beading with tears, Todd knew only one truth, and he said, "I don't want to lose you, Rawlins."

"Guess again—you already have."

"But—"

"Get real." Rawlins clutched the towels around his hand, then pushed himself up. "You know, I thought the same bus that hit Curt missed me, but I was wrong. I just turned my back for an instant and didn't see it coming. And now it's got me under the wheels and it's about to—"

"Stop it!"

"Oh, Todd." Rawlins took a deep sigh. "You can't go back in the closet on this one, you can't hide in the dark. This is reality. This is here, now. And you know what? We're done, we're over."

Todd turned around, stared at Rawlins, who stood in the middle of the faintly lit room. "What are you saying?"

"I'm saying that I saw how freaked out you used to get when we went over to Curt's. I saw how scared you were, how you shut down when you saw his emaciated body. Face it, man, you can't handle it. You can't. You're going to leave me just like that shit left Curt."

"Stop it!"

"Trust me, AIDS is too faggy for you."

"What, you're telling me that I flunked some kind of test?" shouted Todd, wondering at the same time if he'd been that obvious. "Well, fuck off! And if that's the way you feel, then get the fuck out of here. I don't need this!"

"See? You've got your career. You don't need this and you don't want it," said Rawlins with a half smile, and then turned and started for the door.

Todd, horrified at what he'd just said and what was now happening, called, "Wait!"

"Forget it, Todd. We're over, we're done. You can barely take care of yourself, let alone someone with a terminal illness. Trust me, it's better this way. Better that we both face up to things and that the truth comes out now instead of . . . instead of later."

Oh, shit. This wasn't what he wanted. This wasn't how it was supposed to go.

Starting after him, Todd shouted, "Rawlins, you can't go! You—"

As he headed for the door, Rawlins stopped, slowly turned around. "You know what I'd do if I were you? I'd get myself tested again. Of course, you won't be absolutely sure for another six months or so, but I'd go right out tomorrow morning and take a test for the HIV virus. And while you're waiting to find out, you can curse me all you want. I'm sorry, Todd. I really am. I thought I was okay."

As if he'd been slapped, Todd just stood there. Oh, God. He hadn't thought about that. Not really. And his mind whizzed through their history of sex, sorting who'd done what to whom. They'd been wise, they'd been smart, but they were talking about a virus, a little, tiny, microscopic thing that traveled in bits of bodily fluid. So what about the time they'd woken up at something like three in the morning, groping with lust? They'd had sex in some kind of blissful, dreamy fog, but what had they really done? And what about—

"Good-bye, Todd."

He looked at Rawlins, knew there was no stopping him, and realized that right then he wasn't so sure he wanted to anyway.

"Where are you going?" asked Todd.

"To find the guy driving the bus. If it wasn't you who hit me, I have a good idea who did." Rawlins shrugged. "I don't know why it's so important for me to put all the pieces together, but it is. I suppose if I can't understand life, then the least I want to understand is my own death."

Todd said nothing, just stood there in some kind of shock as he let the person he loved most in the world walk through his door and out of his life.

18

First you have to find a thread, thought Lyle Cunningham as he started up his pickup truck. Just one single, loose thread. And then you pull. More often than not, things start to unravel, leading you closer and closer to the crux of the whole damn thing. Right now he saw a number of the pieces—the outspoken and controversial Clariton, the blond woman he'd spoken to at the autographing that morning, later the very same woman in the very same black coat and the two men who'd abducted Clariton—and it was just a matter of trying to find how everything was stitched together. When Lyle had phoned his boss just a few minutes ago they'd both speculated that the gay television reporter, Todd Mills, somehow fit in. After all, who knew what his agenda might be? Was it purely coincidence that the kidnappers were AIDS protesters and the kidnapping had taken place while Mills was doing the interview? Could he have somehow been in on the planning or somehow manipulated the interview or given the kidnappers access to the building? Perhaps not. Perhaps all of the above.

Of all the things, that was what Lyle hated most about gays. On the one hand they wanted to be accepted, to not be discriminated against. Sure, Lyle got that. What he didn't understand, though, was their exclusivity, their reverse discrimination. Either you were a member of their tribe—and therefore trusted—or you weren't. And if you weren't, you were always suspect. In essence gays wanted to be equal but separate. He saw how they hung out together. He knew they preferred to do business within their own community. He saw how they scorned and laughed at the very people from whom they begged acceptance and tolerance. And it disgusted him.

Leaving his home, Lyle headed west toward Uptown, that trendy, very successful, and very gay neighborhood. If he was right, he thought as he drove along, that one loose thread he was searching for could be found over there, in that area. It wasn't going to be easy. Of course not. In fact, now thinking about it, he wished he'd made himself some coffee, brought some food, a pillow. Okay, so he'd stop for a burger, some fries, and a lot of coffee.

Right. He should get tanked up on caffeine because, after all, this could be a very, very long night. There was one residence in particular that he was going to scope out, and who knew how long he'd have to wait before he saw any action.

19

With a cotton swab Matthew dabbed at the spot on his forearm where he'd just been poking around with a special syringe, one treated with the anticoagulant Heparin. Okay, that was done, they'd all contributed, so on with the frigging show. On to the big event. Now if only this goddamn headache would stop. He just stood there in the middle of the room as a swath of pain cut through the back of his head and, seemingly, all the way to the back of his eyes.

"A bad one, hey?" asked the subdued Tina, seated on a chair and still clutching her bottle of Gatorade.

"Yeah . . ." He turned to Elliot and ordered, "Look harder, Elliot!"

"Jeez, I'm looking, I'm looking!" said Elliot, pawing through a liquor box full of pills and medicines. "Sorry, Charlie, it just ain't here." He picked up one bottle, read the label. "You know, you were really stupid to go off your suppressant therapy meds."

"Shut up."

What really scared Matthew was the prospect of a seizure, the one thing he didn't want to happen now. A while back when he'd had a full-blown grand mal, he'd not only collapsed but had also vomited, lost control of his bladder, and been unable to speak for hours. He couldn't afford to lose control of anything right now. Matthew had been on an antibiotic to battle the cryptococcal meningitis for a long time, but then he'd stopped because he was taking so many pills, something like sixty a day. This headache, he realized, was exactly what he had felt before the other seizure had struck, and he'd left whatever pill was designed to battle this specific thing at home. Great.

"Fuck it," he cursed. "Let's just get on with it."

"Oh, fab!" said Elliot, jumping to his feet, then lunging toward a canvas bag. "I'll get the camcorder. This is going to be fun. Don't ya just love home movies? I mean, they're so . . . so *je ne sais quoi* funky. So stupid. So real, ya know?"

Okay, thought Matthew. He could deal with the headache and the possibility of a seizure. But if Elliot didn't stop acting like an idiot he was going to kill him. All this blather. This nonstop bullshit.

"Just give me the goddamn camera," demanded Matthew.

"Oh, a little testy, are we?"

"Elliot, calm down," chided Tina.

"Okay, okay. But can I help it if I'm the only one who feels tip-top today?" Elliot turned, squinched up his eyes, stared at Matthew. "Say, you really don't look so good, ya know. Really pale. How bad's that head, say, on a scale of one to ten? Is it a three or . . . or maybe it's all the way up to a nine?"

"Give me the camera!"

"But, Matt buddy, maybe we need to pay some attention to this. Of course, it could be the first sign of cryptococcal meningitis, as you fear. Or it could be a mere tension headache, a migraine." Elliot put a finger to his cheek, tried to recall that chapter. "Or it might just be a simple sinus infection. Icky. People with AIDS get lots of those. I, myself, have had three bad ones. All that green snot. Say, I know a lot about this stuff, don't I? Did I ever tell you my hero is Commander Data on *Star Trek?* Gosh, if only I could know as much as him."

A thunderlike rumble grew in some distant corner of the building, a rumble that in turn built and built in Matthew's head. He squinched his eyes shut, pressed a hand to the back of his head. He couldn't take it. He was going to go nuts, his head was going to split right in half. But then he opened his eyes because, of course, first he was going to jump on Elliot and wring his neck.

"Goddammit, Elliot, give me the fucking camera!"

"Just be cool, pal. I'm only trying to help. If we know what's happening to our bodies then we can deal with it. It won't be such a mystery, so strange and—"

From the side of the room where she sat on a chair, Tina

pulled back her disheveled hair with one hand and looked at him with sunken eyes. "For God's sake, Elliot, just shut up and do like he says!"

With a shrug and a big, dramatic roll of his eyes, Elliot said, "Jeez, you two are something else, just a couple of big babies."

A lightning bolt stabbed through Matthew's head, he again clenched shut his eyes, and the next thing he knew the camera was in his hands.

"And here's a tape too," said Elliot, slamming a cassette into Matthew's grip. "Have fun, Mr. DeMille, Mr. Great Director Man."

Matthew took a deep breath, told himself to push it away. The pain. Get rid of it. Ignore it. You're not going to have a seizure. You can't. There are more important things right now.

He took a deep breath, turned to Tina. "You ready?"

"Yeah," she replied, and then took another swig of Gatorade.

"That's right, Tina," said Elliot. "Drink up. I think you were dizzy because you're dehydrated. That happened, of course, because you had such bad—"

"Elliot!" snapped Matthew.

"Yeah, yeah, yeah . . ."

Staring at her, though, Matthew thought how she looked so drained, literally so. So white. Sure, she'd just lost a ton of liquid but, God, what was happening to them? And why now? Must be all the stress. The moving around. They just had to make it through the next few days, and then . . . then, well, who knew if they'd even still be alive. And who cared anyway?

"What about the syringe? You got it?" asked Matthew.

"Yep, yep, yep, she does. Loaded and ready," volunteered Elliot. "I saw her put it in the pocket of her sweater vest."

Patting the side of her sweater, the visibly weak Tina nodded and said nothing.

"Very great," said Matthew. "Come on, it's show time."

Matthew turned toward the door, felt his head swell. He took a couple of steps, clutched the metal doorknob, and steadied himself. And then he swung open the door and entered the small white room, followed by Tina and Elliot.

"Hello, Johnny," said Matthew.

Clariton was slumped on the floor, his butt on the blue nylon sleeping bag, knees up to his chest, head folded against his knees. He looked up, face red and sweaty, brow all wrinkled. His striped tie hung open and loose, and his gray suit looked as if he'd been sleeping in it for a week. Sure, it was written all over him. He was scared as hell. Which was exactly what Matthew had wanted.

"You people are disgusting," he barked.

Elliot shrugged. "Hey, he sounds like my father."

"You'll never get away with this."

"I beg your pardon, kind sir," countered Elliot, "but I think we already have. I mean, I hate to disappoint you and everything, but look at where you are, chained to some pipe in some basement. Far as I can tell, there ain't a bunch of Mounties lurking around here either."

"You might as well face it," said Matthew, "from your point of view things don't exactly look rosy."

Clariton stared him right in the eye. "You're sick."

"Now he sounds like my mother." Elliot grinned. "Hey, Matt, this is just like in that film, *Chinatown,* you know, when Faye Dunaway goes: 'My sister, my daughter, my sister, my daughter.' Only now I'm going: My father, my mother, my father, my mother, my father, my mother, my father, my—"

"Elliot," said Tina, clearly exasperated and taking him by the arm. "I think your meds are making you a little hyper. You just sit down here and be quiet. We'll take care of things."

"Oh, okay," said Elliot, leaning against the wall and sliding down into a corner. "Yeah, I guess I am a little cranked up. I've taken about thirty pills today, not to mention all that—"

"Elliot, shut the fuck up!" yelled Matthew.

His voice small, Elliot pulled his knees up to his chest and replied, "Yes, Mr. Boss Man."

How in the hell, wondered Matthew, had they ended up with a nut case like him? Matthew shook his head, then turned, surveyed the place. Okay, now what?

"Tina, you want to just sit down there next to our esteemed guest?"

"Sure."

"What are you doing? What's going on?" demanded Clariton. "Listen, if you let me go now, I'm sure—"

"It's home-movie time," interrupted Matthew, lifting up the camcorder. "It's time to tell the world what's up."

"No," said Clariton, pressing himself back into the corner. "No, I won't say anything."

"You don't really have to. We just want to show people that we have you and that you're alive—though, I might add, a tad disheveled."

"Fine, but just wait until they find me! Do you know what's going to happen to you then? Do you?"

"You know what, Mister Big Shot, we don't really care if a SWAT team bursts through the door right now, because just getting this far means we've already been wildly successful." With a sly grin Matthew added, "I think you had better realize, Johnny, you ain't callin' the shots here. I think you better realize you're in mighty deep shit."

"I . . . I . . ."

"This is how it's going to work. Today Tina is going to tell you her story, which is a real heartbreaker. Tomorrow Elliot will tell you his juicy tale—"

"Trust me, it's certifiably pathetic!" Elliot said with a giggle.

"And the day after tomorrow I'll tell you mine, a confession of sorts." Matthew lifted the camera to his eye, focused, and pressed the ON button. "Say cheese, asshole."

Still wearing her running shoes, Tina edged over to the congressman, braced herself against the wall with one hand, then, biting her bottom lip in pain, lowered herself to the floor next to him. She took a deep breath, then brushed aside some of her blond hair and smiled at the lens with the remnants of her best model face. Almost unseen, her right hand traveled down her side and into the pocket of her sweater vest, where she clutched the small device.

"Hi, Mr. Clariton. My name's Tina. The camera's rolling now, and I just wanted to ask if you have any idea why we kidnapped you today?"

"You people are disgusting!"

Forcing a coy look, she asked, "What people? Oh, and don't

forget to look into the camera so all the nice viewers will be able to see you.''

"You homosexuals! You deviants!''

In the background Elliot started cackling, and he shouted, ''Think again, dumbo! She's not a lesbo—she's a breeder, just like you!''

"That's right,'' said Tina, taking a deep breath of air. "I'm straight. I'm a mother. And I'm a person with AIDS.''

"Well, I don't care. You want to hurt me, don't you?'' Clariton looked right at the camera, turned back to Tina, then started jerking on the handcuffs, rattling them against the pipes. "You can't do this, you can't hold me hostage! This is a federal offense!''

Tina countered, ''And what you've been committing, sir, is an offense against humanity!''

He stopped, sat there quite still, staring at her. "What . . . what are you talking about?''

"Your position on AIDS, of course.''

Clariton turned to Matthew and the lens, said, "Listen, so . . . so I believe in the traditional family, a man, a woman, their children. So I—''

"You fool!'' snapped Tina. "Gay people have been around since the beginning of time. You might as well accept that fact.''

"All I'm saying—all I've ever said—is I don't endorse their lifestyle and that I won't work to defend their special interests.''

Tina shook her head and rolled her eyes in disbelief. "So what you're saying is it's okay for gay people to die, because you don't like them, which is repulsive, of course. But what about me, a straight woman with AIDS? There's an epidemic going on out there, and it's a whole hell of a lot bigger than I can handle.''

"Of course it is,'' said Clariton, slipping into politician mode as he tried to defend himself. "But it's not the duty of any government to support people who've engaged in proven high-risk behavior.''

"How dare you!''

"Listen, basically all I'm saying is that the government should get out of the way and let the private sector handle this mess. There's never been a disease as lucrative as AIDS and—''

"There's never been one as political either." Tina shook her head. "You know as well as I do that the American government would have been all over this—they'd do something like a Manhattan project when they developed the nuclear bomb, or a NASA project to get a man on the moon—if AIDS were killing straight white people in the United States. Or, let me say, straight white men."

Clariton started shaking his head. "This is ridiculous! I can't believe I'm having this conversation. Here I am chained to some pipe basically trying to defend what I was elected for."

"You were elected to be a leader, Mr. Clariton. And as a leader you're supposed to show people right from wrong. Or perhaps you only care about your political future."

In the distant background Matthew heard it again, that thunderous rumbling. He ignored it, kept the camera trained on them. Tina was doing great. Better than great.

"Tell him about Chris," nudged Matthew.

Tina reached into her pocket and nervously clutched the little surprise lying in there, then turned away and stared blankly at the floor. For a long time she said nothing, lost, undoubtedly, in layers of memories, so many of them sweet, so many of them painful.

Then she looked right at the camera and forced some kind of wretched smile. "Chris . . . was beautiful."

"Yes, she was."

Clariton started squirming. "You'll never get away with this, you fools, you'll never—"

"Shut up!" snapped Tina, surprising even herself with her harsh tone. She then laughed and said, "You know, I used to be so polite. Everyone liked me. So pretty. So kind. I was a model, you know. In New York. And I was very successful too. You'd never know it to look at me now, but—"

"She was on the cover of *Vogue* once!" called Elliot from the side. "God, and her hands used to be so pretty. Such gorgeous nails. Tina was even a hand model, you know. They used her hands on lots of TV commercials."

"That's right." Tina blushed, staring down at the nails that

were now ravaged by fungus. "But then . . . but then . . ."
She looked at Clariton. "Do you have any idea who Chris was?"

"Of course not. How could I? I've never seen you before."

"She was . . ."

"Go on," urged Matthew. "Tell him."

"Chris was my little girl. My little baby." Again Tina drifted
away for a long, sullen moment. "Six months ago, just after she
turned two, Chris died of complications from AIDS. She contracted the HIV virus from me in utero. And I . . . I contracted
it from my boyfriend, David, who was also Chris's father and
who'd contracted it from someone—a woman—in Thailand."
She took a deep breath. "David died about a year before Chris."

Matthew zoomed in on her. She was being more strong and
direct than he'd expected. He was shocked, in fact, at how up
front she'd become. Even as recently as six months ago she was
the stereotypical Minnesotan, facing the pains of the world with
a determined smile. Then again, Chris had still been alive, and
there had still been hope. Now everything was as black and white
as life and death.

"Some babies, they . . . well, they're able to . . ." A tear
streamed down Tina's left cheek, cutting through her thick
makeup and finally sinking into a sore. "Some babies are able to
fight it off, somehow get rid of the virus. But . . . but not my
little Chris. I did everything I could, I really did, but when she
died none of the new drugs had been tested or approved for
children. I had almost three hundred thousand dollars saved up,
and I spent every dime of that trying to cure Chris. I flew her all
over the world—London, Paris, India—visiting all the top doctors who were doing the most radical work. In the end nothing
could save my baby. She just wasted away, and she died in my
arms at . . . at . . ." The pain burned all over again, and tears
blistered from Tina's eyes. "Mr. Clariton, my little girl died in
my arms at home last fall."

His voice unusually somber and sober, Elliot said, "Watching
that little girl die broke my heart, it truly did."

Clariton looked at Tina, glanced at the camera and Matthew,
then back at Tina. "I'm sorry. . . ."

"Thank you," replied Tina.

"I'm sorry," continued Clariton, clearly perplexed, "but what does that have to do with me?"

"Oh, fuck," cursed Matthew, wishing the camera he was now aiming at the congressman were a bazooka. "What are you trying to do, dig your own grave?"

Weeping into her hands, Tina shook her head, then looked up and glared at Clariton, saying, "I thought maybe I'd like you even just a little bit in person. I really didn't think you'd be so arrogant. But what am I supposed to think of a man who wants to dismiss AIDS as something he can blame on gay people when I for one am a straight woman who got it from a straight man? What am I supposed to think of a supposed leader who wants to slash research when there are hardly any drugs out there for kids with AIDS, let alone a vaccine? Don't you realize I'm scared as hell about what's going to happen to me? Don't you understand that I'm terminally ill? If I somehow survive the next few days I'll probably die within the next few months. Where? I don't have any money left, I spent it all on my baby. I don't have any family. If people like you, Mr. Johnny Clariton, have their way, I'll probably die in the street!"

This was it, the time, and Matthew aimed the camera on Tina's pocket and said, "Do it, Tina."

"Yeah," echoed Elliot. "Do it!"

She wiped her eyes, further smearing her makeup, and grinned ever so slightly through her tears. "He's really making all this so easy, isn't he?"

"What the hell are you talking about?" demanded Clariton, suddenly nervous. "Listen, lady, I'm sorry about your kid. I'm sorry you lost her, but I didn't have anything to do with it. I mean, isn't that obvious?"

"Right," she said, blotting her eyes with the back of her left hand. "And the next thing you're going to tell me is that both David and I deserved to have our lives ruined because we weren't married, let alone married in a church."

"Listen, as terrible as this is, these things happen. That's reality. That's the horrible side of life."

"Ohhhh," said Elliot, slapping his cheeks with both hands. "So you're the guy that wrote that bumper sticker, 'Shit Happens.' Man, oh, man, I hope you had that copyrighted. You could be making a fortune in royalties.''

Tears dribbling down her face, Tina reached into the pocket of her sweater vest and pulled out the syringe. All eyes in the room focused on the long, thin device, the needle of which was sheathed with an orange plastic cap. Tina held it up and tapped it with a fingertip to get the bubbles out of the rich, dark liquid.

"What's . . . what's that?'' Clariton asked nervously.

"Chris was the sweetest little girl,'' said Tina, her voice small and trembling. "I . . . I always said I'd do anything for her.''

Matthew zeroed in on the syringe with the camera, then pulled back for a larger view.

Horrified, Clariton stared at the syringe and demanded, "What . . . what is that? What are you going to do?''

"It's full of blood,'' said Tina, popping the cap off the syringe. "Our blood.''

"Dear God . . .''

"Do you realize how innocently AIDS is contracted? Just one little stick of this needle and you'd probably contract it. All I have to do is break the surface of your skin and get a little of our blood on you, and then—''

"Stay away from me!''

"But that's why we brought you here, Congressman Clariton,'' she said, calmly recounting the horrible truth. "And that's what we're going to do: give you AIDS.''

"Sweet Jesus!'' gasped Clariton.

All of a sudden he flew into a frenzy of panic. More quickly than any of them could have imagined or anticipated, he lunged out with his foot, kicking Tina's arm. Caught totally unsuspecting, Tina screamed, and the syringe flew out of her hand, hurtled across the room, and broke into a bloody mess against the wall. Pathetically weak, Tina fell back like a raggedy doll, flopping onto the floor in a sobbing heap.

"Tina!'' shouted Matthew as he threw the video camera into Elliot's hands.

Clariton shrieked, "Stay away from me, you fucking bitch! Stay away from me—all of you!''

Overcome with fury, he lunged at her a second time. He got

only a few inches, however, before the handcuffs attached to his left hand jerked taut, yanking him back into place. He shouted more profanities, then swung his foot out again, this time kicking Tina in the thigh. She tried to push herself up, but couldn't, and her face fell to the floor.

"Don't hurt her!" shouted Matthew, who lunged for Tina, grabbed her under her arms, then started dragging her back.

Elliot, clutching the camera and standing a safe distance away, stared down at Clariton and yelled, "We're really going to do it, you know—we're going to give you AIDS!"

"Fuck you!" shouted back Clariton. "You're dead, all of you are dead!"

"Oh, yeah? Well, for your info so are you, Mr. Congressman Asshole!"

It took more strength than Matthew had, but somehow he did it, he dragged Tina out of there, pulling her through the doorway and back into the main room. Elliot hurried after him, turned around, flipped Clariton the bird, and then slammed the metal door as hard as his thin arms could manage.

Lying in a heap on the floor, Tina sobbed, "Chris . . . Chris . . ."

"That fucker!" cursed Matthew. "What an asshole! Are you all right, Tina? Did he hurt you?"

"I just want my baby back!"

"We're going to get him, don't worry."

"You bet we will," added Elliot, his face deep red. "You did real good. And it'll happen, just wait. You'll see. We're gonna do it for little Chris. I swear we will. That bastard's gonna get sicker than all of us."

"Are you all right?" Matthew bent over and touched her leg. "Where did he kick you?"

With a startled, even frightened face, she looked up quickly and her red face blanched. Clutching her stomach, Tina twisted toward the bathroom.

"Oh, my God, I gotta go! Help me! I gotta go *now!*"

"Elliot!" shouted Matthew.

The two of them snapped into quick action, grabbing Tina by each arm and jerking her to her feet, then scrambling across the linoleum. As she was rushed toward the bathroom Tina began yanking up her jeans skirt, and once she was through the door she leapt for the toilet. Matthew spun around, shoved Elliot back, and the two of them fell out of the bathroom, pulling the door shut behind them. A half second later there was a painful explosion of diarrhea and gas.

"Ow!" sobbed Tina from behind the closed door.

Elliot looked at Matthew, wrinkled up his nose, and then reached for a Coke. "Wasting syndrome is the ickiest, ain't it?"

Matthew shook his head. "Oh, Christ."

"I guess we should have expected Clariton to be stronger than all three of us put together."

Matthew took a deep breath, leaned against the wall, and clutched his throbbing head. The tension was growing so much that his ears were pounding and ribbons of light were flashing before his eyes. Of course he knew what was coming, that much was as obvious as a dark thunderstorm on a horizon.

"Listen, I got everything we need on tape," he said, and then paused to catch his breath. "My head's killing me—I've got to go pick up my pills, the ones I left at home."

"What?" gasped Elliot, freezing. "Are you nuts? You can't leave now!"

"Everything's on track, everything's still going according to plan."

"But—"

Matthew snapped, "I'll be right back!"

"Oh, my God, Matthew," said a panicky Elliot, "this is the worst time to—"

"Jesus Christ, you moron, I said I'll be right back!"

"What? But . . . but . . ." Elliot's voice was small and shaky as he added, "Well, I mean, I guess okay. Just don't be too long."

"I won't."

"I mean it, Matt. Tina and I—we need you."

"I know, I know." He stepped over to the bathroom door, put one flat palm against it, and called, "Tina?"

From the next chamber came something not much more than a whimper. "Wh-what?"

"I'm going to go out for a bit, but Elliot will be right here and he'll take care of you. I'm gonna pick up my meds and then deliver this tape to our favorite television reporter, just like we talked about. Are you going to be okay?"

"Sure . . ." Her voice breaking as if she were crying, Tina said, "I'm sorry, Matthew. I should've just done it, I should've—"

"Hey, you did great, babe." Something akin to a knife stabbed his head, and he clutched his brow, then said, "Don't worry, I got everything on tape. It's all happening. It's all going to work."

"But I didn't—"

"Shh, don't you worry. I'll be back soon."

Matthew turned away and started for the main door. He had no choice but to go. He really didn't. And besides, this shouldn't take too long. He'd be as quick as possible.

Off to the side, Elliot dropped to his knees and started pawing through a box, mumbling, "God, I really need a Twinkie."

Matthew looked over at him, and in a weak voice advised, "Keep an eye on her, Elliot."

"Sure, sure. But you just come back as fast as you can." Elliot turned, stared at Matthew, and shrugged. "You come back fast because . . . because I'm scared, Matthew. I really am."

20

Slumped into the soft folds of his black leather couch, Todd just sat there in his dark apartment, overwhelmed with shock and confusion. That Rawlins, the most stable, level-headed guy Todd had ever met, had been poised to take fatal flight from his balcony was impossible. And that Rawlins, who looked so incredibly healthy, was at the very least HIV positive was something Todd couldn't even comprehend. Oh, dear God. He wanted to jump up screaming. He wanted to break down crying. Instead, Todd leaned forward, his elbows on his knees, his face buried in his hands, the painful fear locked in him so tightly that no amount of force could break it free.

Something grazed Todd's foot and he flinched. Peering down, he saw a sleek black creature brushing his ankle. Girlfriend. At first Todd didn't know what to do, for Curt's cat had never been so brazen, so daring. As he watched she did it again, turning around, sauntering up to him, slowly twisting her head from side to side in that seductive kitty way that says you simply must love me. Next, pressing her left shoulder up against Todd's ankle, she slowly dragged the full length of her body across his foot. As if he were trying to catch a fly, Todd carefully moved his hand down inch by inch. Girlfriend's languid tail swished back and forth, and then Todd did it, he touched her for nearly the first time in the month since Rawlins had brought her over, sinking two fingertips into her silken fur. And scratching. As if she'd just woken from a long sleep and suddenly realized how love-starved she actually was, she buckled up her shoulders and pressed her spine deeper into Todd's touch. More brazen now himself, Todd rubbed her head, then ran his hand down the full length of her body and all the way up to the tip of her tail, a gesture of affection that Girlfriend ate up with rapture.

Roused from his shock, Todd sloughed off his inertia. He'd just let Rawlins prance right out of here? What a complete and utter fool.

He stroked Girlfriend one last time and then rose to his feet. Maybe it wasn't too late. Maybe he could catch Rawlins. Somehow they'd get through this. HIV and AIDS were way bigger than one person alone, but together Rawlins and he could make it—or at the very least put up the best of all possible fights. And they really were doing amazing things with drugs these days. No, the AIDS epidemic was far from over—so few people could afford the new drugs—but they were making real, substantial progress. Just because you were HIV positive didn't have to mean you were going to die, and the longer Rawlins could stay healthy the better the chances were for his long-term survival. Who knew, it could even be tomorrow or the day after that the scientists of the world discovered a single pill to rid the body of HIV.

Oh, God, thought Todd. What a chump he was. He should have tackled Rawlins with a hug, held him, and not let him go. Of course this wasn't going to be the end of their relationship; there was no way Todd would walk out on him, particularly not now.

With his coat still on he darted out of the apartment, down the hall. It took forever for the elevator to come, and when it did it took forever to descend. A woman with red hair got on at the eighth floor.

"I just saw you on the news, Mr. Mills!" said the woman as they rode downward. "What a day you've had! Weren't you scared? On TV you looked as cool as a cuke. Thank God you're all right."

"Thank you."

"Can you believe they did that, those kooks? I mean, kidnapping a politician like that? What's the world coming to?"

Consumed by the personal issues at hand, Todd barely nodded, and as soon as the doors parted he dashed out. He charged through the lobby, out the double doors, then turned an immediate right and jogged up the concrete drive. The guest parking was right there, and he scanned the dozen or so cars but failed to see Rawlins's vehicle.

Todd came to a halt, jabbed his left hand into his hair, and pulled desperately at the roots. What if Rawlins really tried to kill himself? What if he went home and took a bunch of pills, or went downtown and hurled himself into the Mississippi? How could Todd have been so stupid to let him leave like that, to let him go off in such a desperate state?

He had to find him, it was that simple. Todd hurried back in, passing through the lobby, up the single flight of stairs, and into the residential parking garage. It was a cold gray space, and he again burst into a jog. First he'd go straight to Rawlins's place. It wasn't that far, just the other side of Uptown. Right. With any luck he'd find Rawlins there and talk some sense into him—

Todd came to his parking space and froze. Where his green Jeep Grand Cherokee was supposed to be there was nothing, just a blank stretch of concrete. Oh, crap. His first thought was that someone had stolen his vehicle, but no, of course not. He'd taken a taxi from downtown because, of course, his car was still out at Channel 10, just where he'd left it this morning.

Things were going from bad to worse, and he turned around. Okay, now what? If Janice were in town he'd call her and make her come right over, but she was gone until the end of the week. And he couldn't beg or borrow a car from a neighbor, because he barely knew anyone in this entire building; for privacy's sake he'd gone out of his way to remain as anonymous as possible.

So?

He'd have to get another taxi, and God only knew how long that'd take. This wasn't New York. You couldn't step off a curb and just hail a cab. He'd have to go to the front desk, have the security guard call one of the taxi companies, and then wait ten or fifteen minutes for a vehicle to come. Oh, shit, he thought. Why had he let Rawlins go?

Hoping that he'd somehow be able to catch him, Todd broke into a run. He jogged out of the garage and down the flight of stairs and burst through a door into the lobby. As he rushed up to the security desk he saw a limousine, a handsome black Cadillac, parked just outside the front door. The chauffeur was just setting down the last of three suitcases and a golf bag, and a very tanned man was peeling off some money while his wife scurried out of the cold and inside.

"Is there something I can do for you, Mr. Mills?" asked the security guard, poking his head out.

"Maybe not."

The guard then turned to the bronzed woman, calling, "Welcome home, Mrs. Fitzgerald. How was Hawaii? Did you have a good flight back?"

"Everything was perfect, but, ish, I can't believe there's still ice on that lake out there!"

Todd scooted right by her, out the door, past the woman's husband, then around the front of the limo. Waving, he caught the attention of the chauffeur, who was just opening the driver's door.

"Hey," began Todd, "I have an emergency and I don't have time to wait for a cab. I need a lift, just a couple of miles. Will fifty bucks do?"

The driver, a young man with blond hair and wearing a black uniform, looked at him and without a pause replied, "Fifty bucks will do quite nicely, sir."

"Great."

Todd opened the rear door before the chauffeur had a chance and threw himself into the deep, cushy seat. As the driver started up the car and began to pull away, Todd gave him Rawlins's address. What choice was there? Where else could he look? Rawlins had said something about looking for someone else, some other guy, but who in the hell could that be?

Wait a minute, thought Todd as the limousine turned right onto the parkway. Maybe Rawlins hadn't parked in the guest parking area after all. Perhaps he'd just pulled over on the parkway as he sometimes did. Hoping that was the case, that Rawlins was parked somewhere on the street and was slumped in his car pondering his life, Todd turned around and looked out the rear of the Cadillac. Along the well-lit road was a string of cars, but none of them belonged to Rawlins, not even the one with the blazing headlights that pulled out after the limo.

21

So if he hadn't gotten it from Todd, then from whom?

Like a refrain from a nightmarish song, those words kept whizzing through Rawlins's head, and he drove through the dark as numb as he was exhausted. It didn't make sense, it was incomprehensible, this death sentence he'd just been handed. Why in God's name couldn't it have been just a chronic sinus problem? Assuming he'd never understand why HIV had struck him, then at least he hoped he'd be able to see how it had happened.

If not Todd, then . . .

His mind started flipping through his lovers. He saw faces of men with dark hair, broad shoulders, quick smiles. Okay, so he had a type, more dark than not, more easy than intense, more traditionally masculine than gender-bender. No matter how sexy or gorgeous, however, none of them had touched his heart, not really—not, at least, until Todd, which was what made him different. Just the sight of Todd's smile always seemed to defuse Rawlins, and that in turn relaxed him amazingly, which always had the wonderful end effect of arousing him.

But now . . .

Whether or not he was HIV positive or had progressed into AIDS seemed irrelevant. The first meant more time—but was that time to loll about in despair and hopelessness?—and the second meant the fire was already blazing and the question was whether it could be controlled.

For a brief moment he wondered if this was really possible, then he stopped himself. Of course it was, not simply because AIDS was what he'd always feared—as if it were the great punishment for being a homo, some corner of himself was always sure he'd get it—but, quite simply, because it made perfect sense. The chronic sinus infection, for one. The nagging sense of exhaustion he'd felt over the past months, for two. So how long? How long had HIV been floating around in his body, nibbling away at his defenses? And how long did he have to live?

And who the hell had given it to him?

He believed Todd. Rawlins had seen the shock, the horror, when he'd told Todd what he'd learned at the doctor's today. He'd stared into Todd's eyes, knew that Todd was telling the truth, that Todd had had a test, just as he'd told him before, and the result was negative. So Rawlins hadn't contracted the virus from Todd, and he prayed he hadn't passed it to Todd, for he couldn't bear that type of responsibility. So that really left only a few other possibilities who could have infected Rawlins, didn't it? And of those possibilities, didn't it really mean only one guy? Sure, and he knew exactly who, the handsomest of them all. With the others Rawlins had been no dummy, but with this one he'd made one critical mistake. Simply, he'd had way too much to drink. End of story.

Oh, shit, Rawlins thought, his eyes filling with tears. He was going to die because of three or four too many bourbon and sodas and a one-night stand.

Images of Curt came at Rawlins, smashing into his mind. Curt, doubled over in tears, sobbing not only because he'd found out that he had AIDS, but that the man he loved more than anyone else—his Mr. Wonderful—had just walked out the door. Curt, laughing at the array of medications—over fifty pills a day—he was supposed to take. Curt, refusing mashed potatoes because the thrush in his mouth was so thick that even the blandest things tasted foul. Curt, blathering a string of nonsensical crap about changing the world. Rawlins saw all that in his mind's eye, and his own future scared the shit out of him. Why not a car crash? A house fire? Why AIDS?

Rawlins drove around Lake Calhoun once, twice. As if circling his past he went around and around the soggy but still frozen body of water. God, how many times had he biked, jogged, walked around this lake? How many times had he swum in it, canoed on it? He recalled that one magical Fourth of July when he and a couple of pals had swum out into the dark waters as fireworks exploded in the night sky and accompanying music was broadcast over the lapping lake. Was there anything better?

And then he was turning on a side street. It could be the absolute worst thing, perhaps entirely stupid, yet Rawlins knew he had to see him. Perhaps get mad. Perhaps cry together. Perhaps find solace. But if it had, indeed, been Matthew who had infected Rawlins with HIV some two years ago, then there was no holding Rawlins back, not now, not tonight. Among other things it would clarify Rawlins's true health status—he'd know for sure that he was HIV positive only, for didn't it usually take eight to ten years to progress into AIDS? Hadn't he once read that?

As far as Rawlins knew, Matthew still lived just a couple of blocks east, right in Uptown. The small house—that was it— nestled midblock. Sure. Rawlins recalled two years ago going down to the Gay Times, that mega gay bar where boys danced for hours to throbbing beats, queens dragged in their finest boas, and lusty connections were made. That steamy summer night Rawlins had drunk way more than he usually did and then ran into Matthew, and right then, that evening, the chemistry had been fiery and fun. As some disco diva wailed away, they had groped their way through one dance, then stumbled out into the parking lot. But then Rawlins was faced with an incredibly complex question: Should he really do this, go home with Matthew? In the end the booze and the lust got the better of Rawlins's judgment, and he hopped in Matthew's car and they drove south toward Uptown and Matthew's house, where they'd parked alongside the garage.

As they had approached the rear of the house, Matthew tackled Rawlins, felling him in the grass and saying, "You are so incredibly sexy."

Rawlins—knowing in his heart of hearts that he shouldn't be there and he shouldn't be doing this because, after all, who in the world had a worse reputation than Matthew?—had stared into that face and replied, "And you are so incredibly handsome. But you know, I shouldn't be here. This is really stupid of me."

"Oh, shut up." Matthew had laughed, rolled across the ground and right up to the back steps, where he reached under one of the stairs and snatched a shiny brass key. "Bingo! This is the key to fun!"

Too many drinks, Rawlins thought now, staring up at the gray house. Otherwise it wouldn't have happened, Rawlins wouldn't have gone home with Matthew. There would have been no pushing at the boundary of safe sex. And he'd be okay today. How fickle life was. Once he'd avoided being broadsided in his car by a mere second or two simply because he'd slowed to change the radio station; otherwise he certainly would have been killed. Years ago, before he'd been promoted to detective, he'd been involved in a backyard chase where the suspect had turned and fired directly on Rawlins; had the bullet not struck his badge and deflected into his shoulder, Rawlins would certainly have taken one in the heart. But not now. No avoiding this. A microscopic virus had burst from Matthew's body into Rawlins's being.

The lights were off, but Rawlins didn't care. He'd heard Matthew was sick. He'd heard he wasn't all that far behind Curt. So maybe Matthew was at his parents' or maybe he was in the hospital. Or maybe he was just asleep, lolling about in night sweats. It didn't matter. Rawlins got out of his car, followed the front walk up to the house, then continued around the left side. The backyard was a plain of brown frozen grass, the trees spindly and leafless, but it was funny how much he remembered. Back then—just two simple years ago—the grass and oaks had been lush with summer. They'd parked back there by the side of the garage. Rolled right here. And, recalled Rawlins, moving toward the rear steps, Matthew had reached under here for a key.

Now groping under the treads, Rawlins found it immediately. There was a nail, and on that nail hung a key. He took it in his palm, and even in the faint light from the alley could tell the key was no longer bright and shiny. He shrugged. So much time. Then he climbed the back steps, inserted the key, unlocked the past, and entered Matthew's home.

He stood in the kitchen and recalled the light in the hood above the stove. Walking through his memories, Rawlins now crossed the kitchen, fumbled for the switch, and flicked on the light over the gas burners. And, yes. Matthew had gone straight for the sink, turned on the faucet full blast, and grabbed a glass.

"Want some of the Mississippi's finest?" he'd asked.

Rawlins had declined, just stood there watching as gorgeous Matthew chugged the water, a dribble of it curling down his chin, his throat, and disappearing into the hair poking from his T-shirt. And then they'd gone through that door.

Rawlins now stepped over to the opening, proceeded through the dark and to a lamp at the edge of the living room, which he turned on, just as Matthew had done that night that had more than likely begun the end of Rawlins's life. And then Rawlins was proceeding up the staircase, the stairs creaking just as they had back when Rawlins, one hand groping Matthew's ass, had eagerly followed him upward. That's right, he recalled. Up and into the bedroom. They hadn't even hesitated. To bed . . . to bed . . .

It was dark upstairs too, and he stopped at the top, peered into the darkness. Just then he heard something—floorboards moaning under the weight of another's step?—and for the first time wondered if someone else was in fact home. If Matthew wasn't here, could there be a lover? A roommate?

"Hello?" called out Rawlins. "Is someone here?"

No reply. Rawlins doubted Matthew was already dead—somehow he would have heard—but perhaps he was in fact lying in a hospital or hospice. Lying and waiting, just like Curt. Rawlins looked to his left, stumbled back into his memories. Yes, they'd gone in there, the front bedroom. He was surprised at how clear it still was, that one night of big lust. As if it were an obsessive fantasy that he'd been playing and replaying—which he hadn't— Rawlins saw it all. Now standing in the doorway to the bedroom, he peered in, studying it as if it were the scene of a crime. The chamber was flooded with pale light from a streetlight, as it was then. But something . . . something was wrong, thought Rawlins, studying the black metal bed, the dresser. Of course. Back then they'd stumbled in here, ripped off their clothes, and collapsed naked on a futon on the floor, which had lain there, right there by the window. Now there was a bed to the right and—

He heard it distinctly now: a footstep. Someone else was here, and Rawlins slowly and calmly turned around. An ancient light switch snapped and the hall light burst on, outlining the tall but excruciatingly thin figure of a man, his head shaved, cheeks caved painfully in. Yes, he had *the look*—even his eyebrows were gray—and there was no way Rawlins would have recognized him had he not been standing in this man's house. Of course this was Rawlins's personal ground zero. Of course he'd gotten it from him.

But why the gun?

"Hello, Matthew," said Rawlins, his voice surprisingly calm as he studied the man outlined by the harsh light. "It's me, Steve Rawlins."

"Gee, long time no see."

He nodded toward the pistol now trained on him. "Don't worry, I'm not a burglar. I just needed to stop by and say . . . say hello."

"I was wondering when the fucking cops would get here."

"Really?" he replied, his police instincts all but nonexistent tonight.

"It just never occurred to me that that might mean you." Matthew asked, "Anyone else with you?"

"No."

"You positive?"

Not at all understanding what was going on, Rawlins replied, "Absolutely."

"How did you find me?"

"We had a memorable night together, I guess."

Maybe Rawlins wasn't angry because he'd used it all up on Todd, blasting him with his cannons of fury. Maybe he wasn't angry because he was shocked at how awful Matthew, the handsomest man he'd ever slept with, now looked. Then again, he realized, this was it, the end of his search. He'd found square one, the spring, the source, the well of his infection. There was nothing else, no more pieces to gather to make the picture complete.

Rawlins turned, stumbled across the bedroom, and dropped himself on the edge of the bed. Right, he'd found what he was looking for. And he immediately understood that it didn't make any more sense than it had before. He bowed his head into one hand, thought perhaps this tough cop was going to cry yet again, but then realized he was way beyond that. Far too exhausted. He glanced back at the doorway, saw Matthew's pathetic frame. And the gun.

"Why the hell are you pointing that thing at me?" asked Rawlins.

"What?" said Matthew, his anger and disbelief quite evident. "Listen, asshole, don't play any games with me. I know why you're here." Matthew hurried to the front window, stood by the sill, and carefully scanned the street. "There are probably a dozen cops out there, right?"

"I . . . I don't know what you're talking about."

"Yeah, right."

Rawlins looked up, not in the least bit angry, merely totally confused. "Don't you know why I'm here? I—" Rawlins stared at him, saw the perplexity in his face. "Remember that night we got so drunk?"

Matthew was quite still, quite focused on Rawlins. Clearly confused, he then ran his hand over his stubbly head, trying to understand what Rawlins was talking about. And then it struck him, and the smallest of smiles eased onto his face.

"Oh, man. Oh, shit," Matthew finally said, lowering the gun. "You've got it, don't you?"

Rawlins nodded.

"When did you find out?"

"Just today." His eyes began to bloom with moisture, and though he wasn't so sure why it was important, added, "After lunch."

Rawlins then watched as Matthew leaned against the windowsill, staring out at the night and the street and the streetlight. He watched as Matthew's shoulders started shaking. As he clasped a hand over his mouth. As he completely lost it and gasped for air.

But, wait, realized Rawlins. This guy, this fellow queer, wasn't crying for Rawlins and his fate.

"Jesus Christ, you're laughing, aren't you? Laughing at me?" said Rawlins, as shocked as he was incredulous. "What . . . what kind of sicko are you?"

With a huge grin spread across that skeletal face, Matthew turned to him. "So you don't know, do you?"

"Know what?"

Rawlins felt a surge of repugnance rise in his throat. How could he have ever been attracted to someone like this, someone who could find humor in another's demise? This guy was disgusting, he was—

Rawlins caught himself. If this guy was nearly as sick as Curt had been, could he also be as nuts as Curt was in his final days? Could that explain this grotesque scene?

Rawlins asked, "What the hell are you talking about?"

"Let me guess. You haven't listened to the news all day. And you haven't been down to the police station either. Right? Am I right?"

"So?"

"Wonderful, I love it!" hooted Matthew. "Here I stopped home for some pills, and I thought you'd caught me!"

"What the—"

"That's exactly what the entire first month was like for me. I just wandered around in a fog after I found out. I didn't hear a thing about anybody else, and I didn't give a flying fuck either. I'm sure that as far as you're concerned the only thing that happened in the entire frigging universe is that you've seen your future and you've solved the biggest mystery of your own life. What I mean, of course, is that you've found out exactly what millions of others would pay dearly to learn—simply, you found out how you're going to die, didn't you?"

Rawlins sat back down on the bed and suddenly felt himself shuddering. "You're crazy."

"No, not at all. I just have a bigger vision." Matthew added, "You're a bit late, but welcome to the party."

It was then that Rawlins heard a voice, weak and shaky, calling out from some grave. He heard an angry voice, one determined to get even. Dear God, was that what this was all about?

"You did something today, didn't you?" asked Rawlins.

"Boy, oh, boy, I'll say so."

"I came here tonight because in all probability I picked up HIV from you. Right in this very room, right over there, actually, where you used to have a futon." He closed his eyes, for he was just beginning to understand. "But no wonder you thought I was here with a bunch of cops, no wonder you thought someone was after you.''

Matthew's eyes opened wide in amusement. "Oh, do tell, do tell. So you know something after all.''

"I guess so.'' Rawlins nodded. "You kidnapped someone, didn't you? In some restaurant downtown, right?''

Matthew gasped. "Very good, Einstein. Now, how did you find that out? Did you hear a bit of something on the radio?''

"No.''

"Overhear someone gabbing at the doctor's office?''

"No.''

"Oh, of course not. How stupid of me. Your wonderful boyfriend, Mr. Television himself, confessed all. Actually, I wondered if your Mr. Wonderful recognized me. You know, I met him once, but of course that was before I looked like this.''

"No, Todd didn't say anything.'' Rawlins looked right at him. "Actually, it was Curt.''

Immediately Rawlins understood that if there was anything that could have shocked Matthew, it was that. The other man's glee crashed in a million pieces. And again he raised the pistol.

"Oh, fuck,'' moaned Matthew. "Don't tell me you've got direct dial to heaven. And don't tell me Curt relayed all this via your Ouija board either.''

"I won't.'' Rawlins thought back to all of Curt's ramblings. "But I will tell you I spent a fair amount of time taking care of Curt just before he died.''

"Oh, goddammit!''

"So apparently he wasn't as nuts as I thought he was.''

"I knew he was going to let it slip! I knew it! Why couldn't that queen have died about a month earlier?'' Matthew shook his head. "Elliot has such a big fucking mouth—he's the one who told Curt in the first place. 'We got this cool thing cooked up, Curt,' says Elliot. 'Man, it's so unbelievably hot, you gotta join us. We're all going to be so famous, dude.' But of course snooty Curt wouldn't have anything to do with it. Shit, it's just like I told Elliot—Curt was going to spill it all unless we didn't do something.''

"Well, he did—blab, that is.''

Rawlins thought back to Curt's rantings, which Rawlins had dismissed at the time. Back then they hadn't made any sense, dribs and drabs of threats and conspiracies sprinkled as he drifted in and out of dementia. Back then they seemed more like the delirious plottings of a hideously ill man about to tumble from the precipice of life.

"So you really did it?" said Rawlins, stitching together Curt's mumblings. "You kidnapped someone?"

"You got it."

"Someone important?"

"Quite. A politician." Matthew grinned. "Mr. Johnny Clariton himself."

After the events of the day, Rawlins was too numb to react. "No shit? And now you're holding him hostage?"

"Something like that." With a sigh Matthew said, "You probably know where we have him too, don't you?"

Rawlins thought for a moment. "Probably."

"Then I regret to inform you, Mr. Rawlins," began Matthew, taking aim, "that I'm either going to have to kill you or I'm going to have to take you with me as, shall we say, Mr. Hostage Number Two."

"Well, you more or less have already taken care of the first option." His years of professional training defeated by today's medical report, Rawlins passively pushed himself to his feet. "So is it safe to assume you're going to insist on driving again?"

22

Oh, he didn't like this. Oh, this scared him. Thinking back on everything he'd read, Elliot knew this wasn't good. Tina had been in the bathroom since Matthew had left, and he knew there was nothing left to come out of her except her insides. And that was exactly what seemed to be happening. If they weren't precisely where they were in these subterranean chambers and if the police, the FBI, and who knew who else weren't looking for them—which they surely were—Elliot would drag Tina to the closest hospital and make them fill her up intravenously with fluids.

"Oh, Elliot, I can't stop it!" she moaned from behind the closed door. "The cramps are so bad."

"I know, dear, I know."

There was another gush from inside her, and she cried, "There's so much blood!"

"Just be cool." Elliot leaned against the door frame and mumbled, "I can't say for sure because of course I'm not a doctor, as we both know, but I think this goes beyond cytomegalovirus colitis. I mean, CMV isn't usually quite so . . . so aggressive. It could be another organism, say giardia, which is definitely not fun. But no, that wouldn't explain the blood, now, would it? Nor would simple food poisoning, say, if you ate some meat that wasn't cooked all the way through or ate some bad mayonnaise. I mean, actually it sounds to *moi* like you've got a lesion or something going on, you know, like one of your intestines has cracked a leak. Tina, hon, you sure you never had any KS?"

"No. No . . . oh, my God, ow!" Crying, she paused, gasped for air. "No, I don't think so."

"Well, I suppose you'd know if you did."

Okay, so what else could it be? He thought through all the typical stuff—lactose intolerance, spicy foods, fatty foods—all that crap, but none of them would explain the blood. Scratching his nose, he glanced over at the huge boxful of drugs they'd dragged down here. Unfortunately, this went way beyond anything he could deal with. Maybe when Matthew returned they should just take her out of here and ditch her somewhere, then call 911 and tell them to fetch her. Or maybe she couldn't wait that long. In fact, listening to her writhe, he doubted she could. What she probably needed and needed now was not only an IV of fluids but a good, strong transfusion.

"Hon," he called through the door, "I can hear you crying in there, but can you tell me, are any tears rollin' down those pretty cheeks of yours?"

"What?" She sniffled. "Actually, no."

He slapped his cheek, rolled his eyes. Oh, this was definitely not cool. No tears meant her body couldn't spare a drop of moisture, which clearly signified that Tina was already acutely dehydrated. Notwithstanding that her kidneys could be seriously and permanently damaged—big deal at this point—she was probably just minutes away from slipping into shock. Shit, when the hell was Matthew going to get back?

Okay, okay, just think, you moron.

Elliot scurried over to the boxes of food. There was nothing he could do about the loss of blood—who knew, maybe it wasn't so awfully bad, maybe it was just scaring Tina—but he'd had, unfortunately, personal experience with massive diarrhea, and he knew just what to mix up. Finding a bottle of corn syrup, he poured about a half cup of the gooey liquid into a big plastic cup.

From the bathroom she said, "I think it stopped. The cramps are gone."

"Oh, that's fab!" exclaimed Elliot as he grabbed a bottle of apple juice from the cooler. "I'll be right there; I'm making you a cocktail. But just stay put, okay? I don't want you gettin' up or movin' real fast."

"Sure . . . I'm just going to wash my hands."

He dumped the juice in the cup, added some water, and

swirled it all together. Oh, and a big dash of salt, of course. Taking a quick sip, Elliot shrugged. Not his best, but not so bad either, and guaranteed to do wonders for the body's chemical harmony.

"Jeez, this is just like being back at the restaurant. You know, I was a pretty damn good waiter. People really liked me. I made tons in tips—unfortunately much more than I ever did on my paintings, but that's a sob story for another time. Tina, how about a graham cracker?"

From behind the closed door he heard a *thunk*, the sound of something solid hitting something hard. He glanced over, heard nothing else.

"Tina? Hon? You okay?"

Everything terrible flashed through his mind, and for a moment he couldn't move. Then, with the drink in hand, he hurried over to the door and tapped. Nothing. No moaning, no crying. A zip of fear shot through Elliot. Standing there holding the plastic cup, he knocked again.

"Tina?" he called, his hand shaking as he put the cup on the floor. "Tina, it's me, Elliot! Open up! You gotta open up, hon!"

Elliot's stomach heaved and his body flushed with panic. Something was wrong, horribly so. Dear God, he thought. I'm not a doctor. I'm not a nurse. And my dear friend is mortally sick.

"Tina?"

No, he couldn't fail her, not now. Tina needed him, and she needed him now. He kicked back in, barely missing a beat, and pushed the door inward, but it opened only a few inches before it hit something. Terrified, Elliot peered in and saw Tina's twiglike body sprawled on the floor, a small pool of blood spilling from her head.

"Tina!" screamed Elliot as he pushed his way in. "Tina!"

23

When the limo pulled up in front of Rawlins's place, Todd proceeded as if he didn't have a clue that anyone was following him. He thanked the chauffeur, climbed out of the Cadillac, and stood in the middle of the street, looking up at the clapboard house and making sure that whoever was in the car that had pulled over at the end of the block saw him.

It had once been a typical home for this area—a Minneapolis "foursquare" with a kitchen, living room, dining room, and staircase each occupying a separate corner of the downstairs—but during the Depression it had been carved into two apartments, one up, one down. For years Rawlins had rented the upstairs place, where a lamp now burned in one window. But Todd knew that the light didn't mean that Rawlins was home or had stopped by. Leave it to a cop to keep a few of his halogens on timers.

Consumed with worry, he quickly crossed the concrete walk, across the boards of the front porch, and to the door. He rang once, barely waited, then took out Rawlins's keys, which he'd gotten in an exchange as symbolic for both of them as the giving of rings. Opening the lock, Todd charged upstairs, taking the steps two at a time and bounding into the living room.

"Rawlins?" called Todd, his voice booming. "Rawlins, are you here? Rawlins?"

There wasn't so much as an echo, and Todd quickly moved through the small dining room, the plain kitchen with the small table, the bedroom, and finally into the bath at the very end. No one, and nothing, not even a single item, out of order. He'd been hoping to find Rawlins here, of course, but had feared something worse, namely that Rawlins might have somehow hurt himself. Instead, everything was perfectly fine, and there was no sign that Rawlins had even been home. Todd hesitated in the kitchen, leaned against one of the white metal cabinets, and placed a hand to his forehead. Okay, there was one thing he needed to find, but where would Rawlins have put it?

His desk.

Todd returned to the bedroom, his eyes falling first, of course, on the mattress where he'd spent a handful of nights in lustful tangle. Crossing to the other side, he went to the small wooden desk and pulled on the long arm of an architect's lamp. He flicked on the bulb and opened the top middle drawer, but found nothing except pens, paper clips, tape, a beat-up old calculator, and a variety of other home-office junk. Pulling open the right drawer, he found boxes of new checks, some bills, and letters. He moved to the drawer beneath that and found what he was looking for: a trove of photographs. Twenty, maybe thirty envelopes of glossy prints that never had and never would make it into an album, for while Rawlins loved to snap pictures he was not an organized soul. Todd opened the first envelope, found pictures of the two of them cross-country skiing. Trying to ignore any sentimental thoughts, Todd moved right on, flying through envelopes of Christmas, a Halloween ball, a family reunion. On and on. Until he found it: the stack of pictures Rawlins had pulled out just a few days after Curt had died. Todd shuffled through the first ten until he came to one of Curt and another man seated on a log. Recalling that Rawlins had mentioned he'd taken it while camping up in the Boundary Waters four or five years ago, Todd tried to remember what Rawlins had said about this guy pictured with Curt. Unable to, he jammed the small print in his pocket, stuffed the others back in the drawer, and snapped off the light.

Staying close to one wall, he returned to the living room, a boxy, rather unattractive space—it was common knowledge that Rawlins didn't have the queer decorator gene—with a pathetic couch, a TV, a couple of chairs, and two windows up front. A single lamp burned on the other side of the room, and Todd slowly made his way up to one of the windows. But it was no use, he realized. The miniblinds were pulled completely up, and Todd couldn't check the street without revealing himself.

He turned around, heading down the hall, through the kitchen, and to the back door. A large exterior staircase had been tacked on to the rear of the house, and Todd now made his way down to the yard, around the edge of the house, and into the dark that sliced between Rawlins's and the neighboring home. Proceeding to the front, he peered out at the street, his breath smoking in the cool night air. Parked cars, most of them older models and most of them pocked with rust scales, lined the street.

There was no doubt in Todd's mind that he'd been followed over here, though he hadn't been able to discern just who or in fact how many people had been in the other vehicle that had tailed the limousine. So what could this be about? It could be the police, he supposed, but why would they monitor Todd's coming and goings unless they thought he was somehow involved in Clariton's abduction?

Somewhere a car door opened and closed, the sound muffled in the cool night, followed by steps on the gritty sidewalk. Todd edged closer to the corner of the house, but didn't see a soul walking along. Scanning the street again, his eyes proceeded up the block, car by car, Ford to Honda to Olds to Toyota. And there it was, the front of the vehicle that had tailed the limo from Todd's condo all the way over here. Bending over carefully lest they spy him spying them spying him, Todd caught a glimpse through the windshield of the driver. Definitely a man. Whether or not he was alone, however, Todd couldn't tell.

Suddenly he heard it again, the footsteps. Or were they different ones? These were quick and fleeting, their noise ricocheting up the street, between the houses. Was someone running up to Rawlins's house? Todd turned his head from side to side, but couldn't see a thing. Wait. The fear plunging through him, he realized that the footsteps were simply bouncing off the neighboring house. Oh, shit. Someone was charging him from behind.

Todd spun around just as a huge figure descended, grabbing and hurling him against the house, flattening him against the clapboard. Todd noted that his attacker had a gun, and he lifted his arms, tried to protect himself, but the other guy was too strong. Too professional. When Todd saw one of the large arms come swinging up to his face, he thought, Oh, crap, this is really going to hurt. But instead of a solid fist smashing his jaw, a massive hand was thrown over his mouth.

"Keep quiet!" demanded the figure. "Don't move!"

Recognizing his assailant, Todd stared at the man. Him?

"Someone followed you here," whispered Lyle, Johnny Clariton's bodyguard.

Shocked by the other man's presence, Todd barely moved his head up and down.

"Who are they?"

The hand was lifted from Todd's mouth, and Todd spouted with a question of his own. "How . . . how the hell do you know I was followed?"

"Because I tailed you too," said Lyle, his deep voice hushed. "There are two guys out there."

"Two?"

"Yeah, two of them in that car down the street. Who are they?"

"I don't have any idea."

"Yeah, right." Lyle flattened Todd even farther against the wall, raised his pistol, and placed the barrel deep into Todd's temple. "Once again, pal, who are those guys out there?"

"And once again, asshole, I don't know," shot back Todd.

"Were you involved with kidnapping Clariton?"

"Absolutely not."

Todd felt Lyle's angry eyes burning into him. And then all of a sudden the handgun was pulled away and Todd was released.

Straightening his shirt, Todd moved a foot or two away and quipped, "I guess I can now comfortably say that no friend of Johnny Clariton is a friend of mine."

Lyle stepped up to the edge of the house and peered down the street. "So what the hell's going on around here?"

"That's a very good question." Right then there was only one thing Todd was certain of—that he didn't want to hang out with

Lyle—and as he started for the street he said, "And I guess there's only one way to find out."

"Hey, you idiot!" snapped Lyle, grabbing Todd by the arm. "What are you trying to do, get yourself killed?"

"You're the cowboy swinging a gun around."

Todd jerked himself free, wasting no time in heading for the street and away from Lyle, who stayed planted in the shadows of the house. Todd cut across the grass, across the sidewalk, and stepped into the street, walking right up the middle of the pavement. The mysterious car was parked about a quarter of a block away and pointed toward Todd. So Lyle was right, mused Todd as he neared the sedan. There were in fact two guys, a balding guy behind the wheel and someone else next to him whom Todd dearly hoped he recognized.

Once a viewer had alerted Todd about a stalker in her neighborhood, and Todd had gone over and staked it out, watching the guy for three days, then finally climbing out of the van and just walking over to the guy, the photographer's camera rolling behind him. The man was so stunned that Todd was approaching him so directly that he did nothing, just sat there until Todd more or less cornered him. And that's what he hoped, he thought as he now raised his right hand in greeting, would happen with this situation.

But the direct approach didn't look as if it was going to work on this one.

The vehicle's engine came to a sudden and loud roar. Todd didn't like the sound of that, but he proceeded on, his hand still held up in friendly greeting and a stupid smile plastered on his face. He flinched slightly when he saw the wheels turning and the nose of the car pulling out, but he pressed on.

However, when the car shot out of its parking place and started racing down the street toward him, Todd slowed and quietly muttered to himself, "Hi, guys. What's going on?"

He stopped dead. Wanting the guy in the passenger seat to be one person in particular, Todd kept his eyes aimed on him. But in fact the car wasn't going to stop, that much was clear, because it was zeroing right in on Todd, gaining speed with each foot. Yet Todd didn't move. He didn't flinch until the last possible moment. And only when he was positive that the man in the passenger seat wasn't Steve Rawlins did Todd jump out of the way, throwing himself between two parked cars as the silver Chrysler roared past him and into the night.

24

They took Matthew's vehicle and Rawlins drove, and the first thing they did was drop off a large manila envelope containing the videotape. The second was to head all the way out here and park just outside this huge box of a building. As they climbed out of the van, a 747 roared overhead as it descended, so low that all other sounds were drowned out.

Having entered a rear door of the large structure, they now walked along, Rawlins all but oblivious to the gun stuck in his side. He did exactly as he was told, for he was a willing hostage—or better yet a listless one—and he turned one corner, another, then proceeded down a narrow hall, just as Matthew ordered.

When they reached a door with a keypad mounted to the side, Matthew punched in the combination, swung open the door, and said, "Welcome to the bowels of capitalism."

"So where are we going?" inquired Rawlins.

"Down, down, down. Someplace no one would ever think of looking, yet at the same time someplace so incredibly obvious. You'll see. It's the one place I hate most in these United States of America." Matthew grinned. "I worked out here for a while."

"Really?"

"Yeah, my modeling days were over, but it was before I got really sick. I needed a job, and, actually, it was the only place that would hire me. Granted, it was only a McJob—you know, a minimum-wage deal—but I needed something." He needled Rawlins with the gun, shoving him down the first set of stairs. "Keep going."

"Why?"

"Because I told you to, asshole. And I have a gun."

"No, I mean, why did you do something as extreme as kidnap someone? Why not—"

"Why not give out red ribbons?" Matthew laughed. "Or T-shirts or posters or coffee mugs with AIDS slogans so that people are reminded each and every day that something big and nasty is lurking out there in lots of bodily fluids? I could have done that or organized something like the Salvation Army—and that thought did occur to me, you know, nice faggots ringing little fairy bells on street corners, asking for donations to help the sick homos—but the problem is only partially tied to lack of funds. The real problem, you see, is here," he continued, tapping his shaved head. "People in America believe in good and evil, white and black, capitalist and commie, straight and gay. But the problem with AIDS is ever so much more complex. For example, some people—some people like Johnny Clariton—are even saying the epidemic is over. First they ignored it, then they blamed it on faggot immorality, and now they say it's over. I say bullshit. Sure, some guys are taking these new drugs and they seem to be getting better—if they're lucky enough to get them in time—but that might only last a year or two. And then what? What if AIDS mutates around all the meds and turns into some sort of supervirus that nothing can control? No, it's way too early to slap a smiley face on this one."

"Matthew—"

"Shit, do you realize that only about a tenth of infected Americans can get these new drugs? It kind of makes you wonder about the other thirty million people on this planet with HIV. I mean, how many people in Africa or Asia do you think are able to get any of these 'cocktails'?"

"Matthew," interrupted Rawlins, "you'll never get away with this."

"I'm not looking to get away with anything; I'm looking to prove a point. And the point is that one battle is being won—yes, progress has been made—but the war is far from over. If Johnny Clariton really thinks AIDS is manageable, then let him manage it himself. Then we'll see how he justifies cutting both research and subsidies to people who can't afford the drugs that are out there now. It's ridiculous, fucking ridiculous!''

Matthew was beyond desperate, Rawlins knew, and that made him the most dangerous sort of perpetrator.

"Maybe, though, I should just give you my gun, my dear Mr. Rawlins, and then you can fire away and be the big hero. Trust me, I'd be delighted to have a quick ticket off this planet.'' With his pistol he shoved Rawlins downward. "Keep going.''

"So you've been planning this for a long time?''

"And here I thought you were the token queer on the police force when instead you're a brilliant dick,'' laughed Matthew. "But yes, I've been working on this for months. I've been alone a lot lately, so I've had a lot of time to ponder the meanings of life and death and revenge. You see, I kept getting KS lesions on my face and scalp, and I just didn't want to see anyone. Call me vain, but I was used to people ogling me for my beauty, not staring at my oozing sores. So I worked out here in the land of the living dead as a janitor for, I don't know, four, five months, from eleven at night to seven in the morning. After all the nice, decent people went home to their safe suburban homes, I came out here like the hunchback of Notre Dame and swept up after them. Frankly, I hate the suburbs. It's just so artificial, all of it.''

As they started down another flight Rawlins said, "So far I haven't really disagreed with anything you've said.''

"Or probably done either. I'm just acting out every queer's fantasy.'' With a nudge Matthew pushed him along. "Just keep going down. And again, don't do anything stupid.''

"I already did. I slept with you.''

"Come on, you stud, you wanted it.''

"Yeah, but it wasn't worth dying for.''

"Say,'' Matthew said snidely, "when this is all over you could open up an AIDS store in one of the malls. Or maybe just a little kiosk, you know, one of those little carts or something. You could sell little red ribbons and CDs and posters, and then donate all the profits to research or a hospice. Wouldn't that be sweet and meaningful?''

"Yeah, except I doubt any of the malls would want something like that.''

"Oh, very good. You're catching on quickly." Matthew steered Rawlins down a final flight. "We're almost there."

Altogether they descended at least three levels, burrowing deeper and deeper on a journey that would have been like sinking into the cavernous chambers beneath the phantom's opera house except that this was all fresh and white, evenly lit and perfectly laid out. Reaching the bottom, Matthew upped the pace, shoving Rawlins past some plastic Dumpsters, then down another hall to a large, empty room.

"Here it is, home, sweet home," said Matthew, who led the way across the room to a plain metal door, on which he knocked twice, paused, then knocked two more times.

Maybe, Rawlins thought as he stood there, these guys were right. When prominent political figures not only marginalized a group of people and a horrible disease, but used both of them as a platform for social division and political gain, what choices did that leave you? How could you fight back against such hate? Then again, what difference did it make? As clearly as he recalled the history of friends like Curt, Rawlins saw his own bleak future.

When the door failed to open, Matthew shook his head, then repeated his sequence of knocks. When that still didn't produce any results, Matthew's face flushed red and he started banging with his fist.

"Elliot, you fool, it's me! Open up the goddamn door!"

Rawlins heard nothing, not a voice or a single step from behind the locked door. Then breaking the silence came a distinct sob, a sharp one at that, followed by nothing.

"Oh, shit," muttered Matthew, who then started pounding on the door. "Elliot! Elliot, you faggot, open up the fucking door!"

"Matthew . . . Matthew . . ."

"This guy," moaned Matthew to Rawlins, "is such a drama queen."

From behind the door came the sound of a few steps, and then Elliot calling, "Matthew . . . you're too late!"

"What?"

"She's—" began Elliot, who then dissolved into tears.

"Oh, fuck, what is it now?" Matthew started beating on the door. "Open the fuck up!"

"Tina's . . ."

There was a click of a bolt as the door was unlocked, and then the door was cracked open and a skinny, knobby man stood there, his red face streaked with tears. In spite of that and his sickly appearance, Rawlins recognized him at once, having met him a number of times at Curt's.

Peering out of the partially opened door, Elliot eyed Rawlins, stopped crying for a moment, and replied, "What in the hell are you doing here?" He sniffled and wiped his eyes. "Are there more of you cops out there?"

"Let's just say I was persuaded to come."

Matthew pushed forward, shoving the door open and saying, "Elliot, get out of the—"

Rawlins had visited any number of crime scenes. He'd seen any number of bodies. And you could always tell death by the stillness as much as the smell, both of which were confirmed by the woman's body in the bathroom doorway.

"She's . . . she's dead," said Elliot, choking on his tears.

"Oh, Jesus!" mumbled Matthew, rushing across the room and dropping to his knees by Tina's side.

"I did what I could!"

"Oh . . . Tina . . ."

"Honest, Matthew, I tried to help her! I was making her something to drink and . . . and she was in the bathroom. She must have stood up and passed out and hit her head. I heard this crash and I went over—she'd fallen. There was a big gash on her head. I tried to do something, but . . . but she was already dead and . . . and . . ." Elliot started sobbing, "Oh, God, what's going to happen to us now? What are we going to do? This is it, we're done! It's over!"

Drawn by the horror of it, Rawlins stepped in, his eyes focused on the body. Was this the way he was going to croak, in some overlooked corner of the world? He glanced to the side, observing the boxes of food and supplies, the clothing, and the streaks of blood coming from the bathroom. Hearing someone call out, Rawlins turned, saw a closed door. Was Clariton in there?

"Matthew, I'm sorry, there wasn't anything I could do. I wanted to—"

"Shut up, you idiot!" shouted Matthew, taking Tina's limp hand in his.

"But what's going to happen?"

"I don't know!"

Elliot, his eyes small and pained, turned to Rawlins, grabbing him by one arm and begging, "Should we turn ourselves in? Do you think that would be a good idea? But what will the police do to us? Do you think they'll hurt us? Oh, God, maybe we should just kill ourselves! We could let Clariton go, and then . . . then . . . well, what do you think, Rawlins?"

He shrugged. "I don't care."

"Come on, tell us what to do! Should we call the cops? Should we—"

Matthew was back on his feet, whipping his gun around, jamming it against Elliot's head, and shouting, "If you don't shut up right this second I'm going to kill you myself!"

Elliot squished his eyes shut and pleaded, his voice shaking, "Go ahead, do it right now! Kill me! I can't take this anymore!"

Seeing the fury in Matthew's face, Rawlins pulled back, certain that Matthew was about to blow Elliot's brains all over the room. But that moment went as quickly as it had developed.

"Oh, shit," said Matthew, lowering the gun.

"Do it, you coward!" shouted Elliot.

"Fuck off!"

When Matthew turned away and rubbed his forehead with one hand, Rawlins thought this was it, his chance to turn and walk out of here. The door was still partly open, he could make a dash for it.

But why?

Even if he somehow managed to get away, even if Matthew didn't come chasing after him and gun him down, where would he go? What would he do? Where would he, in the greater picture, hide? That's right, he thought, unable to see hope or refuge of any kind. He was infected with HIV, and from today on there would never be any certainty again in his life. After all, even a minuscule cold germ was now potentially as deadly as poison gas.

Behind him, Matthew ordered, "Shut the door and lock it."

"Of course," replied a defeated Rawlins, feeling as if he were switching sides. "Like I said, I really don't disagree with what you've been saying."

25

Todd had no idea what was happening. Nor did he have any real idea how he'd ended up in Lyle Cunningham's black pickup truck. All he knew was that he had to get to the WLAK studios in time for the 10:00 P.M. news, and this was the most expedient way. Whether or not he was in any kind of mental shape to go on the air, however, remained to be determined.

"Why the hell did you follow me?" asked Todd as they sped through the night and the flat suburb toward the station.

Lyle shrugged his large shoulders. "Because I saw the way the leader of that group looked at you when they kidnapped Clariton. And I saw the way you looked at him."

"So?" replied Todd, wondering if he was getting at the very thing Todd had failed to relay to the police.

"So you know him, right?"

Now it was Todd's turn to shrug. Glancing out the window at a dilapidated strip mall, he tried to evaluate how much to say, what and what not to filter, and of course how fully he could trust Lyle.

Finally Todd decided not to hold back, and he said, "I recognized him, but I don't know why. I've been trying to remember, but I can't. Of course, it didn't help that he had on a mask, his head was shaved, and he looked sick as hell. Who knows, maybe I've just seen him at the grocery store."

"Or down at one of the gay bars."

"Maybe."

Lyle glanced over. "Or maybe he's a friend of a friend."

"Perhaps," replied Todd, wondering just how much Lyle actually knew.

"Yeah, well, when you do remember let me know. I'm looking for that thread, the one that's going to unravel this whole thing." He reached into his coat pocket and pulled out a business card. "The second number is my voice pager."

Todd took the card, glanced at it in the faint light of the car. What did Lyle take him for, a total fool?

"Right," said Todd, "I'm going to call you, the same guy who just had a gun to my head."

"I wasn't going to shoot."

"Sorry, buddy, but I don't think I'm going to call Mr. Johnny Clariton's bodyguard with any hot information." Todd motioned to the low white building up ahead on the left. "That's the station right up there."

Lyle braked at a stoplight, waited for a green, then turned left and said, "I don't know if it makes any difference to you, but for your information I can't stand Clariton. In fact, I probably detest him more than you can imagine."

"Oh, I see." Todd shook his head, wondered what in the hell this was all about. "So you're just out here doing double duty, looking for Clariton because it's your moral duty or something."

"Actually, that's about right. I was hired to do a job and I'm going to keep on doing it because, I don't know about you, but I'm morally opposed to things like kidnapping and terrorism."

"Oh, the idealistic bodyguard. Sounds like juicy pulp fiction."

Lyle shook his head, then glared at Todd. "You know what I don't like about you gay people?"

Todd's spine bristled. "What?"

"Your inability to see beyond your own fucking nose."

"And you know what I don't like about you straight people? Your hypocritical morality."

"Listen, you're not the only ones in crisis. In my opinion gays are the most self-absorbed group of people I've ever seen."

Jesus Christ, thought Todd, time to be done with this. He said, "You can drop me off at the side door over there."

He couldn't believe this. Of course he should have called a taxi. Of course he should have avoided Lyle Cunningham's offer to drive him out here. And as the truck turned into the drive of Channel 10 and neared the side entrance, Todd, ready to spring out, reached up to the door handle. Just as quickly, Lyle's bear-like hand slammed down on his own door lock, and with a *thunk* the automatic system locked Todd's door as well. No, realized Todd, turning and staring at the other man, getting out of here wasn't going to be easy.

"Not so fast, asshole," snapped Lyle as he pulled to a stop by some large, overgrown junipers.

"So there's a catch to this free ride?"

"I want to tell you a little story."

"Do I have a choice?"

"No, you don't," replied Lyle. "You don't because I want to tell you about a sixty-year-old lady who—"

"Listen, pal," Todd interrupted, "I really don't have time for this. I'm supposed to be on the air in a few minutes."

"Just shut up."

"Oh, Christ."

"So this lady—she moved down to Arizona some ten years ago. Her husband had died and she moved to Sun City, where she met a nice old man. A really sweet guy, very lonely, and very loaded. A while back he'd had quadruple bypass surgery, but had recovered in excellent shape."

Todd was about to get terribly pissed off when it hit him. Was this story going where he thought it was? Did it involve who he thought it did?

"Or so it seemed," continued Lyle, "until the old man started losing weight and developed pneumonia, which was when they discovered that the blood transfusion he'd been given years earlier for the heart surgery was tainted with the HIV virus. It was very sad, of course, but the pneumonia was quite virulent and it killed him quite quickly."

When Lyle lapsed into silence, Todd pressed, "What about the girlfriend?"

"The girlfriend . . ." Lyle looked out and into the dark. "Unfortunately it took about seven more years before AIDS killed the little old lady, with whom he'd slept three times."

Todd saw the intensity in Lyle's eyes. He saw the anger and knew precisely what it meant.

"Your mother?"

"Exactly. She died three years ago, and it wiped us all out—me and my two sisters—both emotionally, of course, and financially." He turned and stared right into Todd's eyes. "So don't even get me started on what I think of people like Johnny Clariton." Lyle popped open the locks. "Just call me if you know anything."

"I will," said Todd, opening the door and climbing out. "And I'm sorry about your mom, I really am."

"Yeah, well, it was about as awful as things get." He took a deep breath, exhaled. "Just remember, call me if anything comes up. I'm actually pretty good at these kinds of situations. After all, I used to be a marine."

"Now there's some reassuring news."

As Lyle quickly sped through the parking lot and out the other exit, Todd stood there, watching the pickup disappear into the night. He then turned, looked at the low white building, the array of satellite dishes. How the hell was he supposed to go in there and in twenty minutes start blathering about the day's events, how Clariton was still missing, how tense the situation was, how Todd had been right in the heart of it all?

He took a deep breath, knew that as soon as he stepped into the building he'd be overwhelmed. First things first, he thought, heading toward his Cherokee, which was still parked in the third row. Before his work swept over him he'd try calling Rawlins from his car phone.

Todd ran his left hand through his hair. Dear God, he was tired. Worried about the Clariton interview, he'd awakened first thing this morning, and then the day's events had hit one right after the other, each one more highly charged than the last. Actually, Clariton's abduction seemed as if it had not taken place just this afternoon, but days ago.

Reaching his vehicle, Todd slipped his hand into his pocket and pulled out his car keys. As he went to unlock the door, however, he stopped. Through the window, he could see that the vehicle wasn't locked. Odd, he thought, for he always secured it. Then he saw a large manila envelope placed on the driver's seat. Todd hesitated and considered the magnitude of what had happened thus far today. Had someone broken in and left something? Something such as what? He'd received threatening mail more than once—particularly since he'd come out of the closet—and the idea of a letter bomb zipped through his mind. No, you're just being paranoid, he told himself. He turned his head, tried to get a better look. Light from a tall lamppost was spilling through the windshield, and Todd could clearly make out some handwriting on the envelope, handwriting that Todd immediately recognized.

Remembering just who had a copy of his car key, Todd tore open the driver's door, grabbed the envelope, and read:

Dear Todd,
      Unfortunately I've gotten caught up in something, and for that reason I'm sure you'll find this tape of interest. Please, please, please, just remember how good we were together.
                                        My love,
                                        Rawlins

In a near panic Todd ripped open the envelope and pulled out a single videocassette. Written on it in someone else's handwriting was: "Show at nine tomorrow morning on Channel 10 or, as they say, he's a goner." This definitely didn't make any sense. What had Rawlins done after he'd left Todd's condo—gone out somewhere and picked up this video, then come all the way out here to drop it off? Quite obviously. Perhaps Rawlins had come out here hoping to catch Todd before the 10:00 P.M. news. Perhaps he'd been here and had actually gone into the studio.

Todd slammed shut his car door and then, videocassette and envelope in hand, dashed toward the studio. He jogged in and out of the rows of cars, past the line of Channel 10 vehicles, and up to the side entrance, where he took out his pass card and swiped it through the magnetic reader. The door buzzed open, and Todd hurried inside and down the hall toward the newsroom.

"Hey, Mr. Mills!" said the janitor, a young guy, who looked up from his vacuuming. "Everyone's looking for you!"

Todd ducked in the first door on his right, entering the large newsroom. Hurrying past the huge coffeepots and piles of daily newspapers, he headed straight through a sea of cubicles for his office.

"There you are, Todd!" called someone from a cubicle.

Two or three other people called after him as well, but Todd didn't stop. What the hell had Rawlins brought out here? What could be on the tape? It could be something about AIDS. Or—and this was what he most feared—it could be something about suicide.

"Jesus, Todd, where have you been?" called Nan Miller, a diminutive woman and the producer of the late news. "You're on in seven minutes! We're planning on you—"

"Not tonight!"

Todd raced past her desk, past the assignment desk, and into his office, closing the glass door behind him. He dropped himself in his chair and glanced one last time at the note on the manila envelope—what the hell did Rawlins mean?—before stuffing the envelope in the waste can under his desk. He then rolled over to the VCR, jammed the tape into the machine, and turned on the monitor. Immediately the image of a very thin blond woman burst onto the screen, and Todd gasped and lunged forward, touching the glass, trying to understand. He recognized her at once, of course, just as he recognized the disheveled man sitting next to her on the floor.

"What the hell do you mean, not tonight?" demanded Nan, bursting into his office. "Don't you realize how crazy it's been here? We've been doing almost continual coverage of this, and you're—" She saw the image on the screen. "Oh, my God, that's Clariton."

It most definitely was. And Todd was too shocked to say anything, do anything, but watch. That woman was one of the three who'd abducted Clariton this afternoon, there was no doubt about that. And that was the congressman himself right next to her. So this had to have been made sometime after Clariton was abducted.

"Where did you get this?" demanded Nan, unable to take her eyes from the screen.

"My car," mumbled Todd. "Someone left it there."

"When?"

"Just now. Just when I came in."

"Is that one of the kidnappers?"

Todd nodded, said, "Shh."

He couldn't stop the tape. It just kept rolling, each moment worse than the one before. Someone else came into Todd's office, then two, three, five more people pushed their way in, all of them jammed around the small monitor, all of them watching in shock. Finally, a general cry of horror filled the room as the blond woman on the tape finished recounting her story, pulled out the syringe of blood, and broke into a scuffle with Congressman Clariton.

"Oh, my God!" gasped Nan. "That was their blood!"

"I hate Clariton," moaned another, "but that's murder!"

"What's happened to our world?"

Todd was as stunned as them all, for though he'd doubted Clariton would survive the kidnapping, he hadn't imagined anything as perverse as this. Whether they'd actually succeeded in injecting him, however, was unclear, and after he punched off the tape he just sat there groping with one and only one question: What did any of this have to do with Rawlins?

"So you just got this, Todd?" pressed Nan.

He nodded. "Seconds before I came in here."

"That means the police don't even know about it."

"No, they don't." He ejected the cassette, stared at it, and read, " 'Show at nine tomorrow morning on Channel 10 or, as they say, he's a goner.' "

The silence that followed was broken by one of the assistant producers who'd crowded into Todd's office. "What a scoop! Channel Ten scores again!"

Frank, the assignment editor, nearly shouted with glee. "This is unbelievably hot! We'll do a special report, maybe get some other AIDS activists to comment."

"Someone should alert the network about this one!"

"Yeah, right! We'll send something out over the wire before the ten o'clock news. My God, we only have five minutes, but—"

"No!" shouted Todd, jumping up. "Now get out of here, all of you! What do you think this is, some sort of carnival game?"

One of them said, "But—"

"Out!"

Nan turned toward the others and in her best controlling producer voice shouted, "Go on, get out! He's right, we can't use it, not just now anyway. Not tonight. This is far too serious. We have to contact the police first."

Clutching the tape, Todd slumped back in his chair as everyone but Nan filed out. He held the tape against his gut, squinched his eyes shut, and thought: Rawlins, Rawlins, Rawlins. How in God's name did you get ahold of this?

"Do you know," he asked, "if anyone tried to get in the building to see me recently?"

"Not that I'm aware of, but I'll ask around." Nan touched his shoulder and said, "What is it, Todd?"

"I . . . I . . ." He took a deep breath. "I don't get what's going on. I mean, how did I end up with this tape?"

"How did you?"

He shrugged. "Like I said, it was in my car, just sitting there on the seat."

"No note, no nothing?"

It had happened before. When Michael was murdered, Todd's personal life and every bit of dirty laundry had been dragged out not only by the police, but by Channel 7, the station he'd then been working for. His host of problems had become public sport, and he damn well wasn't going to let it happen again, not yet, not given the challenges Rawlins and he were about to face.

"Nothing, just this tape," replied Todd. "Listen, I'm not going on air tonight, I can't. You can have someone else report on me, you can have Terri say that I'm recovering or something, that I've spent a good amount of time helping the police. Something like that. I don't care. You can even say we received a tape—say WLAK received it, not me. But I'm not going in front of a camera."

"Todd, you know how big this is."

"I don't give a—"

"Please, just think about it."

"No, I won't go on, period! End of discussion." He rubbed his eyes. "You better go call the police. Tell them they have to come out here. I'll talk to them, but only out here. I'm going to close my blinds. I just have to rest. I just have to calm things down for a few minutes. This day has been insane.''

"I'll say."

Without another word Nan hurried out. As soon as he heard her shut the door, Todd turned and went over to the glass wall of his office and looked out. About a half dozen people stared back, and he lowered the miniblinds, then closed them completely. When he was sure no one could see in, he reached under his desk and pulled the envelope from the wastebasket. He didn't think anyone would have noticed him carrying it in, and he started to tear it in half, but stopped. No, the police might search his trash, tape it back together or something, so he took the envelope, folded it three times, and stuffed it in his coat pocket. He'd get rid of it later, perhaps ditch it in the men's room. Next he pulled out his shirttail and, not even considering if he was destroying evidence, wiped clean every bit of the black video box. In a few minutes he'd take the VHS tape to one of the engineers and have him make a proBeta dub, but for now he put the tape back in the player, rewound it, and watched it one more time.

As the images of the blond woman and her assault on Clariton rolled a second time on the monitor, Todd reached for a pair of headphones, which he plugged into the VCR. Again he listened to Tina's story. Again he heard the sad fate of her daughter, as well as Clariton's repulsive remarks. This time, though, Todd paid closer attention to what else he could hear. There were two other men in the room—surely the guys who'd abducted Clariton this morning—and one of their voices was oddly familiar to Todd. What caught Todd's attention in particular, however, was that odd background sound, the noise of something humming or rolling. It wasn't coming from just that room either. No, it was emanating from somewhere else in that building. And it was familiar, most definitely. Todd clinched his eyes shut and clasped his hands over the earphones as if to press the sound deeper into his head.

Just where the hell had he heard that before?

Another one bites the dust. And, oy, what a mess. I mean, talk about a bunch of gloppy blood. It took all three of us to get Tina's body tucked into a couple of Hefty two-plies. And it took all three of us a good long while to swab up the bathroom. Who could have imagined that the life of such a beautiful gal could have ended like that, a simple fall and a gash to the head?

I just hope when I croak that it's going to be a little more dignified. I mean, I don't mean to be vain or anything, but it's such an ugly way to go, this AIDS. And so fucking drawn out. I mean, you can linger, bounce back, linger, bounce back, linger . . . etc., etc., and so on . . . for months. No, I did Curt right. Here, have a teeny sip of cyanide, and it's lights out. Boom. I mean, his end was long and sad enough as it was, so why should he have been forced out of his home and left to molder in some hospice? It's what he wanted least of all, and I guess I agree. Who wants to die in some strange place surrounded by strange people and strange things? Not I, thank you very much. No lingering in some cold, sterile departure lounge. I'm going when I want.

Which is to say: soon. In other words, ta-ta. I'm next.

26

The FBI usurped the local cops because a federal crime had been committed.

Less than twenty-five minutes after the producer, Nan, called the Minneapolis police, three guys showed up, two white guys and a black man. They flashed their identification as they were ushered into the Channel 10 newsroom, and then the black man explained that he was Maurice Cochran, the FBI's special agent in charge of regional affairs, and introduced the others.

"Earlier this afternoon the President directed the attorney general to treat this matter with the utmost urgency. Consequently Dr. John Ogden," said Cochran, referring to the tall slim man on his left, "was brought in from the base at Quantico as the lead hostage negotiator. And Wayne Morrish, also from Quantico, heads up the HRT."

These were foreign waters, and Todd said, "HRT?"

Morrish, a stocky man in his mid-forties, wearing a black polo shirt and khaki pants, said, "Hostage Rescue Team. Fifty of us flew in this afternoon."

"Fifty of the best men in the country," added Cochran. "They have assault, demolition, and sniper teams. If anyone can safely recover Congressman Clariton, it's them."

"Welcome to Minneapolis," said Todd, who wasn't surprised at how seriously this was being treated.

"We appreciate any information you can give us," said Dr. Ogden. "So what's this about a video?"

Great, thought Todd. This was all he needed in his life right now, the FBI and a crack team of FBI agents, endorsed by the President, no less.

"Come on, let's go into the conference room," suggested Todd. "You've got to see it."

Nan and he led the way down the hall into a plain room with a low ceiling and light blue walls. Filing in, they and the FBI agents seated themselves around a large rectangular table that filled the center of the room.

"I came out here about fifty minutes ago and found this in my car," explained Todd, holding up the tape. "As you probably already know, I was the one interviewing Clariton this afternoon when he was abducted. Just what the connection is and why I got this tape, I don't know, but they're demanding we broadcast it tomorrow morning."

Without further word he got up and went to a VCR and monitor that sat in the corner. He popped in the tape, hit a couple of buttons, and the images of the blond woman and Congressman Clariton filled the screen. As the tape played, Todd glanced at the agents, who were as transfixed and horrified as Todd had been the first time he'd seen it. The woman told her story, Clariton offered his tacky comments, there were a few quips from behind the camera . . .

And Todd focused again on that distant noise, the soft, rolling rumble. He could hear it for a few seconds and then it faded away. Virtually no background noise for a minute or two. All in all he heard it three times over the course of the video, which lasted not quite ten minutes. It almost, thought Todd when the tape concluded, sounded like airplanes approaching a runway. Could that be where they were holding Clariton, in some hangar or something near the airport?

"Oh, my God," moaned Cochran as Todd shut off the machine.

"When did you say you got this?" asked Morrish, taking out a small pad and jotting down a few things.

Todd glanced at his wristwatch. "Almost an hour ago."

"And it was in your car out here?"

"Exactly." Todd noticed that Dr. Ogden, whom he presumed to be a psychologist, was staring and silently judging him. "It was sitting right on the driver's seat."

Cochran leaned over and whispered something to Morrish,

who nodded and reached into his jacket pocket and pulled out a small device.

"Mr. Mills and . . ." began Cochran.

"Nan Miller," volunteered the producer.

"Right. We'd like to ask you some questions. Would you mind if we tape-recorded our conversation?"

An informal interview, Todd knew, was what they wanted. He'd been through one of these before, of course. And he might as well just play it direct and concise. He just hoped he wouldn't have to go back down to police headquarters or the FBI offices, at least not tonight. He was far too tired and exhausted for much more.

"Go ahead and turn that thing on." Once the microtape recorder was running, Todd said, "My name is Todd Mills, and I'm an investigative reporter at Channel Ten in Minneapolis. I agree to a noncustodial interview. I am aware that this conversation is being recorded and I am speaking of my own free will." He looked at his coworker. "Either you agree to speak freely or you have to leave the room, Nan."

Her eyes large with seriousness, she glanced at Todd, then the FBI agents. "No. No, it's okay."

"Does that mean you agree to this interview?" clarified Cochran.

"Yes."

"And your name is?"

"My name is Nan Miller. And . . . and I'm a producer here at WLAK TV."

With the technicalities out of the way Todd went into detail about getting a lift out to Channel 10, then thinking he wouldn't be able to do the late-night broadcast because he was too tired. He told them about walking through the parking lot and up to his car to use his car phone.

"What type of vehicle?" asked Morrish.

"A Jeep Grand Cherokee," replied Todd.

The door was open, he continued.

"Open?" questioned Cochran.

Unlocked, Todd corrected. It was unlocked, which was weird.

So he glanced in and saw the videotape just sitting there on the driver's seat.

"Just the tape, not in a box or anything?" asked Dr. Ogden.

Todd hesitated for the first time. Did he, he wondered, glancing briefly at Nan, want to bring Rawlins into this right now? No, because what would she and Channel 10 do with that information, perhaps use it and Todd as broadcast fodder?

"No, it was just the plain tape sitting there."

Nan interjected, "I saw him come into his office and put it in the VCR. And I was right there—a handful of us were—when he played it the first time."

"And what was your reaction to seeing the tape, Mr. Mills?" asked Ogden.

"My reaction? What the hell do you think? I was and still am disgusted." He knew what they were getting at, and so he laid it out. "Listen, I'm not a Clariton supporter by any means, but what happened today is totally wrong. If they really plan to inject Clariton with HIV-tainted blood, well, I'm appalled."

"Everyone felt that way," added Nan.

"Right," Todd agreed.

So they went over it again, this time in more detail. Cochran, Morrish, and Ogden asked a host of questions, ranging from who gave Todd a ride out here—Todd told them it was a friend, and felt his entanglement draw a little tighter—to if he'd seen anyone else in the parking lot, to why his car was unlocked and on and on. Then they turned to Nan Miller, asking her to have the front-door guard draw up a list of who'd visited the station that night.

"You don't have a surveillance camera on the parking lot by chance, do you?" asked Morrish.

"No, I don't believe we do," replied Nan. "We just haven't had any security problems before."

He turned to Todd and said, "I'm afraid, Mr. Mills, we're going to have to impound your car."

"What for, prints?"

"Exactly."

Cochran said, "We'll get a crime lab on it right away." He paused. "And the tape—has anyone else handled it besides you, Mr. Mills?"

"No." Todd thought for a moment and added, "Wait, one of our technicians handled it too."

"Well, maybe we'll be able to get some other prints off it."

"I'm sorry, Mr. Cochran," said Nan, drawing in a deep breath and taking a bold stand, "but if you're thinking you can just have that tape you're mistaken. That tape belongs to WLAK and you're going to have to subpoena—"

"No, Nan," countered Todd. "That tape does not belong to the station. It was in my car, I brought it inside the building. Therefore, unfortunately, it's mine. Obviously the situation is very serious, so I'm going to have to do some thinking about whether or not to turn over the tape to the FBI."

"Todd, think about what you're saying," she pleaded. "Think about what kind of precedent you'd be setting if you turned over the tape to the FBI or the police without a subpoena."

"Listen, Nan, I—"

"No, you listen, Todd. Giving the tape to the authorities goes against everything we know about good journalism. It really is a dangerous precedent. And what about getting it on the air? What will the kidnappers do to Clariton if we don't run the tape exactly as they say?"

She was right on all accounts, of course, but Todd made a snap decision. Screw subpoenas and all that. Screw the media's freedom. Someone's life was very much in danger.

"Nan, this is my tape, and I've got to do what I think is best not for the station but for someone else," he said. "While we were waiting for the FBI to get here, I had a proBeta copy made, which I will keep in my possession. The FBI gets the original. What you, Mr. Cochran, Mr. Morrish, and Mr. Ogden, have to decide is if we should broadcast that tape tomorrow morning at nine. And I suggest you decide soon, because who knows what they'll do to Clariton if we don't follow their instructions."

"Todd, I wish you wouldn't do this."

"I'm sorry, but that's my decision."

Quite determined that Channel 10 not be cut out of the deal, Nan shook her head and interjected, "You know, management is going to have a shit fit. Todd, at least let us air your copy tomorrow morning. I really don't think we have any choice but to show it.'' Looking at him quite sternly, she added, ''I'm certain that your job depends upon it.''

He glanced from Nan to the FBI guys and said, ''Actually, I don't think we have a choice either. After all, who knows how many other people are involved and who knows what they'll do if they don't get their way?''

''Given the level of stress in their voices,'' advised Ogden, ''I would say that we're dealing with some very serious and desperate people. They are dangerous, no doubt about it.''

''Exactly,'' said Todd. ''And if we fail to broadcast the tape, perhaps they'll kill Clariton right on the spot. Or perhaps—who knows?—they'll attack other public officials with syringes of blood.''

Morrish shifted in his seat. ''No hostage has ever been killed on a deadline in the United States.''

''Now there's something reassuring.'' Todd shook his head and leaned over the table. ''But let me ask you this: Have you ever dealt with any kidnappers who are terminally ill and close to death? These people have nothing to lose, you realize. They're desperate. And if they're willing to use their own blood as a lethal weapon, there's no telling what they'll do.''

Cochran thought for a moment, put a hand to his forehead, and took a deep breath. ''I'm going to have to make a couple of calls to Washington and see what we're going to do on this one. It's going on eleven right now, but I should have an answer within the hour.''

''Good. For now we'll plan on showing Todd's copy of the tape at nine.'' Nan's mind was obviously spinning with producerly orchestrations, and she added, ''Todd, that's when I want you to introduce the tape. By then we can drum up a hell of a lot of interest and you'll have viewers from around the globe.'' She leaned toward him and whispered, ''I guarantee you, Todd, it will be the best thing for your career.''

It was true, they were going to have to broadcast the tape at some point. And it would be seen all over the country and around the world. But was this a horse he really wanted to ride? No, not at all. Yet he had no choice, not really. Better he, a gay person, should do this. Better he should put the right spin on it.

"Okay."

"Unless Washington has any problems, that'll work for us. I agree, I don't see that we have any alternative," said Cochran, glancing at Morrish and Ogden for dissent.

"No, at this point I think the best thing we can do," advised Ogden, "is keep them engaged. We don't want to start out by alienating them."

Morrish said, "Mr. Mills, do you have an envelope or something?"

Todd looked up and pressed his hand over his coat. Holy shit, how did they know about that?

"What?" said Todd.

"My evidence-collection kit is in the car—do you have an envelope?"

"Oh, sure. Of course," he replied, wondering if his relief was too obvious. "I'll go get one."

Rubbing his eyes as he left the room, Todd retreated down the hall to his office, where he fumbled around in his desk drawer for an envelope. Finding one, he started back to the conference room. With any luck there would be no more questions, not tonight at least. Yet as much as Todd wanted and needed to head home for some rest, he wasn't going to. No, instead he was going to have to borrow one of Channel 10's vehicles and head downtown, for there was just one more person he had to talk to tonight.

27

Rawlins leaned against a wall and sank to the floor in the main room. He bowed his head, took a deep breath. Everything was such a blur. All of this, every moment since the doctor had pronounced him all but dead with "unfortunate news." And now he was hidden in some underground chamber, while just across the room was a woman's body wrapped tightly in some heavy-duty plastic bags.

"You okay?" asked Matthew.

Rawlins replied, "I don't know. I can't even think straight."

"Well," mumbled Elliot with an edge of giddiness, "I can't even talk straight, I can't even walk straight, I can't even look straight!"

"Jesus Christ, Elliot, don't start up again!" snapped Matthew. "Now, get the camcorder."

Elliot turned to Tina's plastic-covered body, stared at it, and said, "I don't know, Matthew. I don't think I can do it, not now."

"You don't have a choice!" ordered Matthew.

"Oh, all right, Mr. Cecil B. DeMille."

"We need to speed up our schedule a bit just to make sure everything happens."

"Whatever you say, Mr. Great Director Man."

Rawlins said, "What's going on?"

"It's time for Elliot to tell the world his story," answered Matthew. "And it's time for you to meet our honored guest."

As Elliot grabbed the video camera and loaded it with a tape, Rawlins pushed himself back to his feet. Matthew then led the way to the other door, which he opened. And there, cowering in the corner of the next room and chained to a pipe, was a disheveled man, his fine suit a mass of wrinkles, his tie ripped away, and his face red and anxious. So this, realized Rawlins, was the famed congressman.

"You can sit over there," Matthew told Rawlins, pointing to the floor. "And Elliot, you go over there and sit next to Johnny."

"Oh, God, what are you going to do now?" Clariton pointed at Rawlins. "Who's that?"

"A recruit." Matthew laughed. "Actually, he's a cop. But don't get your hopes up. He's a member of the tribe—my tribe."

"What about that crazy bitch who tried to kill me? I heard all that crying. What did you do to her?"

Elliot wiped his nose. "Tina croaked."

"Oh, Jesus. Why don't you just let me go? You . . . you could just dump me somewhere and take off." He clasped his hands together and started rubbing and folding them over and over. "If you let me go now I could still get you immunity."

"Why don't you just shut up?" Elliot went over and sat down next to him. "And don't worry, I don't got a syringe or anything. We're saving that for later."

"You're pigs! You're complete pigs!"

"Oh, like, hurt my feelings!" replied Elliot, clasping a hand over his heart.

Rawlins stared at the politician, who looked less a commanding leader of the right wing than he did a terrified boy, and asked, "Have they done anything to you?"

"Have they done anything? They tried to inject me with their poison blood, that's what they tried to do! These disgusting people with their disgusting disease almost gave me a shot of AIDS!"

"Oh, just shut up, would you?" said Elliot. "Do you know how famous you're going to be now? The whole world is going to know who you are. Of course, a lot of people already do, but your picture is going to be everywhere, I bet. Like, I'm sure tomorrow morning your picture's going to be on the front page of every major paper in the world. You know, you can't buy publicity like that. And just wait till everyone gets ahold of that video of you and Tina. I mean, every news show is going to play and replay that, not to mention CNN International, which will—''

"You're depraved!"

"Yes, twisted and sick, perhaps, but trust me, several billion people will be tired of seeing your face by tomorrow evening. You'll probably get your own theme song on each of the networks!"

"Boys, boys, boys," chided Matthew. "I'm turning on the camera . . . now."

Taking it all in, Rawlins sat quietly. So this, he realized, was how they were making their point—and why they dropped off a tape for Todd earlier.

Elliot bowed his head, then looked up. "Tina's dead." He let the words hang in the air. "She was so weak and dehydrated that she got dizzy, and then she stood up and fell and hit her head. She passed from this world just a few hours ago. What do you think of that, Mr. Clariton?"

Rawlins could see the fury on Clariton's face. The hatred. It was quite clear that all the good congressman wanted to do was lunge at Elliot and rip out his throat. Instead, some little part of Clariton the politician held himself in control.

So instead of cursing and swearing at Elliot, Clariton jerked his handcuffed arm and demanded, "You have to let me go."

"No problem," replied Elliot. "I for one will certainly be glad to be rid of you. I mean, I find you entirely repulsive. Don't worry, we'll let you go just as soon as we've finished the videos—this one, then one with Matthew—and they're shown on national television. Oh, and after we've given you a little shot of something special."

From behind the camera Matthew the director said quietly, "Tell them why you're doing this."

"Why?" asked Elliot, looking right into the lens. "Why would nice little Elliot do something so terrible as kidnapping a top politician and threatening to inject him with AIDS?" He pulled back the sleeves of his shirt, exposing old scars on both wrists. "Because I won't do this again. I won't try to go quietly so that no one notices, so that I don't bother anyone." He shrugged. "The truth is that I'm really angry. I'm angry that I

28

Todd didn't head home in the Channel 10 Ford Explorer that he'd borrowed. Nor did he proceed directly to his destination. Instead, he took the back roads, cutting through the suburb of Golden Valley and then steering onto the parkway system that encircled the city of Minneapolis. Following the landscaped road, which ran alongside bike and pedestrian paths, he passed the ski hill at Theodore Wirth Park, the golf course, and eventually reached Cedar Lake. Driving slowly, his eyes on the rearview mirror, Todd proceeded along the wooded parkway system, passing around Lake of the Isles, Lake Calhoun, and finally Lake Harriet. Except for a few late-night strollers, the parks rimming the lakes were quiet and still. And the traffic almost nonexistent. Checking behind yet again, Todd was relieved to note that there was no one following him.

After he'd driven past the Disney-like band shell, with its tow-ers and flags, and then around most of Lake Harriet, he cut over to the freeway and headed downtown. Reaching the edge of the central business district some ten minutes later, he found a park-ing place right in front of the Hennepin County Medical Center, cut off the Explorer, and headed into the beige building, a mas-sive, brutal structure that had been dropped onto several blocks. It was almost midnight, much too late for this kind of thing, but of course he had to know. Sneaking into the building via the emergency room, Todd proceeded to the back elevators. The halls on the second floor were deserted, the lights low. He proceeded to her room, which was at the far end. Reaching the door, he tapped lightly, pushed it open, and stepped in. In the harsh glow of the night-light she lay on the hospital bed, an IV

have AIDS. I'm angry that I'm going to die so young. I'm angry that I won't get to paint anymore. And I'm really angry that people like Mr. Johnny Clariton want to declare the AIDS epi-demic over when none of the drugs works for me. It happened before, you see, something like this. Someone tried to sweep me under the carpet, only I did nothing. Nothing! And you know what? It very nearly killed me. Or I should say I very nearly killed me.

"I'm from Omaha," continued Elliot, turning to Clariton, "and when I was a kid there were nine boys in my neighborhood. We did everything together. You know, we rode bikes, we built forts, we went swimming in the gravel pits."

It was something like five years ago, thought Rawlins, that he'd met Elliot, and even back then Elliot had been the trickster, the oddly jovial guy who lit up the room with a kind of manic happiness. Rawlins recalled that first time, seeing the animated face, hearing the nonstop voice, and wondering just what it was Elliot was trying to run from. And here it was, his core, his heart of pain. For the first time since Rawlins had met him there was no jive in Elliot's voice.

"Well, to make a long story short, I had sex with a kid from another town out at the gravel pit." Elliot blushed. "It sounds kinda tacky, but I swear I wasn't a major-league slut. No way. It just happened. Boys will be boys, and we were just trying to figure it out. It was just kid sex, you know."

"This is disgusting!" barked Clariton.

"Oh, shut up! That's the trouble with you, you know that? You're always bossing people around, telling them they're this or that." Elliot shook his head, took a deep breath. "I won't go into details—my modesty overwhelms me—but we were exploring, you know."

"Oh, please," spat Clariton, turning his head away in disgust.

Elliot glared at him, then continued, saying, "The only thing is, we got caught when we were doing it. Well, the other kid just took off, but from then on all my supposed friends made my life miserable. They sent me threatening mail. They spray-painted obscenities on the sidewalk in front of my home. They slashed the tires on my bike. And, worst of all, they told the entire junior high school that I was a queer. Kids are so cruel, and it got so that I couldn't walk down the hall without people taunting me: 'Hey, Elliot, how about a blow job? Hey, Elliot, look at your homo lips. Hey, Elliot, let's see your hairy palms.' '' He shook his head, raised his eyes to the heavens. ''I don't know why I didn't say anything. I don't know why I didn't tell anyone about the other guys I knew who'd had a same-sex experience—that Gary and Ron did it up in the treehouse at least twice, or that Chris and Joe and Pete all did it in a circle whenever there was a sleepover. But I didn't say a thing, I guess because . . . because I was afraid they were right, that I was a homo. And that's when I was sure my life was over. I didn't want to be different, that's all, but I knew I was and I knew there was only one way out— death. That's when I did this, when I cut myself.''

Elliot again pushed back his sleeves, exposing the scars of that time. Staring at the grievous marks, he started to rub them, the thin ridges of skin that time had healed but never would erase.

''I did it in the bathroom with a razor, but of course Mom found me and called an ambulance. And then eventually it all came out—I couldn't hide it. I got sent to the nut house, and the shrink asked me so I told him, and he told my parents. Of course, they nearly killed me. Their boy a homo? Oh, God, it was awful, I mean we're talking thirty years ago in Omaha. I wouldn't go back to the same school, and so my father sent me to his brother's in Rockford, Illinois, which was actually worse. I was supposed to finish high school there, but I stayed only a week, and then I ran away to Minneapolis. I started washing dishes in a restaurant and . . .''

Elliot started crying. Not much. Just a few large tears. He turned his head aside, wiped his face with the back of one hand, and stared off at something no one else could see. So this, Rawlins understood, was the deciding event in Elliot's world. This was what had driven him—driven him deep into the gay community, driven him into his passion for painting, and driven him to the point of doing something like this abduction.

''I was quiet then, but I won't be now!'' Elliot wiped his eyes and breathed in deeply. ''Ever since then I've hated straight people . . . straight people like you, Johnny Clariton! I hate you

for backing the Defense of Marriage Act, because homosexuals are the last thing causing bad heterosexual marriages! I hate you for being against gays in the military, because as long as gays are marginalized we'll never have a truly quote-unquote normal life! And I hate you for calling AIDS a gay disease and wanting to cut research funding and medical assistance, because . . . because I'm dying and nothing can save me!'' concluded Elliot, lookin straight into the camera, his voice full of anger. ''And that's wh I'd do this again, kidnap someone and infect him with HIV yep, he'll be infected by the time we're through—because there's anyone in this world that deserves AIDS, it's Congr man Johnny Clariton.''

As Elliot pushed himself to his feet and stormed out o room, as Matthew switched off the video camera and s cackling, as Clariton pulled up his knees and bowed his against his legs, Rawlins understood. Hearing Elliot's sto like drinking a huge cup of sobering coffee. Yes, today had been panicked, fearful, furious, dejected, suicidal. Rawlins realized that that would eventually pass, for as as he was about what lay ahead, as horrified as he w having contracted HIV, he wouldn't end up like them, or Matthew. No, he was quite different in one simpl profound way: The anger and fury that was theirs wou his.

of some sort attached to her left arm. Her eyes were shut, her blond hair pulled back, her head wrapped with a large white bandage. Todd had never seen anyone so pale.

Going up to the edge of the metal bed, Todd called gently, "Cindy? It's me, Todd Mills. Cindy?"

His former coworker, Channel 7's Cindy Wilson, didn't flinch, and Todd stood there, one hand on the metal railing of the bed. Of course he shouldn't have come.

"Cindy?" he called one last time.

He'd heard that she'd been awake earlier and that she'd answered some questions for the police, but perhaps she'd been given a sedative for the night. He was about to turn away when he saw her eyes flutter and her head move to the side.

"Cindy, it's me, Todd Mills. Can you talk for a minute?"

She gazed up at him. "Todd?"

"Yeah, that's right." He touched her gently on the arm. "How're you feeling? They say you're going to be just fine."

"My head feels like shit."

"I bet it does."

"You . . . you okay? They . . . they didn't hurt you?"

"No, I'm fine. So is everyone else," replied Todd, referring to the others who'd been tied up. "Everyone, of course, except Clariton. And who knows what's happened to him."

"Oh." She closed her eyes. "The FBI was here."

"I know."

"They're such nerds."

Todd smiled. "They can be."

Her eyes slowly went over him. "No flowers, no candy. What is it?" She knew Todd had never cared for her, particularly after what Channel 7 had done to him, and she leveled her eyes on him. "What do you want?"

"Okay, I'm sorry, this isn't a candy-striper visit. I'm wondering if you can help me."

"Great. I'm tied up in the hospital with a fractured skull," she said, her voice faint. "You're out there with the hottest story of the decade, and—let me guess—you want me to help you look brilliant. Well, some things never change, do they?" Her head moved slightly from side to side. "Sorry, Todd, you can take a flying leap. Visiting hours were over a long time ago. Good night. I've got to get some rest—Roger wants me to do a report tomorrow.''

"Cindy, this isn't for WLAK."

"Right, and my name's Barbara Walters."

"Listen, this is strictly personal. I promise it's not for work." He leaned slightly closer and added, "After the way you came after me at Channel Seven last fall, you owe me."

"I was just doing . . . doing my job."

"With a vengeance?"

"What, am I supposed to feel bad because you deceived all of us at the station?"

"Come on, you and Roger worked pretty damn hard at screwing me over, and you know it."

She sighed. "What do you want?"

He reached into his coat pocket and took out the photo he'd found at Rawlins's place. "I want you to look at this and tell me if one of these guys looks familiar."

"I'm a fool to help you." She took a deep breath. "Turn on that light over there."

Rather than illuminating the surgically bright overhead light, Todd turned on a standing lamp. He then leaned over the bed, holding the picture of Curt and the other man seated on the log. Cindy reached up with her right hand, took the photo, and held it close to her eyes.

"You promise me this isn't for Channel Ten, that it's not going to be broadcast all over the world?" she asked.

"I swear."

"Swear harder."

"I promise, Cindy, that I won't use this for a report. It really is strictly for personal use."

"Have I ever told you you were a pain in the ass to work for?"

"Sorry."

"You hogged all the stories."

"I've changed."

"Yeah, right, and *Sixty Minutes* just offered me a job." She moved her thumb so that it rested right on one guy in the picture.

"That one. That's the guy, their leader. His head isn't shaved in the picture, but it was today." She shuddered. "That's him, the one that hit me."

"That's what I was afraid of," said Todd, taking back the photo. "Do you know his name?"

"Like I told the police this evening, the woman screamed at him right before he clubbed me. She shouted out his name."

"Which was?"

"Matthew."

Exactly, thought Todd, now remembering.

Cindy asked, "Do you know him from somewhere?"

"Not really. He's a friend of a friend."

Todd stared at the picture that Rawlins had taken, zeroing in on the image of that one guy, who stood there with one arm thrown over Curt's shoulders. But who was he really? Or more important, how well did Rawlins know him?

Oh, Christ, thought Todd. Was Rawlins involved in more of this . . . or all of it?

"Todd, what's going on?"

"I don't know." He reached down, touched her on the arm. "But I'm glad you're okay."

"Bullshit. You're glad I'm stuck here in the hospital so that you can have the entire story to yourself."

"I'm beginning to wish I didn't."

"Roger was in here earlier, and he told me you were on the evening news with Dan Rather. And let me tell you, Roger just about had a coronary."

"Great." Todd smiled and said, "Now, get some rest."

"Right."

He crossed the room, turned off the standing light, and Cindy and her world sank back into the bluish night-light. He started toward the door, then stopped.

"Cindy, there's just one other thing."

Or didn't it matter? At this point in his life did it really make a difference who had talked to Clariton about Todd's sexuality?

Cindy, her blond hair and pale skin blending into the white pillow, rolled her head toward him. "What?"

"Nothing," he said, catching himself, for it was time once and for all to leave that baggage behind. "Take care of yourself."

"I will, but, Todd, be forewarned that I'm down but not out."

"Good. I'm glad."

29

The same silver Chrysler that had followed Todd Mills and the limousine earlier this evening was once again parked in front of Todd's condominium building. It was 3:14 A.M. The parkway was quiet, the night chilly, and the two men in the vehicle had been waiting for over an hour. Almost anyone else would have found this kind of work—sitting there waiting for someone, anyone, to return home—excruciatingly boring, but the guys in the Chrysler were professionals. They'd sit there until sunrise if need be.

Finally spotting a car with its turn signal blinking, the large man in the passenger seat perked up and said, "Here we are, the last person home."

"Right," replied the bald man behind the steering wheel. "It won't get any better than this."

"I'll be back in ten minutes."

The large man grabbed the device—a small thing about the size of a matchbox—from the seat, opened the passenger door, then quickly made his way down the sidewalk. He was a nice-enough looking man, gray suit, white shirt, unremarkable tie, and had anyone noticed him hurrying along they wouldn't have suspected a thing. Even in the middle of the night he didn't look like a thug, and he turned up the drive and walked briskly past the building's entry. Inside, behind a glass window, he caught a glimpse of the guard, a young man with his head tilted against the wall and his eyes closed in dreamy sleep.

The driveway to the second-floor garage arched up a hill and curved to the left, and the man burst into a run when he saw the car's taillights disappear into the building. The garage door was halfway down by the time he reached the rear of the structure, yet there was still enough room for him to duck inside. Bending over, he slipped in, then positioned himself behind a concrete column. Somewhere up ahead he heard a car engine turn off, a door open, the sounds of two people gabbing and giggling as they shuffled along. Then a door opening and closing. And silence.

Emerging from the shadows, the man started walking up the center of the garage, a cold gray space that stretched around and up several floors. It wasn't hard at all, of course, to find the vehicle Todd Mills had borrowed, for the blue Ford Explorer was clearly and boldly emblazoned with the words WLAK TV, YOUR EYE ON THE WORLD! It was parked about fifteen cars up on the right side, and he went directly toward it. He tried the driver's door, but it was locked, just as he'd expected, which actually didn't make a bit of difference. He returned to the rear of the Explorer, glanced up and down the garage, then bent over. Checking the device one last time, the man reached behind the bumper and slapped the small electronic item into position. It took all of about five seconds.

Standing up, the man wiped his hands, straightened his suit and unremarkable tie. No sense in sneaking out the way he'd come. Nope, he thought, looking to his right and spotting the exit. And so he proceeded through the garage, down a flight of stairs, and right into the nicely appointed lobby with its soft sofas and professionally maintained palms, not to mention the large wall sculpture, the one that was supposed to look like sailboats on one of the city lakes.

Approaching the front door, he passed the glass-enclosed guard's room, where the young man in the red uniform continued to snooze.

"Hey, hey, buddy!" called the man, laughing as he rapped on the window. "No sleeping on the job!"

"Wh-what?" replied the young guard, nearly jumping to his feet. "No, I'm awake!"

"Got to keep an eye out for all the criminals!"

"Yes, sir. Oh, yes!"

Grinning, the well-dressed man proceeded through the glass

doors into the night. A huge yawn swelled inside him and he put a hand to his mouth. Today had had its difficult moments, no doubt there, but the little surprise he'd left behind for Todd Mills should make things substantially easier tomorrow.

30

Todd couldn't sleep even though exhaustion had bowled him over. Lying on his bed, a down comforter pulled over him, he stared at the tape on his bedside table—he'd given the original to the FBI and brought home the copy just to make sure WLAK didn't bump him from the story—and one thought kept crashing over and over again in his mind: What the hell was Rawlins doing? With the exception of the puzzling words Rawlins had written on the envelope, Todd hadn't heard a thing. And it was like torture. This was the first night in months that he wasn't either with Rawlins or aware of his exact whereabouts, and Todd's thoughts ricocheted against every possibility, including of course that this was all a setup, that Rawlins had in fact been involved in Clariton's kidnapping, and that Todd and his interview with Clariton were a mere convenience for a devious plan. It was a horrible thought that didn't make much sense, he realized. But then what did? Certainly not Rawlins's fury and his assertion that he had AIDS. Shit, cursed Todd, flipping over as he recalled the sight of Rawlins ready to jump from the balcony. If the worst was really true, if Rawlins was sick, then Rawlins was absolutely right. There was every chance that Todd himself could be HIV positive, and Rawlins's words—"I'd get myself tested"—echoed like a horrible threat in Todd's mind. Could he himself be sick? He felt perfectly healthy, had displayed no troublesome sign such as Rawlins's chronic sinus infection. Nor could he remember any strong bout of the flu or coming down with an extremely high temperature, as many people reported after their initial infection.

But, shit, he could be HIV positive.

Okay, there was a chance that it no longer meant a death sentence, and so maybe he was lucky in that regard, that if he *had* contracted the HIV virus he was fortunate not only that he had done so this late in the epidemic, but that he was in the United States, where the new drugs were more or less available. Maybe, too, medical science had actually corralled AIDS into a category of chronic but manageable diseases. But who really knew how the disease would mutate over the next few years in reaction to the new drugs? And who wanted to live a life taking ten, twenty, thirty pills a day anyway?

Oh, shit. He was sick of this. Sick of being gay. Sick of having his life defined by a sexual act, when to him being gay meant every bit as much who he wanted to have breakfast with in the morning. It was just too big, all of this crap. So many issues, one after the other. He was so exhausted by the process of coming out, which seemed to go on and on, over and over, every day of his life. He'd thought coming out would be just one enormous moment when you crossed some line, something that you did and took care of once and for all. But no, instead, coming out kept happening in little but significant ways every day of his life, every time he read an article about someone like Johnny Clariton and told someone he was incensed, every time he touched Rawlins in a public place and some straight couple cast a judgmental eye, every time some salesperson called for Mrs. Mills asking if she wanted her carpet cleaned and Todd, who used to just hang up, now said, no, there was no Mrs. Mills, only his boyfriend, Steve, would they like to talk to him? Shit. He wished he'd just stayed in the closet so he wouldn't have to deal with all this crap. But could he have? No, actually, that hadn't been an option. Notwithstanding how it had actually come to pass, if he had managed to remain closeted he probably would have self-imploded out of sheer stress.

Yet the idea, the very suggestion, that he might have to deal with another often-called ''gay issue,'' that of being sero-positive, made him want to jump out of his skin. As he tossed, Todd saw images of Curt. Oh, Christ, was that the fate of every gay man, to be eaten alive by some virus?

Stop it!

He rolled over, punched his pillow. At the very least, you jerk, you have to deal with Rawlins. You love him and you have to be there for him. And you have to be there for him in all the right ways. There's no choice.

Just take a deep breath. Relax.

What is it, he asked himself, that you like about being gay? Not simply the company and touch of men, not the conversation and camaraderie. No, something more profound. What he liked about gay people was exactly what he pitied so many straight people for missing. The honesty, thought Todd. Everything in this world was set up for heterosexuals—all the ceremonies, all the major events of life—which meant that if you were, indeed, straight you didn't even have to think about who you were, where you were going, what you really wanted. But if you were gay you were forced by your very nature to see that there were many layers of many truths beyond the surface of what was presented. And as difficult as the self-search might be, that realization and the personal accounting it always entailed brought a wisdom well beyond one's years. It was something straight people—straight white people in particular—didn't automatically experience and learn, not unless there was a tragic death in the family, a struggle over substance abuse, divorce, or some kind of crisis that split open the crust of the earth. As a matter of fact, thought Todd, it was those straight people—those who could see beyond the superficial markers—who were not only Todd's friends, but the people he truly admired and respected.

Enough. You need, he told himself, to get even the slightest bit of sleep. If you're going to be worth anything to anyone tomorrow you have to doze off for at least a few hours. He got up and poured himself a juice glass full of scotch, which he slammed down. He filled the glass again, downed that, and felt the burning liquid whirl down his throat and into his gut. Returning in the dark to his bedroom, he found a black heap of fur curled up at the end of the bed.

"Hey, Girlfriend," Todd called gently to the black cat.

Before today she wouldn't even come close to Todd, let alone beg for attention as she had done earlier this evening. Nor had she ever spent the night in Todd's room. Yet here was Curt's cat snuggled atop his comforter for the night. Taking refuge from thinking about the unthinkable by tuning in to her needs, he moved quietly across his room and slipped back into bed. Todd forced himself to lie quite still and found himself wondering exactly what Girlfriend, the silent witness, had seen that night Curt had died. He wondered because, of course, what had happened a month ago had just come up again this morning. A witness had reported seeing someone slip into Curt's building, Rawlins had told Todd over the phone. So that proved, didn't it, that Curt's death had been either murder or assisted suicide? Sure, Todd had agreed, hoping it was the second, because that at least made some kind of sense.

Todd's alarm started screeching just before five-thirty, and he rolled over, smashed the OFF button, then grabbed the remote. As he switched on the small color TV that sat on his dresser, he was surprised to look over and see Girlfriend still nestled on his bed. Small miracles, he mused, and lying there he watched as the familiar logo and background music of Channel 10's *DayBreaking News* began to roll. A moment later the camera focused on a desk where the early-morning anchor, an attractive woman with short brown hair, was seated.

"Good morning, this is *DayBreaking News*," she began. "I'm Caroline Roberts, and WLAK's coverage of the kidnapping of Congressman Johnny Clariton continues. It's been almost seventeen hours since Congressman Clariton was abducted by three self-described AIDS activists just after a luncheon with Twin Cities executives. The unprecedented incident has shocked the nation, and at this hour Clariton's whereabouts and safety remain unknown to authorities."

So nothing of significance had happened overnight, thought Todd, propping a pillow behind his head. But was the airing of the videotape still on schedule for this morning?

As if answering Todd, Caroline said, "Last night, however, WLAK's own Emmy Award–winning reporter, Todd Mills, discovered a videotape allegedly made by Clariton's kidnappers showing Congressman Clariton in their custody. Broadcast of this tape, which has been described as shocking, is set for nine o'clock this morning here on WLAK TV. That broadcast will be carried live nationally, and I'm sure that our viewers will want to tune in both to hear Todd's report as well as watch this most unusual footage.

"In Washington yesterday afternoon the President, who has been described as outraged over the incident, ordered the FBI to begin a full-scale manhunt."

The program cut to a repeat and summary of the President's statement, then switched to a reporter who used a computerized three-dimensional map to walk viewers through the scene of the crime. Moments later yet another reporter showed taped footage of the mayhem that had followed the kidnapping, including Todd's first live report. The staff, Todd now thought as he watched all this, must have been up the entire night in order to put the footage and graphics together. That actually wasn't that surprising, and he jumped out of bed and ran a hand over Girlfriend. He proceeded to the kitchen, where he got his coffee maker going, then headed for the bathroom and a hot, hot shower. Thirty minutes later he'd eaten some yogurt, fed the cat, put on a sport coat and tie, and was heading out the door with a cup of coffee in his hand. Traffic at that hour was light, and, driving Channel 10's Ford Explorer, Todd made it to the station in record time.

Less than an hour after he'd risen, Todd hurried through the newsroom, pausing only to grab a mug of coffee, and then proceeded to his office. Sometime during the night the janitor had come in, vacuumed, emptied the trash, and raised the miniblinds on the glass wall overlooking the newsroom. Todd set down his coffee and now lowered the blinds once again. By habit he hit a couple of keys on his computer, which brought the color monitor from overnight hibernation. A series of messages filled the screen, none of them important except the last couple from the morning producer, confirming that Todd still had the green light and that the FBI concurred that the tape should be shown this morning. Todd had, he inquired, remembered to bring the tape this morning, hadn't he?

Todd shook his head. What did they take him for around here, he wondered as he turned to his phone and checked his voice

mail, the village idiot? Of course he had the goddamn tape. He'd
clutched it, slept with it, not let it out of his possession.

On the phone there were six messages: four from fans who
had called to express how glad they were that Todd hadn't been
hurt when Clariton was taken, the other two from friends. But
again nothing from Rawlins.

Shaking his head, Todd turned to the small bank of video
equipment at the end of his office and inserted the copy of the
kidnappers' tape into the VCR. He plugged in a set of earphones,
slipped them on his head, and punched PLAY. As the tape began to
roll, Todd grabbed a pen and a yellow legal pad. How the hell
was he going to come at this thing? What would his intro be, how
much should he and could he say? While nine times out of ten
the angle of any story and just what was said were left to the
reporter, given the circumstances Todd wouldn't be surprised if
the producer—as well, of course, as the station manager—were
all over this one. And he was certain that the FBI was going to
want Todd to slip in something that would have significance to
the kidnappers, who would surely be watching. There was one
thing that Todd was certain of though: He didn't want this to get
personal. So far no one knew about Rawlins's scribbled note on
the envelope, and for now he was going to keep it that way. Nor
would he reveal on camera that he'd found the tape in his car.
No, if anyone—namely the other stations in town, specifically
Channel 7—found out about any of that they'd do their damnedest to turn it into some sort of story, perhaps accusing Todd of
involvement. Who knew, in an attempt to spice up their own
coverage, they might even dredge up Michael's murder again. So
how would Todd put it this morning, merely that he'd obtained
the videotape? Could he simply leave it at that? Sure. Better yet,
perhaps he should even hint that he'd worked his investigative
skills to get the tape.

Hell, he thought. What difference did it make?

He watched the whole tape, hit REWIND, then viewed it a second
time. He focused on Clariton's face, studied his comments and
words. No doubt about it, the congressman was frightened. No,
he didn't think they should show the last bit, Clariton's panicked
reaction, his screaming, and his desperate kicking. They should

stay focused on satisfying the kidnappers, whose primary goal was undoubtedly to show the world Tina's story. So maybe they'd end the footage with the woman pulling out the blood-filled needle. At that point they could cut to Todd, who'd then explain the rest. At least that would be Todd's recommendation.

Or would it?

Watching the tape a third and fourth time he realized it might be all wrong to sanitize the thing and put his own spin on it. After all, where did his allegiance really lie? Perhaps it was better to let the world see the raw terror of AIDS. Tina's story, her pain, her indignation, her frustration, and, finally, her hate. And Clariton's total lack of compassion, his cockiness, his assured righteousness, and, finally, his pathetic fear.

Todd halted the tape, bowed his head into his palms. God only knew what lay ahead for Rawlins and him. Perhaps hope. Perhaps disaster.

He shook his head, took a large gulp of coffee, rewound the tape, and watched it once again from the beginning. Beyond what had been said and done in that little room, there was one thing that Todd kept tripping up on—that odd humming noise that kept repeating itself through the course of Tina's story. Just why in the hell did it sound so familiar? He'd heard it somewhere before, hadn't he? He was sure he had. But where? Could it really be as simple as the sound of jets approaching the Minneapolis/St. Paul International Airport?

This time he ignored Tina's story, Clariton's remarks, and all that happened. Instead, he put his hands on the earphones, closed his eyes, and focused on that sound. There it was the first time. There the second. Right, and a third. And finally a fourth. During the course of the videotape the sound repeated itself a total of four times. It actually could be jets. They came roaring out of the sky that regularly, didn't they? And if so, that meant they could be holding Clariton either in a hangar or perhaps in a house abutting the airport. Sure, that was possible. Just off the northwest edge of the runways was a postwar development of tiny houses now slated for demolition because the noise of the jumbo jets was so severe. Could Clariton be tied up in a basement out there?

No, something wasn't right here. Todd concentrated on the noise. It was kind of jetlike, but not really. No huge roaring thrust, no explosion of power as a huge metal thing tried to force itself into the air. Each of the sounds on the tape was identical too, which didn't make a whole lot of sense. If those were jets he was hearing, wouldn't the noise vary from plane to plane, 727 to 747? He rewound the tape, played it all over yet again. Todd pulled back his sleeve, stared at his watch. The noise cycled on and off with computerized regularity every three minutes and thirteen seconds.

What?

Todd hit the STOP button, ripped the headphones from his ears. No, it couldn't be, he thought with a jolt.

There was an abrupt banging on his glass door, the miniblinds rattled, and the morning producer, a young guy with curly hair, black glasses, and a permanent smile, burst into Todd's office.

"The station manager's here," said Craig, who'd become a producer most likely because he had the unique ability to always be cheery, no matter how tense the situation. "So are the assignment editor and the other two producers."

Knowing it would come to this—that they would try to meddle—Todd turned around and snapped, "Give me a couple of minutes!"

"Oh, no, Todd. Right now. Very right now. You see, all of my bosses are here, as are my bosses' bosses."

"I'm busy!"

"My dear Mr. Mills, the FBI's here too. And everyone wants to know exactly how we're going to handle this—or more specifically, exactly what you're going to say at nine o'clock."

"Shit."

"Don't worry," continued Craig as he kept on smiling, "I've got a draft of something written up. They're all waiting for you down in the conference room. Let's go, Todd. Like now. Like really, absolutely right now."

He took a deep breath, grabbed the tape from the VCR, and pushed himself to his feet. No, he wasn't sure, not just yet. It could be a coincidence, a weird one at that, so he wouldn't say anything to anyone here at the station or to the FBI without first checking something else. But a roar every three minutes and thirteen seconds could only mean they'd taken Clariton to one place, couldn't it?

31

Elliot wasn't sure why he woke up so early. It was either his battery of meds, which, if they hadn't been doing anything else for the past few weeks, were certainly making him, well, perky. Or the fact that he'd never liked sleeping bags—too confining, you had to sleep all zipped up and everything like a mummy. Or that Tina's body was beginning to stink. They'd wrapped more plastic around her, dragged the corpse into the bathroom, and left the fan going, but it wasn't enough. Tina was in the air, no doubt about it.

Whatever the reason, Elliot's eyes had popped open some ten minutes ago and refused to close. He peered around without so much as flinching and saw that Matthew was fast asleep and probably would be for hours, given the number of pills he'd swallowed last night. Undoubtedly he was exhausted after yesterday, all that running around, all that stress of having to deal with Clariton, not to mention Tina croaking and everything. Oh, and the videotaping had been no easy feat either! Just imagine, Elliot thought with a giggle, sometime soon his story would be broadcast everywhere, all over the entire country!

As for Rawlins and Clariton, they were both locked tight in the next room.

"Sorry, pal," Matthew had told Rawlins last night, "but I think it's best if you sleep in here with Mr. Congressman. We just want to make sure you don't slip out in the middle of the night."

Elliot now sat up, rubbed his eyes, and scanned the room. No doubt about it, he had to get out of here, just for a bit. Some fresh air. A change of scenery. This was way too intense down here in this bomb shelter of a joint.

"Psst," he whispered. "Psst, Matthew?"

On the other side of the room Matthew slept like the dead. When Elliot called out a second time and Matthew again failed to budge, Elliot stared at him. Okay, okay, so his chest was rising and falling, so he was still breathing. Thank the Lord, at least Matthew hadn't kicked the bucket too. Wouldn't that be the pits if the two of them, Tina and Matthew, checked out and left Elliot to wrap up this mess?

"Matthew," whispered Elliot to the sleeping man, "I'm going to just step out for a bit. I need to get out. I need some fresh air. Tina, you know, is a little thick in the air, if you get what I mean. I'll be back in twenty minutes. Okay, huh? Okay?" Elliot smiled. "Great. Yeah, I'll be okay. Yes, I'll be careful. No, don't worry, I'll be back long before they broadcast the videotape of Tina and Clariton. Love ya."

He unzipped his sleeping bag, pulled his long, slinky frame to his feet, and stretched. Glancing at the box of food, he thought about grabbing something, a Twinkie perhaps. No. He'd go up top, get some juice, a muffin maybe. Something healthy for breakfast. Yeah, he really needed to get out. Matthew, after all, got to escape for a while yesterday, leaving Elliot to deal with poor Tina. It really was too much, doing all this, playing the bad guys. It just took far too much energy, energy that none of them could spare. His own T-cell count, after all, had slipped to almost zilch months ago—and was probably now on empty.

Elliot slipped on his shoes, ran his hands over his short, bristly hair, then made his way to the door. He turned around one last time, noted that Matthew's mouth had opened a bit. Poor guy. He could probably sleep for another six hours, but that wouldn't do. No, Elliot would come back and then wake him up in plenty of time to watch the broadcast of Tina and Clariton on Channel 10.

"Ta-ta," Elliot called softly.

Elliot closed the door behind him and took a big gulp of air. Yes, much, much better, he thought, peering around the large empty space. But he didn't want to just pace around out here, staring at metal studs and drywall. No, he wanted windows. He wanted daylight. He wanted to step outside and breathe real air, not something that had been circulated down here.

Plus he wanted a muffin, a lemon poppy-seed one. Yep. That was what he was craving, and he really couldn't deny himself anything because, God knew, the big clock was ticking away. He'd get some juice too. Fresh-squeezed orange juice made from real Florida oranges. He knew a place that promised just such a thing. And you know what, he mused as he headed for the staircase, he should get some flowers for Tina. She'd like that. Some sweet petals sprinkled over the Hefty two-plies in which she was presently encased. Lots of flowers, actually. Forsythia. No, something big. Something like sunflowers. And giant daisies. Anything big and bright. That would be cool, he thought with a bit of a smile. Yeah, sure it was a real bummer Tina checked out, but she was with her daughter now. She and little Chris were together. So Elliot should be happy. Maybe he and Matthew should have a little celebration and rejoice now that Tina's suffering was over.

With a grin he started bounding up the steps, then quickly caught himself. No, he chided himself. Not so fast. You have to take it slow. You run up these three flights, you Bozo, and you're going to exhaust yourself right at the beginning of the day. Take it easy. Take it slow. Take it literally one step at a time. You don't want to have to go back to bed for a couple of hours, do you? Well? No way.

Muffin. Juice. Flowers. This little shopping spree would be fun. But then he touched his rear pocket and froze on the steps. Uh-oh, no wallet. He nervously jammed a hand into his front pocket, found two crinkled and wadded-up dollar bills and some small change. Hmm. Now what? Go back and wake up Matthew? Nope. Elliot wasn't a fool. He knew Matthew wouldn't approve of this.

Oh, well, he thought, pressing on. A couple of bucks wouldn't get him very far, but it was a start. He'd just have to scan—*I am the Scanman!*—and keep his eyes open for opportunities. After all, when he was a stupid little kid he used to shoplift all the time, and he was ever so much wiser now, wasn't he?

32

It wasn't clear to Todd who won in the end—the station manager, the FBI, or maybe even him. At first Cochran, the FBI guy, proposed that they skip the beginning of the videotape, including Clariton's cold remarks, and just air part of Tina's story, then cut off before the struggle broke out. Todd flatly refused.

"That's bullshit," Todd insisted to the eight people gathered in the conference room. "This morning I was worrying about sanitizing this goddamn story, but that's taking it and dipping it in a hundred percent bleach. In fact, I don't think you should edit this thing at all. I think we have to let the tape speak for itself. But if that's what you want to do, if you want to cut it way down, then I'm out of here. You're going to have to use the tape I gave to the FBI, because I'm going to take my copy and sell it to some other station."

"Come on, Todd, calm down," pleaded Craig, who looked stressed for the first time Todd could remember. "You're just tired."

"No shit I'm tired, but you can't cut out what Clariton says." Knowing how to play their game, he added, "I'll tell you one thing: Nothing is going to make a bunch of AIDS activists more pissed off than if you cut out what the most homophobic politician in the country has to say, especially because it shows him to be a real ass. And if you piss them off who knows what they'll do, either kill Clariton outright or possibly attack someone else, which is a very real possibility. After all, they're dying, all three of them. They have nothing to lose."

A lot of heads went up and down with that, including that of

Dr. Ogden, the chief negotiator, who said, "He has a very valid point."

"Of course I do," replied Todd.

So in the end nothing was cut from the beginning and the end was only slightly trimmed.

"We have to stop it there," insisted Harlan Benson, the station manager, a trim man with a shock of silver hair. "We simply can't show anything that graphic, particularly not at nine o'clock in the morning. If those terrorists have a problem with that, then we'll deal with it later on."

Todd was then informed that Channel 10's morning anchor, Tom Rivers, would introduce Todd, who in turn would intro the tape. It was quite possible, the station manager also said, that CNN or Dan Rather would want to do a live interview with Todd as well, so Todd should be prepared for that. After all, as far as the media—both local and national—were concerned, this was the only story.

"Absolutely," replied Todd, dreading the idea of having to play the talking head on this one.

The meeting was soon adjourned, and a few minutes before nine Todd found himself in Studio A, seated at one end of the large newsdesk. The coverage of the abduction of Congressman Clariton had been almost nonstop, and all morning promos had been running, claiming that WLAK was about to air a major development. Todd's interview last night with Dan Rather, so widely watched across the country, would pale in comparison to the viewership he would have this morning; without a doubt it would be repeated on *CNN Headline News* throughout the day. Glancing across the studio—a huge two-story space also filled with both a weather and a casual talk-show set, as well as a Milky Way of spotlights hanging from the rafters—Todd saw one of the robotic cameras gliding across the floor toward him. The camera slowed to a gentle stop and the lens automatically extended, then retreated like the eye of a *Star Wars* creature taking careful aim. Controlled by a distant technician's touch on a computer screen, the short tower of metal and plastic then inched to the right.

"Okay, looks good," came the producer's voice via the IFB

transmission and the earpiece discreetly lodged in Todd's right ear.

Craig, the producer, was unseen, hidden in the glass-walled control booth, and Todd stared into the camera with a pressing question: "Is my tie straight?"

"Perfect," cooed the voice through the earpiece.

Nevertheless, Todd straightened his blue tie one last time, smoothed his dark sport coat. His stomach was locked in a hard knot, and he realized that he should have eaten something more substantial this morning and drunk half as much coffee. Sweat dampened his armpits, and he reached up and touched his fore-head. No, at least he wasn't visibly blistering with perspiration. Not yet anyway.

Craig had written the first draft of the script Todd would read, and all the big guns had gone over it. Todd, all three FBI men, the station manager, and of course Channel 10's corporate law-yer had all made comments. And while the resulting story wasn't exactly Todd's angle, he knew that he'd be able to make his opinions more clearly and forcefully known in the Q&A that would follow the tape.

"Todd, we're thirty seconds from Tom Rivers," came Craig's godly voice in the earpiece.

Todd looked over at Tom, a tall, dapper man with thick, dark hair who was quite possibly the most arrogant man on the face of this earth. As Rivers took his position on the other end of the newsdesk, Todd offered a small, friendly wave, then glanced down at the legal pad and his notes of what he might later say. Be objective, Todd thought to himself. Be clear. And keep it simple. Yes, that was the key. If nothing else the kidnappers' desperation would speak for itself, just as Clariton's words would paint him the obvious, even logical target of such desperation.

The floor director took his place behind the robotic camera aimed at Rivers.

And then came the IFB transmission of the distant news direc-tor. "Okay, guys, here we go. And the countdown is: three, two, one, live."

The red light atop the camera that was focused on Tom started burning, the floor director pointed at Tom, and Tom said, "Good morning, this is Tom Rivers, and we continue our coverage with a special bulletin on the fate of Congressman Johnny Clariton, who was abducted at gunpoint yesterday just after one P.M. in downtown Minneapolis. Here to tell us more is WLAK's investigative reporter, Todd Mills, who has been at the forefront of this shocking case."

The floor director stepped over to the other camera and pointed to Todd just as the red light started glowing.

"Good morning, Tom." Staring at the TelePrompTer, Todd read, "The last twenty hours have been filled with a series of dramatic events, not the least of which we are about to broadcast."

Following the script, Todd recapped the entire story, describing the scene at the restaurant, how the President had ordered the attorney general to handle the matter with the utmost urgency, and that he had discovered a videotape of Clariton.

Todd then said, "According to the demands of the kidnappers and under the advice and approval of the Federal Bureau of Investigation, WLAK TV will now air this tape."

The director cued the videotape, and Todd watched it in the monitor for the umpteenth time. He didn't really see it, though. Instead, his mind wandered to Rawlins and his involvement in all this. Yes, that had been his handwriting on the—

Oh, shit, he thought, panicking as the tape rolled, where was the envelope? He hadn't seen it this morning, so it must be up in his apartment, still hidden in the pocket of his other jacket. And unless he could figure this out within the next few hours, he was going to have to turn the envelope over to the FBI. Or was he already in trouble for withholding it—as well as the photograph of Matthew?

Todd suddenly realized that the tape was seconds away from the cutoff point. He looked back up at the TelePrompTer and waited for the floor director's cue.

"The remainder of the tape shows a struggle between Congressman Clariton and the woman and then abruptly concludes." He took a breath. "Beyond that, the authorities have learned nothing and have heard nothing further from Clariton's abductors. By airing this tape WLAK TV has met the demands of the abductors. And WLAK TV management would like our viewers to know that we will keep you up to the minute on this still-breaking story.'' Todd looked over to Rivers and said, ''Tom, the authorities are still baffled, and all I can say is that this has been a most disturbing series of events.''

Tom thanked Todd for his expert coverage, briefly recapped the events once again, and reminded the audience that Channel 10 would remain at the forefront of this unfolding tragedy, with updates given hourly throughout the day.

Starting the Q&A, Rivers turned to Todd, saying, ''So do you have any sense, Todd, of what the outcome of this incident may be?''

Here it was, Todd's chance to put his own spin on this whole thing. No, he couldn't clutch and he wouldn't. There was no script for this, everything was ad-lib. And he thought: Screw the FBI, screw the station manager, screw the producer; I can say whatever I want. Yet how could he put the right angle, the right view, on this? If they weren't watching now, sooner or later every queer person in Minnesota would hear and weigh Todd's words, and—Lyle Cuningham was right—gays were about as judgmental as they came, so Todd was really being set up. Hell, what Todd said now about Clariton's abduction by AIDS terrorists could very well set the tone across the entire country. Todd had already done so much wrong in his gay life, from the pain of his marriage and divorce from Karen, to his stunted relationship with Michael, to his going before the television camera so many thousands of times and pretending to be someone he was not. But just as he couldn't rectify that, neither could he now say the politically correct thing that would appease all gay, lesbian, bisexual, transgender, and sexually questioning people.

Instead, his honest, unfiltered opinion popped out, and Todd, knowing this would blow Rivers away, replied, ''Tom, I have no idea where this is going, but frankly I don't understand why something like this hadn't happened sooner.''

Tom Rivers couldn't hide his surprise, and he cocked his head. ''Really?''

''Don't forget it was only last month that a group of AIDS

activists in San Francisco doused Clariton with a bucket of blood.''

In Todd's earpiece the voice of Craig, the producer, shrieked, ''Jesus Christ, Todd, watch what you're saying!''

''Yes, but—''

''Tom,'' continued Todd, knowing he was being much too blunt for TV, ''we're over fifteen years into this epidemic. Nearly a million Americans—men and women of every race and every sexual orientation—have been infected with HIV, and while the media are suggesting that it's over, there are only enough new drugs for one hundred thousand people. Everyone's frustrated. Clariton's abduction is merely a reflection of the anger around this frustration.''

''But surely you don't think these so-called AIDS activists are justified in their actions? Not only have they kidnapped a government official, but they're threatening to infect him with a deadly virus.''

Like a desperate god whispering in his ear, Craig pleaded, ''Couch it, Todd! Couch it! Please, you're sounding like one of them!''

It drove him nuts, the way producers yakked in their ears while they were on air, bossing them this way and that and expecting them to make any sense, yet he forced the squealing Craig out of his mind and said, ''Let me say this clearly and unequivocally: I don't by any means condone this type of terrorist activity. For that matter, I'm sure that every AIDS organization across the country will condemn the use of HIV as a weapon. However, two things are important to note here. First of all, as the abductors themselves have pointed out, on a global basis AIDS has infected and killed over ten times more straight people than gay. Second, Congressman Clariton has irritated a huge number of people, straight and gay, by misquoting facts and using people's fear of AIDS for his own political gain. These two things, in my opinion, were almost destined to collide. They're both so highly charged emotionally that I think a conflict like this was unavoidable.''

Rivers shifted in his anchor seat, clearly not sure what to say or where to lead the conversation, and he cocked an eyebrow and threw a curveball. "Todd, you've publicly acknowledged your own homosexuality, is that correct?"

At first Todd tensed, then he hit it straight on, saying, "Absolutely. And as a gay man I have to say that the way AIDS is viewed in this country horrifies me. We're talking about a communicable disease—that's all. Congressman Clariton continually tries to turn it into some sort of test, of just what I'm not sure. As a case in point I should add that yesterday I personally found the congressman quite offensive."

Tom's eyebrow shot back up, and he asked, "Can you be more specific?"

"Actually, I have a videotape of my interview with him that will prove my point," he ventured, hoping that the tape was still nestled safely in his mailbox.

"Shit, Todd!" screeched Craig via the earpiece. "What tape? The FBI guys in here are going nuts!"

"However, I don't think it's appropriate to get into this until the congressman has been safely recovered."

"Yes, absolutely."

Craig ordered, "That's it, you're off, Todd!"

Todd looked into the dark studio, saw the floor director pointing at him and then drawing a finger across his throat. Todd nodded. Christ, thought Todd, what Pandora's box had he opened now?

Rivers explained that the heads of several AIDS organizations would be interviewed later in the morning, then, obviously given the word to close out Todd, turned and said, "Todd, I want to thank you very much for your help and your insights. I'm sure we'll be hearing more from you as this shocking case develops."

"Thank you, Tom."

The voice in his ear said, "Okay, you're clear, Todd. Get your butt in here!"

Todd looked at the camera focused on him, saw the red light go off, then pulled the earpiece from his ear and quietly slipped away from the newsdesk. With Rivers and the broadcast continuing behind him, Todd scurried through the studio and out the door. As soon as he was in the hall Craig came hurrying toward him.

"Todd, just tell me, are you nuts?" demanded the producer. "Those FBI guys are freaking! You have to talk to them—now!"

"My stomach's upset," he said, holding a hand to his waist. "I think I drank too much coffee."

"Nothing like a little stress, huh?"

"Just cover for me, will you? Tell them—"

"Yes, I see it now, you're certifiably crazy. What do you want me to do, tell them you've gone home to do your laundry?"

"Five minutes, that's all I need."

Turning away from him, Todd hurried down the bright hallway toward the men's room. As he reached the rest room he placed a hand on the door as if to push it open. Instead, however, he looked behind. Good, Craig had disappeared, the hall was empty. Before he was spotted, Todd turned and started jogging down the corridor, turning to the left, then right, and rushing all the way down to the other studio in search of a tape he'd filmed almost two months ago.

Not as large or as technically sophisticated, Studio B was used for special events, shows that required an audience, and a place to film promos. No one was in here, and Todd quickly passed through it and out a double door at the far end, where he entered the warehouse. Proceeding past standing lights, reels of electrical cords, and a variety of other equipment, Todd reached a small repair room built on one side of the large area. Inside, a single technician sat working on a camera that was lying in pieces on a table like an autopsied body.

"Listen . . ." began Todd, racking his mind for the guy's name.

"I'm Mark," volunteered the thin red-haired man.

"Right, Mark." Todd nodded toward a piece of equipment. "I need to find something in the archives. Can I use your computer for a second?"

Mark, a wire in one hand, a lens in the other, couldn't have cared less. "Sure."

Todd grabbed a stool and sat down at the computer, which was at one end of a long table littered with tools. Okay, what was the keyword? Right, he thought, recalling it and typing it in. And the date? He wasn't sure, not exactly, so he came up with a date parameter, a window of about three months. After typing all this in he hit ENTER, and a moment later the keyword popped up with six entries. Todd scrolled through and found the entry he was looking for. He punched that in, then had to enter the slug, the title of the story. So how had they filed it? What had they called the sequence? Sure. He took a stab, hitting the name the first time, and the script of the entire story came up on the screen. Yes, this was exactly it, just as he'd thought and hoped. But he didn't need this, not the words that were spoken. No, he needed the sounds that had cropped up in the background, and he grabbed a pen and wrote the number of the master tape in his left palm.

With the number of the tape literally in hand, Todd logged off, jumped to his feet, and said, "Thanks."

"No prob," replied Mark without even looking up from his dissection.

Todd dashed out of the repair room and cut across the warehouse to a metal staircase, where he grabbed the railing and started up the grid steps. The archives were all kept up here, boxes and boxes of the actual written scripts on the wall to the right and the tapes on rolling files to the left. Todd glanced at his hand, rolled two tall files aside, then moved down the narrow aisle. He had this fear that the tape wouldn't be there, that it would be like going into a library and finding every single issue of *Consumer Reports* except the one you were looking for, but there it was, sitting right in its place. Taking down the master tape, he next pulled the written menu out of the plastic case. Yes, this was it exactly. This was the story, running time and all.

Videotape in hand, Todd charged off, rushing down the metal steps, out of the warehouse and Studio B, and through the maze of halls, eager to return to his office to see if he could confirm his suspicions. As he passed through the newsroom, he heard Frank, the assignment editor, call out from the raised platform.

"Congratulations, Todd, we need to schedule you with Dan Rather!" the guy said with a smile. "His producer just called again!"

"Not now," snapped Todd, breezing past.

"What?" replied Frank with an incredulous and nervous laugh. "What do you mean, not now?"

"I'm busy."

"Are you crazy? God's messenger just called and—" When Todd failed to stop, the assignment editor yelled, "Todd! Todd, you fool, come back here! Craig's looking for you too!"

Todd ignored him and headed directly into his office, where he shut and locked the door. He jammed the videotape into the VCR, grabbed a chair, then pulled on the earphones. Okay, he thought as he fast-forwarded through a large part of the tape. He checked the numbers on the menu, watched the numbers on the tape fly by, then slowed it a bit. There. This shouldn't be too hard, not if his luck held out. Okay, he thought, his eye on his own figure as it quickly moved along. There he was in one part of the building, the photographer following him as he explored the structure. There he was going down into the heart of the building, down one flight, another, yet another. The camera then cut to Todd in a large underground space. He remembered it well, the Sheetrock walls, the metal studs. A blank space waiting for a miraculous transformation. Todd slowed the tape to normal speed and listened to himself gab about the structure, about how big it was, how many square feet it occupied, how much it had cost. Yes, hundreds of millions had been spent on the place, and millions had visited it and millions more would.

And then he heard it for the first time. He stopped the tape, reversed it, listened to the odd sound again, that dull roaring sound. No, not the roar of an engine, but the deep hum of rubber wheels. It wouldn't be on here a second time, he knew, because the tape wouldn't roll that long. But when he had been standing in that huge space where they were supposed to build the exhibit about the earth's core, Todd distinctly remembered the tour guide pointing that out. Yes, exactly every three minutes and thirteen seconds. Like clockwork. That was the sound of the roller coaster rattling the posts and beams some three floors above, so regular in its passage because the damn thing was completely computerized. Wasn't this place just a marvel? Everything, the transplanted Yugoslav guide had said with a big beaming Midwestern smile, was computerized in this wondrous place. The trash-hauling system, the ventilation, the security cameras, the lights. And even the roller coaster.

Oh, shit, thought Todd, he'd been right: They were holding Congressman Johnny Clariton in the subbasement of the Megamall.

Okay, even though it sounds horribly pedestrian, I want to confess. Before I die, before I do myself in, I want someone to know the truth. I can't help it, but before I leave this wretched life I have this urge to blurt it out: I killed Curt.

Why do you think that is?

Unfortunately that makes me seem not very special, for it throws me in the generic sinners' pot: Forgive me, Father, for I have fucked up. Maybe I'm afraid of what lies beyond and I just want a little extra insurance before I kick the bucket. You know, like maybe the Big Guy will let little old horrible me into heaven if I beg forgiveness.

On the other hand, maybe it's the only polite thing to do. There aren't many mysteries in the world one can actually solve, and just think how much I could simplify, how much confusion I could clarify by telling someone what I've done. I mean, just imagine how much time and energy and money have been wasted trying to figure out who really killed JFK. It's an entire fucking industry—a stupid one at that, if you ask me—and it could all come to a dramatic end if the real killer would only stand up and say: I done it.

Wait, no. I think I got it, I think I know why I feel such an overwhelming need to tell someone I poisoned Curt. I ache and I'm tired, and all I want is to get out of this life, this body, this world. Right, that's it: A sin is like ballast. And unless I tell someone, I'm afraid I'll be stuck here forever, I'm afraid I'll never be able to float away.

Okay, so as soon as I tell someone I'm outta here.

33

To Elliot the Megamall looked like Eden. Almost all his friends hated it out here—a number of them had taken the Anti-Megamall Pledge: If you buy something out there, then you gotta steal something of equal value—but as Elliot stepped through the service door and into the endless hall, he was quite sure he'd never seen anything quite so wonderful. All the color. The glittery lights. The smells. The stuff, piles and piles of it, everything so pretty, everything so picture-perfect.

Jeez-Louise, thought Elliot, all agog, this place was kind of great!

He'd never realized it before. Of course, he'd never spent twenty-four hours underground in a plain white room before. With a dead friend, no less. But here it was, all the fruit of the capitalistic tree. Anything you wanted, from an Armani suit to a chain saw, a bird whistle to a handgun, a deep-fried cheese curd to Argentinean sea bass grilled in a banana leaf. Wow. And all of it under one gargantuan roof. His mouth gaping as if he'd spent the last ten years in Siberia, Elliot shuffled along, oblivious to the time as he admired the sensual arch of the four-story hallway. Unbelievable. Three gorgeous floors, covered with teal carpet, mauve carpet, and gorgeous tiles. Three floors of store after store after store, nearly five hundred of them, and all with such cute displays. Stopping at Cuddle Up, he admired a display of down comforters—wouldn't one of those have been nice this past winter to keep his twiggy little body toasty warm? Then he came to the next shop, Marco Polo, and admired a stack of Peruvian sweaters, so thick, so beautiful. No, thought Elliot, spying the next shop, Stick to Me; he had to have everything in there, every single refrigerator magnet.

He wanted to cry.

And that was what he did, tears flooding his eyes and gushing down his cheeks as one and only one thought barreled right into him: If only Tina could've been here. Long ago she'd brought her kid, Chris, out here, and Chris had loved it, being rolled down the long halls in her stroller, going into the amusement park in the center with its sparkly lights and tropical plants and kiddie rides that went 'round and 'round.

He leaned against a column, burying his face in the crook of his right arm, and just stood there sobbing. This joint was just so beautiful, so perfect, but it wasn't the real world, was it? Hell, no. He recalled the later images of little Chris, so shrunken with AIDS, so bald, so listless, as she faded from life. And then came the all-too-recent image of Tina, so skinny as she wasted away. Elliot sobbed and gasped for air, then sobbed some more. True, no one was getting off the face of this here earth alive, but it just wasn't fair that Tina and her baby girl had to die like that. Nor was it fair that he was headed that way, deflating into nothingness, dying like a pathetic balloon. Really, the only question left in his life was when would it happen—would he croak tomorrow, next week, next month? Maybe he should start taking bets, run his own little Lotto, call it something simple like Kick the Bucket. He could see it now, death driving straight toward him, transforming from mirage to reality. Yes, and there was no hiding, no running. Virtually no escaping, no matter what he did. Yup, his end was fast approaching, of that Elliot was quite sure.

Blech, he thought, first mopping his eyes, then blotting his snotty nose. He glanced up, scanned one way up the hall, turned around, scanned the other way. Gentle, soothing music slipped this way and that through the humongous building. But there was something missing in the Megamall: people. The beautiful corridor scattered with clumps of bushes and benches was totally devoid of shoppers. Oh, that was it, realized Elliot, hearing a vacuum cleaner in the distance. The joint wasn't open yet.

''Hey, you, what are you doing here?'' blasted a voice out of nowhere.

Elliot turned to see a brick shithouse of a hunk standing there in a fascistlike uniform of black pants and white shirt, a badge on the shirt pocket, a walkie-talkie strapped to his belt, and a sneer on his big boyish face. Uh-oh, thought Elliot. This could be big trouble. Matthew wasn't going to like this.

"Me?" said Elliot, struggling to smile at the dairy boy cum high-school wrestler cum security guard. "Nothing."

"How did you get in here? The mall ain't open for another hour."

Okay, okay, okay: Think. Elliot wiped his nose, his eyes. Yes, he looked exactly like what he was: a blubbering sissy. So how was he going to explain himself?

"Haven't you heard what . . . what happened at the air-port?" began Elliot, puffing out his lower lip.

"Huh?"

"The crash—man, a plane crashed this morning."

"You're kidding!" gasped the astonished guard.

"No, it hit the ground and smashed all over the runway. Didn't you hear the explosion?"

"No! Was everyone . . . everyone killed?"

Elliot nodded and put his hand to his eyes. "Including Mom."

"Oh, man, I'm sorry."

He sniffled. "And now I have to go tell Sis. That's her Hoovering down there."

The imposing hulk suddenly turned into a big teddy bear, tromping right up to Elliot and throwing an arm over his shoulders. Elliot fell into the big, hard chest, nuzzled right up to the fellow, and thought: yum. Oh, but if only this butch wonder boy could really make everything right. Granted, the guy's cologne smelled a bit like bug spray, but . . .

The guard asked, "Like, what can I do for you?"

His voice faint, Elliot muttered, "Oh, nothing."

"Here, well, let me at least take you down to your sister."

"No, no, no!" He pushed against the solid pecs and out of the embrace. "I'll go myself. This . . . this isn't going to be pretty. Mom and Sis were like sisters, you know."

"It's okay, man. Let me help you. Maybe your sis is going to, I don't know, faint or somethin'."

"No, no, no. You're too kind. This is a family matter, something I have to do myself."

"Yeah, sure, you bet."

"So, I'll . . . I'll just be going." Elliot suddenly stopped.
"Or do I have to wait until the mall opens?"

"Heck, no."

"Thanks."

"Hey, I'm sorry for you."

"Yeah."

Forgetting about the 9 A.M. broadcast, Elliot moped along,
glanced back once, saw the hulk standing there gabbing on his
walkie-talkie. Oh, brother, he thought, that was close enough.
Too close. And when he reached a break in the stores that featured a staircase, an escalator, and a bank of elevators all leading
upward to more, more, more shopping orgasms, Elliot cut to the
right. He walked quickly past the stairs and entered the amusement park, an enormous square area filled with trees, a roller
coaster, a log-flume ride, sundry other rides, and way, way over
there, so far that it looked small, a towering Ferris wheel. Wow.
Elliot took it all in with one long, sweeping gaze, then followed
an arching pathway past a popcorn stand, turned left on a path
that led through a grove of trees and plants, and then plunked
himself down in a hidden corner. Even if Mr. Future Farmer of
America—a.k.a. Mr. Arnold Schwarzenegger, Jr.—back there
wised up to the status of things out at Minneapolis/St. Paul International Airport, he wouldn't be able to find Elliot squirreled
away like this in a corner of the amusement park. Nope. No one
would. And Elliot was going to be a good camper. Yep. He was
going to sit right here until the Megamall opened its megadoors
to the megaconsumers, until they rushed in here and started suck-
ing up their clothes, their jewelry, their knickknacks, their lawn
mowers. He'd keep nice and out of sight; then when there were
others around he'd get his juice and muffin and slip back down to
the tomb of doom.

Elliot scanned from left to right and his eyes hit upon a gorgeous explosion of color: bright yellow mums.

Well, thought Elliot, staring over at a pot of flowers next to a
bench, those were pretty, perky things, those mums. So bright.

So brilliantly yellow. Those would do. Tina-hon would've liked those a lot. Big blooms, lots and lots of festive petals. Hmm. He glanced through some bushes, scanned. No security guards. No what-do-you-call-'ems. No sanitation engineers. Yes, he needed flowers and God was giving him flowers. Beautiful ones for darling Tina. See, everything was going to work out just fine. He had just enough money for juice and a muffin—and here were the flowers he needed. Cool. Elliot got up, pushing himself out of his little hiding place, and went directly to the pretty flowers. Peering over the pot of mums, he thought, yes, this one would do. And so he broke off that flower, careful to keep the stem nice and long. Yes, that one too. Oh, and this flower was so nice and huge and beautiful. Okay. And that one and that one and that one.

Pretty soon the plant was all but bald and Elliot had a nice bouquet. Well, pretty nice, he thought. Tina, actually, deserved better. A huge armful of flowers, that was what she needed. Yes, beautiful Tina, the onetime model, should be buried in flowers. And so he turned his head, scanned from side to side. And sure enough there were two more pots of bright yellow, big, gorgeous mums. Without another thought Elliot darted across the path, plucked all those flowers, spied another pot, then broke off those flowers one by one. Well, this was getting to be a lot, almost enough, and then he eyed one more burst of color. Okay, just one more, and so—

"Hey, you, what the hell are you doing?" shouted a guard.

Elliot glanced across a little pond filled with goldfish and saw another one of those uptight guys—this one old and fat—in tight black polyester pants and white shirt.

"What? Who? Me?" gasped Elliot.

Into his walkie-talkie the guard barked, "Hey, we got trouble over here, a real nut case."

And when the guard started running around the pond toward him, Elliot screamed out, threw the flowers into the air, and, at as fast a pace as he dared, took off.

34

He punched off the VCR and sat there staring at the blank screen, the headphones still clasped over his ears. Todd didn't know what to do. It couldn't be anywhere else, and if they were holding Clariton at the Megamall, didn't Rawlins have to be there too? Hell, where else could he be?

Someone started banging on the door, and the metal mini-blinds banged and rattled.

"Todd!" called someone, twisting the door handle and trying to get in. "Todd, open up!"

It was Frank, the assignment editor. Oh, shit. Todd didn't care if Dan Rather was out there in person, he didn't want to do another interview. Not now. Not today. There was too much else in his life that wasn't making sense.

"Todd, dammit all!"

He ripped off the earphones, rolled his chair over to the door, and twisted open the lock. Frank immediately burst into the room, followed by Craig, the producer. Todd pushed himself back, rolling all the way to the VCR.

"Todd, we've got to get this straightened out with Rather's producer," began Frank, clearly perturbed. "We can't just blow it off like this. I mean, you do know what this kind of exposure is going to do for your career, don't you?"

Sick of hearing that, Todd sat there, a flat expression on his face. Who cared about the frigging networks?

"Gee, and I don't think you want to blow off the FBI either," said Craig, unable to hide his irritation. "It just wouldn't be a good idea."

Frank said, "Besides, we've got to stay ahead of Channel

Seven. You have heard about their morning broadcast, haven't you?''

Todd froze. "What?"

"They're running promos saying they're going to do a special report from Cindy Wilson's hospital room at ten this morning. That's in about a half hour. They're claiming she's going to identify one of Clariton's kidnappers and provide some big break in the case."

Todd bowed his head into his right hand. Okay, he knew what was up. Cindy was going to give a description of Matthew, not only as of yesterday with his shaved head and shrunken face, but what he looked like in the picture with Curt. The sixty-four-trillion-dollar question was whether she would divulge just how she got this information. She might claim she'd garnered all this via her expert journalistic skills as they'd dragged her away with Clariton. Or she might claim that she'd gotten it from one person in particular, namely Todd Mills, who'd kindly stopped by last night with a nice color snapshot of said kidnapper.

Oh, shit, thought Todd. In the virtuous interest of her career Cindy Wilson had screwed him over when Michael had been murdered, and she might very well do so again. She'd said as much last night. Her big story might not be about Clariton and his abductors. No, depending on how piqued her trashy tabloid skills were and how much she'd already revealed, her story might be about Channel 10's star reporter withholding critical information from the police and the FBI. He wouldn't put it past her. In fact if she was half as conniving, half as good, half as smart as Todd thought, Cindy would do just that, implicating Todd for no other reason than to get him yanked in for questioning. That in turn would not only offer Cindy Wilson and WTCN a searingly hot story—something juicy like STAR REPORTER PART OF GAY CONSPIRACY—but put Todd, her competition, out of commission for a few days. Dan Rather's people would drop Todd in a millisecond.

"Listen," began Todd, wondering just how the hell he was going to explain this, or even if he could, "I went down to the hospital to see Cindy Wilson last night."

"Oh, no, this isn't good," muttered Frank, shaking his head.

One hand to his forehead, Craig said, "This sounds very mucky. Am I right? Are you mucky with Cindy Wilson? You are, aren't you? Oh, God, I just sense it."

"Perhaps."

"Uh-oh," moaned the producer. "What is it, Todd? You know something, don't you?"

"Perhaps." He checked his watch; in a little over thirty minutes he very well might be tumbling from star to traitor. "I need to be real up front with you—there's a bunch of stuff I need to explain. Why don't you bring the FBI guys down to the conference room? I'll meet you there in a couple of minutes."

"Okay, two minutes," said Craig. "No more."

"Don't worry. I just want to get some stuff together to show you."

"Oh, God. I think I have a headache. And I think it's going to get a whole lot worse."

"It just might," Todd replied.

Rising from his chair, he shooed them out and shut the door. Todd then returned to the VCR, took out the tape he'd made months ago at the Megamall, and went over to his standing file cabinet. He pulled out the second drawer, thumbed to an obscure file, and dropped in the tape. Okay, he thought as he slid shut the file drawer, no one was going to find that sucker, at least not for a good long while. Now what? He didn't have any choice, so how was he going to do this? Right. He touched his sport coat. Yes, his wallet was there in the inside breast pocket. And his keys were in the pocket of his pants. He then grabbed a coffee cup he'd used days ago that still had a bit of sludgy coffee at the bottom, swung open his office door, and headed into the newsroom.

"Just going to get some more coffee," called Todd over the tops of a couple of cubicles.

Frank, pacing anxiously behind the elevated assignment desk, glared at him. "Just one thing—don't ruin my career too, okay? That's all I ask."

Todd nodded, continued through the cubicles, and crossed to the commissary area. The large, industrial-sized coffee urns were to his left; Todd turned to the small sink on his right, rinsed his coffee mug, grabbed a paper towel, and slowly dried the cup. Glancing back into the newsroom, he saw that neither Frank nor the producer was coming this way. Todd then went to the coffee urn, pulled on the red handle, and half-filled his mug. He took a sip, glanced around. Two associate producers sat in their cubicles to his right, a secretary was typing something, but all of them were much too busy to take notice.

Todd turned, made his way past the stack of daily newspapers—all of which, he saw with a casual glance, featured the Clariton story in massive headlines—and left the newsroom. Anyone would have thought Todd, rather than cutting through the chaotic newsroom, was going around the back way to the conference room. He stopped in the hall, swigged his coffee, and glanced up and down the corridor. No one, not a soul. Wasting not an instant, he spun and darted for the parking-lot doors.

There was no way in hell he was going to be able to explain Rawlins, their relationship, AIDS, meeting one of Clariton's abductors way back when—at least not quickly, because, of course, Todd didn't understand it himself. And there was no way in hell he had any time to waste answering questions for the FBI. No, the President of the United States and every law-enforcement branch in the country might have one and only one priority, but Clariton most definitely wasn't Todd's. He had only one: Rawlins.

Dashing outside, Todd chucked his coffee, mug and all, into some juniper bushes, and raced down the low steps, across the lot, and to the Channel 10 Ford Explorer he'd been loaned. He jumped in, brought the engine to a quick start, and slammed down on the gas, the tires screeching as he roared out of the lot. Turning right onto the street, he glanced back at the building. Nope. No one racing out the door, no one leaping into a car after him. And though it seemed Todd had gotten away completely unnoticed, he didn't slow, speeding down the road and distancing himself from Channel 10 as quickly and cleanly as possible. If he was correct in his assumption that it was the FBI who'd followed him to Rawlins's apartment last night, he had every reason to believe they would tail him again now.

. As he drove along he kept a steady eye on his mirrors. There was a blue van, a couple of sedans, a motorcycle. He couldn't discern if any of them was the vehicle from yesterday, however. Not on a busy two-lane road like this. Up ahead he saw the gate of a fancy subdivision and he purposely turned on his blinker. Braking, he turned to the left and steered along a gently sloping street lined with what looked like expensive three-car garages with attached houses. He glanced back, but as far as he could tell no one had turned after him. Just to make sure, he turned right at the next street, left at the one after that. Then he slammed on the brakes and turned completely around. Speeding up, he retraced his route, but the subdivision was dead. The street was void of any life, pedestrian and vehicular. As perplexed as much as he was relieved, Todd slowed to a stop and then just sat there. Surprised by his good fortune, he turned around yet again and continued all the way through the winding streets of the subdivision to the gate on the opposite side. He checked his mirrors once again, still could discern no one, and turned onto a busy road. It didn't make any sense, he thought as he headed for the city, but he sure as hell wasn't going to argue.

So how was he going to do this? How was he going to find Rawlins? No, he couldn't do it by himself, that much he knew, just as he knew he couldn't tell the FBI and police what he suspected without endangering Rawlins.

Okay, okay. Think.

He came to a convenience store, pulled in, and went inside, bought a small bottle of cranberry juice. With a fresh quarter in hand, he came out and went over to a pay phone attached to the brick wall. Todd took a number from his wallet and dialed.

A deep voice answered midway through the first ring. "Hello?"

"It's me, Todd Mills. I think I know where they are." Okay, here was the test question. "Will you help me?"

Lyle Cunningham audibly inhaled, then exhaled. "Perhaps."

"It's very complicated, so I don't want the police involved or the FBI, at least not yet."

"After a hot story, are you?"

"Hardly. Things have just turned a bit personal. So are you in or not?"

There was a long pause. "Sure."

"Okay, meet me at Lake and Hennepin. I'll be at the corner entrance to Calhoun Square." Todd glanced at his watch. "Pick me up in fifteen minutes."

Todd hung up the receiver, opened the bottle of juice, and slammed it down. Then he hopped back in the Explorer and took off, afraid of what lay just ahead.

35

Lyle Cunningham sat for a long time at his kitchen table and tried to decide just how he should handle this. He reached for the phone, started to drag it across the Formica surface, then stopped. He envisioned his mother in that hospital bed, wasting away. He recalled holding a paper cup full of scrambled eggs and remembered how hard it had been just to get her to take a bite. He pictured her listless face, her fading memory, and the blood that sporadically dribbled from her nose. The stench. Nothing he'd seen in the Marines had prepared him for his mother's death from AIDS.

Yet despite his ambivalence toward Clariton and everything he represented, he had no choice but to call this one in. He pulled the phone closer, dialed the number.

And when a deep-voiced man answered on the other end, Lyle said, "It's me, Cunningham."

"What's up?"

"Mills just called."

Lyle's boss chuckled. "See, I told you. I knew he was part of this. I knew there was no way Mills wasn't involved."

"Perhaps," replied Lyle.

"So what did he say?"

"He wants me to meet him."

"Excellent. When?"

"Fifteen minutes." Lyle asked, "So what do you want me to do?"

"What do I want you to do? I want you to meet Mills and attach yourself to him, that's what. I mean, I don't want him to move more than two steps away from you. Got it?"

"Yes."

"Mills obviously knows something we don't, and with any luck this will be the break we've been looking for. So don't lose him. Let me remind you, your ass is grass if you blow it."

"Don't worry," said Lyle with a sigh, "I know what to do."

"That's what you said before," replied the man, slamming down the phone.

Lyle hung up and then came to his feet. He'd be more than glad when this one was over, he thought as he left his small kitchen. Entering the dining room, he found Koshka, his sinewy black cat, lying right in the middle of the table, bathing in a pool of morning light.

"Hello, kitty," he said, running one hand over the length of her spine.

His hand passed from his pet to his gun and shoulder holster, which were also coiled on the table. He took out the gun, flipped open the barrel to check that, yes, it was fully loaded, then settled the weapon back in the holster.

Okay, he had no choice. No getting out of this one. And not much time, he realized, glancing at his watch.

He slipped the holster and gun over his left shoulder, grabbed his leather coat from the back of one of the dining room chairs, then started for the front door. From a small entry table he snatched his keys and also a small beeperlike device, which he clipped inside his shirt pocket. He was about to flick it on, but then he thought, nope, not yet.

Shit, thought Lyle, heading out the door. One way or another he hoped to be done with this one by the end of the day, if not a whole hell of a lot sooner.

36

As he sped into the city Todd felt his stomach shrinking into a tight, painful mass. Clariton at the Megamall? Rawlins there too? Todd envisioned that enormous concrete box of a place that except for the flags resembled the nearby airplane hangars. He saw the endless rows of shops, the quite amazing central space that could have held a couple of 747s but instead housed an amusement park. And then he recalled the underground levels he'd toured and filmed. Was that where they were hiding, in the sub-basement destined for the Journey to the Center of the Earth?

Todd ran his right hand through his hair. This was too unbelievable. Reaching the Uptown area, Todd headed up Lake Street, passing Café Wyrd, Lunds grocery store, and finally crossing Hennepin Avenue. A block later he turned right and pulled into the parking ramp behind Calhoun Square, where he steered into a ground-level space and left the Ford Explorer. He then dashed out of the ramp, across the alley, and into the mall—dubbed Updale by some—carved into a block of old buildings. Clariton had been signing books here just yesterday, Todd noted, although it seemed like weeks ago. He'd been out here in the middle of the two-story courtyard, holding court like a prince, completely unaware of what would soon befall him.

Todd glanced to his left, saw the bookstore just opening up, then cut right, hurrying past the fountains to the entrance on the corner of Lake and Hennepin. Checking his watch, he realized that Lyle should be here just about now. He stepped outside, went right up to the curb, and looked down Lake, then searched up and down Hennepin, but saw no sign of the black pickup. This was the place though. Todd couldn't have been more specific. He checked his watch again. Lyle wouldn't back out, would he? No, he doubted it.

Someone crossing the street glanced at him. Another person walking down the sidewalk raised his eyes and studied Todd. Someone driving by did a double take. Shit, realized Todd, sinking back against a column. They were all recognizing him. For a good while now he'd been well-known in the Twin Cities—occasionally a head would turn his way—but nothing like this. These people weren't just noticing him. Not even staring. No, they were gaping.

"Hey," muttered someone in a passing group, "that's that guy who's been on the news—you know, because of Clariton. They almost got him too, didn't they? What's his name, Tom . . . or Rod . . . or . . ."

So they'd seen the local and national news. Possibly CNN on perpetual repeat. Whatever, but Todd didn't want the attention, particularly now. He scratched his forehead with his left hand, tried to shield his face. But the fame he'd sought for so long and that was now his was not something with a switch. It couldn't be turned on and off at his discretion, he thought just as someone came up to him, a guy with a big gut and a big smile.

"Wow, we've been watching you on TV," said the guy, loaded with questions. "Pretty intense, huh? Pretty amazing? You were right there—were you scared? Do you think they're going to give Clariton AIDS?"

Todd was at a total loss. "Well, I don't—"

A second and a third person stopped, as the first man continued, "So what do you think's going to happen?"

"I really don't know."

An older woman carrying a Lunds bag stopped and gasped. "Say now, you're the fella that's been on my TV, now, aren't ya? And you know what, you're even better-looking in person."

The voice of Stella, his agent, echoed in his ears like a righteous mother, a shrill nun, and a football coach all rolled into one: "Todd, you gotta remember that every one of your viewers isn't a potential couch potato, they're a potential customer. *Your* customer, doll. You forget that and it takes only seconds to go from a nice hunky beefcake to a piece of dead meat. Nothing spreads faster than gossip, bad gossip, and people just love to torch a celebrity. Trust me, doll, I've seen it done thousands of times. It can take you years to claw your way to the top of the pile and about two seconds to fall off. Be careful, this is a nasty business.''

The woman put down her grocery bag, pushed up her glasses with her left index finger, and said, ''You wouldn't want to give me your autograph, now, would ya?''

''Yeah, can I have one too?'' said the heavy guy.

But Todd didn't have it in him to be charming, let alone polite. While all that these people saw was a television personality—and probably an encounter to brag about to their friends—all that Todd saw was the chaos now butchering his life. He just didn't know what to say, and he was about to duck out, to say something crude and probably profane, when all of a sudden he saw the black truck racing through a yellow light.

''I can't talk now.'' As he started to push himself away, Stella's voice echoed, and he added, ''Something big's going on regarding the case.''

''Oh, you're working? Are you filming something?'' asked the man, eagerly looking around. ''Where are the cameras?''

''How exciting!'' said the woman, her tiny wrinkled eyes opening wide as if she were seeing Superman. ''Go get 'em!''

Todd tore away, pushing past a couple of people, around a bank of newspaper stands, and rushing to the truck that had stopped. He ripped open the passenger door and jumped in.

''Go!'' he shouted.

Lyle Cunningham calmly checked his mirrors, pressed on the gas, and pulled back into the stream of traffic, heading due east on Lake Street.

He said, ''Your wish is my command.''

Todd glanced out the rear window, then slumped back, leaning his head against the headrest, closing his eyes, and taking a deep breath. ''They're at the Megamall.''

''Who?''

''Clariton . . . and whoever has him.''

''Really? What are they doing, shopping for some new outfits?''

"Yeah, right." Todd rubbed his forehead. "Did you see the tape this morning, the one we ran?"

Lyle eyed him. "Of course."

Todd then explained, beginning with the piece he'd done on the Megamall months ago and ending with the tape they'd received from Clariton's abductors. On both tapes, he insisted, were the exact same sounds, those of the roller coaster.

"And I actually have a very good idea in what part of the building they're holding Clariton," concluded Todd.

"I see," replied Lyle, trying to contain his obvious interest as well as his suspicions. "But why call me?"

"Because I need some help—and you have a vested interest, so to speak."

Todd turned around again, searching the street for any suspicious vehicles. He'd come to understand that being closeted, as he had been for so many years, had made him permanently paranoid, for there was once a time when he'd feared nothing more than his own sexuality. And while he'd worked so hard for so long at running from that truth, the reality had at last come into focus.

Just as the car behind them was now coming into view as a real truth that had to be dealt with.

Lyle continued, saying, "Okay, but the police and the FBI would be the logical choice. You could even get your cameras and be the real hero."

"Let's just say things have gotten radically more personal."

"How so?"

"The guy I've been dating just . . ." Todd could barely force himself to say it. ". . . just found out he's HIV positive. And I'm afraid he's somehow mixed up in all this." Todd eyed the familiar car about three vehicles back and shook his head. "Actually, I'm not really sure what's going on, so for now I need to keep the FBI out of this."

Glancing in his rearview mirror, Lyle asked, "Do you see something back there?"

"Yeah. A silver four-door Chrysler. If I'm not mistaken it's the same car from last night—and chances are it's the FBI."

"Shit, they've probably been following you all morning."

"No way. I checked. I double-checked. There was no way anyone tailed me from the station. It had to have been you—they must have followed you from your house."

"No, I made sure of that," Lyle said calmly as he steered into the other lane and passed a van. "They must have been waiting when I pulled up to Calhoun Square."

"Then your phone must be tapped."

"Or yours."

Todd countered, "But I called you from a pay phone."

"Okay, maybe. But maybe they put a bug on your car." Lyle grinned slightly. "Shall we lose them?"

"Absolutely."

"Brace yourself."

As they approached the busy intersection of Lake and Lyndale, an old business district lined with brick buildings and now swarming with buses, cars, and a few motorcycles, Todd made sure his seat belt was snug. He wondered how Lyle was going to handle this, and he soon had his answer when the light ahead turned yellow and Lyle failed to slow. Instead, Lyle accelerated and whipped the car back to the right, whooshing past a Ford Escort and racing toward the crossroads. Oh, shit, thought Todd, grabbing on to his seat. He glanced at the speedometer, saw the needle still rising. The light ahead popped red. And just as the east-west traffic cleared, just as the north-south traffic began to move, Lyle shot through. A car on Todd's right slammed on its brakes and horn. A motorcycle skidded to the side. Todd was sure they were going to be broadsided, but Lyle whipped through like a race-car driver. Behind them the traffic hesitated, then proceeded, flooding the intersection once again.

Todd turned around, saw the silver Chrysler's unsuccessful attempt to swim through a gnarly jam at the red light, and said, "I think you did it."

"Let's just make sure."

He swerved around a food-delivery truck unloading in front of a restaurant, slammed on the brakes, and jerked the wheel to the right. With a screech of tires Lyle made a ninety-degree turn into an alley, hit the gas, and bombed down the narrow passage.

Someone emerged from a back door pushing a wheeled garbage container.

"Crap," muttered Lyle, veering to the left as much as he could in the narrow passage.

The guy leapt back into the building just as Lyle clipped the garbage can with his front fender. As if a stick of dynamite had exploded, the whole container flew into the air and burst open. As trash rained down, Lyle sped down the alley, burst onto 31st Street, screeched to the right, then raced left through another yellow light and down Lyndale Avenue.

"There," said Lyle, easing back on the gas and checking his rearview mirror. "That ought to do."

Todd took a deep breath, turned around, and looked out the back window. Behind them cars and trucks just puttered along, none of them a silver Chrysler.

"Where did you take driver's ed? A stock car track?" quipped Todd. "Now, if you just keep going straight south we can make it to the Megamall in fifteen minutes, maybe less."

37

Ohhhhh, shit, thought Elliot, dashing away from the pond. This was not cool. Definitely not cool.

"Hey, you!" shouted the old guard, rushing around a mound of shrubs after him. "Stop!"

"Leave me alone!" cried out Elliot. "You don't understand, I'm sick! I'm really sick!"

"Stop!"

"For Christ's sake, man, you don't have to get all Twisted Sister about it! I'm sorry, I just wanted some flowers for a dead friend, that's all!"

He rushed past a drinking fountain, down a sloping path, and swooped around a merry-go-round. Glancing back, he saw the guard hobbling after him and barking something into his walkie-talkie. Yikes. Matthew wasn't going to like this, not a bit! And that thought alone made Elliot freeze. Oh, no, he thought, glancing around. Straight ahead was the roller coaster. Over there on the left was the log-flume ride. And right there the haunted house. But which way did he need to go? How the hell did he get out of the amusement park, and where the hell was that door that would take him back down to Matthew and their hidden chamber?

"Al, he's right over there!" shouted the older guard.

Elliot turned, saw the hunky guard, the same one from before, his face no longer sweet and sympathetic. No, the guy realized he'd been duped and was madder than hell.

"Oh, hi!" called Elliot from across the merry-go-round. "I'm . . . I'm still looking for Sis. You haven't seen her, have you?"

"Stop right there, buddy!"

"Oh, no. I . . . I think I need to go."

"Freeze!"

Yeah, right, thought Elliot. He turned and dashed off, following another path past a cotton-candy stand, around a hot-dog joint, and then bolting toward a gaping exit framed with balloons. If he could only get out of here, if he could only get back into the corridor, then he'd get his bearings. Oh, crap. Matthew was going to kill him. Jeez, and all he'd wanted was a nice muffin.

Chugging along, Elliot glanced over his shoulder as he ran and saw the two guards gaining on him. He wasn't going to be able to escape them, no way. Not with the pain in his knees and his lungs. Starting to slow, he clasped a hand to his chest. He just couldn't get enough air, and he took a big gulp. Oh, God, breathing hurt so bad, like knives cutting into his chest. He coughed into his hand and felt a splatter of moisture.

"Oh, big ish," he muttered, staring at the spray of blood on his palm.

He heard the steps closing in on him, looked back, and knew he had only moments. Oh, jeez, he thought, glancing desperately from side to side. Just to his right was the tiny Cookie Log Cabin, inside of which a blond girl in a frilly gingham dress was shoveling big chocolate chip cookies from a cookie sheet. Elliot dashed over, ripped open the screen door, and burst into the tiny kitchen.

"Hi!" said Elliot, rushing right up to the table of hot treats.

Surprised, she looked up, the spatula in her right hand. "Oh, hi. We're not open yet, but do you want a cookie? This is the kitchen, you see. The counter's right over there," she explained with a wave of her kitchen utensil. "You just go back out the door and—"

"No, I don't want anything."

He looked out, saw that the guards were only fifteen, twenty feet away. Elliot rolled his eyes. What choice did he have?

"You don't know me, but I'm really a very nice person," he began, hurrying around the table.

"Huh?"

"I mean I'm sorry to do this and everything." Reaching the

corner, he lunged for her and grabbed her by the arm. "But what else can I do?"

"Hey, stop it!" she shouted, swatting at him with the spatula.

These days Elliot barely had enough strength to pick up a chair, but somehow he managed to get around and twist her arm behind her back. She kicked and twisted, and Elliot had no other choice but to wrench her arm upward. She screamed and Elliot lessened the pressure, then two seconds later the two guards rushed through the door of the miniature log cabin.

"Stop!" screamed Elliot. "You guys stop right there or . . . or I'm going to hurt her!"

"Hey, just be cool!" ordered Al, the younger guard, who surveyed the situation, clearly noting that Elliot had nothing, not a gun or even a knife. "Now, just calm down and let her go."

"No fucking way!" shouted Elliot, using every muscle as he struggled to control the bucking young woman. "You have to do what I say!"

"It's over, buddy," said the older guard. "Just calm down and release the young lady."

"Guess again, asshole!" snapped Elliot.

Al started forward. "Do like he says and let her go."

"Stop!" screamed Elliot. "I have AIDS. And if you come one step closer I'm going to bite this girl and make her sick too!"

As if she'd just been slapped, the young woman was suddenly quite still. "Oh . . . oh, I don't want to get hurt!"

"I will! I'll do it! I'm one of the guys who kidnapped Congressman Clariton yesterday—and I'm nuts, man!"

Al froze. "Just calm down."

"Oh, God!" cried the woman.

"I'm really nuts!" yelled Elliot at the guards. "Just look at me! Just look at how sick and scrawny I am! I'll make her like this, I'll give her AIDS if you . . . if you . . ." He glanced to the side, saw the walk-in refrigerator. "I'll bite her if you don't go in there!"

"Oh, dear Lord," moaned the older guard.

"Shit," muttered Al.

Elliot ordered, "Go on, get in that refrigerator or I'll come after you guys too! I'll slice off my finger and spray AIDS blood all over you!''

The two guards looked at one another, grumbled. Elliot had won, just as he knew he would, for he'd come to learn that the fear of AIDS alone was as powerful a weapon as kryptonite was against Superman. The younger guard shrugged. Of course there was nothing they could do.

"Move it!" barked Elliot, hoping he could keep it up, this anger, this fake show of force.

The two men started toward the refrigerator, edging along the work counter and the rows of hot chocolate chip cookies, right up to the large stainless steel door. Al pulled the handle, opened the door, and a cloud of cold air fumbled out, pooling around his feet.

"You won't get away with this!" said Al, looking over at Elliot. "We'll get you!"

"Oh, like, I'm really afraid, Mr. Clint Eastwood man. Like, go ahead and make my day, Mr. Heterosexual Macho man."

Elliot shook his head. Oh, brother. What kind of wienie did they think he was? Threats didn't bother him—for Christ's sake, he didn't just have one foot in the grave, and he wasn't knee-deep either. Nope, he was waist-high and sinking all the time. He only wanted to get out of here and get back to Matthew, who'd probably woken up by now. And, man, oh, man, wouldn't he go tilt when he saw that Elliot wasn't around?

"Now, just shut the fuck up and get in the fucking fridge," shouted Elliot, "before I play vampire and bite this young virgin in the neck!"

"Oh!" she cried. "I . . . I don't want to get AIDS!"

The two guards, looking glum and sheepish, proceeded into the walk-in. Okay, okay, thought Elliot, now what?

"Sorry, sweetheart," he said quietly into the young woman's ear as he nudged her toward the refrigerator. "Guess you're going to have to go in there too."

"Just . . . just don't hurt me!"

"No prob. Just do like I say, okay?"

"Yeah, sure. Sure."

Keeping her arm pinned behind her back, Elliot walked her

over, then peered in. It wasn't a big walk-in, just enough for racks of premade cookie dough and other supplies, and the two guards stood there, clearly disgusted with the situation.

"Hmm, what do I want you to do?" began Elliot. "I know— turn around, that's it. I want you two guys to turn around and not move. Got it?"

"Sure," said the older guard.

"Okay, so do it. Turn around. Turn around now!" yelled Elliot, who then watched as the two men rotated their backs to him. "Very nice. Now the young lady here is going to join you, and then I'm going to shut the door. Got it? I warn you, though, don't try anything fancy. If you do I'm going to claw and spit and bleed all over all of you, got it? Huh? Well, do you?"

"Yes," said Al.

"Good." Elliot realized something. "Say, will those walkie-talkie things work from inside there? Will you be able to call out?"

Again Al said, "Yes."

"Then you wait five minutes before you call for help, okay? Not sooner, not a second sooner."

After all, he wanted to get away, but he certainly didn't want them to freeze to death. The guards were just doing their jobs and the young woman was just doing hers, baking cookies by the dozens. It would be bad enough in there, all dark and everything, not to mention freezing cold. Once Elliot had been stuck in an elevator when the power had gone out, and it certainly wasn't any fun. No way. And this walk-in refrigerator, he was sure, would be lots worse.

Elliot nuzzled his mouth up to the girl's ear and whispered, "Hey, I'm sorry, sweetheart, for pushing you around like this. You don't have anything to worry about though, okay? I'm really sick, but you can't get AIDS through casual contact like this, so you're perfectly fine. You can't get AIDS from holding hands or touching or kissing even. You know that, don't you?"

"Sure."

"Listen to me, sweetheart, you can only get it through the exchange of blood or other bodily fluids, so you're fine. And, anyway, I wouldn't have hurt you. I really wouldn't have. You're such a nice girl and . . . and . . .''

Her voice was small. ''Thanks.''

''Now, scoot on in there,'' he said, releasing her arm.

She broke away from him, darting into the refrigerator as quickly as she could. Elliot then slammed the door shut, reached over to the work counter, grabbed an oversize spoon, and jammed it in a small hole right beneath the door handle. Right, that's exactly where a padlock went, so there was no way they were going to get out. At least not until he was long gone.

Fab, thought Elliot with a huge smile on his face. Crisis averted, at least for now. He turned around, scooped up a half dozen warm cookies, and scurried out of the little log cabin. Emerging again into the amusement park, he looked around at all the rides and trees, all the bright colors.

Now, where the hell was that door, anyway, that would lead him back down to Matthew and Clariton?

38

Todd had never been out here this early and hence had never seen the environs of the Megamall so deserted. As the pickup glided off one of the freeway ramps, there were few cars and no frustrated traffic, and he instructed Lyle to turn right and right again, then left into an open lot next to one of the bunkerlike parking ramps. And as soon as the truck came to a stop, Todd whipped open the door and started clambering out.

"I'm pretty sure we'll find them on this side of the building," explained Todd.

"I hope you're right," replied Lyle, jumping out.

"So do I."

They rushed along the blank facade and down the side of the monolithic structure. As they neared a main set of doors, creatively emblazoned with the words MALL ENTRANCE, Todd heard sirens, a screaming mass of them swirling closer and closer. He hoped they signified a fire, but with his luck he feared not.

"I wonder what in the hell that's all about," he said.

"Sounds like a whole posse coming this way."

"No shit. But a posse of what?"

Yanking on one of the doors, Todd found it open, and Lyle and he hurried inside, entering a large space with rest rooms on either side, lockers, an information stand, banks of phones. A large cluster of people gathered around a security officer, a woman with dark skin, short hair, and wearing a white shirt and black polyester pants, who was obviously briefing them.

"So until we know what this is all about," explained the guard, "we want you all to remain in this area."

Two women clutching coffee cups drifted to the side, and Todd went over to them.

"What's going on?" he asked.

"Oh, there's another nut case out here," said one of the women, who held her foam cup with long red talonlike fingernails.

"Yeah," added the other, a tall woman with curly hair, "some guy went after some girl and tried to give her AIDS."

Oh, shit, thought Todd. "When?"

"Just a bit ago." The first woman waved with her red claws toward the innards of the mall. "He's still in there somewhere."

So things were already boiling over, and Todd wondered if he was already too late. If only there was a way to keep the FBI and police at bay, and, more important, a way to prevent some pestilence from dragging Rawlins into the heavens. Was it only yesterday morning when the most pressing things in their relationship were how often Rawlins was blowing his nose and just what they'd do in New York—what plays to see, what bagels to eat, what neighborhoods to stroll?

Todd turned to Lyle. "Come on."

They ducked around the two women and hurried past the crowd. Todd could never find his way around this windowless place; the slightly curving corridors and the endless shops always left him disoriented. He was fairly sure, though, that the perky Megamall tour guide with the Yugoslav accent had led him this way, that they'd descended into the bowels of this commercial giant somewhere over here on the west side.

"Gentlemen!" called a voice. "Please, I'm going to have to ask you to stay in this area!"

Todd glanced over his shoulder, saw the guard who was shouting at them, but kept going.

This time she shouted, "Hey, stop right there!"

Speeding up, Lyle nudged Todd on the arm. "Come on, let's get out of here, let's make a break."

Following Lyle's lead, Todd broke into a trot. Yes, they could outrun her. Yes, they could disappear into this massive place. After all, this guard was alone, wasn't she? As Todd was about to enter the main hall, he checked behind just to make sure there weren't more security people, a group of them that would come barreling after them.

"Hey, speed it up!" commanded Lyle.

But Todd couldn't. Just as he neared the corner of the hall, he looked back and froze in disbelief. Beyond the guard, past her and out the glass doors, he saw first the reflections of a flashing blue light and then a silver car—the very one that had tailed him last night—which came to a screeching halt. A moment later a second car stopped right behind it. No, he thought, staring at the second vehicle as Maurice Cochran climbed out. This couldn't be.

"Shit!" cursed Todd. "It's the FBI! How the hell did they get out here?"

He immediately broke back into a run, tearing past Lyle and down the corridor, which was littered with gargantuan houseplants, kiosks with umbrellas, benches, and a fountain or two. There was no way Todd was going to get this close to the truth and be stopped, especially not now and particularly not by the FBI. He'd almost found Rawlins, of that Todd was confident. He couldn't give up now. No way. Now thankful for all those years of jogging around the lakes, he tore across the teal carpeting, past a jeans store, and sports shop, with Lyle just a half step behind.

But how the hell had the FBI followed them to the Megamall when Todd was so sure Lyle had lost them back in town?

Even as he ran he couldn't let go of the question. Todd's phone might have been tapped, just as Lyle's might have been. Or Todd's vehicle might have been tampered with, which meant Lyle's might have been too. If that were the case, if they had in fact put some sort of tracking device on both vehicles, that would make sense, that would explain how the FBI could have traced them all the way out here to the Megamall even after Lyle had lost them at the intersection of Lyndale and Lake. Or had there been a second car besides the silver Chrysler? Perhaps even a helicopter?

But why?

In some paranoid and homophobic corner of himself, Todd could rationalize why the FBI might view him cautiously, even why they might tap his phone or whatever. He was gay. He was right there when Clariton was abducted. He "discovered" the mysterious videotape of the congressman.

But what about Lyle? What would cause the FBI to track him as well? Todd could see how he himself might be suspicious, yet he certainly didn't know what would put Lyle, a self-employed bodyguard, in the same category.

Unless . . .

Suddenly the truth exploded as sharply as a dart piercing a balloon. In his mind he went back and added everything up, all the events over the last two days, and came up with an entirely different conclusion. Dear God, how could he have been so utterly stupid? There could be only one way the FBI had been following him with such uncanny ability.

"In here!" ordered Todd, ducking past a women's clothing store and down a side hall that shot through to the amusement park.

Todd knew he only had moments, if that, and he slammed himself up against the wall. Lyle came tearing after him, his face flushed red, his forehead blistered with perspiration.

"What are you doing?" he demanded. "Where's Clariton?"

Todd peered back down the corridor, but didn't see any movement, let alone FBI agents. Not just yet anyway.

And then he whipped around, grabbed Lyle by the collar. All of Todd's anger exploded, and he hurled the much larger man back against the wall.

"It's you, isn't it?" he shouted. "You're one of them! You're a fucking FBI agent, aren't you?"

Lyle could have flung Todd off with brawny ease. With his thick arms he could have lifted Todd right off the floor and swatted him aside. Instead, Lyle, big and bulky, just stood there, castrated by the truth. He hesitated for a moment, glanced to the side, then raised and lowered his head in a slow nod.

Todd shouted, "What the—"

Lyle's face tightened in a panicked grimace, his eyes flashed wide, and he whipped a forefinger to his own lips in a desperate attempt to silence Todd. Both understanding and not, Todd caught his words. Lyle then nudged Todd back a half step, reached into his sport coat, and silently pointed to a small device in his shirt pocket, a black thing that looked like a tiny radio and had a dot of a red light burning on the top of it.

Lowering his chin and speaking clearly into it, Lyle said, "Top floor, by the movie theaters. Out."

He then pulled the transmitter from his pocket, ripped loose a wire, and hurled it down the hall, where it skipped along like a rock and finally crashed into bits.

Stunned, Todd shook his head. "I can't believe this."

"Sorry."

Only one question came to mind. "So . . . so none of that was true?"

"I work in the local FBI office," confessed Lyle, "and, yes, I was assigned to watch Congressman Clariton while he was here in town. After that blood was thrown on him in San Francisco, there was a certain amount of concern for his safety."

"No," said Todd, for all that other crap was irrelevant, at least in the bigger scope of things. "I mean you were bullshitting me about your mom. She didn't die of AIDS, did she?"

"Actually," replied Lyle, measuring his words, "she did. Just like I said. Which is why I didn't want this assignment in the first place. I'm being totally honest when I say I really can't stand Clariton."

Stunned, Todd couldn't move. He shook his head. What was he really supposed to believe, and what difference did it make—this guy and his lies—anyway?

"I've got to go," said Todd, breaking away.

"Wait!"

"Forget it."

"But you're going to need some help," insisted Lyle.

Todd hesitated. "And why would I trust you?"

"Because I'm a witness."

"What the hell does that mean?"

"It means I've seen it, I've been there."

Todd stared at Lyle, searching the other man's eyes and seeing something different. What was it—sincerity?

"I took care of my mother for the last month of her life,"

continued Lyle, "and I saw how AIDS ate her alive. Listen, man, I understand what you're facing, you and this guy of yours."

"Oh, do you?" said Todd as snidely as he could.

"Yeah, as a matter of fact I do. I understand AIDS doesn't have a fucking thing to do with anyone's morality. Not at all. It's about humanity."

As if he'd just been doused with frigid water, Todd was stunned by the clarity thrown at him. Trembling, he stood there dripping with some kind of insight. In the same hideous moment Todd sensed he'd caught sight of his own future, which was now hurtling at him with such speed and determination that he feared there was no escaping. Be that as it may, did that mean everything important in his life had already been decided?

No, he couldn't give up. He couldn't let go of the belief that he could make a difference, that he had the power to affect or alter, however slightly, his own destiny. Believing that, he knew he had to move, to jump back into all this. There wasn't time for any banter, any discussion. Only honesty.

And, yes. He did need help.

"Come on," said Todd. "If I'm right there's a door about a hundred feet down the main hall. Clariton should be down three levels. Since you're with the FBI—or were—may I assume you've got a gun?"

Lyle reached beneath his sport coat and pulled out a pistol. "Yes."

"Good, because I think we're going to need it."

39

Matthew couldn't fucking believe it. He'd overslept and missed the whole goddamn thing, the entire broadcast of Tina and Johnny Clariton!

He stomped across the floor, kicked the bathroom door as hard as he could, and it flew open. Inside was the sink, the toilet, Tina's dark-plastic-wrapped body, but no Elliot. Where the hell was he, and why hadn't he awakened him?

Matthew stormed over to the small storage room, took out a key, and with shaking hands slipped a key into the padlock and shoved open that door. Congressman Clariton, handcuffed to the pipe, looked up, his face haggard and wrinkled. Steve Rawlins, lying on the floor against the other wall, raised his head.

"Where the fuck's Elliot?" demanded Matthew.

Clariton said nothing, his face blank and hard.

Rawlins volunteered, "I heard someone go out about an hour ago."

"Damn it!"

Matthew slammed and locked the door. Elliot had taken off? Jesus Christ, it was unbelievable! Matthew tromped across the room, pulled his foot back, and kicked the box of Twinkies as hard as he could, his foot ripping through the cardboard and plunging deep into the treats. He kicked it again and again, until there was sticky cream filling coating his shoe. Had Elliot simply freaked out and left Matthew down here to deal with all this shit? Or had the moron simply lost his mind? Probably the latter, thought Matthew, turning away. Right, more than likely the already borderline Elliot had simply flipped off the charts.

Shit. How was he even supposed to know if they'd shown the

videotape on Channel 10? Call them and say, Ahem, excuse me, but could you tell me if you followed our orders?

And then he heard it. A slow shuffle from somewhere beyond their little hideaway. Matthew's first thought was to rip open the door and start screaming, demanding to know what the hell Elliot was doing. But what if it wasn't him? What if it were a wayward janitor, searching these subterranean rooms for some piece of filth?

An arrow of pain shot through Matthew's head, so painful that he caught his breath and clutched his forehead. Oh, dear God. It felt like a handful of knives, little tiny ones, piercing his forehead right above his left eye. Determined not to make a sound, he clenched his mouth shut and slumped against the wall. No, there wasn't time for this. Not now. Despite all the medication he'd taken last night it just hurt so horribly, those ribbons of pain that were cutting through his scalp, into his sinuses, into his brain! He took a deep breath, tried to push beyond it. Yes. Just take some more pills and ignore it. Focus on those steps, the ones out there somewhere. But where were they? Wait. Yes, they were right out there. Someone was nearing the door.

Opening his eyes, Matthew saw zips of white migrainelike light flashing in his vision. A whole thunderstorm of light. He shook his head, tried to battle them away, and turned and took three quick, furtive steps. Reaching a small canvas bag, he slid a hand into the open top and grabbed one of the guns. He fumbled with it, tried to focus on the barrel. There, right there, that was the butt, the handle. He positioned the weapon in his sweaty palm, then slipped back to the door. A mere second or two later he heard something and looked down. Struggling to see, he was able to make out the door handle as it slipped downward.

Matthew exploded, and he grabbed the door, swung the gun around, and jammed it right into the other guy's gut.

"It's me, it's me, it's just me!" hollered Elliot, throwing his twiglike arms up in the air.

"Fuck—"

"Don't shoot! Don't shoot!"

"Goddammit!" he shouted as he seized Elliot by the arm and

dragged him in, then slammed the door. "Where the hell have you been?"

"Up-upstairs."

"I missed it! I missed the broadcast, and it's all your fault! Jesus Christ, have you gone nuts?" yelled Matthew as he threw Elliot against the wall. "What are you trying to do, ruin everything?"

"N-no," whimpered Elliot.

"Well, then what?"

"I . . . I . . ." Elliot raised one hand, in which he clasped a gooey mess. "Want a cookie? They're . . . they're yummy."

"You're an idiot!" screamed Matthew, beating on the other man's chest. "A big fucking idiot!"

"No, no, I'm not!" snapped Elliot, tears spilling from his eyes.

"Did you see anyone?"

His head bobbed up and down.

"You shithead!" shouted Matthew as he slapped Elliot with the back of his left hand.

"Ah!" cried Elliot, dropping the cookie, clutching his face, and sinking to the floor.

"Who? Who saw you?" demanded Matthew, kicking him.

"Ow, stop it!"

"Who saw you?"

"I don't know. The . . . the security guards, I guess." Elliot collapsed into a ball, his head pressed into his knees, his arms wrapped around his legs, and he sobbed, "I don't want to do this anymore! I . . . I just want to go home! I just want to be in my bed, my own bed! All I ever wanted to do was paint, and now look at—"

"Shut up!"

Suddenly it was like an ice pick was jammed into Matthew's brain, and clutching his head, he gasped and turned away. He dropped the gun, stumbled a couple of feet, then turned and leaned against the wall as the pain sliced deeper and deeper. He opened his eyes, saw only black. He clutched them shut, then opened them again, and a flurry of squiggly ribbons of light filled his vision. Oh, shit. He breathed in, out. In, out. And then tried again. Okay, just get a fucking grip. Okay, just hang on.

But Elliot was right. Slumped against the wall, Matthew knew it. They couldn't do this anymore. Yesterday had not only killed poor Tina, it had pushed the two of them over the edge. They didn't have the strength for this kind of crap. Even if the security people or the police or whoever didn't find them down here, they'd never physically make it through another day of rage and demands, of keeping Clariton and Rawlins locked up.

"Get me my pills, the one in the yellow container," ordered Matthew.

"Yes, Mr. Boss Man."

Elliot did as ordered, getting the pills and a bottle of water, both of which he handed to Matthew. Like an addict desperate for a fix, Matthew grabbed them, gobbled the pills, and slammed down the water.

His voice now calm and low, Matthew glanced over, thankful that he could see again, and said, "I'm sorry."

Elliot sniffled, but didn't look up, and in the smallest of voices said, "That's okay."

"You can go home if you want."

"What?"

"I'm fucking sorry I got you fucking into this. I'll finish things up. Really, you can go home."

Elliot mopped his eyes. "Thanks, but I don't think . . . I don't think I can. I'm afraid it's too late for that." He shrugged and looked up at Matthew with a childish grin. "I kind of think I really screwed up things out there."

"I see," said Matthew, understanding what that meant. "So is now the time?"

"I guess."

"So what do you think, El? Ready for the grand finale?"

"I always did want to go out in style." He nodded. "And actually I think sooner is better than later."

So this was it. This, Matthew realized, was how it was going to end. Certainly not quite as he'd envisioned—who'd have guessed that Tina would have gone so abruptly, who'd have foreseen they'd be saddled with Rawlins. But this wasn't bad either. At least they'd made their point, gotten all the media attention, and the effects of what they had done would live on. Yes, in a way they'd been wildly successful.

"I mean it," added Elliot. "I made a mess of things up there. If we're going to do it, we gotta do it now."

"Okay, I'm ready."

Matthew turned and bent down to his canvas bag. This time he pulled out a cellular phone and a pad of legal paper. There were three numbers on the pad, all for the main television stations in town. He hesitated only for an instant, then punched in the number for the first station.

"Good morning, WTCN TV," said the receptionist.

"I'm only going to say this once: If you want to film Congressman Clariton, go immediately to the middle of the amusement park at the Megamall."

"What? Who—"

Matthew hung up, then dialed the second and the third numbers and repeated the terse message. That done, he folded up the cellular phone and dropped it back in the bag. He then picked up his gun and handed it to Elliot.

"Here, hold this."

Elliot's sunken eyes grew wide as he turned the weapon over in his hands. "I don't think I've ever held one of these things before." He smiled. "I'm a butch kind of Marlboro guy now, aren't I, Mr. Dude?"

"Careful, the bullet comes out of that end there," he said, pointing to the barrel. "And that's the trigger."

"Way cool."

"Now all we have to do is load our secret weapon," said Matthew, reaching into the box of meds and withdrawing an empty Heparin-treated syringe, "then head all the way up."

"Up and up and up," chimed in Elliot with a stupid grin as he fondled the pistol.

Yes, thought Matthew. Up and out of the basement. Up to the second and then the third floor. Right. He could see it now, all the cameras lined up. It was going to make for great drama and great news. Great American news, for it would all be captured, à la O. J. Simpson, on TV. It was going to be shocking and disgusting, and it'd probably run live too. In fact, maybe he'd insist on that, the live part. The networks would eat it up. After all, wouldn't the entire world be captivated by the image of an American congressman held hostage by a couple of sissies with a tiny syringe of blood?

Yes, the Grand Balcony overlooking the amusement park was going to be the perfect place for a dramatic conclusion to this stupid mess.

Matthew pulled back the left sleeve of his shirt and searched his scrawny arm. "God, my veins are shot. What are yours like?"

"The ones in my arms are pretty pathetic, man. I'd suggest my legs, but," said Elliot, pulling up his pants and exposing limbs that were not only painfully skinny, but covered with bruises, "they're not so good either, ya know." He shrugged. "Now what?"

Matthew thought for a moment, then in a low voice pronounced, "I've got an idea . . ."

40

The phenomenon of the Hostage Rescue Team kicked into full gear.

Ferried by a convoy of blue vans, Wayne Morrish, Dr. John Ogden, and the fifty members of the HRT arrived five minutes after Maurice Cochran. The first thing Morrish did was to establish a command post at an information desk by one of the mall entrances. The second was to summon the head of the mall security force.

"Hello, I'm Dick Russell, head of security out here, and—"

Morrish looked up at the gray-haired man and said, "I want the building evacuated immediately. Don't set off any of the alarms—just get everyone out of here at once!"

"Yes, sir."

"That includes your staff as well. We'll take care of the interior, you and the local police will assume responsibility for the outer perimeter. I don't want anyone coming in, and for God's sake, once the place has been evacuated, I don't want anyone coming out."

"Absolutely," said Russell, turning away.

"Wait. I want the head of your maintenance department here right away. And I want a complete set of blueprints for the entire building, including specifications for doors, walls, and a complete layout of the air-conditioning ducts."

"Of course."

Russell vanished, and Morrish looked over as Dr. Ogden distributed a small color photograph of Congressman Clariton to all the members of the HRT. Gathered in the lobby, the men were fully operational and dressed in their black utilities, from Kevlar helmets to goggles to the MP5 submachine guns each of them clutched.

"Okay, listen up," called Morrish. "I want sniper teams posted at each of the four corners of the building and on each of the four floors. You—Smith, Wharton, Reynolds, Krepinski—organize the teams."

"Study the photo," said Dr. Ogden, raising his voice. "Study the man. This is him, this is Clariton. And as soon as you come in contact with the kidnappers, call it in. I want to know everything: how they move, how they talk, anything indicative of their stress levels."

"Demolition Team—over there, and Assault Teams—over there," said Morrish, pointing to opposite corners. "We don't know whether this is going to be a dynamic entry or a stealth entry, but we need you ready. Be prepared for anything, and don't forget the danger involved here. Each of you has been issued a pair of latex gloves, and I want you to put them on now. Our targets have AIDS and should be considered extremely contagious. You must exercise extreme caution and avoid contact with their blood! We have an emergency medical team just outside, and they have full protective gear. Leave any and all medical emergencies to them. Lastly, remember we have just one priority today, and his name is Congressman Johnny Clariton. Nothing and no one else matters until he is safe!"

Suddenly a blond woman with a bandage around her head burst through the doors. Half-jogging behind her was a man carrying a video camera and a variety of other equipment. Oh, Christ, thought Morrish, the last thing they needed was television coverage.

"Out!" shouted Morrish, pushing toward them. "Get that camera out of here!"

"I'm Cindy Wilson from WTCN TV," countered the woman, "and we got a call from the kidnappers telling us to come here. I really don't think you—"

Morrish looked over, saw another reporter and yet another photographer pushing through the doors. Emblazoned on their camera was CHANNEL 8! And pushing behind them came yet a third reporter.

"Oh, Jesus," muttered Morrish, shaking his head and knowing they'd all have the same story.

41

As soon as they turned the corner and started down the narrow hallway, Todd saw the door and was sure. Yes, there was no doubt, this was the way he'd been led into the basement. Through the white door at the end. The tour guide had taken him and his photographer through it and then down three levels to the massive empty space where the Journey to the Center of the Earth exhibit and ride was to be built.

But even from here Todd could tell the door would be locked, for right above the knob was a keypad that obviously required a combination. With Lyle right behind him, Todd raced down the passage and pushed down on the handle. Nothing happened. He then threw himself against the door, which didn't even budge.

"Damn it!"

Lyle pushed Todd aside, took hold of the handle, jammed it down, and hurled his large body against the plane of metal. Again the door didn't even quiver. Great, thought Todd, now what?

"Shoot it!" demanded Todd.

Lyle looked at the thing for a moment, shrugged, then pulled out his gun and fired twice. The lock shattered under the blast and the door drifted open.

Heading in and leading the way, Todd said, "It's straight down."

"Right."

It was a plain industrial stairwell—metal railing, concrete walls, fluorescent lighting, some emergency lights—and their footsteps reverberated up and down as they plunged lower. They took the steps two and three at a time, going down and around, past the first sublevel, then the second. Suddenly Todd felt a firm hand on his shoulder.

"Nice and quiet," ordered Lyle, his voice hushed.

Todd slowed. Trying to recall the layout, he pictured in his mind a large space with Sheetrock walls, a few rooms, and the metal columns. As far as Todd knew, they were still battling for funding for the exhibit, and construction had yet to start.

Now in the deepest level of the Megamall, they approached the last door. Holding his gun upward, Lyle tried to discern what or who might be beyond, while Todd pressed himself against the concrete block wall and strained to hear something, anything. At first there was nothing. Then it came, that soft but firm rolling sound. Somewhere up above, the computer-run roller coaster had been started for the day. And, yes, Todd knew with the utmost certainty, this was the place, the sound on the videotape had emanated from here.

Lyle quietly inched open the door, stepped through, and Todd followed. The chamber beyond was faintly lit with a few long fluorescent lights. He remembered walking through while the proud tour guide explained how the lava exhibit would be here, the dinosaur fossils there, the underground sea over there. And the operations room in the far back. But now, instead of visions of grandeur, there were only blank walls.

Todd slipped into the lead, quietly moving along. Reaching a corner, he hesitated. Yes, he thought, they had to be somewhere back here. He pointed around the corner, and Lyle nodded. Todd was about to move on when he heard something, a shuffle of steps. He paused. Nothing. Then proceeded, rounding the corner and entering a large empty space perhaps thirty feet wide and a hundred feet long. His attention was immediately caught by a closed door on the far wall; at the bottom of the door a strip of light glowed softly.

Todd looked at Lyle and nodded.

Holding his gun high in both hands, Lyle moved swiftly yet carefully across the space. Todd hurried after him, silently crossing to the wall and pressing himself against it. Lyle slid over to the door, listened, then moved right in front of it, his gun held out and ready to fire. He glanced once at Todd, lifted his foot, and kicked in the door, which burst open under his force. Todd rushed after him, entering a small room littered with sleeping bags, boxes, and a small television.

"Shit!" snapped Lyle, finding it otherwise empty.

He quickly checked a side room and then the bathroom, which was rich with a foul odor and an odd mound of plastic.

"This was it," said Todd, adding it all up. "They were here. Look, there's the video camera."

The air in here was too thick, too stuffy. They couldn't have left that long ago, and Todd turned, dashed out. He glanced up and down the long room. Suddenly something started struggling at the far end, and the next instant a person lunged out of the shadows.

"Stay out of this, Todd!" screamed Rawlins.

A second person jumped out, jabbed a gun to the first man's head, and dragged him away. Yet as horrible as the situation was, Todd was struck by a wave of relief, for this meant Rawlins wasn't a willing participant.

"Rawlins!" he shouted, bursting into a run.

Todd charged through the long space, with Lyle speeding after him. A third and a fourth figure appeared and, yes, Todd could tell one of them was Congressman Johnny Clariton. A distant door opened and then all four of them slipped into the innermost parts of the Megamall and disappeared. Sprinting all the way, Todd reached the passage before Lyle.

"Wait!" ordered Lyle before Todd could rip open the door.

Todd resisted the temptation, waiting until Lyle rushed up, readied his gun, and slowly pulled back the door. The next chamber was filled with a mass of gray pipes, huge tubes running horizontally one on top of another through the low-ceilinged room. Exactly, recalled Todd, this was no boiler room. The tour guide had told him about this, bragging about the heart of the Megamall's cooling system. Such a huge structure filled with so many lights and so many people generated massive amounts of heat, so much in fact that the main concern even here in Minnesota was cooling. In this frigid climate the heat was turned on only two or three weeks a year. The rest of the time it was all about cooling, and a massive underground system had been developed, with pipes that plunged several hundred feet down into the earth so that the heated water they carried would be cooled before returning to the air-conditioning system. This room, Todd knew, was only the tip of the system.

Something clanked straight ahead and to the right, and Todd followed Lyle into the next room, one slow step at a time. Peering ahead, Todd saw that in some fifty feet the pipes curved to the side. There had to be another way out, a far exit, and they continued along, Lyle clutching his gun in both hands and swinging it from side to side. Out of nowhere came an odd noise. What was it? Merely water churning through the pipes. Or footsteps? Then it came again, the sound of hushed movement. Todd stopped. Were they over there to the left?

Echoing up and down the chamber, a single drop fell on the concrete floor, followed by a second. Lyle turned around, put one finger to his lips, then nodded and motioned to Todd to follow. They continued another twenty feet, and the sound of the dripping water grew. Breaking that came the slow, barely audible vibrations of something being dragged. Reaching another gap in the pipes, Todd and Lyle hesitated. Something clicked—a door?—and Todd spun to the side.

Straight ahead two people suddenly lunged out, a skinny man pressing something against the second one's neck.

"Don't shoot! Don't shoot!" he shouted, his voice nervous and quick. "I've got a syringe full of HIV-infected blood, man, and if you come any closer I'll inject him with it! And . . . and this is Johnny Clariton, the congressman! I'll pump him full of AIDS, I will!"

"Elliot, please . . ." begged Clariton, not even daring to flinch.

His spine rigid with fear, Todd stood perfectly still, and he forced his voice to sound calm and even. "Hi, we just want to talk. My name's Todd and—"

"I know perfectly well who you are, you TV turkey!" said the skinny one. "I know all about you! Now, go away! Be a good faggot and let us finish our business!"

"But maybe we can—"

"Oh, just shut up! I mean it, either of you comes any closer and I'm gonna give Mr. Gay Public Enemy Number One a full dose of the Supreme Cootie! Courtesy, I might add, of your handsome dying lover!" he said, tapping the syringe with a naughty giggle.

Horrified, Todd couldn't move, didn't know what to say, let alone do.

"I mean, man," chattered Elliot, "my arms and my legs are so skinny. They're just toothpicks, not much left of 'em at all, and my veins are in shit shape, so . . . so we borrowed some blood from the nice cop!"

A voice cracked not fifteen feet behind Todd, coolly pronouncing, "You guys do anything fancy and this one gets it too!"

Todd whipped around to see Matthew, the bald-headed leader, pressing a gun to Rawlins's right temple. Oh, Jesus. Now what?

Looking up, Rawlins pleaded to be understood. "Todd, they took it from me—my blood! They forced me to—"

"Rawlins—" began Todd, taking a half step forward.

"Stop, Todd!" screamed Matthew, his face bursting red. "I mean it, I'll blast his brains out, and Elliot will shoot Clariton full of AIDS!"

Todd was perfectly still.

"You and your friend there get down on the floor!" commanded Matthew. "Now! And you, Muscles, put the gun down and slide it over here!"

Todd looked over at Lyle, saw him hesitate, then watched as he placed the gun on the floor and gave it a shove with his foot. Of course they had no choice, and Todd began bending over.

Matthew scooped up Lyle's gun and barked, "You know what to do, assholes. You've done this for me before, so get down and put your hands behind your fucking heads—now!"

"You tell 'em!" cackled Elliot from the other side.

Todd went first, placing his knees on the floor, then leaning forward and pressing his hands onto the cold concrete. Lyle stretched out to his right, and then both of them clasped their hands behind their heads. Todd glanced over, saw Matthew shoving Rawlins toward them.

"Okay, now you get down too, Rawlins!" ordered Matthew. "Get down on the floor next to your boyfriend!"

In a tiny voice Clariton said, "Please, just leave me here too."

"Oh, shush, you ninny!" Elliot chided.

As Todd caught a glimpse of Rawlins slowly lowering himself, he started trembling inside. Dear God, how crazy was Matthew? Just what was he going to do to them?

Todd closed his eyes, slipped his leg over, and tapped Rawlins on the ankle. Rawlins nudged back. The next moment Matthew was leaning over Rawlins, strapping first his hands behind his back and then his feet with flex-cuffs. He then stepped over Todd and cuffed Lyle as well.

"As for you, my friend, Mr. Todd," laughed Matthew, kicking Todd on the foot, "this time you're the one coming along for the ride."

"What?" shouted Rawlins, twisting on his side. "No, Matthew, leave him out of this! Just—"

"Shut up and stay down!" shouted Matthew. "Sorry to dump you, Rawlins, but Elliot and I are going to need all the exposure we can get."

"Absolutely, *dahlink!*"

"And Todd's a lot more well known than you!" continued Matthew. "Now, get up, Todd!"

His voice low as he lay on the floor, Lyle advised, "Do as they say, Todd."

"You're fucking right!" snapped Matthew.

As Todd slowly pushed himself up, he glanced at Lyle and saw his hands twisting against the flex-cuffs. Just how strong was he?

As soon as Todd was standing, Matthew jabbed his gun into Todd's back and said, "Now, just be a good boy and do like I say, or it's going to be lights out. Am I clear?"

Todd nodded and glanced down the hall at Elliot, who was clutching Clariton, almost leaning on him for support, as he kept the tip of the needle all but pressed into the congressman's neck. One false move by either one of them and Clariton could be on that long, dark road.

"You're crazy, Matthew!" yelled Rawlins, trying unsuccessfully to wrench himself free. "Don't you see that you're doing more harm than good for AIDS? Every straight person in the world is going to hate gays after this!"

"I'm just determined, that's all!"

"Oh, wow," muttered Elliot. "This is so great—now we've got two famous people!"

Matthew nudged Todd with the gun. "Okay, just go over there toward Elliot. We're going to go out another way. Got it?"

Todd nodded.

"And remember, no fancy stuff."

"Todd . . ." called Rawlins.

"I'll be okay," he promised.

Matthew echoed, "I'm telling you, just stay here or Todd gets it!"

Elliot and Clariton went first, Todd and Matthew second. Continuing through the cooling room, they reached a far door and entered a second stairwell, a tall, impersonal space with concrete block walls and stark lighting.

"We're going all the way up," explained Matthew.

Elliot shoved Clariton along and said, "Say, what do you think of the homosexual agenda now, Mr. Johnny Congressman?"

His voice deep and low and full of hate, Clariton glanced back at Todd. "Pigs! That's what these people are—pigs!"

Elliot laughed. "Careful what you say, Johnny. All I got to do is prick you with this teensy-weensy little needle and you got big problems!"

Clariton's face bloomed red, and in a calm but very strained voice he said, "Just let me go. I'll help you, I promise I will."

"Oh, really?" replied Elliot, doing his best to sound earnest.

"Yes, I'll get you all the latest drugs, everything you need!"

"Wow, so now you're no longer the wicked congressman, but Glinda, Good Witch of the West?"

"I swear I'll get you into the best hospital and get you the best doctors!"

"Don't listen to him!" snapped Matthew.

"Girlfriend," said Elliot to Matthew with a laugh, "you think I'd start believing a politician *now?*" Changing thoughts and changing tone, he said, "Hey, Todd, I made a video too. My whole story's back there on tape, back in that room. Remember that, okay? And make sure it gets on the air, okay? Promise me that, please?"

"Sure," replied Todd, fearing that Elliot already knew how this was going to end.

"Oh, and there are three people in the walk-in refrigerator at some cookie place. They've probably already gotten out, but you better check."

"Okay."

With the gun pressed deep into his back, Todd took hold of the metal railing and started up, some ten steps behind Elliot and Clariton. He climbed one step after another, and behind him he could hear Matthew's labored breathing as he gulped and wheezed. By the time they'd climbed one flight Matthew's exhaustion was more than evident.

"Not . . . not so fast," gasped Matthew, reaching out with his free hand and grasping on to Todd's belt for support.

"Holy cow," huffed Elliot, clearly exhausted as well, "I'm not the great athlete I once was."

They rested a brief moment and then, as if they were scaling a mountain, Matthew drove them all upward. The climb proved too much though, and they paused again on the next landing, waiting so Matthew could catch his breath, which he couldn't. When they'd made it up all three levels and were back at ground level, Todd glanced over his shoulder, saw Matthew dripping with sweat.

"Just . . . just wait a minute," said Matthew, his voice faint as he struggled for air.

Keeping his gun trained on Todd, Matthew groped for the wall, leaned against it, and started coughing. He then bent over, clutched his forehead with his left hand.

"You don't look so good," said Todd.

"No shit."

"It can end right now, you know. Why don't you let me—"

"Fuck off!" Matthew tried to straighten up, but swooned and reached again for the wall. "We're going all the way, aren't we, Elliot?"

Elliot struggled to catch his breath as well, and then in an odd, almost serene voice replied, "Yep, we are. All the fucking Thelma-and-Louise way, man."

Oh, shit, thought Todd, fearful of what that implied.

"Elliot, just . . . just . . ." Matthew started hacking, then continued, saying, "Just keep that syringe right on Clariton's neck."

"Yes, my captain," replied Elliot. "I got it right up against his skin. It's curtains if he so much as makes a move I don't like."

"Oh, Christ," muttered Clariton, as beads of perspiration formed on his brow.

"Okay, let's do it," said Matthew, stabbing the pistol back into Todd. "Let's go. Nothing like a dramatic entry, eh?"

Todd said, "Matthew, we can still get you out of this."

"Shut the fuck up! Now, just open the door and head out. I'm going to be stuck to you like glue."

Matthew moved behind Todd, clutching an arm around Todd's waist and jabbing the gun into Todd's temple. Todd took a deep breath, then did as he was told, opening the door and proceeding down the plain white service hall toward the heart of the Megamall. Reaching the three-story main corridor, they emerged between Heavenly, a store overcome with angels, and The Big Stink, which was filled with stacks of perfume. Glancing through palm trees and banners, carts and planters, Todd saw no one.

"Head over to those elevators," ordered Matthew. "You with me, Elliot?"

"You bet," he called.

Suddenly a voice behind them said, "Hey, Mel, look at here. Aren't we glad we're the last ones out?"

"Oh, brother," muttered Matthew.

Todd halted, looked to his right, and saw two mall guards in front of a store emblazoned with the words MEGA BARBIE! While Mel and his partner seemed most determined to do something, anything, they stood weaponless and hence powerless in front of a showcase filled with Pink Splendor Barbie, a life-size figurine all done up in an explosion of pink chiffon.

"Oh, Jesus Christ!" laughed Matthew. "You two turkeys don't even have guns!"

"Yeah," agreed Elliot in a voice that seemed to be getting calmer and softer by the moment, "like, what are you going to do, throw your walkie-talkies at us?"

Matthew swung his gun away from Todd's head, aimed not

directly at the guards but just to the right of them, and fired two shots into the Barbie showcase. In a single instant the glass shattered and Pink Splendor Barbie exploded, her tall plastic body shattering into a thousand pieces and her head and beehive white-blond hair tumbling into the store.

Turning to the guards, Matthew laughed like the devil and shouted, "Now, which one of you am I going to kill first?"

The guards bolted, tearing down the teal-carpeted hallway.

Clearly amused, Matthew continued chuckling as he jabbed the gun back against Todd's head and ordered, "Keep moving!"

With the hot barrel against his temple, Todd led the foursome onward, moving around some planters, past a teddy-bear shop, a music-box shop, an enormous shoe store, and to the bank of elevators. He pressed a button, one of the doors immediately opened, and Matthew, Todd, Elliot, and Clariton boarded the all-glass lift.

Elliot pressed the number three and in a faint voice said, "Going up. Next stop: chaos."

As they rose past the second floor Todd saw a handful of guards come charging toward the elevators. No, those weren't mere shopping-mall guards, not geeky men and women in white shirts and black polyester pants. They weren't even local police, Todd realized as the glass car continued ascending. Dressed in black uniforms and helmets and carrying submachine guns, they were quite obviously Hostage Rescue Team commandos.

A bell chimed, the lift came to a gentle stop on the third floor, and Todd felt Matthew draw closer yet, pressing himself tightly against Todd's back. When the doors eased open, Todd stared out at two marksmen, their guns aimed at him.

"Get back or I'm going to blow this guy's head off!" shouted Matthew, tapping Todd's head with the gun.

"Do it," seconded Elliot, "or this guy's gonna get a big dose of AIDS!"

Suspended between Matthew and the submachine guns, Todd felt his heart leaping wildly, his body trembling and sweating. At first it seemed as if the sharpshooters weren't going to budge, but then, without lowering their weapons, they backed away.

As he nudged Todd out of the lift Matthew commanded, "Okay, turn right."

With the guns trained on them Todd led the way down the hall. Matthew hung on to him, and Elliot and Clariton followed just a few feet behind. Aware that the sharpshooters were looking for that one moment, that millisecond that might give them a clear shot, Todd moved cautiously past a blue jeans store, finally turning a corner and entering the food court, which glowed with sizzling red neon hamburgers, chilling blue neon shakes, and dancing orange neon french fries. Lining both sides of the massive V-shape space were several dozen fast-food booths with brightly lit menu boards offering everything from pizza to minidoughnuts to sushi to deep-dish chocolate chip cookies.

"Go all the way out there," commanded Matthew, whispering into Todd's ear and shoving him along. "All the way to the edge."

Todd led the way around a column on which hung a huge neon Pepsi cup with flashing bubbles, then steered through a mass of Formica-clad tables. As he moved along Todd was suddenly aware that they weren't surrounded by simply one or two additional sharpshooters, but at least a dozen more, all of whom fanned into strategic positions. Carefully proceeding through the food court, Todd headed onto the Grand Balcony, a huge perch covered with still more tables and chairs, which jutted out over the entire amusement park. With Matthew still pressing the gun into Todd's temple, he went all the way to the edge and peered out. Off to one side hung an enormous space rocket and moon constructed of multicolored Lego blocks, while in the distance stood the Ferris wheel, which was so far away it looked tiny. Spying something snaking and curling through the treetops, Todd realized it was the roller coaster, completely empty yet maintaining its computerized schedule. With a quick glance over the railing, Todd saw down below not only another dozen guns aimed up at them, but a handful of television crews and their cameras as well.

"Very good," cackled Matthew, his hand trembling as he ground the gun into Todd's scalp. "Can their telephoto lenses reach this far, Toddy?"

"Yeah, and I'm sure they won't miss a second."

Matthew called, "Hey, Elliot, we're going to go down in history!"

"Yeah, we made it," he said softly.

Out of the corner of his eyes Todd watched Elliot nudge Clariton up to the railing and peer out over the largest of interior spaces. For a long time Elliot just scanned the area, seeing it all—the forest of trees, the huge columns, the sparkling lights, all the rides—as if for the first time. Or was it, Todd feared, perhaps the last?

His voice faint, Elliot said, "So do I do it now, Matthew? Is it time to inflict the ultimate experience upon the evil congressman?"

"Oh, God," pleaded Clariton, "please . . . please don't!"

"But why shouldn't I?" asked Elliot, as lucid as he was perplexed. "Otherwise you'll never understand the damage people like you have done."

"Please . . . I swear it, I'll help you! Just don't, please don't . . ."

"Clariton, you are such a fucking baby," said Matthew, who then turned and leaned over the railing and yelled to the journalists below. "You guys with the cameras, make sure you get this!"

Glancing the other way, Todd saw movement. It was Rawlins, bounding past a hamburger stand and heading straight for them. Several black-clad HRT guys leapt out and grabbed him, but Lyle, right behind, came to his aid, and Rawlins pushed through. Maneuvering in and out of the tables and chairs, Rawlins rushed on, then slowed as he approached the edge of the Grand Balcony.

"Oh, shit," groaned Matthew upon spotting him.

Todd shouted, "Rawlins, stay away!"

Paying no attention, Rawlins calmly said, "Don't do it, Matthew. Don't kill Todd."

"Get the hell out of here!" shouted Matthew.

Rawlins, his brawny frame quite still, ignored him and calmly continued, saying, "It's me you want to kill, not Todd."

"Oh, is that right?"

"Absolutely. You gave me a death sentence, Matthew. You

passed HIV to me. So why don't you just do it? Why don't you just shoot me and finish off what you started?''

"Oh, Jesus . . ." moaned Matthew.

"After all, I don't want to get as sick as you."

"What, it's too much for you, tough guy?"

"And I certainly don't want to get as ugly as you either."

Matthew flinched. "Listen, if you think this is going to save your boyfriend, you're wrong."

"You look like shit, you know, and—"

"Shut up!"

"—and I don't want that." Rawlins waited a moment, then slipped to the edge of a table and added, "You used to be the handsomest man I'd ever seen."

Matthew hesitated, then snapped, "Rawlins, get the hell out of here—now!"

"Everyone said that about you, how gorgeous you were. It was no surprise you were so successful as a model. Everyone lusted after you. All the guys. But now look at you."

"Stop it!"

"People run from you, don't they? I mean, you look like some sort of freak. That must be real hard for you."

"Listen, I—"

"AIDS is so damn ugly, isn't it? I mean, can you even stand to look at yourself in the mirror?" Rawlins shook his head. "I just don't want to look as bad as you do now. All the oozing sores and the wasting and—"

"Shut the hell up!"

"I don't want to rot like—"

"Stop it!"

"No, Matthew, you're going to have to shoot me. That's what I want. I want you to kill me so I don't look as hideous as you."

Matthew shifted from one foot to the other and blurted, "You know, if you don't shut up I'm going to kill Todd!"

"No, you're not."

Todd glanced over, saw Elliot and Clariton hanging on every word. Swinging his eyes across the food court, Todd spied the sharpshooters frozen in position, one against a column, another leaning on a tabletop, another perched by a garbage can, all of their guns trained on Matthew and therefore Todd as well.—"

His body blistering with sweat, Todd said, "Rawlins, I—"

"You know, Matthew, I'm pissed off too," continued Rawlins, ignoring everything and everyone else. "I'm pissed as hell at you for doing this to me, for making me sick." Rawlins started forward. "And I'm angrier than hell that people like Clariton have exploited—"

"Stop right there or I'll blast his brains out!"

Rawlins halted, took a breath, then said, "Actually, maybe that's a good idea. Maybe you should kill Todd. I mean, I don't want to see him get sick too. He's probably got it, you know. I probably gave him AIDS. And I sure as hell don't want to watch him start puking and shitting his brains out."

Todd closed his eyes, bit his lower lip. He took a deep breath, felt his heart slamming against his chest. Was Rawlins as insane as Matthew?

"In fact," continued Rawlins, "I kind of like that idea. You can shoot Todd and then he won't have to suffer. That's pretty good."

Matthew's eyes flitted about, he rocked from side to side, then looked over the edge at the cameras below. "They better be getting this live."

"And then you can shoot me too." Rawlins nodded. "That would be a great relief."

"You think so?" demanded Matthew, turning back and pressing the gun against Todd's temple so hard that Todd's head bent to the side.

"Yeah, I know so. Just go ahead! Shoot Todd and then shoot me! I don't care anymore. What does it matter? We're all going to die! All of us! All the gay men in the world! It's kind of what we deserve, don't you think, for fucking around? I mean, how many guys did you screw in your life?"

With the barrel of the gun digging into his head, Todd pleaded, "Rawlins, just calm down. Just—"

Matthew turned to Elliot and screamed, "Do it, Elliot! Do it now! Shoot the blood into Clariton!"

Rawlins's tone was smooth and even. "I mean, you walked

out on Curt because you couldn't watch him die. And I don't think I can watch Todd die either, so perhaps you should just—''

"Shut up, you bastard!"

"Or did you leave Curt because you were just afraid of getting it, because it freaked you out so much?" Rawlins paused, then said, "Hey, how did you get it anyway? I guess it doesn't make much difference, but it's always interesting to know—did you give it to Curt or did Curt give it to you? Care to confess to us?"

"Stick the needle into Clariton's neck, Elliot!"

Rawlins blurted, "But you have to admit, walking out on Curt just when he got sick and needed you most makes even Congressman Clariton look like a saint."

Elliot gazed at the roller coaster as it whooshed nearby like a ghost of better times, then turned to Matthew and mumbled, "I . . . I . . ."

"Do it, Elliot!"

"But—"

"Do it, you moron!"

"Matthew, you know what Curt's last words were?" taunted Rawlins.

Nervously fidgeting behind Todd, Matthew yelled, "Curt's dead, I don't care!"

"Of course you don't care. You left him. I just thought you might—"

"Shut up!" he screamed.

"Matthew, I was right there when he died. Right there by his side. And you know what he said?"

"I don't care!"

"He said, 'Tell Mr. Wonderful I hate him!' "

"Stop it!" he shrieked.

"Those were his exact words . . . his last words."

His what? Last words? Suddenly Todd switched back to a different time, a different tragedy altogether. Dear God, what was Rawlins saying? That he'd been there that fateful night? In Todd's mind he pictured a man in a dark coat slipping down the street and creeping into a dark apartment. Could that have been Rawlins? Had he been the one? And could whatever have happened in Curt's final moments explain the change in Rawlins in the last month—the sulking nights, the disappearance of his laughter?

"I suppose it really doesn't make any difference who gave it to whom, but you know what's really terrible, Matthew? The fact that you left him, that you abandoned your partner. That makes you a real shit." Rawlins shook his head. "You broke Curt's heart, you know."

"That's not true!"

"Oh, yes, it is. You destroyed him. And do you know what I did for the man who once loved you more than anything in the world? Do you have any idea what I did because I loved my friend so much and he was in so much pain?"

"Stop it!"

"He was bleeding and shitting and coughing and crying, and he hated you for every miserable moment!"

"He did not!"

"Yes, he did."

"I'm going to—"

"He told me how he hated you with all his heart for leaving him like that. He told me you were the worst kind of human being," taunted Rawlins. "And you know what, Matthew? Curt was right. You are the worst. Ten times worse than some pathetic politician like Clariton. And you're going to rot in hell for what you did to the only person who ever loved you!"

Todd sensed it, the subtle change of the gun against his head, the barely perceptible switch in Matthew's grip. Oh, Jesus. He knew what Matthew was going to do a split second before Matthew even moved.

"No!" screamed Todd, elbowing Matthew in the stomach and shoving him back.

But it was of little use. Matthew stumbled just as he fired over Todd's right shoulder. In an instant Todd saw everything great in his life destroyed as a bullet rocketed into Rawlins, hurling him back onto a table.

"Rawlins!"

Todd dove forward, and as soon as he was out of the way the sharpshooters opened fire on Matthew. There was one rapid explosion of gunfire, a half dozen shots that came so quickly they sounded nearly as one. Every single bullet bit into its target, and Matthew's body danced as if suspended, then dropped to the floor, his punctured body spurting his poisoned blood everywhere.

Aware of nothing else, Todd scrambled through the chairs as his lover collapsed. "Rawlins!"

Elliot, his sunken face stretched with terror, abruptly pushed away the congressman and threw aside the syringe. He then clamped his eyes shut and slapped his hands over his ears, standing there in hideous anticipation.

Clariton bent out of the way and bolted for safety, yelling, "Shoot him! Get him! Now!"

Elliot didn't move, didn't open his eyes. He just stood there, undoubtedly expecting and perhaps hoping for a hail of bullets— something, anything to blast him from this world into the next. There was, however, nothing. Not a single blast of a single bullet, nothing to take him beyond.

"Shoot him, you idiots!" shrieked Clariton, tripping and pawing over chairs and tables as he stumbled out of the way.

Instead, four men with machine guns swooped upon Elliot, their weapons trained on him the entire time. In one orchestrated and balletlike instant, they swarmed around and engulfed Elliot, seizing the skinny, frail man with ease.

Todd saw the blood leaping from Rawlins's upper left chest and shouted, "Get a medic! Hurry!"

Falling to the floor on his back, Rawlins clasped one hand over his wound in a desperate but feeble attempt to stem the flow of blood, which was gushing with maniacal pressure.

"Back!" he gasped as Todd neared.

"I'm here!"

Rawlins held out his blood-drenched hand, cried in the weakest of voices, "Stay away!"

Horrified by what he saw, Todd couldn't stop. He grabbed Rawlins's bloodied hand, scrambled down, and knelt in the pooling blood. He touched Rawlins's shirt, looked for some way to stem death. But the wound was so big, the blood flowing so quickly.

"Get back!" whispered Rawlins.

Panicking, not knowing what to do, Todd reached up, ran his own now-bloody hand through his hair, then pleaded and screamed, "Where's a doctor?"

Rawlins closed his eyes, then opened them and looked up. His lips parted, he tried to speak, but couldn't. He grabbed Todd's arm and squeezed. And finally his eyes fell shut.

"Rawlins, stay with me!" shouted Todd, caressing Rawlins's face. "I'm right here! Don't go! Rawlins!"

Beside me I hear pain and confusion, such suffering. It's Todd, and he's crying so hard I'm afraid something's breaking within him. If only I could open my mouth, because there's so much left to say. This really isn't so scary. No, my eyes are closed, but it's not dark. In fact, there it is, that light, the one they always talk about, so pure and white, beckoning me to come, calling me with its clarity.

There, I can still move my fingers. And that's your arm, Todd, that beautiful, wonderful arm that you used to wrap around me. I'm closing my fingers, clutching you. Do you feel that? Do you? I'm not trying to hang on, I'm really not. I just want you to understand, sweetheart, that I'm going to be okay, that I'm fine, really I am. In fact, I feel flush with a kind of overwhelming sense of well-being. If only I could make you believe this, if only I could move my lips and smile. Hey, right this moment I'm realizing that the secret of life is like a ball that you have to keep rolling. So that's what you got to do, Todd, just push on, because, after all, it's like your old boss used to say: This ain't no dress rehearsal.

Wait, the light's getting brighter and there's someone out there, a radiant face, an outstretched hand.

Curt, is that you?

"Of course it is," says the smiling, glowing face. "What the hell are you doing here?"

What is this? Am I going crazy? Am I hallucinating? This vision is so real.

I'm sorry, Curt! Really, I'm sorry! I've regretted it every day since then.

"What are you talking about?"

But—

"Rawlins, you did me a favor. Holy shit, you saw how sick I was. And you knew I didn't want to die in a strange place, that I just wanted to die at home. The cyanide was my idea, you fool."

Yes, but—

"You just followed through on our little plan. You helped me when I needed it most. You did as I asked." Curt's smiling now. "Do as I say: Go back to him. It's not your time. Go back to Todd. He's the one that needs you. And don't give up. Someday— someday real soon—this AIDS crap is going to be over."

The white light is beginning to dim. The wondrous face is receding.

Curt? Curt!

"That's it," said Todd, trotting alongside the gurney as they rushed Rawlins to a waiting ambulance. "Take a breath. Good."

Thank God. Oh, thank God, thought Todd, his eyes beaded with tears as he saw Rawlins's eyes flutter open.

The Hostage Rescue Team had, of course, considered every possibility, including emergency medical care, which they had rushed to the third floor even before Matthew had fired the first bullet. And within thirty seconds of being shot, two emergency doctors and a nurse—all of them wearing heavy rubber gloves, smocks, and goggles—descended upon Rawlins, stopping the horrendous flow of blood and slapping an oxygen mask over his mouth and nose. They'd saved him. Rawlins had been tumbling away and in another minute or two he would have died. As it was, they'd caught him just as he was slipping from this world.

"It's okay. You're going to be okay," coached Todd. "You're on a gurney and they're going to take you to the hospital. I'll stay right with you."

Rawlins tried to say something.

"No, just be quiet, buddy." He saw Rawlins's eyes flit about, and Todd explained, "You've been shot, but you're going to be all right. Elliot's okay for now. They have him in custody. He wasn't shot but he's awfully weak." He added, "Matthew's dead."

Beneath the plastic mask Rawlins opened his mouth and faintly said, "Curt . . ."

"Don't worry, we'll talk later. But I know you did something quite drastic for your closest friend. Everything's going to be okay." Todd lifted Rawlins's left hand to his mouth and kissed it. "I love you, and I'm never going to let you go."